Meredith's JOURNEY BEGINS

Edward Green

BALBOA.PRESS
A DIVISION OF HAY HOUSE

Balboa Press books may be ordered through booksellers or by contacting:

Balboa Press
A Division of Hay House
1663 Liberty Drive
Bloomington, IN 47403
www.balboapress.co.uk
1 (877) 407-4847

Because of the dynamic nature of the Internet, any web addresses or links contained in this book may have changed since publication and may no longer be valid. The views expressed in this work are solely those of the author and do not necessarily reflect the views of the publisher, and the publisher hereby disclaims any responsibility for them.

The author of this book does not dispense medical advice or prescribe the use of any technique as a form of treatment for physical, emotional, or medical problems without the advice of a physician, either directly or indirectly. The intent of the author is only to offer information of a general nature to help you in your quest for emotional and spiritual well-being. In the event you use any of the information in this book for yourself, which is your constitutional right, the author and the publisher assume no responsibility for your actions.

Print information available on the last page.

ISBN: 978-1-9822-8160-1 (sc)
ISBN: 978-1-9822-8162-5 (hc)
ISBN: 978-1-9822-8161-8 (e)

Library of Congress Control Number: 2020908975

Balboa Press rev. date: 05/20/2020

With thanks to Kate, Hazel, Marie, Mira and Ali, without whose encouragement this story would not have been told and without whose help Meredith would not be half the woman she is.

In the Beginning

Everyone people watches; Meredith has long been certain of that. She's played at it herself ever since she and Jess were first old enough to go to the mall together and sit, nursing cappuccinos in a coffee shop window. How could anyone resist the eternal human fascination with other people? Meredith does it to this day; it's a great way to enjoy the thrill of new people, their secrets, the sense of them, and the way they move. She imagines their stories and what has led them to this precise moment in time, sharing it with her—though she, like other people watchers, hopes they are unaware they have been plucked from obscurity and cast in a role.

It makes her feel powerful and filled with knowledge, and does so without challenging her own shyness or insecurity. The game is best enjoyed while sitting with a friend or few. During a lull in conversation, one allows one's eyes to wander, picking out the strange, the new, the out of place, or even, if one's luck is in, the beautiful.

He's just there. She hadn't seen the group of smartly dressed men enter while she was drinking and laughing with the crowd from work. They certainly hadn't been there when she arrived. She looks up and in that moment, he turns and meets her gaze. She finds herself looking into a face studying her from the other side of the bar, and senses that the owner of that face sees more than people often intend. The man's eyes are glitteringly bright and she feels suddenly drawn toward the grey-suited stranger in the midst of this new group. The corner of his mouth turns briefly upwards, and she thinks or imagines she sees him nod almost imperceptibly in her direction before he returns to his conversation.

As time passes and drink flows, her eyes seek him out ever more frequently. She senses his attention on her from time to time too, and fancies he is undressing her with those eyes as sure as craftsman's hands. In her mind his people-watching has no shyness or insecurity at its centre, and with this thought she blushes inwardly. (God! She hopes it's only inwardly.)

The drink after work rolls into late evening as she chats and flirts in her little group, none of whom she is even remotely romantically interested in, and so among whom she feels totally comfortable. She laughs at an anecdote about a crass former colleague, and then nods along to hopes of better bonuses this year. They try to drive the blues of the grey January evening away in the warm glow of her safe space. Between each passage of conversation, she finds her attention drawn back to him. The corners of his eyes have a slight downward tilt that makes her think of sadness, but light up as he smiles, laughs, or speaks. If tonight is anything to go by, that oddly stern face is well used to both laughter and smiling.

When she steps out for a smoke, her thoughts are of him, though she fixes her eyes anywhere else. She walks with all the grace she and several glasses of Malbec can muster, doing so in the hope that her movement pleases him. Stopping to gather drinks on her return, she tries to make eye contact, but is unable to see him from her gap at the bar. She manages o get served in not too long and returns with her laden tray.

A glass later, she sees him go to the bar, and she makes a beeline for the ladies' room to pass close to him. Her valour, though reinforced by the wine, is still not great enough to make her introduce herself, but he and the Fates reward the bravery she does show. He half turns and, with a fluid motion of his arm, hands her his card discreetly with a hint of a smile, murmuring, "Call me," in a voice deep enough to echo in her bones as he does so. The unexpected rumble makes her flush like a child, and this time Meredith knows that her response is external as well as internal. She lowers her face and hurries on, but not before taking in the unusual blue-green colouring of his eyes.

Once inside the restroom, she reads the card:

WILLIAM FARROW, CONSULTANT
DIRECTION CONSULTING

Meredith has never heard of the firm. She rolls his name and title around her mind. "Farrow"—what an ill-fittingly modest name. But she can believe "consultant", with its hint at importance, its room for ambiguity. She rereads it and carefully places it in an inside pocket of her purse.

Meredith wonders what sort of consultant he is. Surely people would tell that penetrating gaze anything, and she at least would listen to that voice even if it were reading the accounts! She avoids his eye as she walks back to her colleagues, but once safely seated, she meets his enquiring look and nods towards him. She flushes again as he smiles in acknowledgement before they each return their attention to their present company.

As he and his friends leave, not long afterwards, his head turns towards her once more, and that hint of a smile plays across his serious mouth again, as he goes through the door. Seeing and feeling it, she does a silent internal jig of self-congratulation—so out of character, but so exciting.

She memorises his name and periodically fishes the card out of her purse, and allows her fingers to play with it for the rest of the evening. Then, having drunk more than she should, she gets an Uber home.

Despite not really being in a fit state to make conversation, she's barely able to refrain from calling him when she gets in. Instead, she heads to the kitchen, prompted by her stomach's reminder that she has not "eaten" anything but red wine tonight. With nothing ready in her fridge, she searches the bread bin and, finding the bread a little stale, decides to make toast. Her efforts at slicing produce two usable though distinctly wonky slices and a small cut on the side of her left index finger.

Meredith briefly mulls over the notion of calling him once more while toasting the uneven slices but, chastened by their doorstop-like shapes and the kitchen-towel wrapped cut, decides against it. She then butters the sort-of slices and eats them as her evening meal before making her way to bed.

She has trouble settling. Her pyjamas, the duvet, and the alcohol she's drunk make her hot, but when she kicks the covers off, she feels exposed. She gets up, pours herself a glass of water, and opens the window on half lock before trying again. When sleep still eludes her, she allows her thoughts to drift back to the evening. She alternates between thinking of the stranger and trying to prevent the ceiling from spinning for long enough for her to find sleep.

★★★

After a fitful night, her alarm comes as a rude shock, as does remembering that she will be at the mercy of public transport for her journey to the office, and so will have to leave earlier than is her custom. She has to make do with a half cup of instant coffee for breakfast while she feeds her cats. At least the morning is clear, with no rain to turn her hair frizzy. She manages to get a seat on the train, even though she has to stand on the bus.

Sitting at her desk, she plays him in her mind a hundred times or more — that devilish smile, his cheekbones, the way his bum and shoulders filled the smooth lines of his suit, his softly rumbled "call me". Her fingers are almost able to feel the cotton of his crisp white shirt as she half dials his number. Then the warm flush suffuses her cheeks and she returns the phone to her pocket for the dozenth time. The bravery of alcohol has deserted her. She could do with being busier, rushed even, but after the month-end things are always a little quiet. Thoughts of him creep into the spaces.

Meredith finds herself searching for him online. *Maybe,* she tells herself, *it's the wine that remembers the chiselled jaw and blue-green eyes.* He must be online somewhere. She needs proof, and so she takes to Facebook and Instagram—to no avail. There are several William, Will, and Bill Farrows. Yet all are clearly not *her* William Farrow, unless he's the one on Instagram with a private account and a comedy photo and, well, he doesn't strike her as the comedy photo type.

The afternoon ticks by, and she wrestles with what to say to him when she calls. There's a comfort in that resolution. *When* feels better than *if.* She will call him for sure, just as soon as she feels a bit more confident. Yet she gets no closer to dialling that last digit.

She finally finds him on LinkedIn, where his picture shows him in another charcoal suit. He's wearing dark glasses on his serious face, so she can't be sure about the eyes, but yes, he's every bit as handsome as she recalls. There's no personal information listed. His network appears to be a series of similarly dressed men, though there are a few women among them. She's relieved that about half of the others haven't gone with the dark glasses look. Mysterious is one thing, but sinister is quite another.

After work she heads home, stopping only to pick up a ready meal and a bottle of wine. Her little ginger-and-white cat is in an affectionate mood, butting her shin and mewling softly as she enters the warmth of her hall from the winter evening. She plays with the cat while enjoying a glass before dinner. Eventually she realises that she's hungry, pops the meal in the microwave, and pours another one while it's heating.

As she puts the TV dinner on a tray and heads for her sofa, she thinks, *such a comedown from the unexpected laughter of last night.* The food is filling, but not satisfying. She pushes the last few morsels around her plate before finishing them, and then phones her friend Jess to ask for advice on how to call a strange man.

Her chattier, more social friend is of little help, instead bombarding her with questions about him that leave her more nervous and more embarrassed than before. *Those who aren't shy,* Meredith reflects after the call ends, *don't understand what the big deal is.* It's all very well for Jess, who passes from one relationship to the next as smoothly as a dancer slides from one partner to another and always seems to be the one to let go. Meredith rarely sees a man who interests her, and even more rarely feels that interest is reciprocated.

Again through the evening, she half dials a dozen times as she struggles inside her head over what to say. After the bottle is empty, she realises once more that she is too tired and tipsy for the conversation. That night she again sees his face and frame as she lies awake, unable to settle. Late-night TV, counting sheep, her fingers, and even her vibe fail to provide her with relaxation or release. The lights and sound of a storm shower interrupt her the one time she gets close. Sleep eludes her into the small hours and, when it comes, proves restless once more.

The next day passes slower still. Shorn of rest, her mind is even harder pressed as she tries to concentrate on her work or resolve once and for all to call him. The morning goes by interminably, with several more cigarette breaks than usual and an impromptu walk to the coffee shop.

The afternoon drags too. She even catches herself dozing and dreaming, as she has been daydreaming of his eyes upon her. When a colleague suggests a quick drink before heading home, she agrees, semi reluctantly. She wants the distraction, hoping to find the words and courage to ring him (or at least a distraction from not doing so), but Emily sometimes annoys her. The tall younger woman has always seemed so confident, especially when it comes to men. At times she has delighted in teasing Meredith's bashfulness with tales of her own adventures.

The two of them return to the same bar. As Meredith suspected, Emily has a new man to boast about. She seems to be inordinately pleased with the instant intimacy she has enjoyed with him. Emily also has enquiries—which Meredith suspects are not quite so kindly intended as they are worded—about Meredith's private life. They make her feel put upon, especially after her conversation with Jess the previous evening.

For her own part, she chats and responds while trying to pretend that Emily's comments are neither accurate nor finding their mark. She seeks words for her call, and they drink their drinks. She's surprised that, as Emily says goodnight, she asks, "Are you okay? Only you've seemed distracted this week." It strikes her as out of character—concern for others has never been something she's associated with Emily, and it puts Meredith off balance.

After a pause, she lies, "It's my aunt; she's been ill." Which Emily appears to accept before departing. Meredith stops to use the restroom before heading off. She resolves, *Yes, I will call tonight*, as she looks in the restroom mirror, promising herself to be a bit more Jess, or even a bit more Emily than is her habit.

2

Lightning

She takes her lighter and cigarettes out of her bag and makes to leave. But as her hand reaches out, the door is drawn open. She looks up in surprise. She finds herself looking into those eyes, and yes, they really are blue-green. The clothes are casual, cotton shirt and jeans, but those eyes are unforgettable. She flushes, pauses.

"You haven't called me, young lady." His deep voice once again seems to reverberate inside her. Her blush deepens and she lowers her head, feeling like a naughty schoolgirl. The side of his index finger touches the sensitive spot under her chin with the gentlest of touches, though the contact brings her the warmest of shocks as he lifts her face towards his. "Did you want to call me?"

She stammers and looks up into his face. Those stern eyes twinkle, the hard corners of his mouth turn upwards – and something inside her melts as her blush continues to burn and she smiles in return.

"Yes —God, yes! I just ..." The finger moves to her lips, stilling her tongue before it can ramble further. The touch sends a thrill through her, and his mouth creases more deeply into its smile.

There's real mirth now in his eyes. "Let's start again. I'm William Farrow." He tilts his head. "Would you care for a drink?"

Meredith smiles and nods her response, moving aside to allow him to enter before following meekly. Being taken aback doesn't prevent her from noting and approving the lines of his haunches and the breadth of his shoulders, which are more clearly visible in what he's wearing today. What's the saying? *A good suit can cover a multitude of sins?*

As he approaches the bar, he doesn't wave or call, merely makes eye contact to get served. He orders himself a beer and then turns to her and asks, "What can I get you? It's red, isn't it?"

"Um, Malbec please, "she responds.

He collects their drinks and heads for a table in a quiet corner, and sets their glasses down, then draws out a chair for her before placing himself close to her, but not inside her personal space. The two seats he chooses each have a clear view across the room."And yours is?"

"Pardon?" Meredith asks.

"Your name." His cheeks and the corners of his eyes crease with a mirth she hadn't thought his face capable of.

"Oh, sorry. Meredith, Meredith Webb."

"Meredith, that's pretty." He rolls the sound of her name in his tingle inducing bass baritone

"So people tell me, though they rarely say Webb is." The joke is an old one to her, but his face indicates that he likes it. "You can blame my Welsh grandmother."

"For calling you Webb?" His smile really is nice."Oh, the Meredith. How long have you smoked?"

She wonders how he knows — but of course, he'd seen her go outside to smoke the other night. Besides, she has the packet and lighter in her hand. Feeling silly, she replies, "Since I was sixteen. I started when I had a shop job on Saturdays. If you smoked, you could nip outside for a ciggie. I should give up; I mostly don't enjoy smoking, but ..."

"Then do!" His eyes crease fractionally, "I understand that if you wish to give up, you should start with the times, places, and reasons." He seems amused, but not to be judging her."When and where do you smoke?"

It seems a bit deep, but it's conversation. "When I'm out, or at work, or my cats are out. I don't like to smoke when they're with me in the house ..." Again her words trail off; it sounds ridiculous when she says it out loud, for all that it's true. She doesn't like to spread the poisons she inhales for her cats to breathe in.

What is it with his voice? It rumbles along, and she winds up saying the stupidest things she can think of! At least it's true.

"So you care more about your cats' lungs than your own?" His words cut, though the upward turn of his mouth shows kindness mixed with humour and his voice is gentle as he says it. "That's admirable, but hardly seems wise."

"Sorry, it sounds pathetic. I didn't mean to say it like that, and I hate myself for—" She stumbles, crestfallen. Here she is with the beautiful man she's been dreaming about all day, and she's ruining things.

His eyes save her. Again the twinkle—how can he be so stern and so amused at the same time? Heat rises to her cheeks again, and she wonders if is he laughing at her. "I shouldn't do that if I were you," he advises.

"Do what?" It's another foolish question, she decides, even as it passes her treacherous lips. She's sure her conscious mind doesn't intend to ask it, but it fails to stop the words escaping before it's too late.

"Hate yourself. It's far less bother and far more fun to have other people hate you." His response is almost a laugh, for all that his words are outrageous. Yet she can see his jaw tighten, as though to cut it off. "Oh, and the smoking too; I wouldn't do that either." And this time his smile is warm as he sips his beer.

Meredith laughs out loud, unable to help herself at his bravura. He allows his smile to spread, making him seem much younger despite the hint of wolfishness in it. Perhaps he's just a little older than herself? "Oh, I'm serious!" he continues after taking a leisurely draught from his glass. Iron weaves into the line of his smile and the timbre of his voice, though the sparkle in his eye made her unsure as the how much his words were serious and home much they were in jest. "A person can always find some fool or other to hate them if they wish, so there's no use wasting one's own efforts on doing so."

She looks at him and senses that, for a fleeting moment, she is looking into him and seeing depths of shadows and of light and feels her insides swirling in those depths and then they're gone, back behind a wall.

"Tell me about your cats," Cats seems a safer topic so he goes with it.

As she describes Agatha, her affectionate ginger-and-white molly and Poggle her sullen, nervous, tabby tom, he listens attentively, smiling at her humour and asking about their ages and characters when she runs out of words.

"Poggle's a great name! Is your office nearby?" he asks.

"Yes. I work at a marketing firm, the Triangulation Partnership. We're a couple of blocks away, and this is sort of our local bar." She catches herself, wondering what this man might want or need of her. She feels somehow inconsequential under his eyes. One part of her feels that she wishes him to take whatever he wants, while another part of her wants to be wearing more. She remembers that the company details on his card say that it's based in London, and she rushes out the first question that comes to mind. "What are you doing in town this week?"

"I'm here for a conference." His mouth twitches into yet another hint of a smile as he lifts his glass in emphasis. "Conferencing then driving is not a good policy." He takes a sip. "The beer's good. Not a bad spot for your office local." When she doesn't speak, it dawns on him that she's probably not interested in the beer. "We came in the other night to escape from talking shop. It was the first bar we came to that seemed far enough from the venue to avoid being surrounded by delegates. And it looked nice. Tonight I was planning on just a quiet drink after the gym."

That explained the casual clothes in place of the crisp suit he had been wearing when she first saw him. It also went some way towards explaining the breadth of his shoulders.

"How about you?" He fixes her with his eyes. "What brings you out on a school night?"

Feeling a little more at ease as the conversation progresses, she positions herself forward on her chair. "Oh, my friend asked if I fancied a glass of wine after work, and I wanted to work up the courage to phone this man I sort of bumped into." She places her hand on the table. He looks into her eyes as he allows his own to brush it; the sparks from her skin and those ignited by his look meet in a tightening ball inside her. After what feels like too long, she smiles and looks away to take a sip of her wine. She feels a little giddier than the one and a half glasses she's drunk should have made her. "Did you hear the rain last night?" She's pleased that she's making conversation.

"Hear it? I had a front row seat. I'm on the top floor of the Novotel—it was like the New Year's celebrations for a while around midnight." He cocks his head to one side. "Are you a 'hang out the windows' or a 'hide under the bed' type when it comes to lightning?" He's clearly daring her to be the former.

"If it's a long way off, then I like to watch," she replies, knowing that no matter how much she might sometimes wish to, she never would hang out the windows. "It kept me awake. I watched for a while when it was coming closer and then closed the curtains and looked after my cats." Realising she has mentioned her pets already, and not wanting to come over as a crazy cat lady, she tries to change subject. "Do you have any pets?"

"I'm afraid I travel and work odd hours at times, so I don't. I don't like the idea at leaving them alone."

"So you aren't the kind of charming man who goes to conferences and picks up women, and then goes back to his wife at the weekend?"

"No, no wife or current girlfriend." He purses his lips. "And yourself? Any wife at home I should know about — not that you've done anything that means I should?"

"No, it's just me, no boyfriend, "she responds flushing at the implication in his words that she might be going to do something of that sort. *Am I that transparent?* "So you're just the kind of man who goes to conferences and picks up women?"

"If I recall correctly, I noticed you looking over first." He sees that his answer has embarrassed her. "And, yes, that's the only answer I could think of that doesn't make me look like a cad or a kid." With that he tilts his now empty glass towards her. "Another?"

Meredith nods her assent. As he rises, she asks, "Can I have a sparkling water too?"

"Would you like some snacks?"

She ponders for a moment. "The honey roast cashews are nice."

While he goes to the bar, Meredith concludes that it looks like another minicab evening, but it's been a while since she has met a man she liked. She glances at her pack of cigarettes, but decides against popping outside to smoke while he's gone. Clearly he doesn't approve, and— for the moment at least —his approval matters to her.

He returns with a tray bearing their drinks and the cashews, walking with a grace that her old dance teacher would have approved of, but which she herself never quite managed. No mother should force a girl with two left feet through the trauma of dancing classes. She enjoys watching him, and noticing her eyes on him, he smiles a smile that goes straight to his eyes and from them to her cheeks.

Sitting, he unloads the tray and slides it to the far side of the table, placing her empty glass on it. While she takes a sip of sparkling water, he opens his pack of nuts, and, after having one of the honeyed cashews says, "These things are almost addictive, aren't they?" with a conspiratorial look that elicits one from her in return. "But they're hardly a suitable dinner." He pauses. She doesn't answer. "I had been going to grab something at my hotel, but if you don't have other plans, we could eat out."

Meredith had intended to pick up something on the way home or, having started her third glass of wine, get delivery alone. She certainly doesn't want another toast dinner so soon. "Yes, I'd like that. What do you fancy?"

"The dining-out app on my phone says there's a good Thai place near here, if you don't mind spicy," he suggests, sounding hopeful.

Her inner voice yells, *He likes Thai food! Check!* The words almost make it out of her mouth, but the part of her trying to play it cool tells it to shut up. Instead she says, "I know it. The food's good."

They chat amiably as they drink. Meredith tells him about her most spectacular thunder and lightning experience, holidaying in Madrid. William laughs along before telling a story of hiding from hailstones under a bridge during a storm in South Africa. She doesn't believe him. When she tells him so, he looks downcast, and she thinks she's ruined things. He takes his phone out and looks at it, then shows her what he's doing. "We knew nobody back home would believe us, so we took precautions!" There on the screen is a video of him and two other men holding up golf-ball-sized hailstones while lightning plays across the sky.

When they step outside, the cool air hits Meredith in a reminder that she's had three glasses of wine and no dinner. She exclaims, "Oops!" She steps sideways and finds he has moved swiftly from holding the door open to slipping his arm through hers.

"Chilly tonight, isn't it?" he says, looking up at the stars. "Takes your breath away a bit after the warm indoors." He loosens his grip once he's certain that she has steadied herself. "Well, as you know the way, lead on."

He's no longer holding her tight, but Meredith decides that she likes the feeling, so, without disengaging from him, she guides them on their way. For all that the night is chill, he seems warm and comfortable in his shirtsleeves for the five minutes' stroll. She thinks, *it's been too long, since*

I walked so with the solidity of a man beside me. They fall into an easy-paced walk together.

A smartly dressed waitress recognises Meredith when they arrive."Good evening Miss Webb. Table for two?" It being a weeknight, there are several free tables. In no time, they're seated comfortably. William requests a bottle of sparkling water to share before inquiring if Meredith would like anything else to drink. She asks for Rioja. He orders a glass for her and a beer for himself and thanks the waitress courteously.

Meredith enthuses about her favourite items on the menu. They quickly agree to her choice of a mixed platter of starters to share. William asks, "How are the scallops?" She is positive about these, and he suggests adding them to the hors d'oeuvres. Nervously Meredith says that she will have stir-fried tofu for her main, and William smiles."I'll do you a deal. I won't tease you about that if you don't recommend it to me."

"Why do men always tease me for liking tofu?" she asks plaintively.

"In my case, I don't like the stuff. But I only tease people who try to inflict it on me. I'm not going to try to answer for anyone else, though I suspect a lot of men fear some woman trying to make them vegetarian."

Their drinks arrive, and Meredith mutters, "I'm sure you'd like it," as she takes a sip.

William initially chooses to ignore her aside. He tries not to make a face as Meredith says "tofu" when she orders. He playfully asks, "Would I be best advised to avoid 'Thai hot' for my main?" When the waitress hesitates, he rescues her, saying, "Perhaps I'll brave that next time." She smiles with relief. "Oh, and would you be able to do another half portion of the chicken for me on a second plate?" he adds, his smooth voice deepening as he speaks.

Meredith wonders about the oddity of his request. The waitress seems a little confused, but whether it's the quietness of the evening or the calm confidence with which he speaks, or the timbre of his voice, she nods."Of course, sir."

When she's out of earshot, he looks Meredith in the eyes and says, "And I'm sure that I shouldn't, and that I don't want to spoil our evening by having a row about bean curd, especially in front of the waitress in your local restaurant." He takes a slow draught and then, more lightly, asks, "So tell me about work."

Over starters, Meredith talks about her current project and her frenemy Emily, whose life seems so much more exciting and who taunts her. She wonders that she is being so open. She takes pleasure in reflected praise when he compliments the satay and shrimps parcelled in lettuce, and thanks him as he agrees to trade the third light pastry bomb for the last morsel of spiced rib.

As they finish William makes a show of washing the sticky sauce from her fingers, his touch, confident without clinging, seems to offer the promise of more but make no demand for it. His questions about plans and deadlines show he has actually listened to her words. In response to her talk of Emily, his voice takes on a kindly, conspiratorial tone. "People who talk about how much fun they're having aren't always having that much fun," he says, and winks. "While those who don't are sometimes having lots, and choose to keep quiet about it."

He releases Meredith's hands, and she smiles. "Why, thank you." He leaves his hands on the table, and she reaches out to squeeze them briefly before they both pull back to allow the dishes to be cleared.

William tops up their glasses with mineral water and asks the waitress to bring another bottle. "I'm not having another beer, but you're welcome to more wine."

Meredith would quite like more wine, but she's feeling light-headed and takes his decision not to have another as her guide. "Thanks, but I have work tomorrow too."

He raises his water towards her in a mock toast. "To adulting!" And they both laugh.

Meredith's main is good. She considers offering him a taste but doesn't want to spoil the mood. Instead she asks, "Are you going to tell me why you ordered one and a half meals?"

He responds with a look of pure mischief, tilting his head fractionally to one side and allowing a crooked smile to grow. "No, but there are three reasons." He pauses for effect. "And you're welcome to guess."

"To take some home?" Her first guess seems the obvious choice to her.

"No. I'm staying in a hotel with its own restaurants, so that's not really the done thing. Good guess though."

"Um." She pauses, then ventures, "You're hungry after the gym?"

He nods and lifts his water glass in salute."That's one, yes."

They eat companionably. Meredith continues to guess without success. Giving upon her questioning she asks, "Can I try yours?"

A grin of impish delight spreads across his face."Yes and yes."

"What do you mean?"

William's lips twitch as he controls his smile. "Yes, you may try mine, and yes, that's the second reason why I ordered extra." His bright eyes focus on her. "A woman usually wants to try something on a chap's plate!"

Meredith rolls her eyes unintentionally as she makes to frame a retort, but is held back by a cascade of memories of herself doing just that, and by the playfulness in his eyes and the lightness of his words. Her voice is sharper than she intends when she speaks next."Well, then! What's the third reason?" She instantly regrets her tone.

He seems not to pick up on the edge in her voice, though as his first response is to laugh."Do you seriously want to know?" She nods. "I really like Thai food!" His frivolity dissolves the tension she feels, and they laugh together.

At ease, Meredith enjoys the rest of the dinner, reflecting that she is finishing a meal out without drinking beyond the point of pleasant tipsiness. Each takes a turn to share an anecdote while the other eats.

The waitress arrives to take their plates. William enquires whether Meredith would like coffee or a liqueur. It's late, but there's only instant at the office. Knowing that the restaurant's coffee is good, she responds, "An espresso would be nice."

"Double?"

"Yes, please."

He orders two double espressos for them as he asks for the bill. Not wanting to feel obligated, Meredith reaches for her purse to offer to pay her share. William is reluctant to let her. "You can if you insist, but my per diem will amply cover this."

She pauses, looking at him for any sign of expectation. Detecting none, she graciously thanks him for his kindness. Not wanting to let the evening end so soon, she asks, "Could I buy you a nightcap to thank you for dinner?"

His responding smile warms her with the knowledge that he too is not ready to part, "My hotel's bar will still be open, and it will be easier for you to arrange a cab there."

Coffees finished, he helps her into her coat. As they step outside into the chill night air, Meredith shivers. "Aren't you cold?"

"No. I don't really feel the cold, especially if I've just had a good meal." He slips his hands into his jeans pockets and opens the crook of his arm, inviting her to thread her own arm through it. "Even if I were, I'd hardly ask to borrow a lady's coat on a winter's night."

She stops and turns towards him. "Are you teasing me, Mr Farrow?"

Tilting his head down towards her under the streetlights, he replies, "Why yes, Miss Webb, I do believe I am."

She isn't sure what the reason is — the wine, the days of wondering what it would be like, the way he drifts from stern to boyish, or the pleasure of his company — but she lifts her head to the teasing smile on his lips. She opens into the kiss as he greets and returns it, drawing herself against him, and barely registers that yes, indeed his body is warm. She melds hers against it and senses the muscles of his chest tighten as he holds her close. She slides her arms around his broad back. His initial touches are intense without being overtly sexual, strong without being threatening, and her body responds to them with unfamiliar speed under his knowing hands.

When they finally break their embrace, she looks into his face. The cool air tingles against her rosied cheeks. She is relieved to see his face is happy, though surprised. "Sorry, umm, I didn't mean to …"

Her voice tails off and he softly places a finger against her mouth as she strives for words. "It was nice." The devilish twinkle in his eyes, visible under the street lights, assures her that his words are true.

He holds his hand out to her and she takes it. He allows her to guide him along their way, though each time she seeks to steer him, he playfully pulls her to a halt. At first she tries to tug him, but it's like trying to pull a reluctant horse, and he laughs at her attempts. His laughter is infectious. Each time, she finds herself joining in with it and allowing him to kiss her lips. And each time she does so, she is reminded that, true to his word, he is warm despite the winter night.

She is sure the ten-minute walk to his hotel must have taken nearly twice that, but the extra time, her body assures her, has been well spent. The cool air and playful interchange with William has distracted her and cleared her head. When they arrive, she feels mostly free of the effects of the wine she has drunk.

The hotel bar is modern, though quiet and not overly bright. Just two tables are occupied, and there's a bored-looking barman. Meredith orders, pleased to find that there's a rhubarb gin for herself and gets William a Laphroaig. He raises his glass in salute to her before they retire to a corner. As they settle companionably, she enquires, "Can I ask why you gave me your card?"

"You were looking at me, and there was something about you. And, well, to be honest, online dating has been a bit of a disaster for me."

Meredith laughs sympathetically. "Dating is a disaster full stop!"

William smiles. "Tell me about it! The profile pictures from five dress sizes ago!"

"Don't forget the ones from when they had hair!" Meredith raises her eyes and her glass. "And then there are the dates! The 'OMG, please don't let that be him' moments when you see someone approaching, dragging a leg behind them because they still haven't recovered from the fight they got into last weekend!"

"Then there's the not turning up, or being late without messaging. There's no excuse these days. It's not as if we still have to send a carrier pigeon to let a person know!"

"Or turning up with a physical peculiarity they have carefully neglected to mention." Meredith sips. "I had one guy who actually did that. It wouldn't have been a deal-breaker, but his not telling me about it before we met in person certainly was!" She rolls her eyes, "Did he expect me to not notice?"

William raises his glass and nods. "Then there's the ones who haven't offered to buy so much as a coffee after three dates. They're brilliant!" He sips and pauses. "But then you go out on your own, and you're the only single adult, or it feels as if you are. So I make a point saying hi to women who interest me."

For once when she looks into his face, she sees a hint of sadness. "So that's why you gave me your card?"

"Safe option. We were both with groups. I didn't want to embarrass you, but I thought I sensed a spark." He drains his glass and tilts it towards her enquiringly.

She nods, not wanting the evening to end. "I'll get these too." Then she looks apologetically at him. "But I need to pop outside for a cigarette first."

His eyes show disapproval, but his voice is kind when he replies, "It's after closing time. They'll only serve residents. I'll get them while you indulge."

They rise, and Meredith gives him an apologetic smile as she picks up her bag and heads towards the door and into the deserted courtyard. Once outside, she pauses to gather her thoughts in the chill air while she takes out her cigarettes and lighter. He's certainly handsome, and good company. She hasn't had an evening like this since whenever. But ...

Here the "buts" come flooding: he's from out of town, she's only just met him, he probably makes a habit of this sort of thing. She only smokes half of the cigarette, sucking down deep breaths. She calms a down little, extinguishes it unfinished, and disposes of it in the ashtray before heading back into the warm.

William and the drinks are waiting for her. She sits close by him and immediately takes a taste of her gin, swirling its bitter sweetness around her mouth to rinse away the taste of tobacco before leaning forward to thank him with a kiss. His mouth tastes of his whisky's rich, peaty fieriness. His hand is warm on her face as he brushes his thumb tenderly along her cheekbone, then gently cups the nape of her neck.

She's unsure how long the kiss continues, but she is sure that her hand is in his lap and her breathing is heavy as it ends.

"It's your choice. I can get you a taxi, or ..." He pauses meaningfully, his face intent but playful, then continues in a rumble barely above a whisper. "But we both know that if I get you a taxi, you're just going to lie awake thinking about me when you get home." His eyes gleam with mischief as they look straight into hers. The tone of his voice borders on laughter.

The words have been spoken so quietly that surely no one else could have heard, but her cheeks flame nonetheless. She tightens her jaw to make sure her mouth hasn't fallen open. The words, *Oh my God, you aren't supposed to know!* shout in her mind. Her "You can't say that" escapes her mouth rather more querulously.

He leans in again to kiss her reddening cheek, then the side of her neck. His hot breath in her ear carries the barely audible words, "Why not? It's true, isn't it? It's certainly what I'll wind up doing if you don't come up with me."

His hand is on her side and his body heat is close enough to her breasts that she can sense it. Unbidden, the thought of him pressed against her runs warmly through her mind and on throughout her body, further raising her temperature. His shirt isn't tight, but she has admired his shape underneath it all evening.

She pulls back so she can tell him she's not the kind of girl who goes to bed with strangers. But pulling back brings his eyes and impish smile into view, and instead she allows him to kiss her full on the mouth once more.

3

That Kind of Girl

His hand tightens on her without crushing, without pulling. She allows her own desire to draw her in, tentatively pressing her body to his. The swirl of reasons and excuses in her mind fight a losing battle with her body. Meredith isn't quite sure how it happens, but she is kissing him again. Then they're draining their glasses, and she is letting him lead her toward the lifts.

There's no wait for one to arrive, presumably because it's so late, and he sweeps her into the waiting car. Once inside he holds himself back from kissing her again, though she can see the playful desire in his eyes. He doesn't let go of her hand either. He hits the top floor button and aims the naughtiest of smiles at her. She waits, expecting him to move towards her. When he doesn't, move she tucks herself against his side. The car glides upwards.

As his hotel room door shuts, she experiences a sense, a moment. Her decision to stay with him hasn't seemed real somehow until now. Here in the silence, seeing the view over the city, alone with him, she with him so close! She realises that yes, this is happening and she closes her eyes for a moment as, with a rush of sensation, her body prepares itself eagerly.

She opens her eyes and finds him smiling down at her, his mischievousness shining brightly in the subdued light. Not trusting her voice, she reaches up to loop her arms around his neck and draws herself against him. Their kiss is long and slow, and within this private space she finds herself sinking into it with a giddy delight. When at last they part, she draws breath. His eyes ask the question one more time, and her own answer yes again.

His kisses and his hands sweep over her, setting off echoes inside. His touch is strong but gentle, with no hint of grabbing. The first contact is like a friend's, before it melts into her flesh in a way most unlike *just a friend*. It sends delicious heat trickling through her.

There's no sense of hurriedness. If anything, she finds herself silently longing for the next touch, longing for him to make more intimate contact with as his caress runs along her side, for it to find her nipples as he allows his arm to brush against the side of her breast. He's knowing in a way she had no idea a man's touch could be. He trails kisses down her neck and the open collar of her blouse until his stubble tickles the moons of her breasts. His hands run slow, liquid warmth down her back.

He looks up at her with that cocky smile as his deft fingers begin to open the buttons of her blouse. Its boyishness has an even more intense effect on her than his confidence. She feels unexpectedly comfortable with him undressing her, touching her skin. He carefully lays the blouse down on a chair and kisses her once more.

He looks at her, waiting and shyly reaching forward in her turn, Meredith works at the buttons of his shirt. His stomach continues firm below the dip between his pectorals. His skin is so warm to the touch. She had known he was muscular already, but as she pushes the soft cotton over his shoulders, her mouth gets ahead of her brain again. "Oh my God, your body's amazing!"

He looks abashed, but she only speaks the truth—his shoulders are from a Marvel film! "I like to keep in shape," he replies.

As his hand touches her own bare arm she is suddenly self-conscious again. The thought *What am I doing?* comes, unbidden and unwelcome. The momentary awkwardness passes and his lips meet hers. Her body knows what it's doing and sends tingles through itself to remind her what that is. *This is what I'm doing, and I'm doing it because I very much want to* and she returns his embrace passionately.

She's powerless in the grip of his strength, yet his touch is tender. He continues to undress her, and the caresses, not only of his lips and hands, even the touch of his arms make her aware of every sensitive part of her body.

The bra she's wearing does up at the back with three hooks. Its thick straps make it comfortable, but it isn't what she would have chosen to wear for a date—particularly one that might end in the bedroom. She's always found it awkward to do up herself. He chuckles softly as his first attempt to undo it fails, but once he uses two hands, it opens, and he slides it from her shoulders.

She expects his hands to reach for her breasts, but instead they linger along the length of her now bare back, first caressing, then pushing meltingly down both sides of her spine with a firm touch as he kisses her. Her sense of self-consciousness and the contrast between her body and his athletic physique eases. Her hands explore the fullness and furrows of his muscular body, and her reticence is washed away by the familiarity of touch.

His hands glide down her sides. As they do so, his wrists brush the sides of her breasts, sending thrills though her. She gasps and catches her lower lip between her teeth. Those hands continue to roam over her skin, seeking out each sensitive place she knows and some she does not, blending light caresses into firm, slow pressure that sends unfamiliar but welcome caramel rivers of sensation through her.

Meredith doesn't like being naked with the lights on even when alone, but she relaxes under his strong hands and soft kisses, remaining calm and comfortable when, at last, his fingers undo the button and zip of her skirt. The skirt's silky lining slides down her legs. Meredith remembers that she hasn't done any tidying up downstairs, she hopes William isn't put off and doesn't say anything. Placing her hand on the side of his waist for balance, she steps out of her skirt and shoes. Contact with living flesh shaped like sculpted muscle feels especially intimate.

Without her heels, the difference in their heights is more obvious. She feels small as he leans down to kiss her lips once more, his hands caressing her back then her bum through the thin material of her tights and the knickers she would not have chosen if she had known this was going to happen. His hands again flow from the softest caresses to deep, strong touch that seems to seek out and dissolve stiffness and tension. She leans into him as she enjoys their effects.

He gently slips the tips of his fingers inside the top of her tights. Bending at the knees, he slowly slips them down her thighs. He presses her, unresisting, into a sitting position on the edge of the big bed before removing them completely. Mercifully he does so without setting off the ticklishness of her feet. He puts his right arm under her thighs and tips her backwards into his left. His chest and biceps turn to steel as he lifts her. Thinking he will have difficulty, she says, "Don't!" in alarm, but finds herself being raised easily and laid down fully on the bed with him kneeling beside her. "Don't what?" He tilts his head to one side like a puppy wanting to play, and she can't help but smile.

She isn't entirely honest when she replies, "I'm not used to being picked up." though she is when she closes her eyes and pulls him down.

He pulls back. She looks up at him, touches the heavy lines of muscle that divide his chest. He takes her hand, kisses the palm, then lays it by her side. Rather than rushing to remove her knickers, he allows his fingers to trace their outline while she wishes she had worn a fancier pair. His touch though makes her feel as special as the simple white cotton briefs are plain. They move inside, brush over the line of her pubes, and return, each motion gentle yet purposeful, and each welcome to her senses. Eventually his fingers arrive, trace her slit and find her lips swollen, her entrance near readiness. They linger and caress without making to drive into her. They pause on her hood and circle, letting her know that he knows precisely where her clitoris is.

When he puts his fingers inside the band of her knickers and looks expectantly, Meredith, knowing what she thinks is expected of her and wanting it to happen, lifts her hips to allow him to slide them down her legs. Instead, he just caresses under the material there also. She enjoys the sensations of his hands on her and reflects that being undressed tenderly is a luxurious feeling.

Again he lingers in kisses and gentle touch. Just as she is beginning to wonder, with some disappointment, whether he intends to go any further, he stands and slides his jeans and briefs down his legs, stepping out of them with a slight kick. It's the first awkward movement she has seen from him, and it makes her giggle with a mixture of nervousness and relief that he is mortal after all. He kneels astride her legs and with a purposeful gentleness draws her knickers down her legs leaving them both quite naked.

He lies by her side, sliding his left arm under her shoulders to hold her close as his right hand resumes its caresses. This time it doesn't take so long to find her centre and once there it finally parts her lips far enough to touch her wet, welcoming folds before moving upwards with tantalising slowness, carrying her juices up to and under her hood. She gasps as his unerring touch finds her clitoris with a sure ease, then sighs as his fingertip circles it. The palm of his hand presses with careful weight on her pubic bone. It creates a combination of sensation that she has not felt before, but instantly knows is right for her and she rocks against it without realising that she is doing so.

Her fingers clench around his stiffness as the waves of her own pleasure wash through her. She relishes the afterglow as he moves on top of her, his hardness easily finding her opening. She feels his weight on her hips. He may be lean, but he is heavy, even with his thick arms holding the weight of his upper body.

Meredith breathes the words "I don't think I'm ready." But as he slowly enters and fills her, she finds that she is. It's gentle and slow and each time she opens her eyes, his are looking into them and there is a tender expression on his face.

As they lie together, she sleepily asks, "What you did with your hands … before we …"

"Mmm, before we what?"

"Before you touched me." She's uncomfortable opening up. "That was so nice."

"Didn't you like cumming?" His tone is surprised, but his eyes are laughing.

In her discomfort, she bats his shoulder with the side of her fist. "No, not that! That was incredible, what you did before was… lovely, unexpected."

"Have you never had a massage before?"

"No. I don't usually feel comfortable being touched by strangers."

"Well," he leans in and kisses her cheek, "now you know part of what you've been missing."

She drifts into sleep as he continues to speak and stroke her hair while his own consciousness fades.

4

In the Night

She feels a hand on her hip and stirs. The hand moves, and it feels good, knowing. There's body heat behind her, and she leans into it without fully rousing. She senses lips, first on her neck and then on her mouth. She doesn't resist or fully wake as a strong, knowing hand rolls her onto her back. She fancies dreamily that she catches a glint in a smiling eye in the near darkness, and remembers where she is.

The hand is joined by its partner, which is just as knowing and just as confident. Lips begin to work their way down her body. They travel along her collarbone and move towards her breasts. Becoming more aware, she feels her back arch in response. Her nipples become tumescent in invitation. Yet the kisses tease their way past them, circling her right breast before continuing downward across her abdomen. Her body warms as they find the line between her hip and thigh, trail toward her mons. She reflexively lifts towards him, her body waking more swiftly than her conscious mind.

He breathes heat from his lips to her slit. His warmth seems to flow into her, though again his mouth merely teases her sensitivity before reversing its journey, this time travelling up the left side of her body. Her hand seeks to guide his mouth to her swollen nipple as it nears, but firm fingers take hold of her wrist and press her arm irresistibly to the mattress.

The kisses continue; her breath catches as they trail along her jawline. She definitely see the glint as they reach her mouth. He takes her other wrist as well, and she felt his hardness as his strong legs ease her thighs apart, pinning her completely. He raises himself and looks down. She senses more than sees his smile. She realises that her body is waiting for him to enter again, and her cheeks warm. The thought *I barely know him* flashes unwelcome through her wakening brain but quickly dissolve in her body's readiness.

The smiling face descends and his lips meet hers. Her hips rise to meet his, but instead of accepting her silent invitation, he kisses his way down her body once more. This time the slow caresses find their way to every sensitive point on her body and linger at each. She tentatively tests the strength with which he holds her arms and finds it irresistible. Her legs, squeezing his between them, find them as immovable as trees.

She may barely know him, but his tongue! Oh, my! Like his hands, it navigates her folds unerringly. It knows her body better than she does herself. For all its knowledge, it seems in no more of a hurry than his cock, though her own urgency is growing. It traces the length of each of her labia, inner and outer. It glides over her hood, around it, and down to her opening. It passes over her urethra and up to her clitoris, swirls around it, kisses it. His mouth makes a seal around it and applies a pulsing suction as his tongue continues to circle the hardening bud.

Her body responds swiftly, nearing climax faster than before. But as she holds her breath, his lips release their suction, and she cries out in frustration rather than passion. She pushes herself up towards his retreating mouth and finds her body still trapped by his strength and solid weight.

His mouth begins to explores her once more. It circles, teases, nibbles, and sucks her nipples. His teeth nip each bud once, making her gasp aloud and again he makes his way southwards.

This time her responses come more quickly, but his reading of them is just as sure. This time instead of sucking, he forms a groove in the centre of his tongue and runs it over and around her clitoris again and again. Once more, in the instant before her release, he denies her. This time her exhalation is a clear cry of "No!"

Moments later he is staring down at her, his thighs still between hers, holding her legs wide, up, and apart, his furiously hard erection teasing her. He lowers his mouth, and despite her frustration and annoyance, she opens her own to it, tasting herself on him. He presses against her entrance. She feels his eyes taunting her as she lies powerless, and that clever mouth begins to tease its way down her body again.

She knows the approximate route it will take by now, but is still uncertain as to where it will travel and tarry and what it will do there. She thrusts her breasts up, uncaring of his intent, hoping they will meet his lips, his tongue or his teeth. This time she holds her silence as he teases, sucks, and nips. Her foreknowledge causes prescient waves of sensation to radiate through her on the paths she expects his mouth will travel.

She tests the strength of his grip on her wrists again, hoping to speed his lips toward their destination, and holding his mouth in place to make him satisfy her burning need. Again she finds herself helpless. He stops as she struggles, looks up, and waits until she ceases and looks down at him imploringly in the shadow. Meredith's eyes meet his steady, unyielding gaze in the near dark. She gives up, drops her head onto the pillows, and spreads her legs wider than his body has held them and makes a sound close to a sob.

Sensing her surrender, he allows his tongue to linger along the lines of her bottom ribs and around her belly button. He descends. The tip of his tongue traces the lines of her inner and outer labia. Time almost stops for her, and her need swells. His tongue makes figures of eight around her hood and urethra. She lies still, knowing this touch will not be enough for her. Then he slides it under her hood, around her clitoris. Her breathing deepens in the knowledge that this most certainly will be enough, if only he carries on...

He settles into a rhythm she can follow and rock with, a swirl, a suck, and a pulse of pressure, and her clitoris, sought and found, rides its movements like a tiny jockey racing for the line. She tries not to hold her breath, tries not to let him know how close she is. But she realises that she *is* holding her breath and that she is there. She cries out under his ministrations. The sound is his signal. He draws her clitoris in with a sudden hard suck and spins the tip of his tongue around it again and again. His arms clamp tight, trapping her wrists and legs even more strongly as she writhes. He draws out her ecstasy.

Eventually, the waves begin to recede, and as they do, his lips and hands release her. He sweeps his strong body up the bed. A fresh breaker crashes through her as he enters in a single motion. Her mouth opens to him as her entrance has. His tongue slides into her mouth as his cock slides into her. Her freed hands clasp him. She crushes herself against him as his hips thrust into her. Her insides, swollen and sensitive from the time before, welcome him anew.

In the past, she'd mostly enjoyed intercourse for the pleasure it gave her partners, though once she'd used her fingers on herself and come close, but her then-boyfriend spoiled the moment. Earlier tonight William, had made the focus of their love making herself and her pleasure. Now she feels thoroughly fucked even before they start again and her senses are instantly alight.

She fears initially that the force of him might hurt. Their pubic bones collide, but the shockwave the impact sends through her is of something entirely other than pain. As he builds a rhythm, her palms are drawn to the hard, powerful, peachy fullness of his bum. As it tenses and relaxes with each thrust into her, she clasps it in time with his remorseless rhythm. The strength of each thrust shakes her.

Though he seems tireless, his endurance has limits. His rhythmic power pushes her over the edge, and his body tenses above her, pulsating inside her. She hears his groans merge with her own. He stills, panting, sweating, and, she is sure, smiling at her.

After a while, he resumes rocking gently inside her, kisses her, and then withdraws. The next thing she senses is him using one of the hotel's thick, soft white towels to tenderly dry their mingled perspiration, first from her body and then from his own, before he kisses her once more and strokes her hair.

5

Breakfast

Meredith rouses to the sensation of lips on her shoulder and the scent of steeping grounds. "Mmm," she purrs as she stretches languidly. The rich aroma, the memory of the night, and the man fill her body and mind. "Real coffee?" she asks, looking up. He's naked and as beautiful as she remembers.

"Hotel's kettle, my cafetière." He smiles. "Never leave home without good coffee." In that moment he is halfway between a boy playing at being a man and a man playing at being a boy.

She laughs and teases, "Were you a Boy Scout?"

"No, just a Royal Engineer. It's amazing what you learn from serving alongside corporals and sergeants about comfort in adversity."

"So you were an officer?"

He nods, "Though my CO always thought I was too keen on getting my hands dirty."

"And a four-star hotel is now your idea of adversity?"

It's his turn to laugh at her joke. "Well, it's better than a snow cave in the Arctic, but it does lack a few of the luxuries of home." He looks hopeful. "However, one thing it doesn't lack is someone else to make a cracking breakfast. Do you mind if we eat before we get ready? I'm starving."

Deep down, Meredith does mind. Her hair is a *mess*. But he's asked nicely and, unusually for herself in the morning, she is actually quite peckish —but then she isn't used to making love all night. Before they leave the room, he quietly advises her to go for tea or espresso. "It's a lovely place, but the filter coffee in most hotels is awful."

"More hardships, Mr Farrow?"

"Ha-ha. It's true, my life is a tragedy, Miss Webb," he jokes and squeezes her hand as they walk to the elevator.

The hotel's restaurant is modern and airy. A waiter guides them to a table with a window view. She can't believe how much William eats. "It's so unfair. How can you eat like that and have a body like yours? he asks incredulously as he piles on the bacon, sausages, beans, tomatoes, and mushrooms. His meal dwarfs her own, though she's surprised at how hungry she is. She rarely eats breakfast, and when she does, it's usually just a piece of toast or a couple of Ryvitas. Today, she helps herself to a healthy portion of bacon and scrambled eggs.

"Three fried eggs?" the woman at the service asks William, unprompted. Her tone motherly.

His eyes light as he smiles a boyish smile of thanks."Thank you, yes. It's good of you to remember."

When they have been sitting for just a minute, the woman from the kitchen appears. "I brought you your fried bread."

"Oh, you are such an angel. Thank you!" He beams at her and she smiles back at him with an expression familiar to every child of a proud mother.

"Are you a regular here?" Meredith asks, amused.

"No, this week's the first time. We got to talking on Tuesday about the perfect breakfast and how it isn't complete without a fried slice. The dear thing has been making me one ever since. Would you like half?"

"No. I've already got more than I can eat on my own plate. You go ahead and enjoy yourself."

He looks slightly disappointed, but says nothing and certainly doesn't offer again. He sets to work on the mountainous breaking of his fast.

"Aren't you forgetting something?" he asks in a conversational tone.

"What do you mean?" Meredith tries to recall whether she's done or failed to do something.

"It might be nice to have your number if you want me to call." The corner of his mouth turns up. "You do want me to call, don't you?"

It's true. In the excitement and intensity, she still hasn't given him her number.

The enormity hits her: she's slept with a man she's barely met, who doesn't even have her number. "Of course. I didn't remember." Her voice trails, as she realises how far out of her comfort zone she is. Her face betrays her embarrassment.

He comes to her rescue once more, "Well, we were a little distracted." His wry, lopsided smile touches her. "I mean, it's OK if you don't, but I would quite like to see you again."

She smiles. "Yes, definitely, that would be nice." And she gives him the number.

He keys it into his phone. Her own phone beeps, signalling an incoming text.

William Farrow x.

It makes her smile. He certainly is playful.

After they've eaten, they head back to his room. She showers and, on leaving the bathroom, finds a new blouse, skirt, bra, and panties laid out on the bed — all in her size, all tastefully stylish. The panties and bra are black. They're sexy, small, and lacy, but not embarrassingly tiny.

"Well, you can't exactly turn up in the office in the same clothes you wore yesterday — and I doubt you keep a change in your desk." He smiles, his mischievous eyes glinting.

She blushes and looks down. She's never gone to work in the previous day's clothes in her life, and certainly doesn't keep a change of clothes in the office!

He lifts her chin and kisses her lips. As they kiss, he loosens the belt of the soft white hotel bathrobe and opens it, causing her blush to deepen. Her shyness strikes anew as her body is exposed again to this handsome, fully clothed, near stranger. Yet his kiss feels good, and she offers no resistance when he slips the robe from her shoulders. The material of his jacket tickles against her nipples. His hands caress and knead her back and buttocks. She closes her eyes and drifts with the sensations as he explores her mouth.

He turns her and continues to kiss her, his hands roving over her breasts, his foot edging her feet apart. The fingers of his right hand trail down her body, over her mons and on to her slit, which, again to her surprise, they find soaking wet. Her vulva is sensitive and swollen from their night of passion and welcomes them. In a few moments, she feels her heat rising. Knowing she has to get to work, she makes to break free only for the heavy muscles of his left arm to stiffen around her as his finger and thumb gently tease her right nipple. "Don't you want to cum again?"

"I have to get to work," she protests weakly.

"It's only a five-minute walk."

His hands feel so good on her, and her body is on his side …

His kiss continues, and she closes her eyes again. He turns her back slowly as her body responds to his ministrations taking his time again, but finds her body is in a rush; and she is on the verge of orgasm in minutes.

"Open your eyes."

She does so and closes them again promptly, seeing that he has positioned her facing the large mirrors over the room's dressing table.

His fingers slow immediately. "Open your eyes if you want to cum."

She resists, not liking to see her naked body so exposed, and certainly not in the arms and at the mercy of a near stranger, but he's taken her too close. Her lips move and she says "Please." Yet she does not open her eyes.

His fingers keep moving slowly. Two of them slide into her and hook, as they did last evening and in the night, onto the sensitive spot inside her pubic bone. The palm of his hand presses against her swollen clit—how does he know to press just there? Men never know …

But he doesn't press hard enough in either place or move his hand fast enough to give her release, merely keeping her tantalisingly close. "Open your eyes if you want to cum." He repeats the words whisper-soft in his calm bass-baritone.

A tear of frustration escapes her tightly shut eyelids. She doesn't mean to say what she says—she's sure of that, and will later assure herself of this. She only means to say yes. But as the sensations become too much and she opens her eyes to her own nudity and vulnerability, she says, "Yes, sir." She will remember it for the rest of her life. She will remember how right it feels.

His fingers gather pace and energy, pressing, probing, taking a part of her weight on the crook of his index finger as the base of his thumb circles and applies pressure to her clitoris.

She feels his hardness behind her as her knees quiver and pleasure flares out from her centre. He holds her and keeps her going. She hears his whispered "Good girl" as the waves carry her away and the tear rolls down her cheek.

The waves fade. He kisses her wet eyes, tasting the salt, looking into them and into her. He holds his wet fingers to her lips as he had last night, and as she did last night, she opens her mouth to receive them without a word. She kisses them, sucks them, licks her taste from them. When they withdraw, he kisses her deeply, then smiles impishly and repeats, "Good girl." The words leave a warmth inside her chest. He kisses her lips again and swats her backside gently with the flat of his hand, saying, "Time to get dressed!" He trails his fingers from her mons to her breast before finally releasing her then sprawling on the side of the bed he hasn't laid her new clothes out on.

She pauses. She can hardly gather the clothing and scuttle naked to the bathroom to get dressed so she dresses under his eyes, despite feeling her self-consciousness rise in a wash of colour as she slips into the new items. In an effort to distract herself and his gaze, she asks, "Where on earth do you get these clothes?"

"I co-opted one of the girls from night reception. She popped out at the end of her shift to pick them up. Are they okay?"

Once dressed, and temporarily forgetting his eyes on her, she admires the ivory blouse and tailored knee-length chocolate-brown skirt in the room's mirrors. "Yes." She's pleased to note that there is only the barest shadow of the new bra visible through the blouse's silky material. The clothes are more than okay. She thanks him, and then blushes as he asks her to turn for him.

William offers to walk her to her office, but she refuses, thinking that, by arriving with him, she would give the game away. She sets off on the half-mile journey by herself. Her own clothes (she almost blushes at that thought, she'd met this man twice and she is wearing, quite literally **his clothes**), are folded in the shopping bags that the new clothes came in. He'd refused to let her pay him for the new things. It feels wrong — deliciously so. She flushes. They fit beautifully.

Her skin feels aglow with morning-after, alert senses. The feeling is exacerbated by the coldness of the air and her recent orgasm, as well as by the memory of her ordeal as she dressed under his penetrating gaze. Meredith pulls her jacket close. Yes, her skin feels different, more alive, as if still under William's clever hands. She's unfamiliar with the physical and emotional sensations of the *walk of shame*. She had not been expecting the strange feeling that every person she passes must know, or at least guess what she has been doing.

Meredith takes the opportunity to pick up a decent coffee on the way. She drops the clothes bags into the boot of her car. The car is covered in hoarfrost, showing that it can't have moved this morning. But it is hardly the first time her little Kia has spent the night in the office car park. She reflects that sometimes drinking and thus having to leave her car has its advantages. as she sips her coffee. At least no one at work will see the shopping bags.

6

The Day After

Having successfully walked past reception and said what she hopes is an innocent good morning, she goes into her office, and, unusually, shuts the door. She sits at her desk to draw breath. Her body is still shouting every detail of the night before. Even contact with her familiar chair is a reminder. She settles in and closes her eyes, focusing on the work.

Then she decides a text to Jess is more urgent.

OMG—call me!

Are you OK?

Meredith hasn't even finished keying in a yes when her phone rings.

"What's up?" Jess's voice is worried, and Meredith realises her choice of words wasn't the best.

"Nothing. Everything. I saw him!"

"What happened?"

"Yes."

Meredith thinks the word says everything, but her friend, knowing her usual habits, doesn't understand. "What do you mean?"

"We did!"

"What? No, you didn't! You? You don't!"

Meredith feels her cheeks flaring. Jess knows her so well. It's true, she barely kisses on the first date, let alone …

"So you've gone to work in yesterday's clothes?" Jess laughs. "Welcome to tramp world!"

"Um, no." Meredith doesn't quite know how to say it. "Um …"

"Come on, details! Have you been doing some crafty shopping on the way to work? That's impressively sneaky for you!"

"No, I haven't. He bought me a new blouse and skirt."

"No! Wow! Come on! What did you do?"

"What didn't I do might be a shorter list!"

Meredith spends the next fifteen minutes relating her evening, her night, and her morning. Jess gets her promise to send pictures of her new outfit.

"When are you seeing him again?" Jess's voice is alive with excitement; her best friend deserves something good.

"I don't know. I only left him half an hour ago. I don't know anything about him!"

"So he might be married?" Jess's voice takes on a note of concern. "You've been hurt before …"

"No. I asked, and he said there's no one." Meredith feels the edge of her joy being torn away. *Why do people have to interfere?* Then, remembering her last relationship, *Why do they have to be shits who turn out to be married?* She feels deflated. What-ifs hadn't been part of today until now. A weight of doubt descends on her despite his assurance, and her thoughts are derailed. *Mind you, this is Jess. She* kicks herself mentally. Jess is the woman who's been there for her after each of her disastrous relationships — and who advised her against starting most of them.

"Ask him to stay tonight. If he's got someone to go home to, he won't, and you can start fretting then," Jess recommends. "You can say you're trying to save him from the horrors of the Friday rush-hour."

Relieved at the reminder that her friend is on her side, Meredith promises to do just that. "Oh, and Jess?" she says after a silence.

"Yes, hun?" Jess's voice is kind.

"Does everybody know? Only I feel—" She stops as her friend's laughter peals out from her phone.

"Nobody knows. You're just buzzing and probably glowing. The better the time you've had, the more certain you are that *everyone* must know every detail, but trust me. They haven't got a clue. Anyway, from what you've said, if they do know, they're going to be jealous—like I am!" More laughter, and this time a furiously blushing Meredith joins in. "Love you. Now go take me a photo of your outfit!" Jess commands as they ring off.

Feeling very self-conscious, Meredith pops out to the rest room to take a picture of herself. Just as she's framing her pose, or trying to, the door opens and in walks Emily. "Look at you! Out somewhere special tonight?" The greeting is a pleasant change and not the sarcasm Meredith fears. Emily never compliments her on the way she looks.

"Um, no, I just fancied dressing up a little today. When I mentioned it to my friend, she asked for a photo, but I'm rubbish at taking selfies."

"Here, give me your phone. It's much easier taking a picture of someone else than a selfie."

Meredith wouldn't normally be willing offer her phone to a colleague, but Emily stands there with her hand out and a friendly expression. Meredith can't think of a polite way out of it, so, despite feeling shy, she hands her phone over. Emily takes a series of pictures. Once satisfied, she hands the phone back. Meredith thanks her and heads for the door.

"That top really suits you," Emily says by way of parting.

Meredith had felt annoyed at having to pose, and the compliment makes her feel bad about it. Back at her desk, she looks at the photos and feels even worse. There are some that she has to admit are quite flattering.

Before she's chosen, a message arrives from Jess.

Sorry to ask about Mr Beautiful being married. Don't forget to ask him to stay over tonight? If there's a wife at home, he certainly won't. x love you.

Then another.

And don't forget my picture ;-)

The pictures Emily has taken are certainly better than Meredith could have done by herself in the mirror. She thinks, *Emily is right; the clothes definitely suit me.* She ponders over which photo to send to Jess. After a few minutes, she selects a three-quarter angle shot that shows off the clothes and flatters her own shape.

She's just getting down to work on a store survey when Jess messages again.

> *He's a keeper! Ask him to stay; those clothes don't scream tramp at all.*

The message is followed by a string of laughter emojis. It makes Meredith laugh. Jess has a long series of Facebook posts depicting clothes bought by men for women. Most certainly fit the *tramp* epithet.

> *Oh, and can I have a rear shot? They really show your curves.*

This message make Meredith feel warm inside. She isn't sure whether her friend is just being nice, but Jess always knows how to make her feel good.

The day is spent failing to work up the courage to call him. He has affected her, but she doesn't know what they are to each other the day after. She's been awake for much of the night. Whenever she stirred, his hands or his lips had found her. She can't remember for certain how many times she woke to the sensations of his mouth or hands pleasuring her, though she knows that on two of those occasions, he finished by entering and fucking her welcoming, if only half-awake body. Whenever she moves, her body reminds her of his touch, the fine fabric of the new clothes against her skin sending flares of pleasure coursing through her. Echoes of the night before. Then there were the clothes themselves, not the sort a man bought a woman in her experience, stylish more than in your face, the sort of thing she might buy when treating herself.

Now she knows how friends who've done the dirty on their first date feel. She hangs on tenterhooks, waiting for him to call or text. Later she'll look back, realising that if he didn't want to see her again he surely wouldn't have gone to the trouble of buying her new clothes. But now, reason isn't ruling her mind.

Eventually he messages.

Thank you for a lovely night. May I see you again?

Yes, I'd definitely like to see you again. I had a great time.
I'm glad you did too.

I especially liked the "yes, sir".

A devil emoji and a kiss follow. Meredith blushes at her desk, aghast. Where had that come from? And why does it resonate when he mentions it to her?

The reminder for the end-of-week team meeting pops up, interrupting her reverie. She heads to the rest room to gather herself before going in. As she stands before the mirror, her memory interferes. *Oh my God! I only met him this week! I've never had an orgasm with anyone before and he made me cum so easily. Then he stripped me in front of a mirror and forced me to watch myself naked and cumming!* She feels panic trying to rise in her chest, warring with the sudden heat that fills her at the memory. *I got dressed while he watched.* She hasn't dressed or undressed in front of anyone since PE classes at school, and she hated doing so then.

It's all very well for him, she grumbles internally; *her mind recalled his own nakedness in all too clear detail. He has the body of a Norse god. And that easy confidence! Where do some people get that from?* Well, she could imagine him finding it simple; the world appeared to wrap itself around his broad shoulders and open before his blue-green eyes.

She pulls herself together at the sound of the tap of the other sink. Emily is standing next to her. "All dressed up and miles away! Are you sure you don't have any plans for this evening?" Emily is—as is usual on a Friday, even when she doesn't have any outside meetings—dressed up, presumably ready to go out and party.

Meredith bristles inwardly and blushes outwardly. She knows Emily is just being Emily, but Meredith wishes she wouldn't be sometimes. "Er, no. I just thought I'd put something nice on today," she lies, looking back to her own reflection and straightening herself before heading for the door.

★★★

Lunchtime rolls around, and with it their ritual Friday lunchtime girls' drink. Emily volunteers to get the drinks. When she returns, she presses Meredith again: "Are you sure you haven't got a hot date after work? You never dress up if you can avoid it."

Meredith, caught off guard, really blushes this time. It's true, she doesn't dress up, but neither does she wish to talk about it. She looks down before replying, "No, I just had these new things, and I thought it would be nice to wear them today." To avoid further questioning, she invokes Emily's self-absorption. "Anyway, you're the one who has hot dates."

The tactic works; Emily launches into her plans for the night. Meredith half listens, her mind on the night before and her own, entirely unexpected hot date.

He messages her again after lunch, continuing the theme of how dull the last day of the conference is.

> *I'm only being carried through it by the memory of your "dress-tease". That could become a thing in our prudish age, you know.*

Meredith can't believe how rude he is — or how this type of rudeness from him affects her.

They keep messaging on and off, silly things and things they've done or seen. One thing leads to another, and when he says he has to travel home that evening, she asks about his Friday traffic, knowing it will be awful. When he says as much, she takes Jess's suggestion and asks if he'd like to stay the night at her place. The moment she clicks to send the question, her heart catches in her throat.

She messages Jess, as she waits, frets to herself. Her phone chimes with Jess's supportive response. She finds herself disappointed that it's only Jess. As the minutes tick by her mind and insides fight a battle about whether she should have asked William. Her mind is just starting to win when his response arrives:

> *That would be great if you don't mind.*

And the matter is settled in favour of her insides. It makes her mouth assume a smile like the one it would wear if she'd just popped a favourite sweet in. Her body gives a brief pulse in celebration.

Meredith messages him her address and—estimating that it will require two hours to clean the place up, bathe, and change— she suggests he arrive at half past five. She's more pleased than usual that her office closes early on Fridays. She enjoys her work and enjoys being good at it, but being able to escape early for the weekend is a definite bonus, even if others use it more enthusiastically.

Nothing too closely resembling constructive work happens for Meredith for the remainder of the afternoon. It may not be their first date, but she definitely finds herself suffering from a surfeit of first-date nerves. She lets Jess know the good news. Then, pleased that he's coming, Meredith decides to take the picture from behind that Jess has asked for.

As she's making a third unsuccessful attempt, Emily once again enters. "Hey, could you hold the fort for the last half hour? I was hoping to sneak off—" she stops mid flow, "What are you doing?"

"My friend wanted a picture from behind," Meredith explains.

"Give me your phone and I'll do it." Emily smiles. "You should hire me as your photographer, you know."

Emily has her try several poses and takes a lot more pictures than Meredith thinks is necessary. "Just delete the ones you don't want," Emily tells her.

"Thanks, I really appreciate it. No problem leaving early. See you next week."

Emily replies, "Remember, if it is a date, you owe me all the sordid details." and laughs at the shocked expression on Meredith's face. "Have a good weekend anyway, and thanks for covering."

Meredith sends Jess her favourite of the pictures and sets about finishing up for the day. She checks with Sophie, their personal assistant, that there's nothing new to prepare for Monday. Then sends Sophie off too and puts her own jacket on.

Her car feels cold when she gets into it. At least with the early finish it's still light outside; she enjoys driving much more in daylight.

Getting home doesn't mean the usual lazy hour of unwinding and pottering, even though she's tired after the long night and day at work. She puts a pot of coffee on, then set about straightening the house. That done she pours herself a cup and changes her bed as she runs herself a bath. As she bathes she reflects that at least rushing around has saved her the worry of waiting.

It also means she doesn't have much time to fuss about what to wear, simply grabbing her best jeans and a top Jess says suits her.

7

Not Rush Hour

She's is pleased when William arrives, but feels awkward as she welcomes him. It had been one thing last night—merry in every sense of the word, and his nice hotel making it seem almost a holiday romance. But having him come into her home in the early dark of a February evening is quite another, far more real experience. The doorbell camera shows him in another dark suit, and there he is, as handsome as she remembers. His smile of greeting is warm, lopsided, and distinctly boyish. He proffers a bottle. "I hope this is OK. It's all I was certain you liked. I'm afraid I don't really know the local merchants."

The bottle looks expensive and has a year on it, 2010, It's more the sort of thing her mother would buy than Meredith would. She gives him "the tour". Her home isn't large, but it's more than adequate for her. It's well appointed, with two good-sized bedrooms, a big kitchen that she thinks she should use more, and a large, open combination dining room and lounge. The cosy area is dominated by her gigantic, newly acquired and loved television and an L-shaped sofa big enough for six.

Downstairs, they pick up a follower when Aggy—the little molly is always curious about people—shows up. William stops and crouches. "Hello," he says in his rumbliest tone, holding his hand slightly in front of him but not approaching the cat.

"Agatha, William. William, meet Aggy," Meredith introduces them. The little creature slowly approaches the offered hand, sniffing cautiously. After a moment she rubs her head and then her flank against it.

"I'm pleased to meet you, Agatha." He ruffles his knuckles along the back of her head and down her neck with the familiarity of someone used to cats.

"You'll have a friend for life if you keep that up." Meredith's happy that they get on. The saying 'love me, love my cat' pops into her head, and she wonders where it came from. But she wants to move the centre of attention back to herself. "I haven't got anything in for dinner, but the local Indian and chip shop are really good."

"That's fine. I live miles from a decent chippie, so that would make a nice change."

Meredith would have preferred Indian. She really doesn't like fish; she usually has a battered sausage with chips when she and her friends go in on the way home from the pub. But she doesn't want to admit this to William just yet, and she's grateful that he is pleased.

There's an off-licence a few shops before the chippie, and William suggests popping in, on the grounds that the Rioja he's brought doesn't really go with fish and chips. Meredith makes a face when he suggests a Sauvignon Blanc that hints at a preference for red wine, "OK, how about sparkling?" he asks.

"Sparkling's good," she responds, glad that he's flexible.

There's a Lindauer in the chiller cabinet. He picks up the first bottle and looks enquiringly at Meredith. She like New Zealand wines and nods her agreement. He puts the first bottle in the chiller again and selects another from the back.

"Colder?" she asks.

"Yes, but not quite—." He ponders before picking up a bag of ice from the freezer with a grin and winks to Meredith. He pays and carefully makes sure the bottle is as well packed against the ice bag as he can.

They have to queue for their food. "Sorry, I should have rung ahead," Meredith says. "I don't often come here." Silently adding *This early* to herself.

"That's okay. It's warm and I like the smell. Besides, the longer we are, the colder the fizz will be."

It is indeed toastily warm by the counter of the busy shop. Meredith stifles a yawn as the heat and late night start to catch up with her. William squeezes her hand in a gesture she finds most reassuring.

When they are served, he chooses a large cod and chips. She is still considering. She toys with the idea of battered sausage, but decides it is not ladylike enough. Plus, there is no telling what the effects of that amount of batter on her sometimes-delicate tummy will be. Eventually, the lady in her settles on a small chips with chicken goujons, which she knows she will only pick at. Before she can object, he taps his card on the shop's machine to pay.

They have to wait for her chicken to be cooked fresh. William is in playful mood, as she is learning is usual for him. He bumps his shoulder gently into her and moves away, then sidles back. Meredith is privately irritated when he's picked up the bill again. He asks if she'd like to carry the cold bag or the warm one. Despite herself, she can't help be amused as she opts for the hot food, even if it will smell of fish.

Once outside Meredith admonishes him, "You should have let me pay. You're my guest."

"Sorry. I would have done, but mine was a lot more expensive. Besides ..." He turns to her, his expression a mixture of amusement and apology. "I get the impression that you're not heavily into fish and chips. I wouldn't have minded Indian, you know."

Meredith gives his hand a squeeze and grins at him, thinking, *He seems to be able to read my thoughts. Gosh, that could be a catastrophe.*

"You can buy me breakfast if that makes you feel better," he adds.

She looks up to say *deal*, but, remembering William's breakfast that morning, teases back saying, "I've seen you eat breakfast! I'm not sure I can afford it! But okay, it's a deal." Then she nudges his wall-like side playfully with her shoulder. "Just how much do you weigh?"

"Ninety-five kilos or thereabouts. Why?"

"Bumping into you's like bumping into a horse!" she complains.

That elicits a mock neigh and an apologetic shrug. "You could always not do it."

"Arse." And this time she presses her shoulder gently against him, and he drapes his arm around her. She can't help thinking that cold winter air is better with the warmth of a man by her side. Even so, her cheeks are beginning to feel the spark of winter chill by the time they get back to her house.

They eat at her large dining table, even though she feels it's more suited to four or six, rather than with the food on their laps, because she doesn't want to be the cause of him getting greasy chip stains on his nice suit.

Meredith likes the way the wine tastes with the saltiness of the meal. "Fizz and chips, who'd have thought."

"I will confess that it was an accidental discovery, but yes, it works, doesn't it."

The smell of food prompts Pog to make an appearance, though he's wary of the large new human in his house. He starts his pleading routine with the familiar Meredith, who he knows is a soft touch.

William is amused by the little creature's antics, all the more so when Aggy joins in. Normally Meredith would have given in and offered each cat a morsel almost immediately, but she doesn't want to show how much in the thrall of her fur babies she truly is. She holds out until she has almost finished eating. Then does she divide one end of her last goujon and, careful that neither carnivore snaffles both morsels, lets the pair have their treat. Pog retreats to a corner to consume his, but Aggy wolfs her piece down close to the table.

"Will they eat cod?" William asks.

Meredith shrugs. "I don't know. They haven't had the chance to find out."

"Should I try?"

"You can."

He pares a little flake of fish and strip of skin away from the batter for each. Agatha is instantly interested, but Poggle hangs back and only approaches the proffered morsel slowly. After an age, and with Agatha beginning to meowl her impatience, he finally gets close enough to crane his neck out and take his share. As he does, William lowers his other hand and allows Aggy to take hers.

"That's so sweet! Are you sure you've never had cats?" She's surprised by his patience.

"Ha, no, but growing up, my brothers and I weren't that different to these two scamps."

He finishes the last of his fish and chips and they take their plates to the kitchen. She runs enough water to start soaking the ketchup off and then turns to him. "So do you fancy TV or …"

"Your television is amazing, but—" he kisses her, "—tell me about 'or'." He says archly and kisses her again.

Meredith likes the way his voice gets deeper when he's being naughty. She insinuates her body against his. "Well," she kisses him back, "you kept me up for most of the night," kiss, "so I might just need to go to bed early." She can't quite keep her face straight and lets out a chuckle. "First, though, 'or' includes washing these plates up so my kitchen doesn't smell of old fish in the morning."

He wipes, and impresses her by remembering which cupboard she retrieved the plates from. He makes a show of folding the tea towel and returning it to her with a teasing half smile.

"Come on, smart arse." She wraps her arms around his muscular frame and kisses him more lingeringly this time before shyly leading him upstairs.

When they reach her bedroom, he takes her shoulders from behind in a firm but gentle grip. He kisses down the side of her neck, sending delicious shivers through her, and she nestles comfortably into his embrace. She feels him stiffen as he continues to kiss her, but she doesn't respond other than with a swaying of her hips. It's early, and she's in no rush.

After a while, he slowly rotates her. She lifts her face, brushing her lips against his and opens to him. One hand explores the crazy folds of muscle on his back while the other finds the hard fullness of his peachy bum. As she does so he does the thing he did the night before — stroking her sides while allowing his arms to brush against her breasts. It's still really sexy, but not too much to start. She purrs softly. They hold, sway, and kiss. It is all very nice, and she feels her body getting ready for the next stage. He seems to read her responses well; his hands slowly move to the buttons of her blouse.

"Why do we have to take my clothes off first?" she asks.

"Hmm, well, it seems appropriate." He winks. "Although these are technically my clothes you're wearing."

"OK, but could we have just the bedside light?"

Surprised by the depth of her shyness, he touches her chin and raises her face to his. He bends to graze his lips over hers, then reaches for the bedside lamp, fumbling until he finds the on switch. He turns the main light off before returning to Meredith. He takes her hand and strokes her face, then kisses her. She whispers, "Thank you," in a barely audible voice.

8

Weekending

On the way to the cafe Meredith admits that she rarely walks as far she has done in the last few days.

"Really?" William asks surprised.

She winces, "I don't do anything fitness-wise at the moment."

"Is there anything stopping you?"

"No, I just don't, hmm…" she tries to pick her words, "If you wanted to see me again…" and lets that hang and looks up at him.

He smiles "Which I would…"

"Would you maybe like to show me some things I could do?"

"I'd love to," He lowers his lips to hers, "But I won't hold you to that if you change your mind." She takes his hand as they walk the rest of the way.

Even the regular cafe breakfast she has is huge by her standards, but William's "builders special breakfast", —which he orders after asking apologetically if it's okay to strikes her as being of comical proportions. Meredith has her own particular way with an English breakfast, though she hadn't indulged it the previous day in William's hotel. This was, however, her own local cafe, and their relationship was no longer just a one-time thing. So she resolves to enjoy breakfast her way.

When the food arrives William's plate is as huge and as heavily laden as she'd imagined. So in Meredith's mind, he has no cause to comment. But she guesses, correctly, that he will. Everybody does.

Everyone has his or her funny little ways and one of Meredith's is with an English breakfast. For starters, there are her hash browns—they need mayo *and* brown sauce. Rather less controversially, she adds red sauce on the sausages, not just the juice from the beans. It has to be red sauce, though either Heinz or Daddy's will do. Finally she stirs a little mayo into her scrambled eggs.

Meredith is about to cut the first piece of sausage when she realises that he's staring. He's already eaten quite a lot and has stopped.

"Do you mind me asking how you worked out that that's how you like your full English?" His voice is amused. "I mean, I have no room to criticise. I like mine delivered by the pallet-load with fried bread, eggs easy over, and bacon cooked just so."

She looks at him, about to get aggressively defensive, before realising his comment is kindly worded and his manner light-hearted. Then she laughs with him. Yes, he's poking fun, but he's poking fun at himself too. "Dad always had brown sauce and Mum always had red, so I tried both and…" she shrugs, still smiling.

It sounds silly, but he seems to like silly, and his "cool" indicates that he sees the matter as satisfactorily closed.

While he demolishes his own mountain, he goes through some of the places he got his preferences from. His mother, an aunt, and a mess sergeant appear to have been the main influences. Though he credits the easy-over eggs to an ex—awful in all other ways, he assures her—who hated uncooked white, while he cordially loathes a solid yolk. They achieved perfect accord on two things: fried eggs and mutual incompatibility.

"Is there anything you can't turn into a joke?" she asks.

"Not that I've found yet." The devil-may-care look gleams in his green-blue eyes, and she feels a girlish one shine back from her blue ones.

They hold hands as they stroll back to her house. Meredith sees their reflection in a shop window. Feeling very much at home in William's company, she leans her blonde locks against his broad shoulder. She doesn't often think of herself as pretty, but she would have liked the courage to take a picture of the two of them just then.

Saturday was supposed to have been busier than she feels up for. Staying up for most of two workday nights has left her tired. After seeing William off, she heads into the kitchen to start the washing. That done, she pops a pod in the coffee machine. While it's heating, Pog shows up. It's typical for the tomcat to arrive once he's sure the visitor has disappeared. She feeds him, then takes her coffee and stretches out on her huge, cosy sofa to phone Jess and pass on at least a few of the latest details.

Her friend again compliments William's taste in clothes. She bombards Meredith with questions and is only satisfied when Meredith agrees to Jess coming over on Sunday evening to hear what her friend refers to as "All the grisly details" first-hand.

After she hangs up, Meredith starts her robot vacuum cleaner on its daily chore of hoovering the ground floor and heads upstairs (her cats are wonderful company but also shed like crazy). Her bedroom is still pretty tidy; he'd even helped her fold back the duvet before he left, so she slips back under her it for what she intends to be a moment. The pillow on the side of the bed she doesn't use smells of him and she pulls it against herself as she settles down for a short doze.

Over an hour, rather than the intended ten minutes, later, a chiming wakes her. *Oh, crap,* she thinks, seeing the time. There's a photo message from William showing three almost-clear lanes of motorway. The caption reads, *"Home safe, much better than the Friday rush hour (shot from dash cam not random phone play) xxx."*

She replies, *"The pleasure was all mine, (at least most of it was ;-))."* Then she calls her brother to apologise for running late.

As Meredith is still a little sleepy, the afternoon with her brother, his wife, and their two young children feels slightly surreal. She plays less enthusiastically than usual with the pair, despite the demands of "Come on, Auntie Merry!" from little Alison. Her brother even asks her if everything is okay in a rare moment of sensitivity. She assures him that it is without sharing details of her new relationship. It feels too soon to tell family.

Deciding that she's too tired to make dinner, she phones the Indian restaurant to order takeaway before she leaves. She hugs her nephew and niece and kisses her brother goodbye before heading home for an evening of curry, cats, and Netflix.

★★★

Meredith sleeps late on Sunday morning. The unexpectedly social week and weekend force her to spend what's left of the morning on chores rather than her usual self-indulgent routine. Lunch is light, comprising a couple of slices of toast and some scrambled eggs, but she catches up on things in time for her guest's arrival.

Jess, who invited herself around to get the gossip, or, more precisely to interrogate arrives by Taxi from the station, bringing chocolate cake and wine with her. It's a tried-and-tested formula among their circle of friends. Meredith knows both that she has been guilty of using the same technique, and that it is likely to work. She isn't quite ready to share yet, but after a glass or two and with the takeaway menu out, she begins to open up. She finds the pictures of William on LinkedIn and proudly shows them off.

"He's handsome, but wow! He looks so serious!" is Jess's reaction. "Come on, Merry, do you have any selfies?" Meredith looks blankly at her. "Surely you've taken a picture with him?"

"He's not so serious when you get to know him. He's always making silly jokes, Meredith says defensively, despite realising that it's true. "And no, there are no selfies. We've only just met. It would look like I keep a photo album of one-night stands."

To Jess the idea of her closest and, in her mind, most proper friend having one-night stands is so preposterous that she manages to laugh some wine up her nose. "Oh, sweetie, you could publish that album as the world's shortest book."

"I'm not that unadventurous."

This is greeted with a disbelieving look. "No, but you are now back down to a grand total of zero one-night stands—unless you've been holding out on me about a secret double life." Jess says dubiously, and with good cause. She pours each of them more wine. "We'd best order food or I'm going to get plastered."

By this point in the wine, poppadoms, bhajis, and naan all seem like a good idea, though Meredith knows she'll regret it later. As always, her local restaurant delivers a well-cooked meal. Over curry and the start of the second bottle of red, Meredith expands on how striking William's physique is, and confesses that she's asked him to help her get into shape.

The now-tipsy Jess has, over the years, made several overtures to get

Meredith into gym, jogging, or even playing netball. She puts "army", "buff", and "fitness" together in her head, and what emerges is a picture of her out-of-condition friend panting and sweating for a loud, uniformed physical training instructor. Inevitably she laughs, though she then feels terrible about it.

"Thanks," says Meredith, though the fact she says it with an overlarge portion of Indian food in front of her rather undermines her case.

"Hey, I'm happy to support you all the way—starting tomorrow at least." A fitness regime begun before the last of the chicken Poona has been eaten isn't destined to end well. "But do you both know what you're letting yourselves in for?"

"I'll show you. How about we put a bet on it? I'll buy you dinner if I haven't dropped a dress size by Easter!" Meredith is defiant. Jess can't see any way out of the bet without making the insulting suggestion that her friend can't do it, so she agrees.

To lighten the mood, Jess changes topic by asking about a more intimate matter, and then makes a fine audience. Meredith wouldn't tell anyone else the details of her intimacies, but Jess has been with her through good and bad relationships since they were at secondary school. They've developed the habit of sharing experiences since their first teenage fumblings.

It's good to talk. Meredith feels, at last, that she is Jess's equal as she relates the take and tells her friend she has finally achieved orgasm with a partner. The second bottle of wine almost seems to empty itself. A third is started, and Jess giggles as she takes two goes to get up from the sofa.

Meredith looks at the time and realises that not only are they both approaching blotto, but it's nearing midnight. "You'd better stay the night, sweetie." It's a sentiment that Jess is only too happy to drink to.

★★★

The morning is chaotic. Meredith finds it bad enough to cope with her own hangovers, but Jess in the morning plus Jess experiencing the regrets of several empty bottles is a different order of farce. At least it provides some distraction. Four days of eating out and two of drinking have left Meredith feeling fat and bloated. As she looks into her bathroom mirror, she's reminded of William's offer and her bet. Curry every night and she'll need a bigger dress, not a smaller one, by Easter!

Eventually she and coffee get them both ready. She drives to work via the station to drop Jess off, sympathetic that her friend has to endure a commute on public transport.

As she continues her own journey, she notices that the mornings are, at last, getting distinctly brighter. She also begins to consider her diet and alcohol consumption more seriously. The idea of William helping her is growing ever more appealing. After all, he's so very patient, and he must know how to get in shape to be in the incredible condition he's in.

And it would be a perfect excuse to see each other regularly.

It's going to be an odd Monday in the office. Meredith often takes some time to get into the working week, but after the last few days, she finds the structure comforting. She's grateful that the company tries to crowd routine matters into Monday.

9

Back to Reality

Work starts slowly, and that gives Meredith time to brood, William may have stayed but… she messages him:

Hey you

> *Hiya, how's Monday?*

Mondayish, but better when I remember the weekend x

> *So you would like to meet again?*

Yes, definitely! x

> *I'm away from Wednesday to Friday, but I could change my flight if you'd like me to stay over Tuesday night?*

Could you?

> *Yes, but you travel next time!*

Deal.

She doesn't have the nerve to mention the exercise thing and anyway she's not entirely sure, but she's still delighted at the prospect of seeing him again. After the exchange though she wonders, and she messages Jess worried.

He's coming over again! What if he doesn't like it?

Don't be ridiculous, they all do!

The response comes as a relief. She's still brooding about her friend's reaction to what she'd said about getting into shape. She doesn't feel the need for any additional stress.

The weekly staff meeting provides her with further cause for thought. There's a stark contrast when Emily sits on one side of her and the company's personnel director sits on the other. Emily has a straight back, slim figure, and youthful looks. The personnel director has prematurely acquired the shape of advancing years. Somewhat uncomfortably, Meredith sees herself as being in danger of sliding from one to the other without having fully enjoyed the former or fought to resist the latter. The last few days spent with William, her nephew, her niece, and Jess have given her one certainty: she is not yet ready to fade into browns and backgrounds.

On the way home, she stops at the supermarket and picks up a Weight Watchers meal, making her way to the till without stopping at the wines. She looks at the receipt as she walks back to her car. The absence of wine and dessert leaves a stark truth on the bill: she's paid three times as much for her cigarettes as she has for her dinner.

When she gets home, she looks through her wardrobe. She gazes sadly at herself in the mirror, then gets on the scales. The scales, like the mirror and some of her clothes, tell her an unwelcome truth, one that she realises she's been ignoring for too long. Her thoughts reach back to the pre-Christmas party-and-drinks season, and she quickly works out that there hasn't been much of a lull in the three months since.

Searching for comfort, she call Jess. "Tell the truth... Am I getting fat?"

Meredith waits through the silence as her friend gathers words of comforting evasion.

"Oh, Merry." It's a question one doesn't ask. Meredith's her closest friend, and Jess doesn't want to hurt her. "You're pretty. It's just that you aren't the girl who fusses about that sort of thing" The intent behind her words is positive, but Jess senses they don't succeed in comforting Meredith. She blunders on a little further."I can eat any old crap, but …"

"So when you laughed last night?"

"It's just that I've never thought the 'get in shape' thing was you. If you *want* to do it, I'm with you!" She realises that her words the night before may have come over bitchier than she intended. "I'll even help you win your bet with me."

Cheered by her friend's supportive words, Meredith allows the conversation to drift. As usual that means it moves onto the subject of Jess, but she doesn't mind.

Aggy recognises the "going to be on the phone a while" look, and the little cat worms her way onto Meredith's lap. There the two stay, settled and warm, Meredith in listening mode and Aggy purring contentedly, until Poggle yowls to be let out for his late evening wander.

Before bed, Meredith messages William.

> *Are you still okay to help me out with my exercise and diet?*

He replies almost immediately.

> *Of course. You okay?*

> *Yes, just had a rough day.*

> *I'm up if you want to talk.*

Meredith is just over her feelings from earlier. Having calmed down, the last thing she wants is to awaken the bad mood just before bed.

> *No, just wanted to make sure you're good with that.*

> *Looking forward to it. Something to do together, no pressure. I'll be up for another hour or so if you want to chat x.*

Thanks, see you tomorrow, x.

Nite xx.

★★★

Tuesday is more productive. In contrast to the way the last few working days have dragged, Meredith finds that the time flies by. The low-calorie meal deal sandwich she chose for lunch is nicer than the dry-tasting tuna she'd picked up on Monday, which cheers her. Following the advice in an article she read online over her morning coffee, she's chosen bottled water instead of a fizzy drink. She isn't sure whether it's just in her head or if the advice actually works, but she doesn't find herself craving snacks as much this afternoon as she did the day before.

William phones at lunchtime. "Are you sure about getting into shape?" His voice is serious. She notices that it gets even deeper when he's in that mood, almost sinking to a rumble.

Meredith pauses. He's so confident in his body. It looks and feels incredible, and he's beautiful. She has an image of herself walking along next to him; it would be awful not to match him at all, ". "Yes. No promises, but I want to give it a go!"

"Then shall I pick up ingredients, and we can cook?"

They spend some time discussing the menu. William is glad that they're on the phone, not together, as he's certain his face would betray some frustration and some amusement at her dietary peccadilloes: no fish that looks like fish, no liver, no venison, no mushrooms (what the hell but okay).

She feels silly but holds her ground. They settle on a simple stir-fry of chicken with cashews and peppers with pineapple-fried rice. "You like Thai, so presumably you have a wok?" he asks.

"Of course," she replies. "Stir-fries are one of the few things I like to cook."

"You'll like the food part then. What kinds of exercise do you like?"

"I don't like exercise at all!" she says, with more feeling than she intends. *Oh, that sounds so petulant!*

William doesn't seem to notice. "Not even walking?"

Meredith thinks. "I like walking my mum's dog, and swimming, I suppose. I'm good at swimming."

"Is there a pool you can use near home or the office?"

They chat for a few minutes. Though he gives her some ideas to think about, he doesn't find anything to convince her that she'll like any of them, except maybe she did used to like swimming.

As well as the shopping bag and his overnight bag, William arrives with an exercise mat and small dumbbells. However, he's a man used to the difference between aspiration and perspiration. The human mind is far more keen on the idea of action than on even the first step towards taking it. He leaves mat and weights in the boot of his car.

Meredith is pleased to see him but also nervous. He's not seen her wearing scruffy clothes before, but said that she should wear comfortable, loose garments for exercise. She's aware that such clothing doesn't flatter her. Her decision to wear them was prompted by a determination to see through on her request to William and to prove herself to Jess. Her doubts prompted themselves.

A part of her also worries that she was just a bit of convenient fun for him while he was visiting, and that, despite their messages and phone conversations since, he wouldn't show up. She's never really been good at the dating game. Having got this far by sort of circumventing the dating stage of their relationship, she doesn't know him well enough to be certain of much other than his sense of humour and his skill in bed.

She opens the door and there he is. He grins lopsidedly when she makes eye contact. His overnight bag is slung casually over the left shoulder of his charcoal suit, and there's a carrier bag in his hand. "Hey you," she says, unable to keep a girlish note from her voice.

His smile spreads further as he holds up the carrier bag, announcing, "Man hunt! Bring food!" The smile that charmed her so completely the week before still has the same effect.

"Lunatic!" She laughs as he steps in, responding to his initial peck on the cheek with a far fuller embrace. She only breaks it when he asks if he can put his bags down.

"Should we do the exercise before dinner?" she asks. Jess's disbelief still rankles, and Meredith is determined, at least for now, to press ahead.

Offering to exercise first up should make sure it happens, unlike the dozen times before.

"Are you sure you want to?" His voice is light, though his eyes strike her as being hopeful.

"Does that mean you think I'm fat?" She tries to make the words sound more like a joke than defensiveness.

He pauses. "No. I'm saying that you asked me to help you get into better shape, and I am reassuring you that I made an offer, not a demand."

Damn his reasonableness.

"I do think it would be something good to do together though," he continues. "Why don't we prep the ingredients for dinner and have a cup of tea? I'm parched. Then we can get started."

Meredith finds her chopping boards, and digs out her second good kitchen knife. They set to work while the kettle boils. Then they tease each other about drinks — her about his drinking tea, and him about her cup of instant decaffeinated coffee. They may have skipped the dating stage, but the ease they find in one another's company makes it feel as though they have simply passed through it.

Once they've chopped and got everything out, Meredith asks if it's ok if they use the thicker udon noodles she has in the cupboard instead of the fine ones he's brought.

"Thick noodles, instant coffee, and no mushrooms." He sighs. "Women truly are from Venus."

"So can we?" Meredith tries to avoid a pleading note. She really does prefer the texture.

"Of course," He winks. "But only if you promise we can tease each other about noodle thickness." He breaks a red pepper baton in two. "Deal?" He offers her one piece, as if that seals the arrangement. "Now, if you're serious about the exercise thing?"

He pauses and she nods.

"Great. I've left a couple of bits in the car."

She nods again.

"Back in a sec then!"

William returns with a small holdall that sags in his hand, making it look heavy. When he sets it down in her living room, it makes a dull metallic sound. Opening it he takes out the contents: two wide, soft yoga mats; several length of brightly coloured elastic material; and two pairs of silver-coloured dumbbells that Meredith presumes were the source of the metallic sound.

The dumbbells look small in William's hands. He moves the larger pair as though they have no mass at all, but even the lighter ones feel substantial to Meredith. The weight of the heavier ones surprises her. "Solid steel's pretty dense," he says, shrugging, his mind-reading trick appearing to be in action again.

"I don't think I can do much with these." She reads the end of one and sees that it's four kilos.

"You'll be surprised." He looks at her. His face is serious, but he hopes his expression looks as kind as he means it to. "Anyway, nobody starts where they aim to finish — otherwise it would be called arriving." He smiles, hoping to encourage his clearly nervous student.

"Did you get that from a life-coaching book?" His words have come over as more trite than she's used to William being.

"No, from a sergeant who used to say it when he was being patient with squaddies and subalterns who looked as lost as you do now." His face shows what she is starting to think of as a "happy memory" expression. "You should have heard the things he said when he got past being patient!"

"Thanks. I'll try to not get past patience then." Meredith doesn't sound or feel encouraged. "What's a subaltern?" she adds as an afterthought.

"Second lieutenant, a newly qualified officer. When you're just out of officer training and you get faced with a platoon, most of whom are older and more experienced than you are, and you're told you're in charge. It can be daunting for some guys, and worse for the ones who don't realise their situation." He looks at her listening and realises what's going on. "But right now a subaltern is a distraction." He takes the holdall and pops upstairs to change.

When he returns, Meredith decides that William is far more at home in gym wear than she thinks she could ever be. If anything, the black sleeveless top makes his shoulders look wider and more defined than either his suits or shirtlessness do. She thinks he looks more like a PT than the one she tried and failed to get along with a couple of years previously then realises he's talking to her and shakes herself.

He patiently and enthusiastically repeats himself. "Lie on your back with your arms by your sides, palms down. Lift your knees until your upper legs are vertical. That's right. Hold for a count of five. Now repeat that ten times."

He takes her through a series of exercises. Most are not what she expects at all. There's no running or jumping or chin-ups or any of the things she remembers with loathing from PE classes. The press-ups are with her knees on the ground rather than with a perfectly straight legs as she had been taught and been unable to do. She can do these!

In fact, she is able to do each of the exercises he shows her, which she had not expected. After twenty minutes, or perhaps half an hour, he decides it is time to stop. She is tired out and sweating.

"Shower, then food," he suggests, his chipper manner for once annoying her. She worries that she may have let that show, because his next action is to step close to her and gently towel her face. "Well done. That was a good start." He follows these words with a light caress of her chin and a brief kiss.

"It was only a few minutes and I'm already tired out!" she complains.

"Hey, you did well. I'm proud of you." He squeezes her lightly in his arms. "It's a journey." He kisses her again. "And we can take you on it together."

"Yes, sure." Meredith is still disheartened, but the idea of more close time with him is appealing, and his arms do feel good around her. "Do you want to go through after me?"

"Please."

The hot water in her shower always takes a while to come through. She usually stands on one side while waiting for it, but, impatient for her dinner and her return to William, she reaches into the chilly stream. The water tingles on her skin. She puts her other arm in, then moves her shoulder under it. The cold on her body is unpleasant now, not tingly, and she pulls back until the heat comes through.

She gets out of the shower and towels herself dry. Whether it's her, her hunger, or the unfamiliar exertion, she finds the shower invigorates her body more than it usually does. It could even be her anticipation of William's hands coming after; she had certainly thought about being in his arms as she soaped and rinsed her skin under the hot stream. She pulls on a pair of slacks and heads downstairs to find William and tell him the bathroom is free.

"You should have let me dry you," he says when she appears. He's obviously been doing more exercise. There's a sheen of sweat under the line of his thick, dark hair. The idea sounds tempting, but her shyness is a stronger force. She's glad he hadn't offered beforehand and put her in an awkward position.

"That's okay," she says. "I can do it myself."

"Probably have since you were a child." He uses a small towel to wipe his face. "But it's nice being pampered too." He pecks her cheek lightly. "Where would you like me to put these things?"

It's something Meredith hasn't considered, that he would lend her the equipment.

"That is, if you'd like me to leave the stuff here for you?" he adds.

"Don't you need it yourself?"

"Trust me, lending you these bits won't leave me short."

"Can I think about it?"

"Sure. I'll just go and get cleaned up."

Meredith is adding the noodles to boiling water as William enters the kitchen. Two pairs of hands make cooking, serving, and cleaning up simple and swift tasks. A bit reluctantly, she leaves the cooking to him as she knows where everything is. She gets out the crockery and cutlery and fetches the spices he requests. She thinks he's impressed by how well stocked her kitchen is. She regrets it when an explosion of spicy aroma erupts from her wok. Watching his confident movements convinces her that he does know what he's doing. The richness of the ginger and onion scent helps too.

He takes a teaspoon and scoops a tiny amount of sauce from the wok. "Here, spicy enough?"

There's a kick of chilli and a warming undercurrent of ginger. "Mmm, yes. I like the fullness the dried onion gives it."

He leans in and kisses her. "You can credit my grandma and my aunt for that. Super cooks." He grins as if remembering something. "If you get another plate out, we can put some away for your dinner tomorrow. It'll be nice if you do some fresh noodles."

She thinks, *Bless him, he's so serious.* Out loud she says, "Thanks, Mum." Then she laughs.

His eyes narrow. She belatedly realises that he's trying to do her a favour. She puts her arms around him. "You're good to me." She looks up into his eyes. "And I am grateful." She lifts her mouth to his, and he allows himself to be pulled down into an embrace.

He laughs as she kisses him. "You are such a minx. But I said I'd help you as long as you want me to, and I shall." He sounds so frank that she can't help looking into his eyes for something deeper. Once more, she finds them unguarded. She gets the feeling that this is the real William Farrow uncovered, and she can't help but kiss his lips again, at a loss for any other response.

He serves himself a huge portion, and serves her one larger than she had expected. He puts a similar amount on the spare plate. When she asks, he says, "The bean sprouts and celery are mostly water and roughage; you'd have to eat a mountain of either for it to be a problem."

They eat at the dining table again, though with sparkling water instead of wine. She admits to herself that his cooking, at least of this dish, is better than her own, though she isn't ready to admit any such thing to him. "Thank you—this is lovely." She squeezes his hand. "I didn't realise I was so hungry."

"Work and exercise should make you hungry. The trick is to do both and then not point yourself at a pile of crap and booze."

She asks him about his trip. He says it's a first phase with a client in Hungary but nothing more. Then he turns the conversation to her. "So, are you good with the exercises?"

She laughs. "No, but yes."

He laughs back. "That's all you can expect at this stage."

"And you're sure I can keep the stuff?" It seems a bit much for him to be giving her this sort of thing so early in their relationship, especially after the clothes he still won't take any money for.

"I'll tell you what: keep it for a month, and then you'll know if you want to carry on. Then we can get you some of your own—or not, if there isn't any point. Either way you can give it back."

"And it won't leave you short?" She doesn't know anyone so into fitness that they have spare equipment.

"No." But his voice is less sure than usual. "I'm afraid I do have spares. These weights are quite a bit lighter than the ones I train with these days." He smiles, and his eyes drift. "I would like them back in the end though. I got those dumbbells as a birthday present from my granddad when I was a kid."

Meredith hadn't thought such things could have sentimental value. She promises herself she will take care of them and return them, and that she'll actually use them.

After they wash up, she says she's popping outside for a cigarette. William joins her. "Sorry about this," she says as they sit on the swing seat on her patio. William tries not to look disapproving. She asks, "Why don't you like me smoking?"

"Because I like you."

"Then why don't you tell me to stop?"

"Because you're a grown-up." He goes to kiss her lips, but kisses her cheek instead.

"Do you really dislike the smell that much?"

"Yes." There's a hint of sadness in his voice. "I'm afraid I do."

"It's a part of who I am, you know." She leans against him.

"No, it's a part of who you are today."

"Why are you always so sweet?" It's intended as a sweet nothing, but once the words escape her lips, she does wonder.

"Am I?" He tilts his head and purses his lips. "Maybe you've just caught me on good days. Maybe you bring it out in me and maybe I just try to see the good in people, if there is any." In spite of the cigarette taste, he kisses her on the lips. "And I think I see good in you."

She allows the kiss to linger. It's nice, and this closeness is something she has missed in her life. After they part, she takes a final drag on her cigarette. "Do you?"

"Trust me, anyone who goes outside to smoke because they don't want to damage their cats' lungs has good in them — and a touch of eccentricity." He touches her chin. "I think someday you'll choose to stop because you don't want to damage yours either." He sees that she's put the cigarette out, so he rises and takes her hand. "Come on, you. You'll get cold sitting out here."

Agatha is waiting on the sofa when they get back inside. She hasn't moved from her warm spot, and doesn't do more than turn a sleepy look on them. As Meredith takes her coat off, she realises that William was right she does feel chilly, even though she's been wrapped up against his warm bulk. She rubs her hands together. "Would you like a hot drink?"

"Yes, thanks."

"What do you fancy?"

"Tea, if I may."

She heads to the kitchen and puts the kettle on. while he settles next to little cat, saying, "Hello, Aggy."

When Meredith returns with two steaming mugs, he's still talking to and stroking the cat. Aggy's half-lidded eyes show that she's enjoying the attention. "One cup of tea," Meredith announces, proffering a mug.

"Thanks," he says, taking it and sipping the hot liquid gingerly. "I like your throws." He's sitting on the short limb of her L-shaped sofa.

"They're okay, and they were necessary. Pog and Aggy were clawing the ends of the sofa to pieces." She nestles in next to him. "I do love them. I just wish they wouldn't scratch so."

"What do they have that they're allowed to scratch?"

"Nothing in here!" she replies indignantly. "There's loads in the garden, and when they aren't collecting animals, I let them come and go as they please."

"How do you know whether they're collecting animals?"

"The security camera I have overlooking the flap messages me when they try to get in." Meredith pulls a face. "I've come home to a terrified live bird and a living room covered in shit one too many times. I could have cried." She goes on to tell him the tale of her escalating war of cat security.

He thinks there's something that can be done about the cats' scratching habit, but isn't about to spoil the mood by interrupting her tale and talking about it now, so instead he kisses her and listens.

First there was the black tom that made a habit of using her flap to get in and steal food." He chased Aggy too," she says. Initially she'd just locked the flap, but then she bought one with a chip sensor when it got cold out. The sensor only allowed her cats through. That had been fine until the following spring. "Then they developed the habit of bringing animals. First dead ones, then live!"

William laughs at this. "People used to keep cats to get rid of pests in the house, not introduce them."

"It's all very well for you. Pieces of frog, sparrow crap, and frightened mice are no fun to come home to at the end of the day's work."

"I can imagine."

"So that's where I am."

"What do you do about feeding them when you're away?"

"If I'm gone for more than a day or two, I have someone stay. Otherwise my neighbour, Mrs Godleman, pops in to feed them."

"That's good of her."

"I pick up shopping for her, so it works out well. Bless her, she's getting on a bit and she's as deaf as a post." She snuggles into him. "I don't think her family visit as often as she'd like."

"So you reward each other's good deeds?"

"Yes, I suppose so." She snuggles in closer.

"And should we do something about rewarding your good deed, starting training?"

His change of tack makes her smile. "Don't you think of anything else?"

"Of course I do." His eyes give away that he's got a daft answer. "Food!"

"You are a bit of a pig when it comes to eating, aren't you?" She pats his washboard stomach. "Not that it shows."

He strokes her jawline. "So, what sort of reward—" his fingers shift to the side of her neck "— would you like?"

Meredith knows full well what sort of reward he wants to give her, and likes the idea, but she doesn't want to end the game too soon. "Oh, I don't know …"

William decides that two can play at teasing, and seeks to discover if Meredith is ticklish. It turns out that she is. She quickly squeals, "Not that!" laughing uncontrollably. Having scored a hit with his first try, he goes on to tickle her sides. "Stop! Please!" Aggy rowls her disapproval and vacates the sofa.

He stops at her request, ". "Well, what then?" His playful expression challenges her to come up with an alternative idea.

Meredith still has the giggles, and they combine with an attack of silliness. She hasn't felt this much like the young woman she is in years and manages to choke out the words "Ch-chocolate cake?" before her giggles and Williams resumed tickling take her voice away again.

Only when it looks as though she might turn blue for lack of air does William relent. "*Other* than chocolate cake?" Humour and an edge compete for control of his voice.

She gathers her breath, calms her breathing, decides she's not done with tomfoolery yet, and tries one more answer she knows he doesn't want. "Wine?" She laughs at his hardening expression and kisses him passionately.

He returns her kiss and pull her towards him. Meredith is half melting, and half worrying whether he'll like what he finds, even though everything she's read, seen, or been told suggests that he will.

The kissing is nice. So is the first part of being undressed. Though she hasn't often allowed her previous boyfriends to do this, Meredith finds she is getting used to him doing so. But she finds herself waiting more for what comes next than for his skilful touch.

William notices her distraction and stops. "Are you sure?"

Meredith responds by biting her lip, then by blushing.

"It's okay if you don't want to."

She manages, "It's just I've done something …"

Her words set his thoughts on a completely wrong track. He looks seriously at her. "What?"

"It might be better if you see." She lifts her hips.

All William can think of is that she's got a tattoo, and that it's a bit early in their relationship for that sort of thing, so it's with some trepidation that he lowers her leggings and panties. When he does so, in place of the tidy bush he remembers, he sees a hairless mons and lets out a laugh of relief and delight. "Smooth!" He kisses her lips as his fingers explore her smoothness. "I was worried you'd got a tattoo of my name!"

Meredith hadn't imagined he might think such a ridiculous thing. "Idiot! I haven't even known you a week!"

William laughs. Yes, it was daft. Making sure his face remains jocular, he adds, "Or someone else's." He receives a punch on his shoulder that he knows he deserves.

His ongoing, curious, and skilled touch rapidly earns him forgiveness.

She moves herself subtly to allow his hand access, thrilling as she sees the look of delight on his face.

He kisses her lips. "I suppose this makes it clear what the first part of your reward ought to be." His kisses move, first to her neck and then further down.

The kisses circle her breasts but don't find their way to their aching tips,. They follow his fingertips down her stomach. She's curious as to how his mouth will feel against her newly bare skin, but he makes her wait for this too, skirting along the crease at the top of her thigh. By the time he returns his attention to her lips, she is breathing deeply. "Can you guess yet?"

Oddly, his levity doesn't break the mood. "I have an inkling."

Meredith thinks his tongue has lavished its full attention on her, but then its tip swirls around and magically feels like it is on both sides of her sensitive bud as his lips suck.

★★★

An hour later, the two of them are wrapped in the throws. "I hadn't thought of using them like this," she muses dreamily.

"Well, they are a bit scratchier than your duvet, but they were to hand." She feels his lips on her head. "We should probably think about going to bed."

"What? Again?" she asks, half tired, half daring him.

"I'm game, but if you're tired out, I'm happy to let you sleep."

"You're insatiable, Mr Farrow."

"And you're smooth, Miss Webb." His words mean it one way, but his hand definitely appreciate her smoothness in another as his fingers trace the line between her hip and thigh.

She giggles, more at his intimation than from her ticklishness. He seems to like it, and she shifts to encourage his exploration.

He kisses her. "A brief word of advice: if you ever have a new boyfriend who isn't insatiable in the first week, dump him before it gets to a month, or he'll be picking out matching shawls and rocking chairs for the pair of you." He continues to joke as he caresses her, his fingers enjoying her silkiness.

"If you're going to go any further, then, yes, let's go upstairs. Otherwise I'm going to wind up sleeping down here." Meredith tries to get up. He smilingly stops her, more like a big puppy than a bully. "I mean it!" she warns.

He lets her with a "sorry, not sorry" look on his face. She wraps one of the throws around herself and gathers her scattered garments. William simply spreads the other out and picks his things up, buck-naked.

"You're shameless, you know that?" she scolds.

"You want me to put something on?"

"No, I quite like the view, but you're such an exhibitionist." Her eyes remain fixed on the exhibition.

He finishes collecting his clothes before she does. "Are you quite finished watching?" His words are offended, but his expression is amused. She blushes and he feels bad when her face sinks. He's forgotten how short a time they've known each other and how shy she is. Unsure how to redeem himself, he does a mocking impression a fan dance, with his shirt in one hand and the rest of his clothing in the other.

Meredith is still uncomfortable to begin with, but his movements are comical. Perhaps he was telling the truth when he said he can't dance? He manages to get her laughing by the time he reaches the door. She catches up with him as he reaches the landing. His peachy bum is at her eye level, and she can't resist giving it a pat.

He exclaims, "Ow!" which is ridiculous. Then chuckles, which is more like him. He turns as he walks into her bedroom, and says, "I see."

Meredith doesn't know what he's getting at. He's used his sexy tone, dropping his voice and narrowing his eyes while smiling in a way that does things to her insides.

Once through the door, he lays his garments quickly on the bed and shifts to catch her. She doesn't even have a chance to put her own clothes down before he wraps his arms around her and pulls her to him. He lifts the bottom of the throw she is swathed in and raises his hand as if to strike her exposed behind. "*No!*" she squeals as his hand falls. Instead of delivering a hard slap, it strokes and then squeezes. "Bastard!" She giggles and kisses him.

His innocent expression is none too convincing, but his eyes are all too seductive. He takes the clothes from her unresisting arms and lays them on her dressing table, moving his own next to them. Then he gently unwinds the throw from around her and holds her naked body close.

He pushes her gently down onto her bed. "Now for some more not getting my nose tickled!"

He makes her smile and wonder what she was worried about, remembering Jess's wisdom as he eases her to the middle of the mattress and crawls over her as though he's stalking her. It's foolish—she's not a child, and she's been with him before—yet she feels a rush of excitement and is tempted to run for the thrill of making him chase her.

He kneels over her, trapping her between his strong arms and his thickly muscled legs. He looks down with a boyish expression on his manly features.

Her lips part in an invitation that he accepts. Once again his kisses do not stop at her mouth. He trails fairy paths of touches over her body. When he reaches her mons, he softly brushes the tip of his nose and then his lips across its new smoothness. Meredith finds the urge to giggle warring with the desire for his mouth to go further. She grins and closes her eyes, lying back and luxuriating in the sensations.

She feels his touch on her mons and outer labia more keenly than before. Though on previous occasions he has neither stopped before she was ready nor given the impression of rushing to his goal, he definitely seems to take more time about it now. He lavishes attention on every sensitive fold, always returning to the focus of her pleasure and she tenderly strokes his thick, dark hair as he caresses her.

Though he takes his time, he brings her to her crescendo again, creasing his tongue around her sensitive bud. This time he continues to drive her on until she can bear no more and seeks to force his head away. He takes her wrists in his strong grip as he pushes her to an even higher peak. She's still shaking and coming down as he enters her with all the surprising gentleness he has shown his powerful body to be capable of.

As they lie together afterwards, now truly sated, he raises the energy to speak. "So why did you do it?"

"It's so much tidier. I feel better having it like this when someone's going to see it."

"It wasn't like that before."

Embarrassment rises before she registers the teasing. "I didn't expect anything to happen before." She doesn't have time to wonder whether it's the right thing to say before he's kissing her.

Meredith bumps his shoulder with the side of her fist, then tries to change the subject. "Why do you sometimes hold my hands over my head when you touch me?"

"Don't you like it?" He's looks playful and sounds amused, and Meredith tries to a avoid his eyes. He seems to know how his actions affect her body, mind, and emotions. Looking into those clear blue-green discs would force her to admit that he's right, and she isn't ready to do that.

He reads her posture and touches her face, lifting her lips to meet his own in a gentle kiss. "Well then."

When he pulls back with a smug grin, she mutters, "I hate you."

He raises an eyebrow. "Would you like me to demonstrate?" There's a note of challenge in his voice, and he holds out a hand to her.

Meredith pouts but allows him to take hold of her wrists. She's unable to maintain her seriousness when his face lights up in childish glee, and giggles as she offers the mildest of resistance to his strong, slow pull. He stretches her out, and she feels a warm, yawn-like sensation flood through her. He explains in a low voice, "The tension in your body activates your muscles and connective tissue." His free hand caresses her as he speaks, his voice even deeper than usual. "It makes you more sensitive." He leans forward, kissing her collarbone and then her cheek. "And if you relax into it"—he free hand presses on her mons—"it opens you." He places his index finger at her opening and his thumb between her folds. "So if you're already wet"—he slips his finger into her—"I can do this." He slides it out again and runs the wetness it has found up the length of her vulva. The feeling is, if anything, even better, knowing how he does it.

Still tingly with the afterglow, she responds swiftly, "H-how do you know I want you to?"

He stills the hand on her body, but still maintains his grip on her wrists.

"If I see from your face or feel from your body that you aren't sure, then I'll stop." He kisses her and then looks intently into her eyes. "And the same goes if you ask me to."

She absorbs the words. She can tell from his face that he's waiting for permission to continue. She lifts her head from the mattress and finds she can't raise it far. He leans down to meet her. They kiss, and she grants him permission to continue by rocking herself against his touch.

He marvels at her as his hand does its work. *How has she not learned this? This is so captivating.* He feels his face respond to her innocent enjoyment, wonders at how much he's smiling, and then decides he likes it.

★★★

William must have got out of bed during the night and opened the bedroom door, because it's ajar and Aggy has found a spot to curl up next to her head. She wakes with the cat's little face asleep a few inches from her own, and her usually cold feet warm against William's legs. She recalls guiltily that the previous time he stayed, he'd been up first and made a pot of coffee. She sneaks out of bed as quietly as she can to put the kettle on and enjoy her first cigarette of the day.

He appears in the kitchen as she's pressing the cafetière. "Mmm, coffee." He wraps his arms around her. They kiss, and he's taken off guard, still unused to her smoking. Seeking to make light of the unexpected taste on her lips, he adds, "And cigarettes." He smiles, though he's not sure how convincing the smile is.

Meredith has her own concern and is too busy with it to notice his. His arrival has jogged her memory too late—she's run out of eggs, and there's nothing in the way of breakfast food other than bread. Even that may not be in any fit state to eat.

She decides that coming clean is better than fretting. At least a quick check in the bread bin reveals an absence of mould. The loaf is definitely stale, but fine for toasting. She pours them each a coffee. "I'm really sorry. I forgot to get any breakfast stuff."

"That's okay. A piece of toast will be fine. One has to check in so early these days—I'll have plenty of time to pick up a full breakfast at the airport." He kisses her on the cheek. Noticing that her breath now smells of coffee instead of Marlboro Lights, he kisses her mouth too. "Would you like to come to my place next weekend?"

It's tempting, more than tempting, but she has plans. "I'd love to, but I'll have to arrange to move a few things around." Then she remembers the family dinner on Friday night. She really can't get out of that, but her friends will forgive her for bailing on them on Saturday. After all, she's the one who usually has to put up with working around their boyfriends. "I can come over on Saturday."

"Would you like to stay Sunday night too?"

She's not doing anything on Sunday; Saturday's girls night was going to be an alcoholic affair, and she makes a point of freeing up the day after such events for recovery.

Oh gods, this is too sudden though. Thinking on her feet isn't her thing; she wants but doesn't want to commit.

"If you like, you can pack for two nights. Then we can play it by ear?" he suggests.

Relief floods through her. If she doesn't feel comfortable, she can just come home on Sunday. "Yes, then; that would be great."

That decided, William kisses her goodbye happily and sets off for the airport.

★★★

Meredith checks her phone when she gets to work. Jess has messaged.

So?

So what?

Did he like it?[Smile and wink]

Even sat at her desk Meredith is blushing.

Yes. You knew he would, didn't you?

Of course I did! Now when do I get to meet him?

The question catches Meredith. Is she ready to start introducing him? What will his reaction be?

I've only been seeing him a few days!

How many other men have you slept with before I met them?

Okay, I'll ask at the weekend, if all goes well.

Jess accepts she's not going to manage to snoop any further.

I'm free on Saturday week (smile)

Oh well, thinks Meredith. She knows the two will have to meet sooner or later, if not so soon. At least it's not her mother asking—but then she hasn't told Mum yet.

Just when she finishes her exchange with Jess a picture of William's breakfast arrives, with a caption of "£££" followed by several shocked and laughter emojis then "Airport prices and monopolies but so necessary!" She replies, wishing him a safe flight and asking him to let her know when he arrives in Hungary.

The main task of the morning is a regular report for a long-term client. It's an important job, but one she can do with only half of her mind awake. Which is just as well.

Early in the afternoon, William messages her a picture taken in front of St Stephen's Basilica. *"Never been inside before, but the client said I couldn't visit Budapest without seeing it. It's stunning! We'll have to come together."*

During the days without William, her time with him seems like a dream—apart from the pictures of food and the Hungarian capital, and check-ups on her progress. He seems to know her better than she does herself. Several times he catches her just as she's about to either skip exercising or cheat on her meals.

For some reason she finds herself cherishing the company of her cats even more than usual. Her mother and father, both often oblivious to her moods, pick up that something has changed, and each comments on how happy she seems. Even Emily annoys her less than usual.

10

Meredith Makes a Discovery

M eredith has never been fond of driving on unfamiliar routes. She sets off early and nervous for her weekend at William's place, despite the reassurance of her phone's satnav and its uncanny ability to guide her around jams and roadworks. It even warns her about traffic cameras. By the time she's halfway there, it's clear that she is on course to arrive unfashionably early. She makes an effort to slow down—she's eager to see him, but not to seem needy.

Despite her efforts, she arrives in plenty of time for a late lunch, having enjoyed the drive under winter sun more than she expected to. The house is large—not overwhelming, but nice. It's detached, with a gravelled driveway. She draws up, slipping her driving shoes off and her heels on.

The heels are awkward on the crushed stone as she gets out of the car and straightens her dress. She has half a mind to put her driving shoes back on, but they'd look wrong with her dress and stockings. She worries that the dress is too short, though she can hardly change it now! She retrieves her case from the car's boot. Glad that she's not packed too heavily, she makes it across the driveway to the door—heels, stockings, and dignity intact—and presses the doorbell.

Then she waits. She'd fondly imagined that the door would spring open the moment she rang the bell but seconds pass. She resists the temptation to tease her dress down to cover more of her legs. The cold air begins to penetrate its thin material, and the thought of him not being home rises, unwelcome, in her mind.

After what has probably been moments but feels like minutes, she hears the sound of the lock. An unwanted image of waiting nervously outside the headmaster's office drifts into her mind. The heavy oaken door swings open, revealing his eyes, and they dispel the chill that had begun to take hold of her.

William's greeting is a smile one might save for a friend unseen in years and sorely missed. She picks up her bag, returns his smile, and steps over the threshold into a house filled with the rich scents of food cooking.

"Would you like me to take that?" He asks. She hands it over, and his fingers brush hers. "You're cold! Would you like me to put the heating on?"

Meredith would prefer not to be any trouble, but she *is* chilly. "If you don't mind."

"Of course not. Now, tea? Coffee? Or wine?" He places her case by the foot of the stairs.

"Wine would be nice." She steps towards him and angles her head. William takes the hint and kisses her.

The kitchen is spacious and the surfaces contain numerous gadgets. In here the cooking smells are more intense still, the aromas of baking bread and a rich stew fill her senses, There are already two glasses out, one of which is empty. William pours red into it for her. The wine is cool and fruity. He bends forward to brush his lips against hers again. "Chianti and a kiss. I hope you don't mind. I went for something fairly light as it's lunchtime. I'll just check the casserole and start the veg, she sees a neat little cup of frozen peas and bowls of carrot batons and broccoli. Then we can sit and chat for a bit." He lifts first one, then a second, smaller earthenware cooking pot out of the oven.

"How on earth much food have you made?" she asks, somewhat incredulous.

"You said you don't like mushrooms." Bless him, he looks apologetic. "So I did some with and some without." He takes the lid from the first pot. The stew's rich, meaty aroma blooms. Each pot gets a stir, and William produces two teaspoons. The first he uses to taste the sauce in the larger pot. The second he uses to scoop a tiny amount from the other pot and offer it to Meredith. "Here. How's the seasoning?"

It's richer than she's used to, almost overpoweringly so, but delicious. "Mmm, what's in it?"

"There's marrowbone stock, redcurrant jelly, honey, thyme, basil, a bit of tomato paste, and some red and yellow peppers. Oh, and black pepper and a couple of chillies for the kick." He runs off the long list as matter-of-factly as if he'd just put a tin of soup on. He starts a saucepan of carrot batons and petit-pois. "I'm glad you like it. I went a bit light on the chillies and pepper in yours."

"Very impressive, Mr Farrow." She takes a sip of wine. "I could get used to this, even if I might have been put off had I found out about the marrowbone before I tried it."

He smiles with a boyish bashfulness that contrasts with her mental image of him, and picks up his own glass. "Would you like a quick wander around?"

He gives her a cursory look at his laundry room and the small pantry leading off from the kitchen. The dining room opens into a conservatory that actually has plants. William takes some pleasure in showing her the herbs, then a pair of plants with tiny, white, star-like flowers that he cheerfully announces as his chilli plants. "So a tiny amount of your lunch was grown in here." The boyish grin, "Which sounds even less impressive when I say it than when I think it." Followed by the roguish one, and once again she can't help but laugh. "I use sunlamps to try and keep at least one or two things in flower or fruit all year round, sort of my vegetable babies."

Next is a well-appointed—no, a more than well-appointed home gym. Meredith thinks, *I'm not sure I could handle seeing myself all sweaty in those huge mirrors.* Aloud, she says, "No wonder you're in such good shape!"

"Travelling," he says by way of explanation. "Having this here means I never have an excuse to let things slide."

The final room he shows her is the lounge, which has a definite male quality to it, except (as Meredith notes but does not say) that his television isn't quite as big as her own. There are two large, comfortable sofas, a pair of huge armchairs, and a sound system of ludicrous size and complexity. Every wall is covered with shelves of books, CDs, DVDs, and even vinyl records.

"If you tell me now I will let you escape the demonstration," he says solemnly.

"Boys and their toys?"

"Well, yes. Pride and joy, after all—and I need to do something to make up for my tiny television."

How does he know? And why does he tease me? And why does it make me laugh when he does?

"Vivaldi okay, or something vocal or a bit more modern?"

"Vivaldi's fine."

It's been a while since she's heard music except from a phone or online dock, but he has a few discs ready.

The opening bars of "Winter" spring up with a menace that surprises her before the sweet tone of the lead violin rises above them.

"Drink." His voice is a church whisper, but nonetheless a command.

She sips the wine. As its fruit fills her taste and smell, those senses seem to merge with her hearing. A tear half rises in her eye. "It's beautiful." The words, like the tear, come unbidden. When she looks at him, his face shows that the feeling is shared, and her heart swells.

He squeezes her hand. She leans against him, his solidity adding another layer to the chorus of the senses. She's unsure how long she has remained thus when a gentle kiss rouses her from her reverie.

"I'll just whip the bread out and pop the broccoli in."

With that he leaves her with the melancholy music.

She takes a seat on one of the armchairs facing the main speakers. Closing her eyes, she thinks that she can almost reach out and touch the musicians. She takes another sip, experimenting. The same sensations are there but do not take her off guard in the same way. Yes, they all join together and carry her away, but without overwhelming her this time.

She doesn't notice his return until his lips touch her cheek. "If you'd like to listen, lunch can wait."

She turns and opens her eyes, surprised to see no humour in his face, only gentleness. "No, ah, no, let's eat now."

"There's couscous if you'd prefer that to bread."

"The bread smells too good to eat something else." It's nice to be able to say that without telling a white lie; the kitchen really does smell incredible.

They eat in the dining room. Meredith feels the two places, a steaming fresh loaf on a platter between them at the big table, are incongruous. At least they are together at one end rather than more formally arranged. She stifles a smile at the memory of a comedy sketch depicting a couple dining at opposite ends of an even longer table.

The rich aroma prompts her to accept a larger portion than she would normally eat, though her meal is dwarfed by the contents of William's plate. Like his strength, his appetite borders on the ridiculous. She teases him for his gluttony, but he raises an unrepentant eyebrow and asks if she'd rather he didn't keep his strength up.

The casserole's flavour is powerful, its taste even longer lasting than the sip of its sauce she had tried in the kitchen. The beef has been slow-cooked to the verge of melting softness. The bread's crust is crisp and sweet. The Chianti's fullness complements the meal, and the soft music continuing in the background is pleasing to the ear.

Meredith tells him about a presentation she is due to give, and that she hates giving them. He has her rehearse some of the points while playing footsie with her under the table. He enquires about her cats, chuckling as she launches into a narrative.

He pours a little more wine into her glass as she chatters on. Noticing that she has stopped eating, he asks if she is finished. When she nods, he uses a piece of a fresh bread to mop up the last morsels from her plate while making meaningful eye contact. "Would you like to retire to the music room for dessert?"

"William! I'm too full to eat another thing."

"I wasn't thinking about food." He gives her the softest of kisses, the deepest of tingles.

"It's the middle of the afternoon!"

His mouth says "Then we can just listen." But his expression makes it clear that *just listening* isn't the only option. Meredith decides to wait and see.

William puts on a playlist. Though he apologises for the quality, she can't tell any issue—the sound is clear and vibrant. She insinuates herself under his arm as Rihanna, Disturbed, and others play. They drink sparingly and kiss frequently. When the opening bars of Beethoven's Fifth roll over her, she finds herself contentedly swept along with the music's passion. By the time the triumphant crescendo fades, she is not only well fed but well sated. They lie sweaty and dishevelled on the rug.

"He wasn't a virgin when he wrote that, was he?"

Her words bring a rumble of laughter from him.

She blushes, then joins in. "Well, it's so passionate."

"It is, and no, I don't think he can have been."

They lie companionably until she begins to feel cool. The room is pleasantly warm, and William's side is like a radiator, so this takes some time. "I'm going to have to get dressed before I get cold."

"You should have said. I could have turned the heating up or brought a blanket down."

"That's fine; I need to clean myself up anyway. Is it okay if I have a shower?"

"Of course. I'll tidy up the lunch things while you do."

"I'd rather we did it together. You cooked," she replies, not liking to feel like a passenger.

Between the two of them, the clearing up takes hardly any time. He sets large meat safes over the still-cooling casserole dishes and loaf while she rinses and loads the dishwasher. The dishwasher is so convenient— she has to get one.

As they finish, he asks, "Is it all right if I do a few quick bits in the gym while you bathe?" She is agreeable, thinking it will give her time to pamper herself.

Meredith luxuriates in and then finishes her shower. She does her hair and applies her make-up before he is done with his training session. She finds him shirtless and sweating in his gym, swinging a kettlebell that, from the way his body sways, must be almost impossibly heavy. After a minute or so he places it down with a soft thud that confirms its solidity. Breathing heavily and sweating he reaches for a drink. "Sorry. Five more minutes and I'll be done. You can stay if you want."

She enjoys watching his body. But, aware of her non-existent fitness regime, she declines and leaves him to it, opting to start coffee instead. She reminds herself that her regime is only *near* non-existent now.

She finds an espresso machine and several cafetières in the kitchen.

Chooses one of the latter, she puts the kettle on. As it heats, she decides to dress and heads up the stairs to his bedroom.

It's a large house for a man who lives on his own. The "grand tour" didn't include the upstairs apart from his bedroom, and her curiosity gets the better of her. The first room she looks into is a small box room. The second a well-appointed bathroom. Then there's a good-size (though smaller than his own) bedroom with an en-suite shower. A person could certainly keep exceedingly clean in this house.

The next door is shut and has a lock, so she doesn't try the handle. She guesses it must be his home office. Before his room, there is a last door, also closed so she turns the handle...

She can't believe her eyes at what she finds within. She isn't a total innocent, and, well, everyone has fantasies. But she's never imagined anything like the display on the walls of this bedroom. If she were still clothed—if she didn't feel so much that she belongs when in his arms—she'd have made her excuses and fled, though her heart might have later regretted it. This is a moment her dreams will revisit time and again.

From the doorway, she sees one display that is striking—ah, a poor choice of words if ever there was one! It contains over a dozen varied crops, canes, and whips. Another display showcases an array of feathers, brushes, and strange, spiked wheels that look like spurs.

The room smells richly of expensive leather. As in the rest of the house, the decor is conservative, for the most part. But in place of a modern bed is a four-poster, and instead of bookshelves, there are tall, elegant mirrors and dark cabinets that indicate the owner delights in their outrageous contents.

Despite her shock, and as there is no sign of William coming upstairs since she thinks she can faintly hear the sounds of his continuing exertion she steps inside.

Meredith has always mocked the girls in horror movies who go into the unknown. Now that the unknown has presented itself, she's finds herself looking over her shoulder and, with a quickening of her heart, taking a few short steps deeper into the room. She moves toward the cabinet filled with whips. To her right is a display of restraints. If these are the items on display, she hesitates to think what must be hidden in the tastefully matched cupboards.

After looking at the whips, she pauses at the display of restraints, all polished leather and gleaming steel. There is no denying the visual artistry... She allows her fingers the lightest of touches on several items and is surprised by the weight of even the slimmest steel chains, and the soft yet unyielding nature of the leather cuffs. The tactile richness matches the sight and scent. One set of chains has strange clips at its ends, which distinctly worry a part of Meredith's imagination. She quickly moves on.

She returns to the whips. The array is even more daunting close up. There are long, thin ones that remind her of what a coachman might use. She recognises the riding crops and canes—there had been a cane on the wall in her headmistress's office. She remembers being teased about it by Nancy Turner. She lived in fear of it for almost a year before she learnt that corporal punishment had been banned in schools decades before.

On an impulse, she lifts a cane from its peg. She feels the fine, harsh grain of the wood, tests its springiness, and taps it against her hand. When she gives it a practice swing, she is surprised by the sound it makes through the air. Then tries a tap on her hand and jumps as it makes a slapping sound. Heat spreads through her palm from the point the cane struck.

A shade of the naughty schoolgirl she hadn't dared to be rises. She slides the sleeve of her robe up, pauses to gather her bravery, and brings the cane down. "Fuck!" she exclaims, dropping the cane in shock at bright pain that flashes through the soft skin on the inside of her forearm.

She almost leaps out of her skin as William's voice suggests, "If you're a pervgin you should start with something a little milder than a cane." from the doorway.

"But... why? Why on earth do you have these things? Do you use them on people?" Meredith feels intimidated. She's wearing nothing but his borrowed bathrobe, and wishes dearly that she had more on. She also wishes she were not alone with him, that she hadn't read certain books when she was younger, and that she hadn't stepped into this room. She wishes many wishes in a rush of quickening heartbeats.

"Which things? The fur mitts? Feathers? Soft skin brushes?" he asks, stepping into the room. He's the devil staring deep into her, but even in her alarm she can see the boy dancing in his eyes. Stopping just short of where she stands he stoops gracefully, and retrieves the fallen cane.

A wave of terror passes through her as he reaches past her and she freezes. But her simply returns it to its place. That done he takes a wide blusher brush from its place and holds it up for her inspection. In a slow, deliberate motion, he lightly presses its soft bristles against her cheek and caresses her skin. The effect is completely unlike using a brush to apply make-up on herself.

The stroking makes its way back down the V at the front of her robe. His free hand passes over her breast. A jolt of pleasure shoots through her. The hardness its tip confirms her arousal. Not trusting herself to speak, she tilts back her head and raises her mouth towards his.

She thinks, *Damn you, you know which things.* Aloud, she only says, "Th-the other things. The whips and canes." She can't believe she's barely clothed in this man's home, talking about these things, trying to stay calm while he seems on the verge of laughter. Her heart tries to escape her chest.

He looks into her eyes as if for permission and then slowly draws the brush's softness down the length of her neck as he enquires, "Have you liked the things I've done with you?" Sparks of unexpected pleasure radiate from the touch as his bass voice sounds inside her.

"Yes, um, of course I have." She wishes she were enjoying the things he's doing to her right now just a bit less.

"And have I done or forced you to do anything against your will?" Eyes dead serious as they seek her attention, he trails the brush down the robe's collar. She's glad the belt is done up, though she is becoming aware that her stiffening nipples don't agree with her.

"No, of course not. I wouldn't have."

She remembers him holding her on the edge of orgasm, insisting that she open her eyes and watch herself before being allowed to cum. She remembers the overwhelming surge of pleasure as she surrendered to his demand. She remembers how he partially undressed her and used her own clothing to keep her arms immobile while his gentle caresses worked their magic. "I trust you, but …"

"But what?" he challenges in the softest of tones, and raises an eyebrow. She is amazed that he seems genuinely curious. The fine bristles, softer than any in her own make-up bag, move upwards, to her relief and disappointment.

"But what if I didn't want you to do something?"

"I imagine that either you'd ask me not to or you wouldn't appear to be enjoying yourself, and that would make me stop." He carries on caressing her with soft, confident motions of the brush, each a delightful note as he plays her warm, glowing freshly bathed skin. "Why? Is there something you want me not to do to you?"

Damn his seriousness, and damn that laugh hiding behind it!

"When people play physical games, there are signals and words. For example, if you chose *pineapple* as a word meaning 'stop' …" He loosens her robe and trails the brush down the curve of her breast. "All you would have to do to make me stop is to say 'pineapple'."

The strange, soft caress is tantalising, one more thing unlike any other that Meredith's body has experienced. She opens her mouth, but in the hope of his kiss, not to say "pineapple'". His lips find hers as the robe's belt falls. One of his hands reaches to the oh-so-sensitive skin of her waist, sending a delicious shiver through her. The brush continues to the underside of her breast and slowly spirals towards her suddenly aching bud. As it nears then circles its destination, sparks of pleasure radiate throughout her body. Time slows.

After a moment or an age, William pulls the brush away. Her body leans forward, as does his. First his warm breath and then his lips find her breast's tip, drawing a gasp from her.

He pushes her robe wider, exposing her other breast. Once again he strokes her skin softly with the delicious device. She finds herself standing in a passive reverie, warm and comfortable. For the first time in her life, she is brazenly exposed, lulled by his tender attention despite the knowledge that she's a bare few inches from an array of torture instruments.

He mirrors his earlier ministrations: collarbone, sternum, the curve of her breast. Her skin is even more sensitive, each nerve alive with anticipation as the brush's gentle caress approaches. Her eyes close as it nears her nipple and she gasps as it lingers there, sighs as it eventually trails downwards. It tickles its way to the crease between her thigh and hip. His lips replace it on her breast but he breaks away just as the brush grazes her outer labia, and she moans at the loss of its touch.

He moves closer. She feels the heat of his strength on her skin as he bends. He gifts her mouth the briefest of kisses. Then takes hold of the open sides of the robe and draws her forward. He seats himself on the bed in front of her, his face level with her still-aching nipples. He kisses each as his hands ease her unresisting legs apart their confident touch.

"Stay there," he commands. The corner of his mouth turns upwards, igniting the gleam in his eye. He stands and moves past Meredith. She turns her head after him, but he stops her. "No peeking," he says as he kisses the base of her neck.

Meredith's curiosity burns. Her trust wars with mental images of whips and chains. She jumps a moment later when his arms encircle her and his lips again find the melting spot on her neck. He resumes his place on the bed and takes up her left hand in his. He raises his right. There are three items in it: the brush, a strange spur-like wheel on a handle, and a peculiar black object shaped like a microphone with a bend in it. He places this last object on the bed and then slowly trails the brush and the spur wheel softly along the length of her hand. The tiny needles and soft fibres ignite contrasting sparks of pleasure.

He looks intently into her eyes. "Is this okay?" he asks, back in his Mr Stern tone.

And it is, for all that it's bizarre and unfamiliar. Meredith takes a moment to respond, the mix of delicacy and intensity quite overwhelming her. "Yes, more than okay," she confesses, her eyes lowering to watch him touch her with them.

"Do you trust me?" He releases her hand and transfers the brush to his left. He takes her silence for assent and reaches forward with the two devices.

Despite her experience the spur wheel still looks alarming, and Meredith finds her voice a moment before either touches her. "Will it hurt?"

"No, it shouldn't and remember 'pineapple'." As he says the safe word, he allows the devices to make the lightest of contact with her skin just below each collarbone. The contrasting sensations wash through her body and escalate further as she recognises the pattern of movement; it is the same with which he caressed her with the brush earlier. The spiked wheel mirrors the motion of the brush, delivering delicious tingles with an occasional sudden peak of something more intense.

Despite her trust, and the pleasures flowing like hot rivers throughout her body, the sharp spikes approaching her now painfully erect nipple cause a thrill of fear in Meredith's heart. It's all very well for William to tell her this won't hurt, but ... At the same time, she finds her breath quickening, and not merely in fear. Her body yearns towards this strange touch. The tingles turn to tiny lightning strikes as the wheel nears her tender bud, each strike grounding deep inside her. She catches her breath as the spikes prick ever so gently around her areola and stay circling there. The tip of her nipple waits achingly; Meredith waits fearfully.

The thunder that has been following the sparks of light arrives in a rumbling wave as the tiny needles finally make contact with their destination. The last flashes of lightning ground blindingly in her clitoris. Meredith's knees buck involuntarily, and she cries out.

He stops.

She is panting, afloat in a near-orgasmic state. Her eyes find William's. He fixes her gaze and places the miraculous items down by his side. His hands caress her: breasts, stomach, thighs, inner thighs, and finally her labia. One finger traces a gentle line from her anus to the top of her slit, brushing over the outside of her hood despite her hips' best efforts to make this contact more intense.

"Are you ready?" he asks.

Her only response is to widen her stance and press her mons towards him.

He lifts the black object and presses its handle. It buzzes into life. Meredith, outwardly voiceless, begins an internal commentary as she hovers in an almost out-of-body state. *Oh my God, it's a vibrator, and I'm so close!* He presses its round head against her opening and twists it, sending a shaking through her. *So smooth. I'm so wet.*

Satisfied that the toy has collected sufficient of Meredith's lubrication, William runs the wand from her anus to the top of her slit and back in slow motion. He barely presses, but Meredith finds herself rocking against the bulbous head to increase the intensity. His left hand and his lips claim her breasts. Her body reverberates like a drum skin stretched between the three points of contact.

He stops moving the vibrator while it is directly on top of her clitoris. He allows her to push herself against it for one moment and then another, until she feels the tide inside her is about to break. She catches her breath.

Then he returns to stroking the round smoothness over the length of her sensitive vulva as she wails in frustration. It moves down to her perineum, then her anus. He doesn't push, but her muscles clench and spasm against even this gentle contact. He lets her ride it briefly before moving the wand back upwards. Meredith's guttural cry dies into a whimper as it moves away.

She places her hands on his shoulders and leans down, her muscles twitching now. Barely in control, she's never cum standing up. Ten days ago, she had never even cum while in the same room as anyone else. Now she is riding this toy as though her life depends upon it.

Once again he pauses over her clitoris. The device's buzzing intensifies and Meredith lets out a sob. It moves down, pauses at her entrance, and again over her anus. She's unable to control the muscle there; it pulses against the soft pressure. He moves it upwards once more, and again it comes to rest over her clitoris, eliciting a moan. The vibrations become more insistent and he presses a little more firmly. His teeth and fingertips tighten on her nipples and she spasms, leaning heavily on him and groaning out loud. But there is no release; she wails as he moves tortuously down once more.

William slips the head of the wand into the crook of his hand. He cups it against the base of her pubic bone. The tips of his middle and index fingers enter her. The pad of his ring finger rests flat over her rose, while that of his thumb presses into her clitoris. Meredith feels vibrations through his hand as well as through the wand's direct contact. Her hands clench fiercely. He presses the fingers inside her hard against her pubic bone, and she stops breathing.

Slowly, he rotates his hand, caressing each point of contact strongly. The power of his arm takes some of her weight through the head of the vibrator. Meredith lets out a long, animal cry. When her lungs are empty and burning, she draw in another ragged breath and cries out again. Her knees buckle against his. She feels her breasts and pelvis take their share of her weight.

William holds her, his hands unrelenting in their subtle motion, until her cries turn back to sobs. Only when she is at the point of collapse does he remove his touch—and the wand. He lifts her crumbling form and lays her on the bed, kissing her unresisting mouth and letting her rest.

In the afterglow, Meredith nestles against him, meek and content. He lazily caresses her softness through her open robe. Meredith blushes, and her blush deepens as his touch grazes the areola of her breast. "You called me a pervgin!" She chuckles, and it feels deliciously warm inside. "What even is a pervgin?"

William laughs the rich laugh that she can never hear enough. "Well, you were. It's someone who hasn't tried anything a bit more imaginative sexually." His face becomes more serious and he looks into—or is it through?—her eyes. "So do you like what this is for?"

Her colour rises even higher. She buries her head against him and resists when he lifts her chin, but not when he bends and kisses her mouth. "It was unexpected." Her eyes fight away from his, looking down. "Incredible!" Her hand presses against his muscular chest. "What do you get out of all this?"

"All what?" He seems genuinely puzzled.

"The toys, the way you touch. I've never felt anything like it."

"What do you mean? Doesn't everyone like to please their partners?"

"They do. At least, I do. But ..." Meredith pauses. "All this is so much more. I'd never even had an orgasm with anyone before you, but you make me cum so intensely, so easily." She blushes, "Easier than I can myself. But that? That was more than anything I've known, even with you."

His eyes gleam boyishly, "I must have a knack." he replies, and that devil's smile of his twists the corner of his mouth. "I like it when my partner is completely satisfied." He leans forward to kiss her.

She allows him to do so, her mouth opening to him as her body does. "The other things—the chains, the whips ..."

"They can make the experience—and the pleasure—more intense, if you like them." The gentleness of his voice is at odds with the topic. She can't quite believe that in the aftermath of her overpowering orgasm, she's lying in his arms and discussing torture.

"I don't think I'd like to be hit with those things," she says, looking at the display of cruel instruments. Her heart beats wildly at the thought of her body being beaten. "Especially if I couldn't move!"

"You don't have to be, but you do seem to like it when I hold you still and caress you."

She feels as though she's arguing with a voice in her own head as much as she is with him. She's never been with a man so physically strong or so skilled. She loves her own sense of powerlessness, but now, in her vulnerable state, in his home surrounded by these frightening things the thought of it scares her.

He takes up the brush again. "You've eaten my cooking and been with me. Have I done anything to harm you?"

She shakes her head silently.

"Besides ..." He pauses while his eyes, his hand, and the brush continue. He lifts her hair and strokes the back of her neck under it. "Do you seriously think I'm the sort to enjoy prison food—or a look in your eyes that tells me I've betrayed you?" He smiles, kindly, and questioningly.

No, she doesn't, and she nestles into him.

The brush makes its way down the *V* at the front of her robe. The fingers of his free hand tease her nipple, sending a new jolt of pleasure through her. The tip stiffens again. Hardness against her hip makes her achingly aware of him. Not trusting herself to speak, she tilts her head back and raises her mouth towards his.

He rises to his knees beside her. She pushes his shorts down, running her hands over the full, muscular curve of his haunches and his thick thighs then takes hold of his stiffness as he kicks his underwear to the floor. She runs her grip up and down his length, relishing its increasing rigidity. Her insides clench in time with the motion of her arm. The last orgasm was better than nice, but she wants him inside her.

She pulls him towards her by his cock. Her strength is a fraction of his, but his body follows eagerly. He drops the brush and pushes her robe fully open, all playful eyes and hungry mouth. She raises her hips and guides the head of his cock into herself. Wrapping her arms around his broad torso, she revels in his sheer physical solidity.

He enters her in one slow, gentle motion. Her body is completely open to him, welcoming his intrusion and eager for his full strength.

★★★

Meredith wakes warm and content, the memory of him in every nerve, to find him caressing her once more. "Don't you ever get tired of ..." Her sleepy voice trails off as he kisses her. Despite her sleepiness, her body responds to his touch eagerly.

"Of what?" he asks, all innocence and mischief. He continues to toy with her body, stirring the glowing embers within her. "Though we should do something about dinner. You've been asleep quite a while." He allows his voice to trail off but his fingers continue to tantalise her.

He takes her close, and then leans forward. His smiling lips deliver the briefest and most chaste of kisses. "I'm going to shower; then we can sort food." His fingers leave her just as she is about to crest.

She sighs her frustration and reaches out for him, but he's already off the bed. He teases, "You can pick some treats for after dinner while I shower. But if you aren't feeling brave, I'd investigate those drawers." He indicates one of the dark wood chests. He departs, only for his head to pop back around the door. "And no cheating. I'll know!"

Meredith briefly considers finishing herself off despite his admonishment, but lets her hand fall. The ride has been good so far, and permission to explore this Aladdin's cave of forbidden things is tempting. Wrapping the robe around her and tying its belt, she rises and pads across the room allowing her earlier experience with the cane and William's words guide her steps.

In one drawer, she finds an assortment of glass and steel objects on a velvet bed. The shapes of some of the items leave her in no doubt as to their purpose. She's never had anything so rigidly implacable as glass or steel insider herself. She only tried her own plastic vibrator inside once and, not finding it erotic at all, never tried again.

Some items have narrow necks, the purpose of which evades her at first. Then, with a blush, realisation strikes, and a matching tightening in her sphincter confirms their purpose. She moves on quickly.

She lifts one gleaming steel item that looks like a modern art sculpture. She's struck by its cold, unyielding solidity and its great weight. Its surface is perfectly smooth, ridged at one end, and curved to small, rounded head at the other. It's completely unlike any of the few sex toys she has encountered or seen online—alien, lovely, and so heavy she thinks as she returns it to its velvet bed.

The strains of a Haydn symphony drift upstairs.

The second drawer contains objects that are obviously vibrators and other, more mysterious objects. Two huge mains devices dominate one end. There is an empty depression, the size and shape of the device that she recently experienced. Seeing it sends a rush of warmth through her. Several things are shaped like slender mushrooms or tiny fir trees with bases. Her body responds, but her mind says a definite no once again.

Almost all of these objects have a firm yet soft surface far different from glass or steel. Most have plus and minus buttons. A number have no buttons on them that she can see, or just a single one, subtly marked with an on/off symbol. Each of these is next to a second, small item like a rounded car remote key. The range of sizes is surprising, she owns just one! She doubts his collection would shame a high-end adult store!

She reflects on the enjoyment she has already received from this drawer. Something from here might do very nicely. Her eyes settle on the smaller but not diminutive devices—ones without the strange key fobs. Several are shaped like riverside pebbles, the perfect size to fit into the palm of the hand. She touches the silky warmth of one; the texture is not unlike that she recently felt. Another has a strange, rounded groove at its slimmer end. She has no idea what this is for, but her mind and body suggest that William probably does, and that the purpose might be one she will enjoy. In a spirit of adventure, she resolves to allow him to try this one on her. A pleasant rushing sensation flows to her nipples and down inside her as she makes this decision.

She closes the drawer and opens the third. It is filled with neatly arranged locks, clips, lengths of chain, and leather straps. She doesn't linger inspecting these, though her fingers do trace the length of a chain and a couple supple lengths of soft, polished leather. She lifts one of these, tests its strength, and finds it far beyond her own.

The bottom drawer is the deepest. One would normally expect it to contain winter wools, fresh towels, or spare linen. This is filled with neatly coiled ropes of various lengths and textures. Some are soft, with fine fibres; others are course, and there are several textures between.

The idea of struggling against bonds has some attraction. The memory of William holding her down while he caresses and makes love to her is certainly delicious, but the thought of being completely immobilised scares her. She goes to the display of restraints to take a closer look.

There are numerous cuffs. Some are of steel, but most appear made of soft or stiff leather. There are belts, collars, and a few things whose use she can only guess at. Some have buckles, others locks. All have metal rings set in them. There's no question that their purpose is to bind and control the wearer. The look of those displayed is exotic, each item finely crafted as though it were fashion wear or jewellery in her arousal and nervousness The thought *Only the best-dressed naked captives* makes her smile.

She inspects a particular pair of slim, soft cuffs with buckles takes one of them down. She touches the polished metal fittings and runs the soft hide against her arm. She holds it under her nose and draws in its rich leather scent. These things certainly are a delight to the senses when not being used.

This is how a naked, freshly clean William finds her. How and *why* does he move so silently? Her brother always made a noise like a trampling elephant whenever he moved about their house!

"Interested?" he asks softly, and colour rises to her cheeks yet again.

"I suppose I could try just a pair of cuffs," she says, looking down.

He raises her face gently to his own. She sees a light in his eyes that excites her as he kisses her lips.

His hand snakes inside her robe, and she moves her legs apart to welcome him. He finds her wet and welcoming to his touch. "But a spot of dinner first." He offers his fingers to her mouth.

She feels like stamping her foot at being denied once more, but takes them nonetheless and gets a little of her own back by swirling her tongue around his fingers. *He's going to get his revenge anyway … but I don't mind that in the slightest.*

William finishes drying and grabs a robe for himself before they head downstairs. "There's a choice: I could heat up some of the casserole of we could something else with bread, salad and cold meats; or I could rustle up scrambled eggs or omelettes?"

"An omelette and a little more of that bread would be nice."

They talk of small things as they work, moving about the kitchen with comfortable ease: how she has done some shopping for her elderly neighbour, Mrs Godleman, who pops in to feed the cats when she's away; her work plans for the week ahead; his next business trip. Between each task, his hands find their way to her body, whether to knead a muscle with slow strength or deliver a caress. The touches and his eyes keep her constantly aware of her body, of the events of the day so far, and of those planned for the evening.

They finish the wine. Conversation slows as the omelettes cook— two, of course, because the smaller one has no mushrooms. They prepare a small salad of watercress, rocket, and vine tomatoes. He cuts more bread and tops the finished omelettes with herbs.

In a short while they have two handsome plates. They dine at the kitchen table because, she says, it is more comfortable than the breakfast bar.

"Water?" he asks.

"If you have sparkling?"

He fetches some from the fridge. "Slice of lemon or some lime cordial?"

She opts for lemon and enjoys the icy shock of the chilled water.

The meal is flavourful. Though the kitchen is large and bright, it still feels more intimate than the dining room. They continue to chat as they eat, the conversation fading again as they finish. When an expectant silence has filled the room, he takes her hand and she does not resist.

William leads her upstairs and into the playroom. He tenderly removes her robe, kisses her, and asks if she has chosen. She feels like a sacrifice as she moves shyly towards the drawers and retrieves the strange pebble-shaped vibrator. After a pause, she adds the curved steel sculpture. The contrasting textures of each item impact her far more intensely now that the reality of their use is so close.

She offers them to William, and he smiles and bends to kiss her. "And the cuffs?"

She retrieves these too. He leads her to the bed before collecting a single long leather strap with bright metal rings at each end.

She sits—naked, nervous, and excited—on the side of the big four-poster bed and offers up her wrists to him as her heart thumps in her chest. The leather feels deliciously soft and warms quickly. He wraps it closely around each wrist and buckles it fast., her wrists and hands are so slim that it takes him two attempts to fasten the cuffs tightly enough to secure her. She admires their polished black leather and gleaming steel. A dozen wild fantasies rise in her mind.

When he is satisfied, he leans forward and kisses her. "Are you ready?"

She nods, unable to vocalise her response.

He loops the thick leather strap around a bedpost and has her lie with her arms stretched above her. He threads a stout metal clip through each end and the D-ring of each cuff. She tests the bonds and, with a thrill of delicious fear, finds herself truly trapped.

His lips, strong hands, and words provide comfort. "Remember, *pineapple!*" He smiles down at his willing prisoner.

He takes his time with her, enjoying the liberty her state allows him. Though she would gladly allow him that liberty if she were free, being stretched out this way somehow makes her breasts still more sensitive to his knowing touch. She eagerly parts her thighs and presses upwards like an offering as his hands stray lower. He runs the bulbous steel head along her entrance, its chill touch sending a thrill through her as it gathers her moisture. Then it is at the mouth of her canal, it's cool smoothness moving irresistibly inwards.

The feeling of the cool steel insider her, is both exotic and alien. He presses it with expert skill against the front wall of her vagina. She is used to his touch. (Used to it? She's known him how few days? And yet her body *is* used to his strong fingers pressing ... and stroking ... just ... there). This is entirely different, though—the hardness, the coldness. There's a steel bar inside her, stronger and more rigid than any part of her. Her body responds as urgently to it as to the warm, firm softness of him, invading her, possessing her in a new way.

She rapidly nears the point at which he previously denied her. Two strong fingers tease her outer labia. Something runs through her wetness and lifts her hood. Its silky texture caressing either side of her clitoris. She jumps when it suddenly begins buzzing. Its effects quickly overwhelm her, and she crashes over a cliff into an internal world, unable to vocalise, muscles spasming again and again.

Eventually the storm ebbs. His lips crush hers in a welcome, passionate kiss. The steel now feels hot, though it can be no hotter than the warm flesh of her insides surrounding it.

His eyes twinkle. The palm of his hand presses hard on the top front edge of her pubic bone. He firmly rubs the irresistible steel intrusion against the matching point inside her, and she is lost in herself once more. She quakes uncontrollably, her arms trapped by the leather and steel bindings, her legs by the iron strength of his own. She has never, even when ill or falling-down drunk, felt so profoundly not in control of her own body.

Timelessness arrives and passes. Her body weakens. As it does, he relents. The buzzing slows and stops, and the pressure stroking her inside and out eases. His kiss is breath-gentle and then gone.

Nimble fingers free her cuffs from the link joining them together and to the bedpost, but leave the cuffs in place. His arms enfold her, and she buries her face against the thick muscles of his chest.

"How did you get all these things? And how did you learn to use them?" she asks at length when reality returns for her.

"I look and I shop, in the real world and online. I imagine. I've done a little practicing, I see reactions and ask how they feel. I, um, I read and watch some references, and I read the reviews," William replies earnestly.

"You what?" Meredith exclaims. For some reason she is on the verge of laughter. Her stomach muscles ache from cumming so many times and with such intensity, but the pain of her efforts to control her mirth only makes the situation funnier.

"I read the reviews," he says again, a little defensively, sending her into a painful peal of hysterical laughter.

Between gasps for breath and groans of pain, she manages to get out, "So do I have to ..." She loses it again. "... write an orgasm ..." Tears roll down her eyes and she curls up in near hysterics. "... an orgasm review as my homework?"

Despite his initial attempts to remain serious, her laughter gets to him and he joins in. "If you wouldn't mind—but if you're too shy, you can just ask for any favourites to be repeated." He rolls her on the bed, and again she feels powerless as he tickles her mercilessly. Only when her squeals sound pained does his tormenting touch turn to caresses. She becomes acutely aware of his hardness against her, and of her own desire. She offers no resistance as he re-binds her arms and stretches her imprisoned body out. Her hips rise to welcome him.

Meredith loses herself completely in the contrast of being trapped in her bonds while greedily accepting and reflecting every ounce of his passion. When at last he erupts into her, she is exhausted and sated. When he frees her, she feels a moment of regret. But this soon passes, and she embraces him. Her body delights in his warmth wrapping around her.

11

Lazy Sunday

Waking in the strange room to the aroma of coffee, Meredith takes a while to come to. She needs another moment to work out where she is. She's aided in both tasks by William's softly spoken "Good morning, sleepyhead."

"Mmm, morning you. You should have woken me."

He chuckles and hands her a steaming mug, then climbs back into bed. "I tried! You were out for the count." He tries to kiss her, but her mouth feels quite morning-y and she doesn't let him. Instead he gives her a peck on the cheek.

After rolling the first sip of coffee around her mouth, she says, "You're not being so bossy this morning."

"Do you think you'd like following orders before you're awake?"

Her instinctive response is *Oh, no! He's laughing at me*, but he's seems light-hearted about it. So she says, "No, I don't think so." She takes a second, longer draft of coffee before asking a question her mind has only half framed: "What adventures do you have planned?"

"There are a few things we could try if you'd like: a salad recipe or two, maybe a country walk." He kisses her successfully this time, and his lips taste of coffee. "Would you like me to show you some more exercises?"

"Those are the only options?" She snuggles into him to hint that his suggestions are not the sorts of adventures she has in mind.

★★★

They relax in the lounge with music playing. "Donizetti," he says. "*L'Elisir d'Amore.*"

It's beautiful, and the sated Meredith is both relaxed and in a playful mood. "So how did you start?"

"With what?"

"You know." He's so embarrassing! She elbows him and tries to smile off her embarrassment. "With being kinky!"

"It just developed, I think—holding someone still and them liking it, getting deliberately teased to the point of swatting a girl's backside and her saying 'ooh' after she said 'ow'. then giggling and winding me up until I did it again." He slides down on the sofa and she snuggles close. "It grew out of that: playing, finding out what I like." They kiss. "And finding out what other people do."

"How do you know whether someone will like it?" She thinks, *Is that why this beautiful man picked me?*

"There are bad girls and good girls—and doubtless boys—who like or feel the need to be controlled sometimes while they enjoy themselves."

Meredith listens to his words, though her body is listening more to his wandering hand as it moves inside her borrowed robe. His palm lightly strokes her nipple to full erectness.

"Others like a little stinging or squeezing mixed in with their caresses."

His fingers tweak the aching bud, making her yelp in surprise. A spark of warm sensation arrows downward from her breast as he says this last. "But you never quite know until you get to know a person. Some like the idea, but the actuality scares them off. Others don't even know it's an option until they find out that's how they're wired."

Her eyes begin to dilate as her focus shifts inside herself. He can easily feel her heart rate rising as he continues his ministrations. Sliding forward to allow his left hand to join in, he undoes the belt of her robe.

"A nice tight bind allows the dom to do whatever your body needs without having to expend too much effort holding you down. He is able to concentrate fully on you."

He takes one end of the belt and ties it to one of her wrists.

"Would you really use those whips on me?" she asks.

Sternly, William says, "You know what I might do if you tease?" as he secures her other wrist.

She looks at him and quite deliberately says, "Yes." And she pokes her tongue out at him.

He seizes her by the lapels of the bathrobe. She cries, "You wouldn't dare!" She's giggling as he flips her easily over his knee, and squeals, "Nooo!" when he slides the robe up, exposing her bum.

"I'd only use them on you if you wanted. *But,* concerning the teasing, I did warn you, young lady." He strokes her derriere, his touch moves down her legs, tickling her inner thighs. She struggles, and begins laughing uncontrollably, but her struggles are to no avail. He uses the robe's loose sleeves to pin her without hurting her.

"Don't you dare!" she tries to order him, but can't resist wiggling her exposed bum at him.

"Is that a challenge? Or a funny way of saying *pineapple?*"

Meredith protests, "You wouldn't!" But she doesn't use the safe word, and her question is answered by a firm slap. The blow isn't hard enough to hurt. Yet the impact and sound shock Meredith to the core, resonating in her already heated insides.

"Apparently I would." He slaps her bum again and then turns his hand to caressing her sensitised skin. "Now are you going to say you're sorry for teasing?"

"No, I will not!"

Another light spank makes her yelp in surprise. She struggles and kicks, but doesn't scream out for help or demand that he stop.

"Well, there are two ways you can stop this," William continues in a matter-of-fact tone as his hand strokes her. "An apology—"slap," —or mention of that deliciously sharp—"He emphasises the word with another slap," —sweet fruit."

The light blows bring the barest hint of rosiness to her skin. He caresses her. When his hand makes its way between her legs, she tries to trap it but finds he is far too strong. He removes his hand from her grip and caresses the line where her thighs clamp shut, stroking with slow, deliberate movements.

"William! You can't do this!" In her position, she can't do anything much with her arms. When she flails her legs she not only can't reach him but the movement allows him to slide a hand back between her thighs. He continues his caresses more intimately.

"I clearly can do this. I've told you how you can stop me." He pushes his thumb into her opening, and, to her surprise, she finds herself eagerly receptive. "And you have chosen not to stop me." Two of his fingers slip between her labia and slide up either side of her hood and clitoris. "So you must want me to." He twists the belt in his left hand and presses down, holding her trapped over his knees. His fingers inside her rock in slow circles, pressing into her most sensitive flesh.

Meredith says nothing—if moving her legs farther apart constitutes saying nothing.

"That's good, but not quite an apology." His fingers continue to work their magic on her. "Do you have anything to actually say?"

Unable to roll with his thumb inside her, Meredith's initial response is to try to free her hands. The knots in the belt hold them quite securely at her sides. Instead she turns her head to the side so that she can see him. Her breath quickens as she senses that she is getting close. Then she holds it, closes her eyes, and waits. Just a few moments more of this and …

And he stops. "I think it's time for that apology, young lady."

Again she cries "No!" This time her response is to what he is no longer doing, not to something he has done.

"Very well!" The tone of his voice is disappointed, and when he removes his hand from her, she is too. Instead of giving her pleasure, it cracks sharply down on each buttock, one after the other, bringing loud complaints from her lips and renewed kicking from her legs. "That didn't sound like an either apology or a tropical fruit." He strokes her slightly stinging bottom and moves his hand back to her opening, where he finds her body welcoming again.

It hurts a little, but Meredith can't help laughing. A warm sensation comes afterwards and joins with the return of his knowing touch. It's so ridiculous and so naughty. She turns her head and looks into his eyes as if daring him to try that again. With emphasis, she says, *"Kumquat."*

He raises his hand once more. It falls onto each of her buttocks in turn, striking the same spots and causing the pain and the warmth to come more intensely. As he goes back to caressing her, he reiterates with laughter, "You know how to stop this; it's either *pineapple* or *sorry.*"

William doesn't give up. He teases and tantalises, then stops as she gets close. He repeatedly asks if she wants to apologise or use the safe word. When she does neither, he spanks. Each repetition sees him taking her a little closer and spanking her a little harder.

In the end she isn't sure if it's her need, her aching bum, or the game itself that causes the words to escape her mouth, but as he goes to withdraw his touch, she says, "I'm sorry," in a barely audible whisper.

"For?" His fingers continue to caress, but not firmly enough to grant her release.

Meredith can't believe she's smiling. "For poking my tongue out at you."

He bends and kisses her back as his touch sets her in flight.

★★★

"I want you to cum too." She slides down from the sofa, legs first, and kneels on one of the fallen cushions in front of him.

He's handsome. His stubble is longer than she has seen it before, and his hair is certainly what he would call mussed. His shirt is still done up, and she reaches to correct that. She pauses long enough to be sure she has his permission to continue, then unbuttons and pushes the soft material back across his broad, flat chest. She brushes her thumbs over his perky nipples, looking him straight in the eyes with an impish grin. A jolt of satisfaction runs the length of her body when she sees his breath catch in response.

She strokes and kisses his chest, gently taking each of those perky nipples into her mouth. His body is even more of a joy to touch than it is to see. Next she reaches for the button fly of his jeans. She wishes she knew a sexy way of opening them, but manages without feeling too clumsy. He half lifts to assist her as she tugs the stiff denim and the soft cotton of his briefs over his strong legs. She marvels that even as he relaxes, there are lines of heavy muscle visible on his thighs and calves even his shins are muscular she notes as she yanks the wretched clothes over his big, bony, male feet.

Satisfied that he is now fully available for her eyes, hands, and lips to explore, she leans up to kiss his lips and then his sternum. She strokes the roundness of his shoulders and the fullness of his arms, and a warm contentedness fills her. Perhaps she would have paid more mind in her art classes if she had been allowed to touch the statues.

She takes her time, relishing the taste of his skin and of his precum. She savours the texture of him—feeling him twitch, hearing him stifle sighs, and seeing him hold himself back. She wonders if this is how he feels when she abandons herself to his ministrations. If it is, she can certainly appreciate that he does indeed get something out of it.

His cock begin to throbs and its head swells. She presses the pad of her thumb against his pulsing urethra as she prepares herself, then lets him release into her waiting mouth. She delights in a sense of control and feminine power as he does, though she's not a great fan of the taste. She holds him in her mouth a moment before rising and kisses him briefly. She reaches for her sparkling water, hoping he won't deduce that she's washing away the taste.

Once she's half drained the glass, she curls up next to him on the big sofa. "I still can't believe you spanked me!"

"You teased me into it."

She buries her face in his chest to prevent him from seeing her cheeks flare.

He seems to read her like a book anyway. "I gave you every opportunity not to play that game, young lady, and you took every opportunity to make sure you did."

"Is it always like that?"

"What do you mean?" He asks, his attention fully on her.

Meredith tries to explain to him and at the same time process the experience for herself. "It was exciting, and so … naughty? So intimate. It didn't really hurt though."

"It's not supposed to hurt much unless you want it to. —"

"Spanking someone who's turned on by it is exciting and intimate—watching her responses, feeling her arousal rise." He kisses the top of her head tenderly and pulls her close. "When you deliberately teased me into starting, and when you relaxed and let me …" He squeezes her shoulder and drops his head back, causing her to look up and make eye contact. "Those were special moments."

Meredith feels an intense sense of closeness with him. More than that, she feels a sense of intimacy with herself that she cannot recall experiencing before.

"We really should get dressed and enjoy what's left of the daylight, you know," he observes.

She tries a pout, but he doesn't look impressed by her attempt. She knows she'll feel better for a brief walk.

"Afterwards I can show you those new exercises you asked about this morning." He winks.

"You know very well I didn't!" She thinks guiltily that she should have done. She's not enjoying exercise any more than she did the first time, though she had fun doing them with him. "It's not getting any easier, and it's not doing any good."

As they stroll outside arm in arm, he asks, "Are you sure you're not finding them easier?"

"No."

"But you can do more than you could on Tuesday."

"Yes." She feels daft. "So I am finding them easier?"

He winks. It's a sweet gesture, much better than the *I told you so* she'd expected. "And that's after just a few days. Imagine what a few weeks will do."

Meredith's cheeks are rosy from the dusk chill by the time they step back into the warm house but she feels enervated. William suggests getting their training for the day out of the way. Meredith really doesn't want to, but she also doesn't want to give up so soon. His enthusiasm helps her through her twenty minutes, and he gets her familiar with a few new exercises.

William's training takes longer than hers, so Meredith uses the opportunity to check up on her house via remote cameras. He finds her curled up, contented as a cat, in one of the armchairs in his music room. She's found some Purcell, *Dido and Aeneas*.

"Not many people know this," he says, leaning over the back of the chair. She jumps, still unused to how quietly he moves.

"I love Purcell. I don't know many other fans either. It's a shame that most people miss out. Mind you, I was tempted to go Fleetwood Mac." She smiles, thinking he might disapprove.

"It's my collection. There's nothing in it I can't stand, so feel free to choose." He sees her living room on her phone's screen. "What are you up to?"

"Checking in on Aggy and Pog."

"You're such a good mum to your fur babies." He leans in and kisses the side of her neck. The two of them watch the remote camera for a while as they listen.

Once Meredith tires of watching and closes the app, William asks, "So, what do you like least about your job?"

"That's easy! Presentations and pitches." She rolls her eyes. "I like people, the work's interesting, and we really help our customers to get more out of their businesses."

"So you like your products and services, and the benefits you provide to your customers, but you don't like telling people about them?" That smile—he has so many. It's hard to keep up with the way he uses his face to talk. "Have you got any coming up?"

"Yes, a retail one."

"What will you talk about?"

"Well, for this client we track the loyalty customer hand scanners as they move around the store, so we can tell what displays draw the most attention. It's cheaper and more effective than asking people, and it gives us a competitive advantage. Stores can use the information in all sorts of ways, like sending out discount vouchers for high value items a customer looks at but doesn't buy." She stops and looks at him.

He's grinning. "Would it help to practice? You should see yourself. You really do care about your work, don't you? Speaking like that when you present to clients, you must get good responses."

"I've never really thought of it like that."

"Don't you video your rehearsals and presentations?"

"No. We don't do rehearsals, and I'd be too shy to be on video."

"Why? Nobody else ever has to see them. Video helps you improve and focus and appreciate what you do, just like your clever scanners do for your customers."

"You mean you get together like actors and rehearse your client meetings?" She pictures William and his serious-faced colleagues as actors; the idea strikes her as funny.

"Of course. One team does its presentation and the other plays the role of clients—asking questions, criticising, negotiating, and generally trying to put the presenters off their stride."

"That seems a bit involved."

William shrugs. "It works. We get the business. And with presentations, the client gets a copy so they can hold us to any promise, of course." He grins wolfishly. "We retain one so that we can hold the client to theirs."

"It's all very well for you, you're so confident!" she complains.

"I'm not always. I just project it, and with work I practice until I feel as confident as I can be. Very few people are 'always confident'." He looks rueful. "Unless they're too stupid to realise everything that can go wrong. They just learn to behave confidently. Then, if they're lucky, the good habits stick." Cocking his head to one side he asks "Fancy giving it a go?"

"What do you mean?"

"Do a bit of your pitch to me."

It's the enthusiasm—that's what gets her. Somehow he persuades her to let him record the session, using the camera on his mobile. She only realises she's got wrapped up in it after about a half an hour and his fourth or so helpful question. Even then, she has little idea how long she's been talking for. "You make a much better audience than some of our customers do."

"I can be less helpful if you want," he offers.

"Why would I want that?"

"So you can get used to it when it doesn't matter if you stop and start again."

What seems like just a few minutes later, Meredith doesn't know why she's said yes. She feels foolish, embarrassed. This is the third time she's fluffed this question.

Her discomfort must show, or his psychic powers must be working because he gets up and turns the camera off. "Break time." He kisses the side of her neck. "Coffee?"

"End time and wine?" she asks, tired. She can see his enthusiasm for his new project and doesn't want to disappoint him, so she doesn't insist.

Instead of using the espresso machine, William puts the kettle on to make a cafetière. He uses the time it takes to gently massage her shoulders. After a minute he senses that she's tired from the stress of talking on camera, and changes his mind about maybe carrying on. "You did well. It's not an easy thing to do." Warmth flows in his voice and in his hands. "I think you're right—a glass of wine while we watch, and if you hate watching too much, we can delete it and never mention it again."

Meredith calms. She's not felt uncomfortable with him before, except about being naked, and she hasn't found talking on camera easy. "It was horrible."

"It was fine. You'll see." He kisses he again, trying to give her further reassurance, and holds up a bottle of Rioja that looks far more appealing to Meredith than coffee. "Small bite?"

"I didn't realise I was hungry, but now you mention it …"

"Post-performance." He winks. "Experience, not mysterious powers. Even when I'm only in the spotlight for a few minutes, it leaves me peckish."

Knowing William's appetite, Meredith imagines "peckish" is an understatement. "I'm not sure my hungry is as hungry as your peckish."

"My larder is your oyster. Cheese, fruit? The clementines are nice, though they're better with water than wine." It's a good try, or at least he thinks so, but it doesn't work, Meredith is set on wine.

With refreshments of both solid and liquid nature on hand, he puts his phone in the dock and hits play. Meredith surprises herself by managing to watch the whole thing through. The wine and food help; they certainly lift her mood.

"How do you like it?" That impish grin is back after how grim and intimidating he'd been while she gave the presentation.

"Well, that depends. It's a good idea, I can see that, but …" Meredith swallows. "I hate it." Her face says sorry, while his breaks out in laughter.

"Everyone, or pretty much everyone hates it, but it works." He does his best to rearrange his features into a supportive expression, and hopes he has succeeded better than he suspects he has. "You saw what you liked and what you want to do differently. You'll get more used to video and presenting, even Q&A."

Meredith enjoys the moment of praise, and considers his words. It hadn't been as bad as she'd expected, once she forgot the camera—apart from afterwards, when she'd seen herself rolling her eyes when William pretended not to understand one of her answers! She would have to make sure she never did that with a client and hoped that she hadn't done it often before. "Okay, you win. Yes, it was useful, and yes, I'll try it at work." His face lighting up is worth the cost of that admission. "Now, is my homework finished?"

"Do you mean 'is it playtime'?" He's chased the humour from his face except for a hint of devilment in his eyes. He's impossible when he's like this too, but more enjoyably so. She wonders if she will ever stop blushing when he hints. Her only answer is the rosiness rising to her cheeks. He continues in a deep, growly whisper, "It can be if you want. After all, I'm quite sure you've earned a reward." He moves forward. "Of course, I might make you write an orgasm review too."

She feels tempted to hit him for his cheeky confidence, but settles for, "You're pretty sure of yourself, Mr Farrow!" She raises her hand between them ineffectually.

"I am, aren't I? I wonder why that might be." His mock-quizzical tone belies the way his face has creased into quite the filthiest smile Meredith has ever seen. "Would you like to choose your reward? Or would you like a surprise?"

How does he do it? Meredith wonders. A moment ago they were all seriousness, and now she realises that she is ready, almost as if he and her body have been having a conversation that she hasn't been a party to.

"I'm not sure. Is there something you think I should try?" Her tone and thoughts are playful, but a more cautious part of her mind makes her add, "Nothing extreme though."

"I wasn't even sure you'd like what you've tried so far!"

"If I hadn't, what would have happened?"

"We wouldn't have carried on, or wouldn't have done them again." He pulls her close and looks at her seriously. "I think most people can like some of this, if there's enough trust. To be honest, I hadn't considered broaching topic with you yet because I wasn't sure."

"But would you stay with me if I didn't like it?" She feels a need to know. This is all new to her, and so is the way she is feeling.

"The person and their response are more important than the activity." He frowns. "The pleasure in this rides a delicate balancing act of trust and desire. For normal people, it needs both." He leans forward to kiss her, but she's not ready.

"And if I don't want to try it all?" Some of the things in his playroom are frightening to her in ways she doesn't like.

"It can be best to always have something you know you don't want to try." His eyes are asking a question he can't put into words. "It would be more worrying to find you instantly wanted to try everything. Remember I hadn't even decided to offer you a vibrator yet."

Meredith laughs. Two days ago, no boyfriend ever had, and now it seems such an innocent thing. Her emotions rise. A tear threatens to spill from her eye. She holds him close, takes a deep breath, and lets him kiss her once more.

"If you want to try something now, I'd suggest a soft flogger or a blindfold. But don't push yourself too fast."

"Why?" She thought he'd be keener.

"Both things can be gentle, but you've tried a few new things this weekend. If you're not in a hurry, it can be nice to find new things slowly and learn to enjoy them properly."

Having brought up the idea herself, Meredith is reluctant to let it go. She already knows what a blindfold is. "Could you show me a flogger?"

Her shy smile dissolves his resistance. He offers her his hand and leads her upstairs to the playroom in silence.

Standing with William in front of the display of whips after having asked about them, seems different to gazing upon them by herself. There's the same quickening of her pulse, but her experiences over the last two days have given her the sense that she can trust him. He's opened doors inside her that she hasn't known were there. She's still scared of the implements, especially the hard ones like the cane she had slapped herself with the day before, but she feels a deep curiosity about the others and the sensations they might create.

"There are different kinds." He lifts down a whip with a short handle and a dozen or so slim rope strands. "Their effect depends on the weight, material, number of falls, and length of the falls and handle." He holds it out to her. "This one won't cause pain unless you poke a person in the eye with it."

After her experience with the cane, Meredith is nervous about holding of it, but when William nods, she takes it from him. The thin ropes are soft and light. She runs them over her hand; they feel soft and warm. A swish makes no sound, and an experimental swipe indeed causes no pain.

Next he shows her a flogger with myriad short, fine strands that feel as though they're made of rubber or PVC. They're cool and silky to the touch as she runs them over her skin. "The ones like this can sting, depending on how you use them."

"You should be a sex education teacher," she says. She plays the falls along her forearm. Then, realising what she's said, she laughs and blushes. "But then again, maybe not!" She swishes with gusto and, he's right, the tips sting sharply. "Ow!"

"I did warn you." He takes the little toy from her unresisting grasp. "Then there's this kind." The thing he takes down is altogether more ornate, with thick suede falls. "Here. Touch and smell."

She takes it. It's far heavier. The tassels—no, the *falls*—are soft and have that heady leather smell. Its caress is warm and weighted, almost like a velvet dress. When she swings cautiously, it lands with a thuddiness and wraps around her arm. "Oh!"

"Used gently, this kind can be very pleasurable."

He steps close to her, takes the flogger in one hand, and opens her robe with the other. He trails the suede falls lightly over her skin, bringing an instant rush of warmth wherever they touch.

She leans into him and purrs. "So much to learn," she murmurs.

"And so much time to learn it in." He kisses her, slides the robe from her, and leads her to the bed.

★★★

"Hot chocolate before sleep?" he asks as they lie sleepily on the playroom's big bed.

The idea is appealing, though she doesn't think she's had a hot chocolate with a boy since she was at school. She opens her mouth to say yes, but instead finds herself saying, "We've hardly been out of bed this weekend!"

"We have! Just today you got a new work idea, and we've cooked, gone for a walk, and trained. Besides, we did it downstairs too." He jumps out of bed.

Meredith's phone rings shortly after she joins him in the kitchen. She lazily glances at the screen, then smiles and taps to answer. "Jess, how are you?"

"I thought I'd better check you hadn't been murdered."

"Of course not, I've just ..."

Jess's mind fills in the blank."Good for you. So do I get to meet him then?"

Meredith realises that she's completely forgotten about asking William to meet Jess. "Sorry, I haven't found the right moment yet. We've only been seeing each other for a couple of weeks."

As far as Jess is concerned, the sort of bloke who won't meet his girlfriend's bestie is the sort of bloke who will turn out to be a shitbag. Meredith's married ex had never been keen on meeting Jess. Protectively, she presses the issue. "No, you've been *devouring* each other for a couple of weeks. You don't normally let a man stay the night for ages. So you've effectively been going out together for a few months."

Jess's view of reality can be a bit fluid sometimes, however she's usually able to persuade Meredith to go along with it.

Meredith begins, "That doesn't make sense at all!" But Jess's persuasion works its magic. Meredith can almost see the hope and disappointment on her friend's face. "But I'll ask. Next Saturday, yes?"

"Perfect. Can I stay?" There's a smugness to the reply that Meredith would probably find annoying from just about anyone else.

She always stays over. Though Meredith isn't quite sure about being with William with someone else in the house, she can't say no.

She hangs up. William has heard it all, and suggests, "If you'd rather, she could come to mine. I've got more space." To him it makes perfect sense: his spare room is large and comfortable, and it has an en-suite.

Meredith though imagines Jess standing in the doorway of his playroom with an expression of horror on her face. "Um, what do you do about *the room* when people come and stay?"

"I don't take them in there unless, well ..."

"And they aren't curious?" She's surprised, but more amused.

"Why should they be? It's just a bedroom."

Meredith tries to control her mirth. "How can you know so much about women and so little at the same time?" He still doesn't seem to get it. "Jess might understand your office being locked, but other than that, she'll want to look around. Even if she didn't, she might go to the wrong door, looking for her room."

"Why should she? The room she's be in is just opposite the stairs."

"How many women other than your lovers have you had visit recently?"

"Not many."

"Then trust me. And I'm not ready to have that chat with Jess just yet." She kisses him, finishes her hot chocolate, and goes to get ready for bed.

When she emerges from the bathroom, she finds William using a wooden back scratcher. He stops on seeing her and puts it down on his bedside cabinet.

"You keep a spanking stick by your bed?"

"No, it's a back scratcher. It's for the muscles I can't reach to scratch. I don't like getting out of bed to find a door frame to rub against in the middle of the night.

He tries to carry on with his explanation, but Meredith is laughing too loud to hear. *The Jungle Book* was a childhood favourite, and an image of her serious, spanky boyfriend as the carefree Baloo is blotting everything else from her mind. She hums the tune to "The Bear Necessities", though her laughter interrupts and it takes him a while to recognise it.

"It could definitely be pressed into service," he says attempting to sound threatening. William can't help feeling a tad put upon, but also can't help seeing the funny side. "I don't spank everyone! And I certainly don't keep my back scratcher by the bed on the off chance that a stranger will stop by for a quick whacking!"

"Have you ever spanked anyone with it?"

"No, I haven't!"

"Perhaps you should try—" A sudden giddy rush has the words out of Meredith's mouth before she realises. She can't believe she's said them, but once she's spoken, she knows she wants him to.

"Seriously?" His face is sceptical, unsure as to whether she's joking.

"Yes." She blushes. "I think so ..." then feels less certain, *"Pineapple, right?"*

"If you're sure you want to, then get on your hands and knees in the middle of the bed."

He picks up the back scratcher and flicks his wrist. She flinches at the sound of it whispering through the air. He hears her intake of breath. He strokes the cool wood across the fair skin of her bottom, sending a ticklish tingle of anticipation through her. Then he lifts it away. "Sure?"

"Yes."

He slaps it down onto the round of her right buttock. The sound is louder in her ears than the sting is in her bum. As before, the sting is followed by a spreading warmth. He strokes her with his free hand, then the scratcher. He lifts it away again, and this time she tenses in anticipation. Again the smack seems to reach her ears before her nerves register the impact. It stings the left side of her bottom this time. She realises he's stroking the area he's about to hit with the stick before he strikes.

Knowing he's not hitting hard, Meredith tenses less before the next strike. This time it lands across both sides of her bum. She finds herself breathing harder after it. The impacts against her skin are talking to her body in an unexpectedly wonderful way, signalling readiness for him and anticipation of him. The next blow falls in the exact same place. This time the stinging is more intense and takes longer to merge into the warmth building inside her.

★★★

Meredith speaks softly as she lies curled up against his shoulder. "Well, that was different too." He looks pensive. She adds, "Good different, though." She's starting to realise that, for all his knowledge about women's bodies and minds, perhaps he doesn't understand her as well as she imagines.

She puts her arms around him and says, "Oh, and William? You are the most Baloo and least Baloo person I know." She kisses him, feeling happy and sad, as well as very fond of him indeed.

12

At Home with the Cats

William's alarm goes off at an ungodly hour on Monday. Meredith grumbles at being woken by a peck on the cheek and the Offspring screeching at high volume. At least he isn't insufferably cheerful this early. Nor does he remind her that the early wake-up was her idea. "I'll put the kettle on and dive through the bathroom while you get yourself together," he murmurs.

Emerging from her shower, Meredith smells good things—definitely coffee and toast. She finds William in the kitchen, putting the finishing touches to a sandwich. She's unable to resist a teasing, "You're so domesticated!"

His response, a firm but not painful swat on her bottom, doesn't surprise her or her bottom. She makes a complaining noise anyway. He kisses her and hands her a cup of steaming hot black coffee. He resumes work, quickly wrapping the sandwich and popping it into a small cool bag.

"Is toast and yoghurt okay for you?" he asks, indicating a place setting. "And, speaking of domestication, you can load the dishwasher," he adds as he sits at the breakfast bar with a bowl of porridge.

She thinks she may as well give up on trying to fight him over breakfast, especially as it smells nice. "Thanks. I could get used to this." She yawns. "Well, maybe not the six a.m. alarm or not being allowed to smoke in the house."

William laughs. "If it helps, you can think of me as a cat." He pokes his tongue out at her before going back to pottering.

Meredith finishes her small breakfast and tidies the things away. She's surprised to be handed a small cool bag and a flask.

"Lunch and coffee," he says. "You said your work only had instant and the local shop's sandwich selection isn't always great."

"That's so sweet. I don't think anyone's made me a packed lunch since I was at school." She doesn't intend to sound belittling, and regrets her choice of words.

He smiles in response, and she's relieved that he's taken it as intended. "Don't get used to it. I just had time today because somebody had an early start. Do you want a cup for your drink holder?"

It's tempting, but she decides against it. "Thanks, but I'd better not risk getting caught short on the way!" Conscious of the time and keen to beat as much of the traffic as she can, she kisses him on the cheek, rather than the lips, to avoid dallying. "I'll call when I arrive."

Meredith lights a cigarette as soon as she gets into the car. Her chest tightens as the first drag hits her lungs as it often does, and she opens the window a crack before clipping her phone into its bracket on the dashboard and starting the satnav. The navigator takes the strain out of the first, unfamiliar part of the journey. But it's "voice" does start to annoy her somewhere between stubbing the cigarette out half-smoked and closing the window because the air outside is cold.

Setting off early, the traffic isn't as bad as she'd feared. She's glad she has a set of keys for the office, though she more often uses them to lock up than to open up. It's still dark when she arrives, but she's not quite the first person in. One of the directors' parking spots is occupied. Meredith finds the financial director in kitchen, making herself a drink when she fetches a cup for her coffee and they exchange pleasantries.

Taking William's flask from her bag, Meredith sits down in her office to start her week. The real coffee is a pleasant change and reminds her to message him.

In early, journey not so bad, thanks for the coffee!

Were you first in?

No, the FD beat me.

> *Excellent, brownie points if he's seen you! Make sure to send your boss an e-mail nice and early too.;)*

> *He's a she, but yes, she has, and not everyone is as calculating as you are, Mr Farrow. :(*

She follows this with a frown emoji, wishing he weren't so …

> *Their inadequacies are hardly my fault.*

His replying emojis, an angel a shrug and a wink signal his lack of repentance. He's impossible, but he does make her smile. Nevertheless, her suspicion that he's right to be the way he is is vaguely depressing.

> *Haven't you got anything else to do?*

> *Checked my mail. Bloody train's too full to get the laptop out, and I'm stuck outside the London terminus. So, unless you want me to turn my wit on my fellow passengers, no.*

This time he send a devil and a wink.

> *Well I have! x*

> *Have a good day x*

She uses the quiet time before the office fills up to finish reviewing the proposal she prepared the previous week, and sends it off to her boss by nine o'clock.

Feeling proud of herself, she sips the excellent coffee from William's flask. Scheming or not, he's good to her.

It sets the tone for a productive day. Once finished with the "must dos" and "should dos" for the day, she thinks about the video rehearsal as she eats one of William's sandwiches. It hadn't been fun, but it had been highly informative. With some trepidation, she emails her manager with a brief description of the exercise and her feelings about it, and asks him for a meeting.

They meet in his office near the end of the day. She's pleased to find him genuinely supportive, even enthusiastic about the idea—so much so that he suggests she do a short presentation to the directors later in the week. When she gets out, Meredith excitedly messages William about how his idea has been received and confesses that she's even more nervous now than she had been speaking on video.

Tired after her long day and content with her efforts, Meredith doesn't feel any guilt at all when she leaves work on time. On the way into the supermarket to get some things for dinner, she sees they have some pretty potted jasmine and picks one up as a thank-you to her neighbour for feeding her cats over the weekend.

Her home seems empty, but she has only been in a few moments when she feels the familiar but unexpected rubbing of a feline head against her leg. The cats are normally sulky when she's been away. The contact is followed by Aggy's meow for attention. Suddenly the idea of having the place to herself—with the TV and purring companions— doesn't seem so bad after all. There's something about the knowledge that she was missed which makes the place more home-like and she gives the little molly a couple of kitty nibbles while she's put the shopping away.

In her cupboard, there are a couple of the tiny bottles of wine they sell in supermarkets. William picked them up. She'd complained about her trouble leaving a bottle unfinished. Her first reaction was a thought that it was mean, but he hadn't been so sweet about giving them to her. She pours herself a glass and sets to work preparing peppers and fresh chicken breast.

Pog, her tom, predictably shows up within moments. She starts the chicken cooking and then carefully divides the trimmings into two tiny portions. He headbutts her shins and circles her feet. Meredith puts a portion into each cat's bowl. Pog growls. No sooner has his meat touched his bowl than he is racing toward the cat-flap with it in his jaws.

Aggy—always ladylike, Meredith thinks—mews and settles down to eat from her bowl. Meredith finishes getting her own food ready. She pops the kettle on for her noodles and remembers to weigh out a serving rather than just cook loads.

The meal is quickly ready and fresh. It even looks nice when she arranges it in one of her white china bowls. She snaps a picture and messages it to William before she settles down to eat in front of Netflix.

Her meal is enjoyable but light. It leaves her feeling not quite full, though she resists the temptation to supplement it with dessert.

His reply is a thumbs-up emoji, a shot of a plastic tub of chicken salad on a desk, and the caption *"Working late, yours looks nice."*

After tidying up, she stretches out on the sofa to watch another episode of her latest series. She updates the family WhatsApp group with her progress so her brother will know how much of the story he can gossip about.

While she's at it, she messages William to ask if he's watched the show. He hasn't, so she tells him the general theme. He says he'll give it a look sometime if it's on anything other than pay to view. Meredith isn't sure how he manages without it; William isn't sure why anyone pays for it.

When she curls up in bed, little Aggy, as usual, makes a nest on the duvet next to her. It's not the same as being with William, but it is familiar and Meredith is very much content.

Tuesday proves busy. Her borrowed idea has received a great deal of attention at work—mostly desirable, though she receives considerable teasing from Emily and others. They want to know if she spent the *entire* weekend discussing work with her new lover. Still, Meredith thinks, perhaps that's better than being quizzed about the main events! If she were to accidentally let on about the things she got up to, she would combust.

By lunchtime she has met with the directors and been asked to try out the idea. She and Emily will present to colleagues at the end of the week.

Then, just as she is looking forward to a respite and her thoughts drift towards seeing William later, Jess calls to arrange a drink on Thursday before the two of them have dinner with William. Jess is also eagerly awaiting a blow-by-blow account without him eavesdropping! Even her carefully worded description has Meredith blushing at her desk. She's thoroughly glad that this part of the conversation is over the phone, not face-to-face.

Jess, bless her, interprets Meredith's reluctance as a hint that she wants more of an audience. "OK, Merry, shall we make it a general girl's night?"

"No! Just the two of us. And I can't make it a heavy one—work's mental." The extra work she's landed herself with is at least good for something, even if only as an excuse. She certainly doesn't want to drink heavily enough to spill too many details—or to do the trial presentation with a hangover!

13

The Price of a Cigarette

O n Wednesday, Meredith manages to leave work at five for the second time in the week. She rarely does except on Fridays, Meredith rushes home, vacuums her already spotless lounge, showers, dries her hair, and re-does her make-up. She is about to dress when, exactly on time, the doorbell rings.

She races downstairs and opens the door to greet William. He lifts her from her feet with ease. His hug squeezes but stops short of hurting, though his strong arms stiffening to iron. The perception brings a memory of steel and a rush of heat. She crushes her lips to his and opens her mouth eagerly.

After long moments, he breaks their embrace and lowers her gently to the ground. "Are you ready to go?" he asks with his most impudent smirk.

She isn't dressed yet. Indeed, she's wearing a baggy T-shirt and a robe she dragged on to come downstairs. "Yes, of course, can't you see?" The sarcasm drips but the corners of her mouth twitch. Now that he's here, she is reluctant to end the intimate moment. She would rather enjoy the twinkling in his eye and all that it intimates for a little longer.

"If not, then ..." He takes her by the unresisting hand and leads her into her living room. Between the sofa and the coffee table, he swirls her to face him. His kisses trail under her jawline and down her neck, warming one melting point after another. Heat blooms through her. It's a pattern of touch and tenderness that she knows, though he wraps it in different ways. She knows that it always builds to good things.

"We can after dinner," he says sternly. Her face drops in disappointment."So get ready quickly." He grins.

He's doing it again. She wonders at his strange mix of youthful charm and seriousness — but even more, she wonders what adventure he has in mind.

Meredith considers asking, demanding, even begging. She's only known him a couple weeks, but he's already inside her head. She'd never cum with a man before, and now she's on the verge of begging for the orgasm he can give her. Sod the booking.

She excuses herself and goes to dress. She pulls on bra, knickers, top, and jeans and checks her hair in the mirror. "Fuck, frizzy." She ponders waiting and doing it properly, then discards the idea when her stomach and other parts overrule her vanity. The thought of making him and the orgasm wait reinforces her decision.

She picks up a fresh pack of cigarettes on their way out the door, and he looks disapprovingly at her. "If you're going to spend some of the evening amusing yourself by smoking, then might I suggest a deal?" he asks, placing his hand on her hip.

"That depends on the deal. Are you suggesting a spanking when we get home?" She wiggles her bum and looks challengingly over her shoulder.

"That doesn't seem appropriate. Firstly, you seem to quite enjoy it, and secondly, it still leaves me bored and inconvenienced while we're out this evening."

"Well, what would you suggest, then, Mr Clean-Living?"

She knows her smoking is at risk of becoming a bone of contention, and she knows it's bad for her. She even wants to give up. But she isn't prepared to bend herself completely to a man she's known for such a short time, and she hasn't yet worked out a way of staying clear of her habit.

"How about we try these?" He reaches into his pocket and withdraws a pair of lacy knickers, handing them to her.

"Cheeky! I'm already wearing some, thank you! If you think I'm going out without any in this weather, you're a mile off! I wasn't even a little bit pervy till you came along and corrupted me."

The knickers are nice, lacy but not too much. She know she likes to buy her clothes and is privately pleased that his taste doesn't run to bright red and crotchless. But there doesn't seem to be anything especially noteworthy about the silky lace. She looks at him, puzzled.

He reaches into his pocket again. "This might give you a clue." and holds out a small, curved, purple object, perhaps four inches in length.

The first thing she notices is the silky texture, the material feels luxurious in her fingers, and all of those are familiar, though they wouldn't have been a few days beforehand. As she's still confused he takes the knickers and device and slides the device into small pouch hidden in the double thickness of material at the front. As she accepts them back from him, the device begins to vibrate. She looks up at him. A devilish smile plastered across his face, he shows her a small remote control. The vibration becomes more intense.

"When you indulge yourself, I get to indulge myself," he pronounces. "It seems fair to me."

The suggestion begins to sink in. "In public? You're kidding!"

His fingers trace lines down either side of her neck. "The cigarettes hurt you. This will give you pleasure." His fingers meet under her chin as his lips brush hers. "If you want to take the cigarettes with you, then you'll wear these." His voice falls silent, he places the vibe and knickers into her hand as his own continue their work.

Damn, the way his touch makes her feel! She is taken by an image of her cats curling contentedly. She says hesitantly, "But people will be able to hear."

"Not where I'll be using it. they won't." His expression turns from stern to boyish. "You'll just be certain everyone knows I'm edging you. In reality, they'll be completely ignorant."

She curses the devilment in his eyes as the rumbling warmth of his voice continues to wash her resistance away.

He puts his arms around her. They are thick and strong, making her feel powerless and safe at once. She returns his embrace, pressing her suddenly needy breasts into the warmth of his chest. Thoughts of being unable to do anything about the vibrations while she sits in a restaurant with him fill her mind and flush her cheeks. "If you aren't brave enough to try it, you can just leave the cigarettes at home." He kisses her and steps back.

She hesitates. "No, wait. I'll put them on, "But don't—"

He presses a finger to her lips."Put them on and don't give me orders."

For a moment she has the terrified notion that he will make her put them on in front of him. But he voices no objection and makes no move to follow her as she heads for her bedroom.

I must be mad, she thinks, once safely behind the closed door. She peels her jeans down. As she removes her own panties, she realises they have the first beginnings of dampness. She imagines his voice asking, *"Are you wet,"* in that tone of his that says, *"I know you are."*

The lace feels soft as she pulls the new knickers on. Their tie sides need some adjustment, which her fingers find awkward. At least they fit neatly. She admires the pretty lace in the mirror. How little they leave to the imagination! She's grateful that she is wearing jeans.

Here goes! She slips the little purple device into the pouch at the front. She uses a finger to ease a little of her wetness along the length of the toy, then wiggles it into a comfortable position. Bending to put her jeans back on, she feels the hardness of the plastic against her as she pulls the stretch-denim up and smoothes it *Oh, my!* She realises her jeans tightness will make her constantly aware of the vibrator's presence even when it's still. As she walks down the stairs, each step rotates the device's little nubbin against her. *I hope this isn't going to be too much,* she thinks as she returns to the hallway and faces his smiling eyes.

The corners of his mouth turn upwards and her cheeks flame. His fingers trace across her jeans, directly over the toy, and her colour deepens. His eyes gleam and the vibrator bursts into life. Meredith jumps, and her heart skip a beat. His hand and her tight jeans hold the device trapped in place and it sends waves of stimulation shooting through her pelvis and even up to her breasts.

"Good girl!" he says, kissing her, and the vibrations stop. He turns to go.

She holds back. "Please ..."

He wonders how she will continue.

"... let me cum? I can't ..."

He doesn't give her the chance, turning he kisses her.

"Trust me!" He kisses her again and the device comes back to life.

"Fuck!" The sensation is intense; that little nubbin is right over her ...

He winks and it stops, sucks his lips in to stop himself laughing and then says, "Are you going to wear shoes?"

"Very funny." Hurriedly she pulls her ankle boots on. The vibrator provides an unyielding reminder of its presence as she bends, *at least it's off ... for now anyway.*

As soon as she's got the boots on, he opens the door, keen not to give her time to back out of the adventure. She obediently follows him out, locks up, and takes her place in the passenger seat of his car. Sitting with a vibrator in place is another new experience. Her weight pushes it against her sensitive opening. She wishes he'd let her cum, though maybe that would make this worse.

He seems to read her mind. "c"—he looks straight into her—"you can cum before we eat."

Gratitude and a desire to shout, *How dare you!* war in her mind. In the end she settles on, "I'm not a child." The phrase sounds weak in her ears.

"Then, young lady, decide whether you want to smoke or cum."

She almost lights up just to spite him, despite feeling that it would be rude to do so in a non-smoker's car. She chooses not to confront herself over her motivations for not doing so.

He resists the temptation to drive anything other than smoothly but also the one to play with the remote. In truth he's concerned that he might have pushed her a bit far. After all, it's the first time Meredith has tried anything like this. For all that she's feisty and fun, it might have been wiser to give it a go at home first.

He parks and turns to her. "Well, a promise is a promise." He leans in to take a kiss, but she is reluctant and he respects her reticence. "You can cum now if you want, but I won't force you."

There's relief in her eyes, Meredith feared he would presume, after last weekend, that he has the right to coerce her into any further adventure he wishes. That is certainly not the case, no matter how exciting the adventures so far have been.

She considers. At the start of the drive, she would have leapt at the chance to cum. But she's had time to cool down have given her mind a chance to recover.

They walk the short distance from car park to restaurant. She lights a cigarette and is relieved, though disappointed, that he doesn't use the remote control.

The restaurant is Italian; set in the countryside a drive from her home, it's her recommendation. The place is always busy, the food being good enough to draw people out of town. The staff are friendly, giving regulars the sense that they are members of the family. The chef does a risotto that Meredith adores. She wants to order straight away, but William is torn between a couple of dishes.

He orders wine while he's deciding. "Do you have any preference?"

"Red."

He picks a Sangiovese based on the description in the menu and it's pricing. Once the waiter departs, he confides, "I should learn more about Italian wine."

"Poor William, never satisfied." She takes his hand from across the table. "Can I ask you something?" Meredith always feels nervous asking him about himself; he seems so private.

"Of course."

"I looked you up on LinkedIn. Um, your picture ..."

The corners of his mouth start to twitch in the way she has learned they do when he's relaxed, but trying to suppress a smile. She feels silly.

"... and the ones for your contacts ..." She recalls the dark-suited figures that looked like something from a stylish Hollywood take on the US Secret Service.

He laughs, sets the vibe on a low hum and leans forward. His voice drops even deeper, as it always does when he speaks quietly. "Customers pay for the smoke and mirrors. Often when they hire us, they know deep down what's wrong and how to fix it. But they're too frightened of change. Being told what's good for them by scary men in charcoal suits seems to help them over their fear."

Fuck, she thinks. The vibrations combine with those words in that voice, and his eyes looking straight into her ...

"The image is intimidating at the same time that it projects trustworthiness and dependability. It's beloved of consultants and bodyguards the world around." He grins a grin that could intimidate a crocodile. "And is generally envied by the clients of both."

She realises she's chewing on her lip and clenching her pelvic muscles against the deliciously humming intruder. So close!

She grips his hand and allows herself to be drawn towards him. Their kiss is as sharply electrical as it is tender.

"Our clients have concerns, or their stakeholders do, so they call us in." William's devilish side is enjoying itself tremendously. He increases the intensity of the vibrations, knowing that with Meredith forward on her chair like that the little toy will be hard against her. He leans further and whispers in her ear, "And we ride in and play the dark knight, the white knight, or the stern protector."

She laces her fingers with his. Suddenly it's very close to being too much. She catches her breath at the sound, the vibration and the intimacy and, lowering her eyes, murmurs, "Please, no ..."

He relents. This is too public and she is too shy. He stills the device, smiling kindly into her eyes.

Meredith squeezes his hand in gratitude and slowly regains her composure. "Thank you," she breathes.

She goes outside for two cigarettes during the course of the evening. Each time he teases her just a little with the tormenting thing, but each time he also gives her time to clear her head and enjoy her cigarette. By the time he has flirted and teased their way through dessert, she's more interested in home than she is in tiramisu. They get the bill and head for the car park.

In the car, she makes a decision. They're on a country road and there's no one around. As they sit at the give way of a T-junction, she bites her lip. In a whisper thick with need, she says, "You can."

He glances across to her. "Are you sure?"

"Yes...please..." She stops, closes her eyes, and smiles to herself as much as to him. She imagines it happening and feels the weight of convention and expectation lift. "Do it if you want to. No one can hear."

He leans across and allows his lips to brush hers. The buzzing starts again, and so does the big Jaguar.

She's already close. It isn't long before she's clinging to the seat belt with both hands. He pulls up in a lay-by. As the car comes to a halt, she reaches out one hand to him and squeezes his. He puts the car into neutral. They kiss fiercely and he holds her—powerfully at first, then just close.

As her breathing recovers, he says, "Are you ready for me to get you home?"

"Yes," she says. "Please, I can't wait." Her liquid eyes make her words a promise.

Not long after they turn onto her road. "So was that more fun than smoking?" he enquires.

She's annoyed at his flippancy, but amused too. Laughter wins, releasing the last of the tension that has built up with their taboo-breaking adventure. "Arse," she says, and he can't help but agree.

That night when they get to bed, Meredith is more in the mood to be held than held down. She's happy that William reads this and takes account of it in their lovemaking.

14

Jess Interrogates

Thursday is also busy. Meredith and Emily try to get their assistant Sophie to help them prepare by asking sample questions after lunch, but the poor girl's stumbling and Emily's attacks of giggles mean the exercise is of dubious value. However, by the time Meredith finishes, she is not only feeling quite good about Friday's presentation, she's even developed a suspicion that she and Emily may be becoming fond of one another. She heads to the station to catch the train up to London and see Jess.

Meredith has never liked the commute to London. At least her journey is against the rush, which is good while on the trains, but means walking against the flow of pedestrians at the terminus. The streets are even more crowded when she gets out. Crowds are worse for those who aren't tall and, though not short for a woman, Meredith feels claustrophobic in the crowd.

As a result, she's feeling flustered by the time she gets to the wine bar. She is relieved to find that Jess has booked a table in a quiet niche. Jess herself has not yet arrived.

Meredith dumps her bag, sits down, and opens the wine menu. After a few minutes, she selects a Beaujolais Villages as something light enough for Jess to really enjoy without a heavy meal. She also picks a sparkling water so she can pace her drinking. It takes her a while to attract a waitress's attention; she wishes she had Jess's knack of getting servers to arrive on cue.

Much to her relief, the wine arrives quite quickly. Glad of this oasis away from the bustling streets she pours herself a small glass she happily recalls her decision to take a local job. Lack of familiarity has made her less, not more, fond of the city's constant jostling. She catches up on social media as she waits.

Jess arrives, not too much later than when she was due, and tells Meredith all about her day. She has a knack of making her life sound entertaining, but then she has a knack of entertaining Meredith no matter what.

Eventually, though, she gets down to the serious business of satisfying her curiosity. "So, Merry, what did you two get up to at the weekend?"

With previous relationships, Meredith has always found this conversation easy. But previously, things have gone slower. She's not had anything as intimate what she does with William to tell—or not tell—Jess about. She wants Jess and William to get on. Yet even his present of the vibrating knickers is something far beyond what Meredith is happy to share. It's beyond anything Jess, always the more adventurous of the two, has shared with her.

She finds that, although she filters the details of what and how, her far more worldly friend seems impressed. Meredith ventures to ask if this is what she'd been missing out all these years. Questions of whether Jess's lovers ever did such-and-such seem to make Jess a little jealous.

They chat and time passes. An imperceptible raising of Jess's eyebrow summons the waitress back, and nibbles are ordered. They're consumed with laughter and the rest of the wine.

Meredith is reluctant to bring the evening to an end. But her desire to be fresh for her big day at work—and her determination not to give up on her diet—help her escape the suggestion of a second bottle.

Jess bites down on an instinctive desire to wheedle in favour of being supportive as soon as Meredith mentions the diet. Jess kisses Meredith goodbye and, with assurances that she's looking forward to Saturday, waves Meredith off to the station and her train.

At home, Meredith has second thoughts about the trial run of the presentation. She messages William for advice.

He calls instead of messaging back. "If you're brave enough to walk into a restaurant wearing a remote-controlled vibrator and risk everyone hearing you cum, you can face a few colleagues. You've already seen them make fools of themselves at the Christmas party." William is ever practical, ever sardonic. "You're a lot braver than you realise."

"I still can't believe you made me do that!"

"Did you enjoy it?"

Damn him, he knows I did! "Yes, and you know it." The memory has her cheeks flaming.

"And could you have said *pineapple* any time you wanted."

It's true. She knows it. Looking back, she's surprised. Somehow, she hadn't said the magic word. She'd gone in with half of her mind quaking and the other half trusting him. She had almost dared him to make her cum. She'd even had been a rebellious thought to dare the people around her to say anything. Afterwards, in his car, her body had rewarded her. "I'm braver when I'm with you," she says plaintively.

"No, you're just learning how brave you are. All I'm doing is helping."

Meredith isn't sure whether she believes him, but she finds his confidence reassuring. She can't help laughing when he gets her to tell him some foolish anecdotes about the people who will be there.

Perhaps it's the wine and laughter with Jess. Perhaps it's guiltily tiring herself even further by doing exercises before bed, having forgotten too often lately. Perhaps it's William's reassurances. Whatever the cause, she sleeps better than she expects.

15

Showtime

rriving at work on Friday, Meredith is amazed to find Emily
already there and bouncing with excitement. "We're so going
to rock this—it's going to be amazing!" her colleague effuses.
It's a side of Emily Meredith has never seen before, at least not so clearly.
Is this what men see in her? she wonders.

Meredith is initially irritated that the presentation is scheduled for
the morning, but quickly comes to realise her manager's wisdom. She
and Emily are too distracted by the prospect of it to do anything else
constructive beforehand.

William sends a message wishing her well and telling her she will
excel. He advises her to put the presentation onto both their laptops—and
on a memory stick too, just in case—then follows it with:

> *Yes, my laptop's battery died while I was doing a presentation
> at university, seriously embarrassing:-) Oh, and when it's for
> real, make sure you know what their facilities are like. Done
> that one too :-(*

She shows Emily, who laughs and resolves to find out more about the
new boyfriend later. "He said that before we start, we should remember
daft stuff the boys have done too," Meredith adds. They are to present
to John, Adrian, and Nigel—the boys' team, as Meredith thinks of them.
Emily, being the more outgoing of the pair, has more stories, and the

two are laughing like old friends by the time they're ready to get down to business.

When they go into the meeting-room, Meredith makes a point of choosing the chair furthest from the camera.

It takes them a while to get going. The boys don't know the client's business as well as the client would, or as well as Meredith and Emily do, which affects the flow. Adrian doesn't help by making a series of flippant comments. He stops after a sharp response from Emily. Then they get into the swing of things, and by the time they finish, both women are happy with their efforts, though Meredith is nervous about how she has come over to the boys as well as on video.

Mr Rossi suggests each team watch the recording separately, then head off to the pub for a quick drink before meeting again to review the experience. Meredith presumes he can't be too unhappy, since he offers to buy them a drink.

Watching with Emily is a salutary experience for Meredith. Her colleague sees far more positive in Meredith's performance than she does. Meredith admits that Emily comes over as very confident. Her own knowledge and ability to manage questioning is also better than she'd imagined. It is one thing to talk to her boyfriend and hear his compliments, but quite another to face people with detailed knowledge, and to receive praise from an unexpected source. All in all, she feels quite good about the whole thing.

Emily drags her into the boss's office on the way out. "So pleased you let us try this, Marco," Emily enthuses. "Meredith can't pretend she's rubbish at presentations now we have the evidence."

Meredith, who usually has to remind herself not to call him Mr Rossi, can barely believe Emily's comment or how her boss responds. "The two of you make an even better team than I hoped when I put you together." His pleasure is clear in his voice and on his face. He puts his jacket on to accompany them to the pub.

The other team arrive shortly after. John and Nigel join them while Adrian goes to the bar. Marco begins, "I put my card—"

John cuts him off. "It's okay. Adrian has these."

The two older colleagues share a look. With a half nod and a smile, they change the subject before Adrian arrives with everyone's usual drinks and an apology.

Meredith is grateful, though Emily accepts her drink without smiling. John makes light of the matter, saying that it worked out well, and the ladies managed the situation admirably. Emily doesn't brighten up until Marco points out that the next time around, the girls can have fun asking awkward questions.

16

William and Jess

J ess arrives early. Her timekeeping is dictated more by her own level of interest than by any host's invitation. Meredith is usually of the view that her dearest friend would be perfect if it weren't for her customary lateness, but today Jess is in time to be a critical audience to Meredith's efforts to select her clothes for the evening. Meredith decides, as she is made to change for the third time, that lateness has it's good side.

"I get dressed perfectly well when you aren't here, you know, and he has seen me before!" she complains, to no avail as Jess sits, wine glass in hand, and passes comment. *At least it's too late to get dragged to the shops,* Meredith thinks, remembering being managed through preparation for other dates.

"I'm here, Merry, so you should take advantage!" Jess's confidence, like her enthusiasm and her fondness for wine, is hard to stand in the way of. Meredith surrenders and changes again.

The fourth outfit is a black wrap-around skirt with a matching top that has see-through material at the shoulder. "Perfect!" Jess exclaims. "Just slutty enough that he'll want to fuck you, but not slutty enough that he'll realise that's why you chose it."

"Behave, okay?" Meredith pleads. "I really like him."

"So I can't say things like, 'You'll know she's really into you if she goes bald from the waist down'?"

"No, you cannot!" Meredith flushes. "Anyway, I already have—as you well know! So you certainly can't. He'll think I'm weird."

134

"Please tell me you've started waxing!" Jess has long since dispensed with what she considers the untidiness and inconvenience and, as is her habit, delegates that task to a paid professional.

"No, I have not. I don't understand how you can lie chatting to someone while she rips all your pubes out! I used a cream."

Jess thinks she might have gone a bit far, judging from Meredith's tone. "Hey, listen." She stands and hugs Meredith. "I really like you in this, and I won't embarrass you in front of your new boyfriend."

After an hour as Jess's mannequin, Meredith has to admit that the results are impressive. She even suspects that she may have lost a couple of pounds. She hasn't been able to wear this outfit for at least a year. But she also thinks of how they've used up the time she was supposed to spend preparing dinner, and have started drinking the wine that was supposed to accompany it.

William gets there just after she manages to persuade Jess into the kitchen. He duly admires Meredith and greets Jess warmly. The old flicker of jealousy ignites in Meredith at the way everyone, especially men, falls under Jess's spell.

William though turns his attention back to his girlfriend, proffering goodies. "Wine and sorbet for dessert," he says and grins. "And stuff for breakfast."

Jess's face betrays what she thinks about the idea of sorbet for dessert, but the Sauternes is a different matter.

Meredith would complain about the breakfast items, but she has again forgotten to get any herself again. "William," she jokes, "follows a religion of which the most important observance is breakfast." Jess, for whom breakfast is a foreign country, laughs.

William takes the joke in good part and isn't visibly annoyed when Meredith admits that dinner is running late. Instead, he gets her to do a twirl, glows with pride when she says she couldn't wear this outfit a short while ago, and praises Jess for her advice. All of which is much to Jess's approval.

Jess preens, as she always does when complimented. He's certainly handsome and charming. She offers him her hand, which he takes in an old-fashioned way, as if holding it to kiss, though he just nods and smiles.

His next actions cause Meredith to look sideways at her best friend.

He sets about "organising" Jess to lay the table. Long years of experience have taught Meredith that it is hard to get Jess to do anything that isn't her own idea, or at least something she enjoys. She will happily chat while Meredith prepares food, or artistically fold a couple of napkins while Meredith lays the table, but …

William is a man with patience and a capacity for wordlessly but sternly expressing a sense of expectation. Meredith knows how meltingly well this works on her, but doesn't have high hopes of it having any effect on her friend.

He doesn't shout or bully, as she half expects he might. She knows that would be a huge mistake and might stop them getting on. His technique is simple and effective, and his cheerfulness and capacity for flattery and "shooing along" are apparently boundless.

As Jess leaves the kitchen, laden with placemats and cutlery, Meredith stares at him open-mouthed. "What's up?" he asks.

"I don't think I've ever seen Jess allow herself to be ordered around before."

He chuckles. "I don't think I'd want to try to get her to do anything she didn't want to. But I'm fairly certain she'd rather make the table pretty than have anything to do with chopping food or stirring over a hot stove."

"Seriously, that was incredible."

William hands her the vegetable knife. "Anyone who can build bridges in a country where not everyone wants them built should be able to get a table laid."

"Is that what you do now?"

"That was in the army." She thinks he looks wistful. "But the same rules apply to what I do now."

"Do you miss it?"

"Yes and no. It came time to change, and this is the road I took. I'm happy right now." He pecks her cheek.

"Merry says you're a good cook," says Jess, returning.

"He is," Meredith assures her.

William looks sheepish. "I try." He directs his boyish grin at Jess. "You can decide if Meredith's just being polite."

Jess sits and observes the two together. She's pleased that Meredith is so comfortable with him, impressed that Meredith lets him have full rein in her kitchen, and impressed by the easy confidence with which he cooks, serves, and bustles them to the table.

"So, does everyone except me call you Merry?" he asks over dinner. It's the first time he's heard her nickname, and it certainly suits the way she acts around Jess.

"Not everyone, no." She tries not to remember what people called her at school.

"Is there anything else people know you as?" For once he doesn't pick up on her body language.

Jess's face tenses. Meredith answers, "My dad used to call me Ditzy when I was little. My uncle Derek still does, but I hate it now." She'd liked the name when she was at primary school, but when it carried on into her teens and became a matter of teasing, it bothered her.

"I should think so." He squeezes her hand in sympathy. "For me it was Billie." He grimaces. "I'm not even sure why I didn't like it, but in the end I just stopped responding when anyone mentioned it."

"That's very mature. How old were you?" Jess asks.

"Fourteen." He smiles. "And it was more trial and error." Another grimace. "First I tried making up versions of other peoples' names, but one of them complained that my version was racist. I didn't mean it that way, but I got into trouble anyway. Then I opted for physical violence. That worked on the rugby pitch, but I got detention elsewhere." His more familiar warm demeanour returns. "I got lucky. I was the only one there, and the teacher supervising was a guy I got on with. He asked me why I started the fight, and I told him."

He takes a sip of wine and puts on a chagrined expression. His accent changes to a lilting highland brogue as he plays out the conversation. "Is Billie your name?"

"No, sir."

"Do ya want it to be?"

"No, sir."

"Then why d'ya answer to it?"

Back in his own voice he says, "Then he shook his head sadly." Before finishing, "It's not as if the cat gets angry when his fool owner talks to the dog, is it?" in the accent. He grins fondly and returns to his usual tone. "It's a lesson I've not forgotten."

"That's sweet," Meredith says, smiling at him. He rarely reveals anything about his past. "Who was the teacher?"

"Mr McDonald. He taught geography." He raises his glass. "Now, shall I fetch the sorbet and let you two talk about me?"

Jess waits for him to leave the room, then beams at Meredith. "He's lovely!"

"He is, isn't he?"

"Bossy, but lovely."

They chat. Meredith enjoys her relief that the two are getting along. She doesn't think William will ever stop being bossy, but she also thinks Jess is a fine one to complain about that particular personal quality.

William returns with Meredith's rarely used large tray. It's laden with three dessert bowls, the tub of brightly coloured sorbet, and a steaming jug, as well as the bottle of amber-coloured Sauternes and three of Meredith's best glasses. She doesn't normally get them out, but William wasn't to know that.

He lays the tray down, revealing that the dessert bowls contain small chocolate puddings. "Confession time: the puddings are bought but the sauce and the raspberry sorbet are mine."

The little puddings are liquid-centred and very rich. Without the sharpness of the sorbet, they and his chocolate and caramel sauce might be a be sickly pairing, but Meredith thinks the combination is just perfect. She happily devours hers while Jess talks.

"So this is your idea of 'just some sorbet for dessert'?" Jess asks. William smiles and regales them with stories of restaurant meals, successful and otherwise.

Jess watches Meredith interact with William, looking for telltale signs. Meredith's ex was such a dick, constantly undermining her. And he'd paid Jess more attention than she felt was appropriate. But William seems different. He's attentive Jess, but he reserves his lingering looks and touches for Meredith.

He's also scored more brownie points with the dessert.

Then there's the Sauternes. Jess savours a sip. "I think you're very good for Meredith, and I approve." She twinkles. "Of course, if that brogue were your real accent, I'd have to steal you for myself."

Meredith looks complainingly at Jess. Her friend shrugs and William laughs.

Meredith suggests they move over to the sofa. Jess makes herself at home on the short arm of the *L* while Meredith and William occupy the long one. They talk and sip well into the evening. Jess and William take turns telling stories until, tired and a bit tipsy after her long week, Meredith dozes off on William's shoulder.

★★★

Meredith wakes as William is leaving the bedroom. He's wearing a robe she doesn't recognise; he doesn't usually bother with clothing first thing in the morning. "New dressing gown?"

"Yes. I thought I'd better bring one and wear it." He grins. "Didn't think your friend would approve if she came out of her room and found me naked, and I didn't think one of yours would fit me!"

That's right, Jess is in the spare room. And no, she wouldn't approve. Even so, Meredith is sure Jess would like the view. But Meredith doesn't want to share that view with anyone, even her best friend. Especially her *beautiful* best friend.

William brings up a tray with four mugs, one of them steaming (doubtless that's his tea), and a cafetière. There's also milk and sugar. "I don't know how Jess takes hers, so I brought all the necessary. You can take it in to her."

Aggy has found her way into the bedroom and Meredith is stroking her, she gives him an amused look, and then laughs aloud as she checks the time. "You don't know Jess!" As far as she is aware, her friend hasn't seen this hour on a Sunday morning since they were children—if one discounts staying up all night.

"Does that mean I get a lie-in with you?" he enquires, leaning forward and holding a mug out.

Worried that she has morning breath, she sips the piping hot coffee—then wishes she hadn't, because it's still a bit too hot. She allows him to kiss her. "Mmm, you taste gingery." The taste on her lips stirs a thought.

He brought a packet of ginger nuts over, and must have had one while he was making the coffee. "Did you bring any up?"

"I thought dunking biscuits in the morning was a kid's thing?" She'd teased him for his habit, and now it was time to extract payback.

"I didn't say I wanted to dunk." She knows she's busted. No, she hasn't done it since before university, but she remembers how indulgent it felt.

"Would you like me to get some?"

She assents. When she gives in to the temptation and dunks, he winks at her and she pokes her tongue out at him.

Meredith is as vocal in her enjoyment of their "lie-in" as ever, much to William's amusement. Afterwards he jokes that a stone-deaf neighbour and a narcoleptic best friend might not be a bad combination. She's still chuckling about it when he gets back from his shower and announces that he's going to start breakfast while she takes her turn.

Emerging from her shower, Meredith finds that Aggy has deserted her, and after a few moments her nose tells her why; the unmistakable aroma of bacon is drifting up the stairs. As a mortal human, she's unable to resist its call either so, wrapping her dressing gown around herself, she follows her nose down to the kitchen.

The sight that greets her makes her burst into laughter. Aggy and Pog are perched like a pair of sphinxes on her kitchen table, staring fixedly at William, who is slicing something that looks disgusting. Both cats' tails are twitching. "I wasn't sure if you and Jess like liver, so ..."

Liver! The word cuts through her humour and takes her back to memories of dry, metallic-tasting strips of stringy leather served in lumpy gravy on powdery mash. "No, thank you!" She shivers. "And I'm sure Jess doesn't either!"

"Oh well, I'm sure I can find some willing takers." He nods at the unblinking felines. "Just eggs for you two then?"

"I'm not sure they'll like it either." Meredith knows her pets are fussy.

"I don't suppose you'd care for a small wager?"

"No. No, thank you."

"Wise plan." He takes a portion in each hand and places them on the table. Two tiny pairs of jaws make quick work of their morsels. Then the cats' eyes return to the chopping board.

"Do you know they aren't allowed on the table?" Meredith asks, though she's quite well aware that she lets them trample this particular rule whenever it suits her.

"I don't live here, so until you tell me I can boss your cats around, I'm going to stay out of that one." *It's the safe bet*, he thinks. *"Never get on the wrong side of your girlfriend's cat" is probably a rule written down in a book no woman ever lets a man read.* He finishes slicing liver and washes his hands, then adds hot water to the cafetière.

Meredith humphs. She's reluctant to admit that he was right about her little carnivores.

"Toast or bread?" he asks. "The bread's white and fresh."

Deciding that her disapproval is getting her nowhere, Meredith hugs him and gives him a peck on the cheek. She finds it hard to fake anger with a man who makes her coffee and breakfast.

The addition of toasting bread to the aromatic melange draws a sleepy, shuffling Jess into the room. Her "Mmm" at the smells in the kitchen is swiftly followed by "Ugh, liver."

The sound draws a hiss from the surprised Poggle. Meredith announces victory by two votes to one.

William is entirely unconcerned. He neatly lays two fried eggs next to toast and bacon on a plate. He then sets about removing the cats from the table by the simple expedient of more liver into their bowls. The little monsters' claws skitter in their rush to eat. "Three-two," he says quietly and presses the coffee.

Meredith would have carried on the argument if it weren't for the arrival of her food. William turns his attention to Jess. "Toast or bread, and how many eggs?"

Normally the idea of breakfast would have sent Jess scurrying, but Meredith's smells delicious. "Bread and butter and one, please."

"Mushrooms?"

"There are mushrooms in Merry's house?"

Meredith looks embarrassed but decides she'd better say something herself. "We have a deal. He doesn't try to feed me mushrooms so long as I don't try to feed him tofu." She looks at the fondly smiling William. "Even if he would like it."

"Then yes, please."

Meredith mouths *traitor* to her friend behind William's back. He sautés his liver and fries Jess's egg, then serves them both.

"How did you know my cats would like liver?" Meredith asks him watching them lick their bowls clean.

"I didn't *know*, but I was pretty sure. My grandmother's did." The explanation seems the most palatable of the ones that spring to his mind.

Jess is trapped into helping to wash up by William's casual yet confident offer of a towel for drying. Jess points out that the dishwasher has been around for a number of years, but takes the towel. Meredith grins.

The three lounge around with mugs of coffee until Jess announces that she's "going to leave the love-birds to it", to Meredith's chagrin and William's amusement.

When she picks up her phone to call a taxi, William offers to drive her to the station. "Are you coming too, Merry?" Jess asks. They head off together. Jumping out at the station, Jess thanks them, kisses Meredith goodbye, and orders William to look after her best friend.

Meredith and William detour on the way home to take a country walk. It's only a short one because the paths are slippery from spring rain, but it's something. The daffodils and snowdrops are out.

17

What? You Didn't Bring Any Toys?

M eredith misses Jess's cheery presence, but her body doesn't miss having a gooseberry in the house. She launches herself at William. Much hilarity and some lovemaking later, she asks, "So, do you like her?"

"Yes, she's nice. Different to you," he kisses her, "but nice." He winks. "Now, are you going to show me the evidence?"

"What evidence?"

"The video of your presentation!"

"How do you know I have one?" Her tone is guarded. He just grins a knowing grin. "You're such a smartarse."

Meredith doesn't really want to, but it was his idea, and she's had a lot of positive comments about it, so she lets him persuade her. She watches with trepidation, but William seems both interested and impressed. He asks about each of her colleagues and pauses the video to get her to expand on some points.

Afterwards he asks, "Have you ever seen one of those programs about meerkats or mongeese?"

"No."

He grabs his laptop and fires it up. "Should have a shortcut here somewhere."

She's happy to change over to watching some of her favourite animals rather than herself, especially when William works out how to feed the stream to her television. Several times he pauses and replays scenes in which the meerkats are hunting dangerous prey or trying to drive off a poisonous snake. "See how, when one is unsure, another steps forward?" he asks.

"Yes. They're cute."

"Well, that's how you and Emily should learn to work in a presentation." His enthusiasm is brimming. "One takes the attention while the other gathers her thoughts."

"So you think we're meerkats." Meredith asks impishly.

He grins wolfishly in response. "It's politer than calling you chimps – they all do the same thing." He doesn't complain in the slightest when she bashes his shoulder with her fist.

"You are such a monkey," she tells him.

"Ape, I'm an ape. 'Ook-ay'."

"So you wouldn't be interested in getting up to any more monkey business, then?" she asks coyly.

His face lets her know that he would.

"And did your apeship bring any more exciting things to teach me with?"

"I'm afraid not, I thought as Jess was over, sorry," he hadn't been sure how she'd feel about that sort of thing with Jess staying, "Next time."

Meredith is disappointed. The adventures of recent days have been eye-openers, and she definitely wishes to continue.

"Hmm." He nuzzles up to her. "I'm sure we can find some way of amusing you anyway." He kisses her cheek. "Even if we have to make do with the bare necessities." He sings the last two words and tickles her neck with his stubble.

After dinner, they watch the 4K copy of *Guardians of the Galaxy* that William has brought. Meredith agrees to watch the sequel because she loves the soundtrack and she loves baby Groot. William jokingly threatens to steal her television, then settles for swearing to make an upgrade at home.

18

Cats Get Treats Too

On Tuesday the kitchen is already smelling of distinctly dinnery smells as Meredith drinks her morning coffee. That aroma from her slow cooker and the grey weather outside tempt her with the sickie she sometimes promises herself but never takes.

Reluctantly she says goodbye to her cats and locks the house. Grey turns to drizzle as she pulls out into the road. Driving to work is never fun in the rain, and this morning is no exception. People seem to either dawdle or rush. A speed camera pointing at the other carriageway almost blinds her by going off just as she passes. She slows while her eyes recover and is glad she did, because there is stationary traffic ahead.

When she gets to work, she sits in her car for a moment to catch her breath and offer a silent prayer of thanks for her safe arrival. It's still raining. Checking her bag, she finds that she's forgotten to bring an umbrella. She curses then remembers her car being "Williamed", he got her to put an old spare in the footwell of the front passenger seat. It's got one wonky spar, but it's more than adequate to see her across the car park and through a quickly smoked cigarette.

The busy day provides a welcome distraction from the near miss on the way in. Meredith hasn't been aware how much extra work she would be taking on with the new approach to presentations—nor how interesting it would be.

She and Emily spend a lot of the day together, going through notes and swapping ideas from their previous pitches. They start by treating it as a bit of fun, then it turns into a salutary lesson as they work through mistakes. They compile a list of questions, argue surprisingly good-naturedly, and move forward. It's the first time Meredith has truly enjoyed working with Emily. She has to admit her bosses wisdom in teaming them to work together.

Their collaboration is so engrossing that it's only when Emily points out the office is getting quiet that Meredith realises she's running late herself and will have to hurry to be home before William arrives.

Her slow cooker is putting the finishing touches on the beef dish from his sampler of easy meals that she'd set cooking last night. It had indeed been as simple as anything. There isn't much to do when she gets home from work. She sets new potatoes simmering on the stove leaving the veg for them to prep together and quickly spruces the house.

His Jaguar pulls up half an hour or so after she arrives home. She hears the rumble of the V-8 still. This absence of sound is followed by the slam of a heavy car door. Then the sound of its boot shutting with a low thud. She makes her way downstairs, arriving in her hall as the doorbell rings.

Meredith swings the door open and finds his arm still stretched towards the bell. "Anxious to greet me?" He smiles. "I hope you haven't been waiting there long!"

She's embarrassed and feels her face show it. She wonders at how is she always so easily inflamed in his presence. Then she rallies—what is it she learned from his silly seminar? Don't react. Observe, think, and then respond. She does just that.

He has two bags, and he's here early, she observes. He must have been keen to arrive. She replies, "Not long, but then as you're moving in today ..."

Teasing him like this is new. She's nervous, but after all, he set her on this path. He can hardly blame her for trying—at least she hopes he can't. Possibly too late, she wonders if her face has betrayed her nervousness about her feisty response.

William's smile broadens. Everything is okay! "Touché!" He waves the overnight bag and holdall with easy control as he steps in, "Overnight bag," then he lowers his voice, ""And I've brought the promised delivery from the toy department."

She steps aside to allow him in, and turns so that he can embrace her. "Mmm, this is nice!" Their conversation from the weekend before comes back to her. Her mind follows that train of thought and her mouth takes up the story. "You've had that in your car while you've been at work all day?"

"It's okay; I didn't lock anyone else inside my boot with it." He sets the bags down. The sound makes it clear that the holdall is far heavier than she expected.

"What on earth have you brought?" she asks, more than curious but also a little worried. Meredith is certain that rushing to open the zip and investigate would be bad form.

"I must confess, the contents aren't just for you." He tries to look mysterious, but she's up to the challenge today.

"Who else have you invited?" Her voice rises by several notes. She likes adventure, but is quite certain that she wants to keep it between the two of them.

"Ah, wait and see!" He's twinkling. There's something about his face that puts her in mind of her brother when he was a child and the two of them about to help hand out the Christmas presents, there's no guile there for a change, just boyish enthusiasm.

"Would you like something to drink?" she asks, meaning, *What's in the bag?*

"A mint tea would be nice. I've had a long day talking to clients who weren't listening, followed by a row with the sales people about how much we're going to surcharge the clients for not listening."

"Of course, you're never wrong?" she teases as they move to the kitchen.

"Ha. Frequently. But if I don't know I'm right, I'm less pushy. Sales always want to be the client's friend even if it means we lose money."

The kettle boils and she pours him a mug. The mint smells nice, but she doesn't much like the way it smells more strongly than it taste so she has sparkling water for herself. He has an odd habit of not taking the bag out of his herbal tea before drinking it. He picks up the steaming mug and heads to the living room, pointedly not stopping to pick up the holdall.

By now, Meredith is about ready to explode with curiosity, but she continues to wait.

They kiss. He puts his drink down on a coaster on the coffee table.

She stares at the doorway to the hall. Finally, he deigns to notice that her attention is not exclusively on him. "If I fetch the toys, will you look at me instead of the doorway?"

William is pleased that she has the good grace to blush. "I might."

It's enough; he turns to go fetch them.

Aggy has already discovered the new items in the hall and is sniffing at them. He collects the holdall. She follows it and him back to the sofa. He sets it on his lap as he sits. "Do you want to do the honours, or shall I?"

Meredith doesn't wait to be asked a second time and reaches around the curious cat's head for the brass zip. At the top are two large, gift-wrapped parcels: one blue with mice on the paper, the other pink with rabbits. "What on earth are these?"

"Well, the pink one is for Agatha, so why not help her open it?"

Meredith is a bit disappointed that this isn't for her, but picks up the parcel. It weighs several kilos, much heavier than she expected it to be, the easy way William had swung the bag had deceived her. It's definitely for Aggy it's even got a gift tag written out to her! Tearing the paper, she finds a box showing a cat scratching post. "It's got a little fluffy ball too," he explains. "Only you said they scratch things, so I thought you could put these by things they scratch and encourage them to attack these instead."

He looks so hopeful. "That's such a sweet thing to do."

Meredith doesn't unwrap the second present, which is labelled "To Poggle"."Is it okay if I save the other one for when he's here?" Saying it aloud sounds it even sillier than she had feared.

She worries William's response will be mocking. After all, he doesn't have any pets. But he responds, "Of course, more than OK." His smile is warm, and his kiss is a gentle "I think you have done a good thing" kiss. Funny that he can say so much in such little ways—and that she can hear it when she's only known him a short time.

Setting the blue-wrapped parcel aside, she resists the temptation to delve further into the bag. The crafty William has put a cloth between the toys for the cats and the ones for her. It's not easy waiting to find out what adventure he has planned, but the growing anticipation makes it worth it.

William has idly balled the pink wrapping paper and thrown it for Aggy. The little molly is happily batting it. Meredith peels the cellophane from the box. Funny how opening presents for her cats makes her feel a childlike thrill. The scratching post has a heavy, wide base. A cylinder wrapped tightly with rope screws into it.

"I read that you should put them next to the places they scratch. Not sure if it works, but it's worth a try. If they don't get the hint you can put catnip or cat mint in the little ball that goes on top." He grins. "Even if it doesn't work, the look on your face was worth it. And Aggy likes her paper ball."

Meredith hardly knows what to say. "It's kind. Thank you." She kisses him and lingers against him. Becoming aware once more of, the half-explored holdall against her she sits up, looks at him, and glances down, smiling a shyly curious smile of her own.

"Here, it's lighter now." He lifts the bag onto her lap. "Enjoy!"

Curiosity finally gets the better of her. Her eager fingers pull back the cloth. She pauses to investigate it. The material is so soft! It's a light woollen blanket that he has neatly folded to fit while hiding the items below it.

Underneath, she finds a strange mixture of things. The soft suede flogger she remembers with a rush of pleasure. The cuffs are simple enough, as—once she touches it—is the vibrator. But the purpose of the leather straps with steel eye rings set in their ends escapes her, as does that of the thing that resembles a typist's wrist rest."May I ask what all this is for?"

"You may." He purses his lips. "But if you do"—his expression changes to one of decision—"I'll tell you, and that might spoil the surprise."

Meredith likes his playful mood. "If I ask you to show me instead?"

Oh, she loves the way his face lights up. "Then I'll demonstrate." The little-boy smile becomes the even sexier demonic one. "Before or after your exercises and dinner?"

"How about instead of my exercises?" Her pout is fake, but some of the sentiment behind it is real. She cannot bring herself to like this part of her new daily routine, though the food is unexpectedly enjoyable. She realises she's getting nowhere and stops pouting. It's that look on his face.

"Do you want to stop?" He knows she doesn't. Already this week, she's texted him, *Lost 3lbs!* The inclusion of a happy emoji said it all. He wouldn't let her quit till she wanted to quit. "And do you want to miss out on the reward part?"

She doesn't—of course she doesn't, who would? And not just

because she is still wondering what the straps and pad are for. "I should, shouldn't I?"

"Do you want to have to tell Jess you gave up after a week?" He looks at her sincerely. "If you do, just say the word and I won't mention it again."

Of course her friend would laugh, and then be sympathetic. But Meredith wants Jess to be impressed, not sympathetic. "What kind of reward?"

He eyes her over the top of his mug. "What kind would you like?"

"Someone to clean the house, perhaps?"

"You seriously want me to hire you a cleaner?" He brandishes the flogger in a gesture that might have been menacing if it weren't for the mirth obvious in his tone and expression.

"Maybe I'd better let you decide then."

"Wise of you." He kisses her. "A reward I think you'll like." He's trying not to give anything away, but there's a twinkle in his eyes. He clearly wants to show her soon.

They exercise, and once again she is able to do a little more. They shower separately. She is barely able to control her excitement while he finishes. When he emerges from the bathroom, she is waiting. "Are you ready?" he asks, and her response is closer to a squeak than the firm yes she intends.

Back downstairs, he has her remove her robe and sit on the sofa while he carefully attaches the cuffs to her wrists and ankles. *It's so weird*, she thinks. *They're so attractively made, far prettier than some fashion cuffs, yet they're for tying women up*. It's even weirder that she's so eager for them that she's almost bouncing up and down.

Once he's satisfied that the cuffs are neither so tight as to restrict the blood flow nor so loose as to offer any hope of escape, he stands and genteelly offers her his hand. She rises. Again the contrast in his actions strikes her as peculiar—and incredibly hot.

He takes her over to the table and has her stand. He lays out the pad and puts the vibrator about a quarter of the way along. Folding the pad over so that the vibe is in the middle, he places the bundle in the middle of one side of the table. He looks at her with a close, caring expression on his face. "Are you ready?"

She nods.

"And are you sure?"

"Very!" She leans forward and he kisses her, his strong fingers stroking down her arm. He briefly squeezes her hand. "Remember, *pineapple*." And he kisses her again.

Then he's businesslike. "Face the table, please." She nervously obeys. He loops a leather strap around each leg of the table on this side, and has her stretch her own legs wide so that he can clip her cuffed ankles to the straps.

"Now bend over, please." She stretches onto her tiptoes, wide open, and presses her breasts to the table. Her mons is over the pad, with vibrator pressed against her clitoris. She gasps and blushes, recalling what the small black wand has done to her before even when she has not been so stretched out and vulnerable.

He steps around the table and takes hold of each wrist in turn, binding them to the far legs of the table. He stretches her further still, denying her breasts any help in supporting her weight. They start to ache almost immediately. Her nipples harden. She thinks about the stretch. It feels different to when he uses his strength to stretch her—less intimate, but just as exciting.

In this position, she feels far more exposed than she had in the hotel, his playroom, or either of their beds. She has a sense that she is less protected downstairs in her own small semi-detached than she was upstairs in his big house.

His hands caress her bound form. As ever, his touch is sure, confident, and delightful. Her vulnerability, the way she is tied and stretched, unable to move any of her limbs even an inch, heightens the experience.

He sets the vibrator to a low, steady, insistent pattern, and she gasps again. As turned on as she is, the little wand's low hum has her immediately working to control her breathing.

"Are you okay?" he asks.

Meredith pants, "Y-yes."

The flogger's falls trail lightly along her back and over her buttocks. A rebellious part of her mind considers changing her yes to a no and crying *pineapple*, but the rising heat in her body burns the notion to a crisp before it can reach her vocal cords.

As he did at the weekend, he strokes her repeatedly with the soft suede. She revels in their touch. This time, however, after every few languid strokes, he flicks his wrist and sends them slapping against her vulnerable flesh. At first, he concentrates on her bum, drawing gasps of surprise more than of pain. Even though there's almost no pain she wriggles against her bonds each time the falls are lifted away from her skins, and finds that as she does she is pressing against the vibrator.

Meredith feels a change in tactics. William runs the hard, smooth leather of the flogger's handle up the inside of first one thigh, then the other. *Fuck*, she thinks. *That's so sensitive, and I'm so vulnerable.* She doesn't know whether he's psychic or can see her body tense in alarm, but he murmurs words of comfort and goes back to using the falls on her. Light slaps wrap around her thighs. Meredith's ears tell her these slaps are gentler than those that fell on her bum, but her nerves tell her their impact is closer to pain. Her imagination wonders how this would feel if he were to strike harder: How much would it hurt? Would she like it? Could she bear it?

The caresses and slaps combine with the buzz of the vibrator and constraint of her bondage to consume her senses. She jerks against her bonds as the flogger's tips brush her open vulva. After a moment, she realises he has not hurt her, but her breathing doesn't slow. She's never felt so helpless.

The flogger is no longer touching her. He strokes her bum, then between her cheeks. Finding her opening warm and ready, he pushes a fingertip between the vibrator and her clitoris, and, in doing so, doubles the intensity of the contact. His other hand worms its way between her stomach and the tabletop finding the handle of the vibrator and—

"Ohh!" she can't help exclaiming as the intensity of the vibrations surges. In moments she's close to losing control.

The warm touch of the flogger's heavy falls returns, stroking, slapping lightly. Pleasure makes her cry out. With each cry, he swings the flogger harder. It thuds heavily into first one bum cheek, then the other. She begins to lose herself.

As her orgasm builds towards its crescendo, she realises she has never felt so free even though she has never been less so. She is comfortable in her helplessness with William, trusting him completely, as her body has trusted him since that first night.

Meredith doesn't register when it finishes, or when he releases her and carries her upstairs. She comes back to herself on her bed, looking up and welcoming him.

★★★

As they lie together, Meredith comes to a decision. She's worried that she may hate herself for asking, or that he might give a truthful answer she doesn't want to hear, but she asks anyway. Better to be hurt now than later. "The morning in the hotel? What you said?"

"Yes? Which thing I said?"

"About me not being the sort of girl who keeps a change of clothes in her desk."

"Yes?" He tilts his head. Well, you didn't strike me as the sort. You still don't."

"What sort is that?"

"A girl who's prepared like a scout." He clearly regards the topic as frivolous.

"Does that mean you're the kind of boy who does?" She frowns without realising it. "Keep a change of clothes in his desk, I mean."

"Yes—one in the car, one in the office, and one in my gym locker." He clearly hasn't a clue as to what she's asking, nor does he realise he's digging himself a hole. "You never know when you'll get rained on or someone with spill something and the shops will be shut and you're supposed to be somewhere."

"So ... not because you spend every night with a different woman?" She hopes the words don't sound like an accusation.

"No! Certainly not if I'm seeing someone! And right now I'm sort of under the impression that I'm seeing you." He sounds a bit hurt. It's hardly the way he'd planned to raise the "are we going out together now" question.

He'd never asked it. But then, he'd never told her otherwise. She certainly hasn't presumed it would be okay to sleep with someone else. Not that was that there was anyone else for *her*, but he was *him*, with his good looks and confident ways.

Meredith thinks, *I wish we had wine.* But it's too late to start a bottle, and she feels it would hardly fit with the new-her campaign. She also thinks *wow*, and feels guilty over her question. "Sorry, I didn't mean to ..."

She's glad that his arms wrap around her in response."Hey, it's okay. We have moved a little fast in some ways; we just need to take some time catching up in others."

★★★

Aggy has managed to sneak into the bedroom again. She's sprawled on her back on the duvet, purring happily as William tickles her. Meredith wakes.

"Hope you don't mind, I used your capsule machine to make us coffee," William says.

"If it gets me coffee in bed, you can do anything you want."

He responds with his oh-so-suggestive smile.

Despite her feelings on the subject of mornings, Meredith can't help but laugh."You have a dirty mind, Mr Farrow!"

Her attempt at chastisement only serves to encourage both William and his smile. He moves from stroking Aggy to tickling Meredith, and his grin becomes positively filthy. When she yelps in surprise, the little cat yowls in protest. Meredith complains, "Traitor!" at Aggy then, looking up at William, she adds, "If you turn my cat against me, not even coffee in bed will keep you in my good books!"

He desists and sips his coffee. "You're no fun." Despite the obvious theatricality of his put, it still plucks at her heart strings. *What it is about him?* Her face falls.

William is caught off guard. He curses himself for not making allowances for how unconfident she is, and quickly raises his palm in apology. "Okay, no attempts to seduce your fur babies away from you!"

Her face lifts a little, showing at least a measure of forgiveness and he leans his warmth gently against her. "We good?"

She nods and holds him. "But you've got to hurry to beat the traffic, haven't you?"

"I do, sadly."

19

The Trouble when Relationships Meet—Or Don't

Jess is happy for her friend, but not with the way the new relationship affects their ritual monthly girls' night. Since their university years, Meredith and Jess and two other friends, Beverly and Julia, have met up at least once a month. In recent years, the planning effort has mostly fallen on Meredith, as Jess moved up to London and the other two had husbands. Now that William is on the scene, the task of organisation has fallen to Jess, to whom such effort does not come naturally.

Meredith has also become a scheduling problem in her own right and Beverly is in 'new mum' mode again! Jess's first suggested date is none too successful—Meredith is taking her mother to Florence for a short break. The other weekends Jess is free are "William weekends". Her next move is to try to wangle her way around Beverly for the only other possible spot but it's no dice there, her parents are visiting to see their grandchildren.

It looks like a bust until Jess remembers William giving her his number. Jess has only met him once, but she's always been able to twist men around her little finger. She puts herself in her most persuasive frame of mind and dials.

"Hi, you're through to William Farrow's voicemail. At the tone, please leave your name, number, and message, and I'll get back to you."

Bugger, she thinks. She hates voicemail. "Hi, this is Merry's friend Jess.

Nothing serious; I was just hoping to ask you a favour. Could you give me a bell back when it's convenient?"

A couple of rounds of telephone tag later, William leaves her some time windows when he can take a call. When Jess rings again, he answers, "Hi, William Farrow."

Merry's right, she thinks. *He sounds even taller on the phone than he is in real life.* "Hi William, it's Jess."

"Oh, Jess, hi. What can I do for you?"

Jess uses her persuasive voice. "I'm trying to organise our regular girls' night, and I need a favour."

"Okay, what is it?"

"Well, we always do it at the weekend, and the two nights everyone else can do it, Merry says she's with you." She gives him the dates.

"I'm driving, so I can't check my calendar. I'm pretty sure we're just having a cosy one at her place that weekend. I think she'd be happy to have me down on the Saturday instead, if you wanted to plan something for the Friday night."

"Um." She tries to put it as gently as she can. "She wasn't too keen on asking you. Is there any way you could sort of ask her for the Friday off?"

It seems odd to him. "Wouldn't it be easier for you to ring her when we're together, and I can say then?"

"Can't you just ..." She leaves it hanging; guys usually fill in the blanks with whatever they think she wants them to say. "I'd be very grateful."

He doesn't want to let her push him around. However, gym, then a boys' Friday night is appealing, and he doesn't want Meredith to lose touch with her circle of friends. "Okay, but you owe me. And next time the three of us meet up, we're going to talk about this. I'm not a fan of three-corner conversations that not everyone knows about." His work is complicated, and he's had long and bitter experience of the damage caused by lies of omission. He has no intention of letting them poison his new relationship.

"I'll see if I can sort something out." Jess isn't used to men bargaining back, but then she'd been geared up to this being harder.

William takes a moment, his friend Jack has been on about drinks, so maybe... "If she gets annoyed, you're going to tell her we agreed."

She gets the feeling that she's just been outmanoeuvred, despite having got what she wanted. "All right, thanks."

William decides to strike while the iron's hot, and uses the hands-free again. "Hi, Meredith. Do we have anything in particular planned for the weekend of the twenty-third, other than me coming over?"

"Nothing special. Why?"

"A friend's are trying to organise drinks, so I was wondering if we could do Saturday to Monday morning?"

As Meredith can come up with no reason not to, and the date fits in conveniently with Jess's proposed gathering, she agrees readily. She's further gratified by—though mildly nervous about—his promise that they "will do something fun".

All that remains is for him to rustle up a couple of friends to turn his friend's idea into reality.

By the time he's sorted that out, he's home and cooking pasta and defrosting ragout. He is able, in good conscience, to message Meredith with his thanks and tell her that he and the guys are looking forward to their get-together. Then he has to feign happy surprise when she says how sweet it is that she has scheduled a girls' night while he has a boys' one.

He messages Jess a thumbs-up and a plea that she respect the progress Meredith is making.

★★★

Meredith meanwhile is having her own scheduling difficulties. She really doesn't want to introduce William to her mother yet, but she's struggling to explain why she is now busy at weekends. There are only so many "friends in need" who can be visited. Moreover, her long-planned weekend trip with her mum is coming up.

Her solution is simple: to recruit her brother's assistance. Well, not exactly his, but he's the one with the children, and her mother is no different from any other grandmother. There is a hierarchy of relationships in the heart of a loving mother. Grandmother-grandchildren time is the only thing that trumps mother-daughter time.

Of course, this leads to its own set of questions. Her brother tries to play the fatherly role. It always sets her in the wrong mood, even though she knows he means well. He's two years younger than she is, but he settled straight into his career and married young. Her life has gone a little less smoothly. She promises to make time for their mother during the week if he does more at weekends. She tells him all she knows about William and his work, and promises to arrange for the two to meet.

When she asks William about meeting her brother, his response is unexpected. He offers to accompany her to her brother's home for tea when he's next at her house for the weekend. Mental images of her little niece Alison telling Grandma about Auntie Merry's new boyfriend mortify Meredith. She suggests making it a grown-ups-only affair.

William doesn't mention his own family at all.

★★★

Meredith finds that preparing to listen to the boys' team give a sample presentation is another stack of work; she and Emily have to learn enough about the potential client to be convincing. It's interesting, but they have to put time into it, test each other, and work out a plan of action. Given the rest of her duties, she has a feeling that she's gone back to school while still having a job to do.

Meredith suspects she will remember the result of their effort for the rest of her life. She'd known Adrian fancied Emily, and that Emily could be a bit of a minx, but the way Emily *points* herself at him at the start of his pitch is positively cruel. The poor guy completely loses his lines, and does so on-camera in a room full of colleagues. Meredith actually pities him, she and John exchange amused looks. Fortunately, neither laughs aloud.

Other than that, it goes well. Again it's praise all round—and nobody makes Emily buy anyone a drink.

The incident brings another busy week to a good end, and leaves Meredith feeling content. She and Emily enjoy reliving Adrian's discomfort over a glass of wine after work. Meredith isn't normally on the side of a woman acting like that, but this was comedy gold, and Emily isn't a bitch about it afterwards.

★★★

Meredith finds that knowing she's going to be away from home makes her appreciate her time with Aggy and Pog more. She wants to keep her bond with the little creatures strong, so she tries harder to play with them rather than sharing her house with them like a mum with two teenagers who merely grunt in passing. Her latest attempt—a toy mouse on a string attached to a small fishing rod—is proving most successful.

William calls while she's on the floor playing with Pog. "Do you fancy trying something different this weekend?"

To Meredith, it seems a strange question. Everything with William has been different. "What kind of different?"

"There's a vineyard near me that does a tour with a tasting dinner. I've never been around a winery before."

It isn't the quiet weekend she's been planning for, but it does sound fun. Despite being a good customer of the wine industry, she's never been to a vineyard either.

Suitably warned, Meredith packs outdoor clothes for her visit to William's, and they set off after lunch. As his Jaguar sweeps along the country roads, she decides that being driven around is something she could happily get used to. He's booked them into a little pub hotel, just a short walk from the estate. They aren't the only guests doing the tour, so they and an older couple enjoy a companionable stroll together.

Meredith's a bit disappointed to learn that very little red wine in produced in England, though William assures her that English sparkling wines are excellent. She's pleased that the winery they're going to is one of the few estates to produce reds. They're both amazed to learn how many growers there are in the country and how much wine they produce. All this information is provided by the other couple, who are very well up on wines.

Meredith notices that William, whom she's grown used to seeing as a font of wisdom, is happy asking questions and listening. He even looks bashful when he declares his preference for rosé sparkling wines to the more conventional white. The other couple are divided on which they prefer, but assure him that the estate produces both and suggest Meredith will enjoy comparing the two side by side.

The vines bursting into life after the winter, strike Meredith as a pleasant sign of the changing season, even if she is glad of her warm jacket. The winery is hilly, and the afternoon tour in the pale sunlight is enough walking to satisfy Meredith. She suspects William, with his glowing cheeks and fleece unzipped, could keep up his easy stride for hours on end without becoming either tired or cold.

The winery has a curious mixture of old and new buildings. Part of the manor house and some of the outbuildings date from Tudor times. The presses and bottling equipment are housed in what looks like a modern factory that is only two years old. Most impressively to Meredith's eye, there's a huge cellar underneath with more champagne-type bottles going through their aging process than she can believe.

They manage to sit with the couple at their hotel for the tasting. Dinner is an interesting affair. Numerous dishes are each accompanied by one or two small glasses of wines chosen to complement them. The presiding sommelier must be very used to these events, because she manages to keep both connoisseurs and dilettantes entertained. Meredith definitely agrees with William: the white sparkling wines are lovely, but the pink ones are something else.

At the end of the evening, there is what the others assure her is a rare treat—an English dessert wine. It's the only wine they've been served that's not from the estate. It doesn't have the heady quality of the Sauternes William brought to their dinner with Jess, but its complex, fruity flavours are a delight.

As they walk back to their hotel in the dark, Meredith and William use the torch settings on their smartphones. Meredith is pleased to take a turn at passing on knowledge, as neither of the other couple know how to use theirs. The walk is refreshing after the food and wine. They arrive back at the pub in plenty of time for a nightcap.

Next morning, William drives them home after a breakfast even he considers adequate. They detour to the winery's shop, where he gets a mixed case of wines they particularly enjoyed tasting. Meredith wishes she trusted herself to keep wine in the house as he does, but she's certain that stocking so many bottles would be too much of a temptation.

Ever the pragmatist, William insists on stopping for groceries as well. This has the benefit for Meredith of giving her some input into what he buys. It also means she gets company while doing shopping for herself. She isn't stuck with picking up a couple of things in the local co-op, as she so often is.

They opt for a chicken-and-sausage cobbler when Meredith asks about dumplings instead of potato. William being William, he does some quick mental arithmetic to ensure there will be enough not only for dinner and his own freezer, but also a couple of dinners' worth for her to take home. Meredith can't resist saying, "Little did I realise when you turned up with your limousine that you'd be sweeping me away on your spreadsheet."

"Be nice or I'll put mushrooms in yours," he threatens with a smile that says he doesn't mean it.

Meredith chooses to chop vegetables instead of mixing up the suet and flour for dumplings. Nevertheless, she manages to get floury when she teases William about his messy hands. He's successfully covered her cheeks and denim-clad bottom with hand marks by the time her squeals of laughter and protest stop him. She calls him an arse and gives him a warning look when he playfully raises his hand as if to spank her. She showers while he cuts the chicken, and then adds it to the already browning sausages before loading the dishwasher while he gets cleaned up.

She tries to get his attention when he emerges from the bathroom. She's not staying tonight, and the previous night they fell into a contentedly tipsy sleep not long after getting into bed. After her earlier teasing, though, he's in the mood for a little payback and feigns disinterest until he has the cobbler assembled and in the oven.

By the time their early dinner is ready, Meredith feels very much attended to. They chat about their week ahead. Meredith has prospective clients visiting, and William is spending the next three days in New York.

20

When Clients Come to Call

Spending time with William and returning home after dinner on Sunday evening rather than doing the long early-morning drive make a nice change of pace. Having a boyfriend is something Meredith is thoroughly enjoying, but having one who lives and works a long way away is far from easy.

Aggy and Pog appreciate her return. Only Aggy is at home when Meredith arrives, but either Pog is close by or some instinct draws him home soon thereafter. His fur feels cold when he rubs past her as she sorts things from car to kitchen. The cats appreciate the cooking scraps she's brought, and she sends William a picture of them tucking into his trimmings.

Having changed her bed and cleaned the house on Friday night, Meredith's only remaining task is to ringing her mother. They go through last-minute shopping needs for their trip, and Meredith arranges for the wonders of internet delivery.

★★★

Meredith's shortened week is made busy by Tuesday's visit from the prospective clients. William, bless him, follows up their conversation by emailing copies of their annual report, current shareholder prospectus, and other published information. His note suggests she print the documents and have them in view in an open file when the prospects arrive. She isn't sure she has the nerve to really do that, but she prints the documents out anyway and collects them from the colour printer on her way to Monday's strategy meeting with her boss.

When Mr Rossi stops to say hello, he asks about them. She explains the reasoning, and he's impressed. He mentions it in the meeting, in the context of praising the way the department has started the year. He suggests having her assistant Sophie bind copies. John chips in with another thought—they should have details of the company's electronic point of sale provider on show too. Emily offers to handle that.

William messages to say he's landed. The message arrives in mid-afternoon when she's busy. By the time she checks her phone again, she's received a photo of his view of a snowy New York from the hotel window. His message says that he'll call after work. She messages back a hug emoji and sets off to visit her friend Beverly and Beverly's sticky children. Meredith loves them, especially the way the boy cries out in delight when he sees her. They're adorable and she spoils them rotten.

She's home and getting ready for bed when William calls."How are you?"

"Tired," she replies. "And nervous about tomorrow."

"Join the club. Jetlag and stage fright aren't a pleasant combination!"

"You? Stage fright?" Meredith finds it hard to believe that William is nervous about anything.

"Of course. I worry about whether I'm prepared and whether I'll remember everything and whether I'll judge my audience correctly." He pauses, one of his thinking pauses. "Everyone gets a bit excited and a bit nervous. We just do it differently." He chuckles. "Then there are the daft things, everything from 'unwanted erections' to 'is my skirt stuck in my knickers', as far as I can work out."

He can always make her laugh. and the images he conjures have her chuckling, "Are you just saying that to make me feel better?"

It's her turn to make him laugh. "No, I say it to make *me* feel better. You can thank Mr McDonald again, though he said he learnt it from his father."

"Is there anything you take credit for?"

"Not if it isn't due," he says simply.

★★★

Arriving early for the big day, Meredith feels great. She knows her part and her material, and is wearing her favourite jacket with the blouse and skirt William bought her. However, when she compares herself to Emily and some of the boys …Even the balding Mr Rossi looks dapper in a dark suit.

There's an almost unreal feeling to the office as he leads a trial walk-through of the visit. Everyone joins in the mutual appreciation. Indeed, the staff look so well-dressed that the MD suggests photos for the next brochure. Several of the keener people dutifully snap them, even capturing those, such as Meredith, who are reluctant to have their pictures taken.

The visitors arrive. They seek to evaluate the Triangulation Partnership while the staff seek to fine-tune their understanding of the prospect's needs. Despite the nerves she always feels, Meredith is certain that it goes well. The presentation overruns on time a little due to people being engrossed. This being the largest project she's been involved in from the start, Meredith is impressed by the way the company pulls together. She feels that she and Emily are at the centre of a well-run machine.

By the time the visitors leave, Meredith has forgotten her usual reticence around strangers. She's immersed in her role. A part of her mind seems to stand back and watch, reminding her of William's observation that it's like a performance.

The remainder of the day is spend in writing up and reviewing while the buzz fades. Shortly before five, the MD calls the involved together in the main meeting room to thank everyone for their efforts.

★★★

Five time-zones of difference are a new experience for Meredith. She heads to work, while for William it's the small hours of the morning. She goes to bed while he's sitting down to dinner. It leaves little time when one or the other isn't at work. However, being able to have a good-night phone call does make her feel closer. She messages him about her day before leaving the office.

Seeing her mum after work provides a nice unwind. Her mum's dog, Roley, has learned that Meredith's appearance in the early evening means *walk time.* His enthusiastic wriggling while her mother gets ready amuses Meredith even more than it exasperates her mum.

They take his favourite fetch ball and the thrower he got for Christmas. When her mother has walked far enough, they sit on a bench and chat while Roley gallops after the ball and they chat. She mentions it to her mother while walking Roley her mum says how much she'd have liked being able to do that when her dad travelled for work.

The conversation concentrates on the presentation and how Meredith and her colleagues dressed. Putting her favourite things on had felt good, even if she did feel outshone by some of the others.

So, when Meredith dresses the next day, she looks in her wardrobe for inspiration. She finds little. She has a busy day ahead and doesn't have time fret. She grabs an old skirt suit and heads in.

Talking with Emily in afternoon, Meredith reluctantly gets dragged into looking at the network folder of pictures from the day before. Emily's eagerness has obvious reasons, not only do her looks stand out, but the pictures she took are better framed than anyone else's. She has an eye, and Meredith tells her so.

Meredith, as always, is critical of her own appearance. She expects Emily to join in, but instead Emily pulls up the Christmas party pictures. Even Meredith sees the difference in her face. Emily says, "You look much better, especially when you dress up."

That evening, Meredith takes a longer look through her closet as she packs for Italy. It confirms that she doesn't have many things that look or feel special to her. When William calls, she bemoans the lack. Her words catch him half wrapped in work. Instead of being wise, he offers to go clothes shopping with her the next time they have a full weekend to themselves.

21

Away with Mum

The afternoon flight is a blessing; as they before the business crowds. Meredith loves her mother dearly, but the combination of a crowded airport and her mum's flying nerves wouldn't have been the best way to start a relaxing break. Once they're safely checked in, she messages William to let him know all is well. He responds that he loves City Airports—apart from the cost of breakfast.

Her mother is surprised that Meredith favours spring water instead of joining her in a glass of red wine with their meal. "Are you all right, Merry?"

"Yes, Mum. I'm just trying to be a bit more careful at the moment."

"I wish I had the will power," her mother says in a light tone that indicates she doesn't wish it too hard. Her mother likes the good things in life. Meredith manages to stop herself before she quotes from William's library of encouraging comments, though she's unable to help herself smiling at the thought of what he'd say.

By not trying to be anything more than it is, the in-flight food manages to satisfy them both. They arrive at Florence's compact airport refreshed. It's still daylight, so they get to see something of the city in the cab to their hotel.

Meredith snaps a few pictures on the way and sends them to her friends and family WhatsApp groups. She sends them separately to William and includes a link to the restaurant they have booked that evening. He says it looks good. He messages again a few minutes later, praising the menu and reviews. He asks if she's doing her exercises before or after. She laughs as she reads this.

You're kidding, right?

"Are you sharing a twin room with your mum?" Is his oblique response.

Yes, we always do when we go away.

Then you can let her go through the bathroom first and do them while she's in there. [angel]

Apparently he isn't kidding. Meredith has half a mind to tell him where he can stick his exercises, but decides against it. It's easier to just not. He means well, and she asked for help, but this is her holiday.

Their room is on the hotel's fourth floor. There is a decent, though not spectacular view of the city. The room is spacious and well-appointed, with ample wardrobes and mirrors.

Meredith hasn't noticed, but she is getting less shy of her reflection, her mother however has noticed something. Catching her normally shy daughter glimpsing her reflection, she asks, "You're looking so well at the moment, Merry—have you lost weight?" Looking at Meredith she sees her standing straight and holding herself with a new confidence.

Her mother is always nice to her, but when it comes to her appearance, Meredith has grown used to the automatic praise of a caring parent. This is something new. The kind-hearted, well-meaning woman seems genuinely impressed.

Buoyed by the compliment and in a moment of weakness (or is it strength?) Meredith says, "Would you like to go through the bathroom first?" And she does the exercises before it's her turn to get ready.

But she definitely doesn't report this to William, it's one thing taking his advice but...

★★★

The food at the restaurant is simpler than Meredith imagines Italian cuisine as being, though it's beautifully presented, enough so that she asks their waiter in her A-level Italian if it's okay for her to take pictures of their plates. The home-made pasta and sauce dishes and classical desserts are little works of art that would grace any table in London or Paris. He's delighted and offers to take the pictures himself.

Over dinner, her mother asks the question she's been working up to. "All these little changes, Merry—is there someone special you're seeing?"

Meredith's face gives her away before she has a chance to say a word. "I've only been seeing him for a couple of weeks, but, yes, he is special."

"I understand, darling," her mother says in a voice that means, *I don't understand.*

"I'll introduce him to you when I'm a bit more certain." Meredith blushes. "Would you like to see his picture?" She may be shy of sharing her new relationship, but she's also proud of it, and of her handsome William. The photo breaks the tension. She takes pleasure in her mother's interest and support now that the secret is out.

"I'm just glad you've been seeing someone, not just avoiding me lately." Her mother's words strike at Meredith's heart. She hasn't realised she might have hurt her mum and certainly hasn't meant to.

They stroll back to their hotel, arm in arm through the narrow streets. Meredith feels her steps lighter. "You can tell Dad if you want," she suggests, glad that her parents have put their divorce behind them and are able to be friends again.

Her mother is only too pleased, both because she's the first parent to hear, and because it gives her something good to tell the family. Meredith is glad that she can get out of the task of telling any more relatives. She knows her dad would certainly grill her about William's "prospects", though she also knows he would mean well in doing so. She's still nervous about how her family will take her tall, confident lover, and how he will find them with their various quirks, but at least the task of telling them is out of the way.

★★★

Mother and daughter breakfast on light pastries in their room. The windows are open to the sound of church bells. Her mother drinks a latte and Meredith a macchiato. The weather is fine, so they plan their day loosely. Much to her own amusement, Meredith messages William to say he might have more luck getting her to eat breakfast in Italy.

When the business of the main shopping streets gets too much for Meredith's mother they walk along a street by the river Arno. The shops are still lovely and expensive, but, like their fellow pedestrians more spaced out. Most are boutiques, jewellers, or bespoke fashion stores. One has a display of silk ties, and Meredith decides to look in. She's still conscious of the things William bought for her, and a tie might be a nice gift. "Mum, is it okay if we look in here?"

"Of course." Her mother could shop for England. "Are you looking for something for your young man?"

Meredith sifts through the stock. Her eye is caught by subtly patterned red-and-blue design. The colours would brighten the look of William's dark suits without being too much and he has a set of cufflinks she thinks would match.

"This grey one looks nice." Her mum's voice attracts Meredith's attention. Given the book she's brought to read—the notorious *Fifty Shades of Grey*—and the nature of her relationship with William, it raises her alarm too. Meredith looks up sharply and studies her mother's face, but there's no hint of a double meaning. She starts breathing again, and makes a mental note to tell William when she gives him the tie.

She does, however take her mother's advice when it comes to selecting a gift for her neighbour, Mrs Godleman.

Meredith quickly becomes aware of how much fitter she has become. For the first time she can remember, she finds herself having to wait for her mum as they play tourist in Florence's narrow streets. The buildings and boutiques give her plenty to look at while she waits.

The Cathedral of Santa Maria del Fiore is striking, with black-and-white stonework, as is the baptistery facing it. Remembering William's fondness for church architecture, Meredith takes a number of pictures. She chooses the best while they sit in a local's café, drinking coffee she is sure would delight him. She messages him as she enjoys another espresso.

Do you have any Italian ancestors?

No, why?

The food and coffee :-)

She can imagine him laughing as she sends this. She can see something of his passion in the city's art too, though she can't imagine him as the arty type.

I love Italian music too, but no, afraid not.

She remembers, there's a lot of Italian music in his collection, but then there's a lot of Austrian and English music as well.

She and her mum rest briefly and eat a light meal at their hotel, enjoying bowls of ribollita and a couple of disapproval-free cigarettes while her mother has a nap.

Their evening excursion takes them to the opera. The exterior of the modern opera house divides them. Meredith likes it, but her mother thinks it's an eyesore. The elegant interior is something they agree on, and so is the performance of *Rigoletto*. Both are in tears for Gilda as the final curtain falls.

Her mother, a keen chorister, bubbles enthusiastically about the singers as they dine in another handsome restaurant. Meredith surrenders to her love of ravioli while enjoying her mother's selection of a vintage Chianti.

★★★

Waking tired on Sunday, Meredith is initially reluctant to get out of bed. Her mother reminds her of the day of pampering ahead, and she forces herself to get up. Over pastries and coffee, they peruse the spa menu. Both are agreed on hot stone massages, mani-pedis, and facials.

"I think I'll start with a sauna." Her mother lets the words hang. She thinks the sauna would be good for Meredith and her smoker's lungs, but knows her well.

"You know I don't like the sauna!" Meredith feels defensive. It's hard to breathe in the steam, and she isn't sure being fitter and slimmer will help. She also doesn't want it to start her coughing, because that will lead to the inevitable "when are you going to stop smoking" question. "I think I'll just wait for you in the hot tub, and we can go on from there together."

"Okay, Merry." Her mother lets it go. "You're going to love the hot stones." Her mum has been on about them for months since she first tried it.

When they get to the spa, Meredith feels less self-conscious than on previous spa visits. Perhaps it's all the time she's spent naked with William, or the weight she's been losing. The charming staff and the fun of practising her Italian while they try out their English probably has something to do with it too.

Meredith enjoys a detoxifying smoothie in the hot-tub until her mother emerges from the sauna to collect her for their massages. There are two beds in the dimly lit room. They talk amiably until the therapists and their smooth, heavy, basalt stones begin their work. The women have to be gently awakened and guided to the recovery room when their massage ends.

"Well?" her mother asks.

Meredith smiles. "From what I can remember, it was divine. I certainly feel relaxed."

The spa restaurant is separate. They decide to eat there rather than nipping out for something exciting, but the food is actually very good. The only imperfect part of their final day is the way Meredith feels when standing alone outside in a light drizzle to smoke. She can't forget the look on her mother's face as she goes.

★★★

When she lands on English soil once more, Meredith messages William to let him know she's arrived safely.

I can't believe I slept on the plane as well as during my massage.
[laugh]"

22

Night Out-In

onday is busy, particularly as she has to catch up on the events of her Friday off. William calls Meredith, who's looking forward to the next evening when he's due to stay at hers. The news he gives—that he's got to go overseas for work—is the last thing she wants to hear. It's of some comfort that he sounds as regretful as she feels. Still, she won't see him for nearly two weeks. She'd been looking forward to telling him about her trip in person.

Her disappointment shows in her voice, and he searches for something to make it up to her. "We could have a web date instead?"

"What do you mean?"

"We pick a film, a play, or an opera, and we watch it together over dinner, even if we are in different countries."

"Have you done that before?"

She's caught him there. It's a new idea to him, but it seems logical. "No, but I'm game to give it a try if you are. It isn't being together, but it's better than nothing." He sounds more confident of the idea as he continues.

"Is it something other people do?"

"God knows. I'm a bit old-fashioned, but I suspect so."

"Okay then, it's a date," she agrees. "What shall we watch?"

"Not a musical," he says immediately, making her chuckle. He knows she loves them, and she knows he hates them.

"Oh, spoilsport. How about *Dido and Aeneas?*" It's her favourite opera, and she knows he likes opera.

"I was thinking something a bit more cheerful." When they listened to it in his music room, she'd cried at the tragic ending, even though she knew the story well. "I won't be there to dry your tears. How about something a bit more cheerful? *Così fan tutte*'s light."

She concedes, reluctantly, that he has a point. It's not as if the Mozart isn't good, and the music and libretto are far more romantic.

He tells her how much he's missed her and suggests that there is nothing to stop them getting a little frisky. Meredith playfully complains, "I wish I had your selection of toys!" She doubts many girls own fewer vibrators than their boyfriends do.

"Well, if you need me to go shopping with you some time ..."

He would too, she thinks, then blushes at the thought of him taking her into a shop and ordering up a selection.

"There's the one from your knickers, if it's charged," he suggests helpfully.

She laughs and sends him a picture of the little purple toy in her hand. "I'm sure you're psychic."

★★★

On Tuesday, the prospect of the evening takes Meredith's mind off how overloaded she is becoming with additional work from their prospect, now a new client. She and Emily send Sophie out for sandwiches at lunchtime, but none of the three manage to finish anywhere near on time. It's a weary Meredith who falls into the bath to soak herself in preparation for her evening out-in.

William, in his hotel, tries to sort out the communications. He has a laptop, phone, and tablet; however, they don't seem to want to work in perfect harmony. He tests calling himself from the tablet while listening to music through his headphones. He curses when he finds that calls and music won't merge on his Bluetooth headphones.

After a quick, unfruitful search for software, he falls back on running YouTube from his laptop through the room's TV, leaving the phone and laptop free. It's a bit of a faff, but he misses Meredith. Once he's got things sorted, it could certainly ease the boredom of quiet nights travelling. He gets it working just in time to let room-service in.

When he calls her, Meredith isn't quite ready. The beauty of this way of doing things is that they aren't bound to table bookings or performance times. Guessing correctly that Meredith won't be doing a starter, he enjoys Parma ham and melon while she finishes up. They sit down together to eat their entrees, and 3-2-1 their way to starting the stream.

As Act One opens, Meredith admits to herself that Mozart's light-hearted masterpiece is perfect date material. She can't imagine herself as one of the faithless lovers in the story, but the playfulness and humour are delightful. It very much suits her experience of being with William. The music and William's sort-of company enhance the taste of her noodles, tofu, and peppers. She teases him that he's missing out on tofu and gets a picture of the calves' liver he's dining on. Amid a string of laughter emojis, they eat and chat through the act.

During Act Two, he messages, flirts, and pauses to listen as Dorabella wantonly falls for her fiancé's disguised friend's advances. Meredith flirts back, teasing him for needing subtitles (though, in truth, they also help her).

As William speaks softly Meredith recalls how his lips touched her on their first night together. She lets her hands move under his guidance. Her neck … the insides of her forearms … the line where her side meets her back—these are places she had no idea were so sensitive until she met him.

His voice and his memory are as impressive as his hands and his mouth. She lets his words guide her fingers. For a moment, she chuckles. This is certainly something she couldn't do if they were really in a box at the opera.

As she vocalises her pleasure, his words become more intimate. She unbuttons her blouse as William likes to, imagining the devilish look in his twinkling eyes as she does. It feels wickedly decadent. It's one thing to touch oneself alone, but quite another to do so under skilled and loving instruction. She bites her lip when he bids her to slow her caresses to prolong her pleasure *the novelty of teasing herself, and of giving her hands over to him excites and amuses. No,* she thinks, *this is certainly something I couldn't do at the opera, even if...* She takes up the little vibrator and wishes he could see her smile.

Afterwards, she lies back on her sofa, watching the lovers' reconciliation. She messages him instead of speaking over their connection.

> *It's a shame you can't use the remote control when we're apart.*

> *Yes. At least not on that one.*

> *What do you mean?*

> *Well, you can get remote controlled toys that work over the web [grin, shrug, laugh]*

> *You're kidding!*

She finds out he isn't when he sends her a web link.

> *Oh, you aren't! [grin] Maybe I'll let you buy me one for your birthday.*

She washes up after the opera finishes, then settles down with Aggy. She calls him again to chat while she drifts off to sleep. It isn't as good as her expected night with him, but it has made an intimate and original evening.

The strange date leads to a long and restful sleep. But work is hectic, and on Wednesday evening Meredith finds herself running late to help her mother take her enthusiastic pup for a walk. Her mum, noticing that she looks tired, insists that she stay for dinner after. While they eat, she tells Meredith that she's working too hard, as many a mother does, but having got in early and left late without making enough of a dent Meredith suspects she has a point.

On Thursday, Meredith's work diary reminds her that Emily has Thursday and Friday booked off the next week. Meredith has the Friday off as well. With more pitches to potential clients in the pipeline, it's clear that something has to be done. She and Emily share a grumbling session over a glass of wine after finishing late once more.

At least she has a simple home-made meal ready to go at home. That part of her life is running smoothly. She even manages to get her exercises in, knowing that there's little chance she'll do so on Friday with the girls coming over.

23

Girls' Night

Meredith feels guilty leaving work on time on Friday, but she has to collect Jess from the station on the way home. They have fun shopping for wine and nibbles. To Meredith's surprise, Jess insists on picking up celery, rice cakes, and alcohol-free drinks as well as their usual fare. Meredith doesn't say anything, but she knows her eyes must.

Julia is the only one of the group not delighted by Meredith's new look and new confidence. She's known she's not the prettiest or wealthiest—that's Jess, and they all know it. And she isn't the motherly one, a title Beverly with her three children and doting husband owned. But until now she hadn't been the plain one either. That has always been cheerful, helpful Meredith, never without a kind word or a cigarette or drink in her hand. It seems to Julia that it is now she, and not her friend, who occupies this role."I never thought you'd be running around changing yourself to please a man."

She doesn't intend an edge in her words, at least not consciously, but in Meredith's ears there is one.

Jess leaps to her defence. "Merry's getting fit, and I think it's great." She smiles at Meredith. "We might all have to be on our guard."

Meredith is certain it's only said in jest. Jess is much prettier than she is. But it doesn't stop her chest from swelling with pride. "Actually, I asked him to help me, and I'm loving it. I was fed up after my winter binge. William's been very supportive. I've even got some of his home gym things to use."

The party proceed up to Meredith's spare room to view William's loaned exercise equipment. Each woman light-heartedly tries the dumbbells. Meredith is privately delighted that she is now far from the least able. She's certain that, a month earlier, she would have been.

"Oh, that reminds me," says Beverly. "I saw a funny one on the internet—exercise I mean." She gets out her phone and shows them a video. The exercise involves picking up a chair. It looks simple, but Meredith finds it hard to bend over a chair then pick it up without moving her feet.

★★★

For William there is work to do between his flight home and his evening out. Being out of the country has messed up his training, so he sets out to correct things. He doesn't have all the equipment he needs at home, and he can't often find the more serious kit in hotel gyms, so he heads to his regular haunt to lift.

"Hello, stranger. You didn't decide to get fat and lazy then?"

It's been a while since William's seen his old bantering partner."Me? I thought your missus must have finally nailed your balls to the sofa."

The two laugh, and William tries to remember the guy's name. They've chatted and even spotted for each other for perhaps two years now, and he knows they've exchanged names, but for the life of him he can't think what the man's is. He knows the details of his family life and training regime, and decides to ask if the man would like to train together some time—that would mean exchanging numbers and give him an excuse to ask the guy to spell his name.

The two swap encouragement and good-humoured comments between sets, in the Friday night quiet of the gym, His nameless friend makes a joke about the young lads who train nothing but arms and chest, then bids William goodnight, leaving him alone with the squat rack.

When William gets into his car, he checks his phone. There's a message from Meredith. *"Hope you're having fun, got the girls over."* It's followed by a row of wine-glass emojis. He's running late, so he uses the hands-free to let her know he's driving to the pub. She doesn't answer, so he leaves a message.

The phone rings as he pulls up. "I thought you were going out for the evening?"

"I am. I've just arrived—had to train first."

"Nobody has to train, William!"

There's a hurt silence, "Everybody should."

Bless him, she doubts that on this they will ever see eye to eye. She doesn't always think to do her short sessions at home, and even when she does, she doesn't always bother.

William's mates are of the view that he had two to catch up on; they're already sat at the table when he arrives. Archie greets him by emptying his glass and cheerily informing William that his first two are going flat and it's his round.

"If you're okay to do without a chauffeur?" William cautions.

"You buy your round and supply breakfast, and I'll sort the cab," Jack assures him.

William snags one of his two waiting beers and strolls to the bar for supplies.

The beer is clearly flowing, as it usually does on these evenings. William is glad he suggested a pub that does decent steak. The place also has a good carpark, and it's only a short trip to pick the Jag up in the morning.

While he's at the bar, he messages Meredith to ask what the girls are up to. She messages back about showing off her keep-fit things and the game with the chair. She says it might be fun to see if William and his friends can do it.

Easy.

Really?

Yes!

Prove it.

Meredith has little experience of boys' nights, let alone the sort of boys' nights that army messes engage in. Had she known, she might not have made the challenge.

A few moments pass as the boys discuss it. Then William makes a video link. Her screen shows William demonstrating, followed by Jack and Archie, who shows off by holding a full pint in one hand while he lifts the chair in the other. William, not to be outdone, does it with Jack sitting on the chair.

At this point someone in the pub suggests they stop messing around before they break something. Archie looks set to argue, but William apologises. The three sit, looking somewhat sheepish. In the safety of Meredith's living room, the girls laugh. Then Meredith messages a follow-up.

Aw, sorry. The video made it look like it's easier for girls.

I suspect TikTok is not a science-rich environment
[smile, beer, kiss]

Jess suggests that they send a group selfie to William. Some dozen snaps and a few squabbles over choice of image later, William receives the picture. He laughs and, innocently enough, shows it to the others. Jack is suddenly interested and demands they send a return photo, Archie? Archie takes the piss, but then, well, Archie takes the piss.

The three of them successfully persuade the landlord that their order for four main courses isn't the result of a counting error or a plan for more larking around. There's a scramble for the onion rings from William's second plate and he defensively claims that there was nothing stopping anyone else ordering two mains.

"You are such a pig, young William," announces Archie.

When the girl who brought the food returns with condiments, she sees Archie's face and asks if there's anything wrong, to general hilarity. She shrugs and says the kitchen will be open for another hour if anyone is still hungry.

Jack casually asks William if he can see the selfie again. "Who's the pretty one with the dark hair?"

"That's Meredith's best friend, Jess."

"Have you got her number?"

"Yes, and no, you can't have it." William knows his friend; he's great fun but a notorious philanderer. William would rather have no role in his love life except as an amused commentator.

Jack does his best to look hurt, "As a true friend, you'd give me her number."

"Your true friend or Meredith's?" William asks archly.

"That seems a rather unreasonable attitude to take."

"Jack, my friend—" William raises a glass "—I love you like a brother." Jack clinks glasses with him. "But that means I wouldn't want you to sleep with my sister."

Archie almost sprays beer as he stifles a guffaw.

"I'm hurt!" Jack feigns offence and receives disbelieving looks from his two grinning friends.

"Okay I'll tell you what: I'll give Meredith your number and a brief appraisal of your character." Archie considers this hilarious. "Then she can decide what to do with it."

"Never play cards with young William!" Archie proclaims with a laugh. "I'd have thought you'd learnt that by now."

It's chucking-out time when the three take a taxi back to William's to wind down over Scotch.

★★★

At Meredith's house, Beverly and Julia pour themselves into a cab in the wee small hours, leaving Meredith and Jess to their own devices. Jess was right—girl time was the perfect antidote to a long week.

24

Saturday Morning Doesnt Exactly Happen

In each household, the late night and drinking have their effects. In Meredith's case, it combines with Jess's allergy to weekend mornings, though this does give Meredith some quiet time to wish she had a perfect antidote for the after-effects of red wine.

For William, the unfamiliar alcohol intake unites with the need to roust his friends out of bed, feed them, set them on their ways, and retrieve his car. The break in his schedule also sits ill with him. At least he has guests who manage to finish his idea of a proper breakfast, even if they do need bullying into helping load the dishwasher.

The overall upshot is that when he phones to say he's running late, his apologies are greeted with gratitude by the still-groggy Meredith. She thinks, *I'm never going to drink again*, and says, "That's okay! I'm not even crawling yet. We had such a good time, but we stayed up talking so late!"

"And drinking?" He asks archly.

"Of course! You've met Jess!"

"Ha, us too," he confesses. "I haven't tied one on like that in a while." Breakfast has made a dent in his hangover, but he wants another hour before setting off on the drive. "Is she up yet?"

Jess is actually snoring; she must have been drunker than Meredith noticed. "You really don't know Jess, do you?"

"She'd get on with the boys. Jack crawled downstairs at the first scent of bacon, but I had to wave coffee under Archie's nose."

She can see William doing it; he's woken her up with the smell of coffee and other delectables before. "So do you tease everyone?"

He smiles. "Everyone I like."

They end their chat so William can get his head together. Before he finishes packing, he checks the fridge. There are things that need using—French beans, broccoli, and some carrots. Being away has, as usual, messed with his eating (as has getting drunk with his friends, he admits). So, rather than take Meredith out, he grabs the veg, a bag of potatoes, and a cottage pie base from the freezer. He doesn't even glance at the wine racks.

★★★

Meredith hasn't long got back home from dropping Jess off when William's car pulls up.

"You didn't bring wine?" she asks teasingly as he unpacks the dinner things. She doesn't want wine; in fact she's having a "fat-day" and wants the control she finds it easier to retain when he's there.

"I don't even want to see wine." He laughs.

She smiles her agreement."That bad?"

"Not exactly, but I'm definitely not ready for another drink today." He's sheepish, which she decides makes him look sweet. It's nice to know he's not altogether saintly outside the bedroom.

"Did you bring anything else?" Meredith asks expectantly. He almost always brings something from his toy room. Finding out what it is is something she looks forward to.

"I was wondering whether you'd done your exercises yet?" he asks innocently.

She wishes she were a better liar. She knows she isn't, and she has missed him, so she decides to confess as cheekily as possible. "No, I haven't. I've been *busy*." A challenging smile accompanies her words.

"Busy doing what?"

"Stripping the beds, loading the washing machine, and recovering from my hangover." Meredith laughs and steps back.

"Can I take it that you skipped your exercises last night too?" he asks sternly. She hasn't mentioned her training all week.

Meredith thinks about the night before. There was no thought of exercise, unless one counted the silly chair video. "No, but you're bad too! You got told off in the pub last night!"

William grins ruefully. "I was just showing you how silly your friend's game was."

Meredith, feeling playful, pushes further and tries to do an impression of the landlord's complaint. "There's a clown school down the road if you fancy enrolling there, gents."

Her impression isn't great, but the landlord's comment had been quite snappy and William is unable to stifle a laugh. He's pretty sure she's taunting him on purpose, and decides to play along. "I think that's quite enough of that, young lady."

"Or what?" She wiggles her bum and skips out of reach, giggling.

He laughs as he gets up and pursues the still giggling Meredith. "Or I might have to put you over my knee again."

It seems to be the sort of answer she wants as her smile widens though she moves to put the dining table between them. "That is SO unfair! Meredith teases "You're the bad boy, so why do I get spanked?"

"Maybe because you're going to tease me until I spank you anyway?" God his smile is just so naughty! "Or maybe because you like it?"

It's her turn to laugh at his audacity. "I'm pretty sure you aren't supposed to say it like that!"

Since she discovered this world, she's done some reading and even some browsing. William's approach doesn't seem to be the way other people do this, at least not in fiction. The way he sees through her is exciting though. It's been nearly two weeks since she's seen William, and she's missed him. She's missed his presence and his physicality. She's missed handing herself over to him. Perhaps most of all, she's missed the sense of peace she feels in his arms afterwards.

"Oh, really? And suddenly you're the expert in this sort of thing?" He raises an eyebrow as he tries to get around the table before she can escape.

"Yes, I've been studying," she says defiantly, still trying to play the role even though she's been well and truly busted.

The thrill Meredith feels in taunting William, thinking she knows where it will finish but not being sure, and of seeing his face and his body respond, chases the last of the fog from her head. She suspects its one hangover cure she's unlikely to read about even in the most risqué women's magazines. It's another new insight: maybe she is braver than she realises, just as William assures her she is.

"Hmmm." His face assumes a thoughtful expression. "I'm pretty sure that as long as you're laughing, I'm doing something right." He smiles as he chases around the table again.

He has a point. On one level, this is like the way she played with her brother when they were kids, only more exciting. On another, it's like being with a lover, only more erotic.

She makes a break for the door, but it opens inwards and he catches her. She cries, "No!"—though not *pineapple*—and she laughs while he drags her back to the sofa.

She struggles and giggles as he forces her over his knee. Once held in position, she stops giggling as she concentrates on the rising warmth inside her. He caresses her through her jeans. She feels disappointed that he hasn't undressed her, but cannot deny that he has excited her. She is ready for this.

His caresses continue and she feels her anticipation rise. He lifts his hand and brings it down with the now-familiar sound and sensation. Meredith, safe in the certainty that her face is hidden, allows herself a smile and then bites her lip.

Her eyes are dilated when he helps her up. The look in them is urgent, though she wishes he'd carried on even after those last few hard swats. Looking up at him, she understands. She isn't the only one who has been denied by their separation. "Here?" she asks breathlessly.

"No, bed." His tone is final, and the kiss that follows his words is overpowering.

For all the urgency of his need, he undresses her gently. She can see in his eyes that he's holding back from tearing her clothes from her. She wonders what that would be like. He even lets her unbutton his shirt and slide it from his broad shoulders. It still raises colour in her cheeks when she unveils her classical statue.

The gentleness lasts until her body welcomes him with an urgency to match his own. Then he unleashes the full fury of his need. There are no whips or cuffs or even clever toys; his strength and his presence burn into her. For the moment, she feels no need for anything other than to be with him, to cling to him as fiercely as he does to her, to feed on his desire and be consumed by it.

They lie, sweaty and panting. Meredith is on her back, looking across at William, who is on his side with a satisfied grin plastered across his face. "So, I've been meaning to ask," he drawls, "should I start calling you Merry?"

It's what her parents and most of her friends call her, but she thinks of the nickname as from her childhood. Besides, the way his deep voice rolls the sound of her full name does something to her. "No, I like the way you say Meredith."

"Very well, Meredith." He grins. She knows he's laying the syrupy depth of his voice on, but it still does something to her insides. Then his face gets more serious. "And, other than last night, have you been doing your exercises?"

She rolls over and embraces him, not wanting to see his face when she confesses. "Not as often as I should." Saying it hurts; she doesn't want to disappoint him. "Work's been crazy lately."

"Well, you can change things up a bit sometimes. Maybe go swimming with your mum when you see her. Or take that lunatic hound of hers for a long walk." He kisses her hair and says with kindness in his voice, "And remember, ten minutes is better than nothing."

Meredith feels his arm squeeze her gently. "Roley's not a lunatic. He's just young, and Mum's not always good with him." It's easy to feel good in William's arms. "He's brilliant with the kids."

"What breed is he?"

"A retriever. He's dark brown." Thinking about her mother's enthusiastic dog lifts her.

"A Labrador?"

"No. He's slim with a long coat." Meredith thinks a Lab would suit her mother far better, but the older woman fell for her young enthusiast at first sight, and none of the family had been able to dissuade her.

William has seen pictures of Meredith's mother, and has a fair idea of the type of dog. He smiles a little, he wouldn't have put them together, then returns to the subject. "Do you want to start back on your exercise regime tomorrow?"

"Yes, please." She kisses him. "Thanks for not being cross."

"Hmm" He gives her a peck. "But do better." He follows up with a gentle swat. "Now, shall I show you?"

Meredith glows as he unpacks. There's a lovely glass phallus, some cuffs of course, and a set of make-up brushes. "Nothing extreme this time," he says, and kisses her again.

"I've got something for you too," she announces and takes a slim, elegantly wrapped package from her bedside cabinet.

The tie is a surprise, and a nice one. William has more often been the giver than the receiver. The gift is all the more welcome because Meredith has picked out one that's bright enough to be fun but conservative enough to be work friendly and that matches his favourite cufflinks makes her gift all the more welcome, ""It's perfect. You have a good eye."

"I'm glad you like it." Meredith basks, then confides, "I was with my mum in the shop, and she tried to get me to buy a grey one." She bursts into giggles.

"Oh, you've read those?"

"I'm on the second volume." Then giggles, "I just hope Mum hasn't!"

Joining in with her laughter, he replies, "Who can tell? I wouldn't ask though! Just don't get too disappointed when you find out I don't own a yacht."

She can't help saying, "You're such a daftie!"

"Guilty as charged." He grins with the naughtiest of looks in his blue-green eyes.

In its way, his boyishness charms her as much as his manliness. More free of tension than she's been for days, she drifts.

William puts Meredith's quietness down to her being tired after her late night. He's feeling a bit that way himself, so he leaves her sleeping while he starts to sort out dinner.

When the aroma of defrosted cottage pie base joins that of buttery mash, the cats are on station. Meredith too comes downstairs to join him in the kitchen. "Have they been leaving your sofa alone?" he asks.

Meredith thinks he doesn't quite get that animals aren't as smart as people. But they mostly have, and the posts and her encouragement have certainly helped. "Yes, they've been good." She ruffles the fur at the back of Aggy's neck.

Both little creatures ignore the exchange as they wait for their morsels. William's got fond of the pair and of this ritual. He looks fondly down on them as they eat their tiny titbits, each in their own distinct way.

Once he's put the pie in the oven, William fulfils his promise to Jack. Meredith is amused that he's worried. Jess can't look after herself! But she agrees to pass on both Jack's phone number and William's caution.

Dinner is a contrast from the curry and wine of the night before. There's Chopin playing instead of raucous chatter, and a fading hangover in place of a rising alcoholic buzz. They enjoy each other's company, the quiet, and the food.

William's calmness and the tactile physicality of his company are the perfect antidotes to her blue mood. By the time they've washed up, Meredith is feeling snuggly. When he kisses her and asks, "Playtime?" Meredith nods.

His manner is gentle, almost hypnotic. He takes each hand in turn and kisses the inside of her wrist before gently applying a soft leather cuff to it. The effect is a curious sense of double seduction, first by his tenderness and then by her own conscious, physical consent. Meredith drifts in thoughts and then looks up to see that playful, filthy look in his eyes. The blue seems to her to get brighter when he does that.

She finds the cuffs have been linked in front of her without her noticing. How does he do these things without looking at his hands?

He stands without breaking eye contact, wearing a smile that ought to be illegal. One of his fingers is hooked around the clip joining her cuffs, forcing her to rise and follow him as he leaves the room.

William's sure feet make their way elegantly up Meredith's staircase to her bedroom, despite the fact he's facing her and stepping backwards. He unclips the cuffs, but, when she moves to embrace him, his eyes stop her. Instead he begins to undress her. First he raises her T-shirt and slides it over her head. Then he smoothly undoes her bra (*Mmm*, she thinks, *he's getting better at that*) as he kisses her lips.

Once he has laid her shirt and bra down, Meredith moves to unbutton his shirt. Again he stops her, this time with gentle hands and a wicked smile. It stirs mixed feelings in her. She loves his playfulness, and what he does to and for her when she places her body in his hands. But she loves to touch and tend his body too. With the slightest of pouts, she reluctantly lower her hands and allows him to clip them behind her back. His kisses melt her pout. She may not be able to touch him, but she can still enjoy his touch

Once satisfied that she has accepted her situation, he eases his lips from hers and resumes undressing her. Even though she loves and trusts William, even though he has seen her body many times, and even despite the evidence of her own eyes, she still feels hopelessly embarrassed. He undresses her with a care that would do credit to a lady's maid: undoing and lowering her jeans and panties, easing her down on her bed, and then removing her shoes and socks without the slightest tickling.

He smiles and kisses her once more, briefly freeing her hands and permitting her to hold him before gently unwinding her arms from around him and tying her cuffs to the ends of her headboard.

Meredith expects him to leave her legs free, but instead he cuffs her ankles and secures them to the legs at the base of her bed. In her mind's eye she sees herself, how open and helpless she is. She tests the bonds cautiously. There seems, as usual, to be no way out except with William's assistance.

His face radiates an incongruously innocent delight as he shows her the selection of make-up brushes. That is definitely interesting, she has very fond memories of the way he used one—so fond, in fact, that she feels her nipples stiffen before he has even touched her.

"Close your eyes," he murmurs.

She looks at him quizzically. "No blindfold?"

"It's different. Try."

His smile is reassurance enough; he's never led her wrong. With an answering smile of anticipation, she takes a last look at her lover and closes her eyes.

She would never have believed it if she weren't experiencing it. Her body responds to the soft bristles slowly, but his patience and skill steadily feed her senses. He doesn't approach any of the obvious focus points for what seems an age. At last, when he does, he hears her breath quicken, sees her bite her lip. He slowly draws one large, soft brush along each of her outer labia. She thrusts her hips up as far as her bonds allow.

"You like?" he asks, knowing the answer, but loving her purred reply all the same. He takes her close, lets her breathing deepen ...

then pauses and eases away, delighting in her mewls of expectation and disappointment.

He repeats the cycle. When she fears he will deny her again, he whispers, "Look."

She opens her eyes. William is holding up the glass toy. It catches the light. If it's as nice as the steel one, Meredith muses, then ... "Ow! Fuck!" She strains against her bonds. The glass is *freezing*!

He immediately pulls the chilled toy away. "Don't you like it?" he asks, all innocence.

"No, I bloody don't!"

"Too cold?"

"Any cold is too cold, you bastard!" Cold isn't something they've discussed, but she HATES cold.

"Oh. Some people like it." His voice is disappointed. "Sorry."

Meredith isn't quite sure how sorry he is. "Well, I'm not one of them!"

William can't help it—he laughs as he puts the pretty glass toy into the bowl of warm water he'd prepared in case. "Do you want me to untie you?"

She may have lost the moment, but it doesn't take her long to decide that she wants to find it again. "No. I want you to do it properly."

Her disappointment at her lost release has a greater effect on him than her shock. Lying down next to her, he holds her, touches her, but it doesn't get her body responding. He tries using one of the brushes—nothing. He trails kisses down her ribs to no effect.

He hums in frustration and props himself up on an elbow. "I don't know what to try next: tickling or ice cubes?"

His suggestion and his grin are so outrageous that she can't help laughing. She responds with a barrage of obscenities. The outburst breaks through her reserve, and when he kisses her, she feels the familiar warmth flowing through her.

Again he takes his time. Again she floats to the edge but not quite over it—once, twice. Then, when he slides the now warm glass inside her, her release is explosive. Her cries are animalistic as she strains against her bonds until she can bear no more. Only then does he free her, cover her with the duvet, and hold her.

Her breathing returns to normal, and William's touch starts to indicate his own desires. "Perhaps I should let you get close, then put an ice cube on your neck," she threatens.

He might feel bad about the cold, but he's not prepared to let her turn the tables on him. Looking her steadily in the eye, he takes hold of a nipple and pinches lightly, but with steel in his gaze.

"You wouldn't dare!" Her voice says the words before her brain can assure her that he would. Sure enough—"Ow! Bastard! OK!" *Not pineapple*, she notes. *Fuck, why does it hurt but feel so good at the same time?* Heat flows through her again, and in moments, it isn't just his gaze that's going deep inside her.

Lying with him in serenity, Meredith laughs, drawing an enquiring look from William. "I was just thinking how glad I am—"

"—that I warmed that little glass toy, or that I guessed 'Ow, fuck', when spoken in that tone, meant *pineapple*?"

"No! Well, yes, but I was thinking how glad I am that Mrs Godleman is as deaf as a post." And they laugh together.

★★★

They walk on Sunday morning, both glad of the bright spring sun. They catch up with each other's weeks. William's project is proceeding "satisfactorily", he says in his inscrutable way, though the workload is heavy. Meredith tells him about her concerns that her team is falling behind.

"If you're getting snowed under, you either need to be more productive or get more manpower," William opines.

Meredith isn't impressed. "That's not very helpful, you know."

William lets the conversation lapse. After a while, he asks, "Let me guess—you're counting the days rather than the things you've achieved right now?"

"What?" She thinks, *Damn, that's true. How the hell did he know?* She asks the question aloud, and he gives her a gentle nudge and a wink.

He thinks, *Page one of cod psychology: when stress and work levels reach the point at which something has to be done. Been there too many times and seen it too many more.* Out loud, he says, "Watching and listening."

They continue to chat as they walk, and William realises that work pressures really are building up on Meredith. "Would you like to sit down and go through things when we get back?" This is, after all, the sort of thing he does for a living.

If it weren't for the times he's been helpful and his way of not forcing his ideas, she'd never have agreed, but then he adds, "And I won't even video it ..." His lopsided smile makes her laugh, as it always does.

She laughs, "Why not?" and feels a lessening of the weight on her shoulders.

★★★

"What you need to do is identify anything that can be automated and anything that doesn't need as much skill as you have. If there's anything that doesn't either make you more productive or generate a profit, it's disposable, so list that too." He sips his coffee. "You'll be left with everything that can't be speeded up or offloaded. If there's still more than you can manage, then you need more staff.

"It's worth talking to your colleague and your other team too. Don't take everything on yourself when you don't have to." His face assumes one of his cunning looks. "And the more other people are involved, the less work you have to do and the more supportive they'll be."

"You are so sneaky!" She bats at him at him.

He shrugs and grins shamelessly."Hey, I didn't make the world—"

She laughs and joins in with his "I just live in it."

They talk for an hour or more. Mostly William asks questions, listens, and clatters away on his laptop.

"Thanks. You always give such good advice, even if you are sneaky. How did you learn all this?" Meredith feels better for having talked through her concerns, and hopeful that they have come up with some ways of tackling them.

William actually blushes. Meredith doesn't think she's seen him do that before. "Mostly what I know I learnt one mistake at a time. Beyond that, I get people to tell me or show me what they do. This—" he points at the screen of his laptop "—is mostly what you already knew. I've just asked you about it and written it down."

He saves the document and sends it to her personal email. "Back to the weekend?" he asks with a grin, changing as suddenly as the English weather back into her playful lover.

"God, yes!" she exclaims, glad of the clarity their efforts have given her, but even more glad to put those efforts aside.

★★★

When she gets in on Monday, Meredith waits for Emily and they take the notes she and William have made to John. He first looks at the women appraisingly, and then appears to come to a resolution. He suggests the three of them raise the ideas in the staff meeting.

So much of the Monday meeting is spent discussing Meredith and Emily's workload and that of John's team, and floating ideas for managing them. Thanks to their preparation, Meredith and Emily aren't just presenting a problem but also ideas for addressing it. To their relief and surprise, John has more thoughts and some measures.

Mr Rossi doesn't immediately agree to anything, but he receives their input positively. Anders, the technical manager, is more supportive still.

As Meredith suspected, solving the problem feels like even more work in the short term, but she's glad to find her colleagues eager to help, but that several have additional ideas.

Adding in preparation for the next proposal and service for their existing clients, the to-do lists are even longer, but Meredith now sees not just the mountains in front of her, but the beginnings of a path through them.

25

Shopping with Jess

Illiam remembers his promise. The offer to go clothes shopping seemed natural and generous on the phone, when he was going through papers with half his mind. Now that he's due to do it, the idea seems less appealing. Women are lovely, and women's clothes are lovely; however, experience has taught him that such loveliness palls for him relatively quickly, and that recriminations for his opinion on any garment can spoil a whole day.

Eager not to let Meredith down, he tries to do the next best thing.

Jess doesn't like to be indebted to anyone. Having begged a favour of William, she owes him. Not knowing him at all well makes it worse. So, when she sees William's name on the screen as her mobile rings, she answers with mixed feelings. "Jess Parfit."

"Hi, William here — Meredith's one."

"Hi, William," she replies, wondering what he wants, but glad his tone is light, and that he's referred to Meredith.

"I hope this isn't an inconvenient time. Only I've got a small favour to beg."

Here it comes, she thinks. "What do you need?"

"Well, I'm seeing Meredith at the weekend, and I was going to take her shopping for something that fits nicely for work. But I'm not really all that up on women's clothes, and I think you'd be much better at helping her choose."

She wonders what the catch is. "Is this the favour I owe you?"

"If you put it like that, yes. Meredith's got presentations coming up, and most of her office clothes are a bit loose on her. I'd be awfully grateful, and I know she'd trust you and take your advice."

Perhaps he isn't the shrewd negotiator she thought? "Sure, I'll try, but I can't promise. Meredith's not as fond of clothes shopping as some women." Meredith isn't, but Jess certainly is. She's also fond of Meredith, and would have done this without him asking.

William has a long-held the view that whenever possible, getting people to do things they don't mind doing is a good idea. It makes for better long-term relations. The favour she asked wasn't exactly onerous— it's not as if he minds going out for the evening with his friends (except when his hangover is at its freshest).

★★★

Meredith is glad when Jess calls to suggest meeting up again. "What are we going to do? Are you coming over to mine?"

The demands of work and family have shifted, given she is spending so much time with William. Meredith had felt in danger of letting her most enduring relationship wither, and now she's glad they're back to getting together regularly again. She knows Jess can be a bit, "boy blind" herself and drop out of circulation during honeymoon periods, but Meredith isn't that kind of girl.

"I'm taking you shopping."

"What? Why?"

"We're going to see how you're doing on our bet." It's politer than William's "her clothes are loose" comment, bless him, and easier to wheedle her friend around with. "And I've got to get a frock, so we can kill two birds with one stone." It's not as if there's any doubt she'll wind up seeing something she likes.

Meredith has been very conscientious about some aspects of her new regime, such as the food, and somewhat conscientious about others, but she's been shy of climbing on the scales. "Do we have to? It's not Easter yet!"

"Yes, we do. I may have made the bet with you, but I really don't want to win it. If you aren't getting close, I'm going to start taking you swimming."

This is a big sacrifice for Jess; she hates wearing a swimming cap or damaging her thick, shiny mane with pool chemicals. Meredith finds the gesture touching. But she doesn't normally like going shopping with her friend because it usually turns into the Jess show. Jess is better off and looks good in anything. "Can't we just wait a bit longer?"

"No. The two of us haven't gone out and done anything girlie together in too long. I can't take you out and get you properly sloshed without feeling guilty about it till you fit into a size twelve." Jess wants to be supportive, but she also wants her partner in crime back.

Meredith thinks about it, but not for too long. It would be nice to do that, and, yes, she's been more stay at home-y since she met William. He's told her that she needs to take the odd meal or day off her routine to stay focused, and so has Jess. "Okay, then, where shall we go?"

They plan the evening loosely. She'll pick Jess up from the station and they'll go to the shopping centre, followed by dinner at a Vietnamese restaurant. The food will be light enough not to break too many rules, and spicy and different enough to feel like a treat. The restaurant is close enough to Meredith's house that they can park at home and grab an Uber there and back.

As far as Meredith's work goes, positive responses from management haven't brought any major results yet, but they have made her feel better. The experience has not only made her more impressed by William, but also by herself and her colleagues. Even Mr Rossi (*Marco, Marco—must remember to call him Marco*) has been supportive of "his guys". Now she has the evening with her best friend (even if she thinks it will end up with her not having lost a dress size and Jess dragging her around twelve boutique shops) and a long weekend with her lover to look forward to. What more could she want?

★★★

The first store they visit is more expensive and more fashionable than anywhere Meredith has ever shopped for herself. She hopes Jess is getting ideas or just plain teasing, because many of the dresses are so skimpy she can't even imagine her friend wearing them, let alone herself. She does admit, when Jess prompts her, that the materials feel amazing, and she wonders if that's part of the trick. Do Jess and William put their confidence on with their immaculate wardrobes?

Jess gets Meredith to look at several garments. She tries one dress on herself. It clings to her curves, its beading catching the light. Meredith thinks, *Wow*. Looking at the assistant, she guesses that's what she's thinking too. Meredith would give her eye teeth to look like Jess.

Jess beams. "How does this look, Merry?" Surely she knows?

"Unbelievable" is all she can think of to say. Her friend normally looks incredible, but this dress could have been designed for her.

Jess changes back and returns the dress to the disappointed assistant, saying she has to look around.

The next shop is still more fashionable than anywhere Meredith would normally look in, but by comparison with the first, she feels far more at home. At least most of the clothes cost less than a week's wages, and only a few of them are see-through! Jess picks out a stylish A-line dress in blue, then tuts and switches it for red. She holds it in front of herself and then in front of Meredith. "Bingo. Hold this, Merry."

Meredith looks at the dress and then at Jess. She worries that the red will match her blushing and make her look like a tomato, whereas she thinks the colour makes her friend's darker complexion glow.

"It sets off your hair," Jess assures her. "You're lucky enough to be a natural blonde, and it'll show off your bust without making you look tarty." Jess laughs at the idea; Meredith is the least tarty person she knows.

When Meredith still hesitates, Jess says, "Come on, Merry, we'll both try it on." Because Meredith isn't good at saying no to Jess, she agrees, even though she's sure the dress will still be too small for her.

They change in adjoining cubicles. Much to her surprise, the dress does fit. It fits noticeably better than the one she wore to work today. *OMG*, she thinks, *I'm a twelve*! It even looks cute—she never thinks of herself as looking cute.

She's still smiling when she emerges, to find Jess looking predictably stunning. Jess's face lights up when she sees her. "Merry, it looks great on you!" They look at themselves side by side in the large mirror outside the changing rooms. "We could almost wear them together."

Jess is rights. The size difference and their contrasting body shapes make their dresses look like separate designs. "It's nice, but I wish I had your figure," Meredith says.

"And I wish I had your boobs," Jess retorts with a laugh.

"Really?" Meredith always thinks she's being teased when Jess says how much she envies her cleavage.

"Yes, Merry, you'd be surprised how many women would kill for your breasts," Jess says straight-faced. Meredith looks for some hint of insincerity in her friend's eyes but finds none. Jess's face tells her she's not just saying kind things because they're friends.

They walk out of a third shop in moments, and Jess leads her past several more, dismissing their merchandise as too cheaply made or too old. Meredith's limited shopping tolerance is starting to wear thin.

In the next store Jess considers worthy, Meredith sees a familiar sight. There's a skirt suit and blouse combination that remind her of the things William bought her that first night. She stops to take a look while Jess walks on. They have the suit in charcoal, navy, and black, as well as the chocolate colour of the skirt she has.

When Jess returns bearing a cotton shirtdress, she finds Meredith comparing the colours. "Definitely the charcoal," Jess opines. "And this in navy."

Meredith takes the dress, the suit, and a white blouse that Jess picks out into the changing rooms. The dress, with its white detailing, is tailored and elegant. She wouldn't have considered trying it on an hour ago, let alone a couple of months, but once again Jess is right. It's size twelve, it fits, and when she looks at the price label, it isn't too expensive. Changing into it, Meredith imagines that William will find unbuttoning it all the way down irresistible. She does it up high so she can wear it respectably for work or days out as well as for her deliciously lecherous boyfriend.

Jess approves and encourages her to get the suit and blouse too. "You need to look the part, and in this you do." She then badgers Meredith into a new set of underwear, saying, "If you get these, I'll buy you the red dress for our bet."

The clothes are nice, and Jess is right, she does need some new things. So they head back to the earlier shop. Meredith is laden with bags and Jess is very pleased with herself. Jess negotiates a small discount on the two red dresses. Meredith is ready to depart, but Jess continues on to the first store and the first dress she tried on. "I've been looking at this for weeks," she confides as she parts with an eye-watering sum.

"Thanks, I enjoyed it. And thank you for my lovely dress," Meredith says on the way back to the car. "We haven't been shopping together in ages."

"Well, you weren't interested for ages," Jess replies. "It's like getting my friend back from school and uni. I've missed her ... I mean, you're cool and all, but you're cooler Merry." smiling.

★★★

Meredith enjoys her first experience of Vietnamese food. The flavours are very pleasant, even if they're lighter than she expects as a lover of Thai cuisine. Nevertheless, she apologises in case the tidy little restaurant isn't up to the London standard Jess is used to.

Jess assures her that the food is good and advises her to eat there regularly, because sooner or later their chef will get nabbed.

They chat away. One bottle of wine turns into two, and as they're getting an Uber, that's okay. "You could do personal shopping, you know."

Jess waves Meredith's compliment away. "It's easy. Everyone likes to play dressing-up games with a pretty girl as their doll."

"Not everyone. There are a lot of gay men."

Jess laughs so loudly she almost spits her wine out. "Oh, Merry, especially them—why do you think so many of them work in fashion?"

26

Friday Off—And a Country Walk

illiam arrives after lunch. They each had family obligations and chores to attend to first. It has given Meredith time to see her mum, who is still having a hard time coping with Roley. Her mum thinks the puppy needs training, while Meredith is strongly of the view that it isn't just the puppy. She loves her mother, but the woman's dog manner leaves a lot to be desired. She'd taken details of courses and trainers with her in the hope of helping. She also hope to quell her growing fear that her ageing mum will find herself being dragged through the park at the end of the young enthusiast's leash.

"Hey, why don't we go to that forestry commission site near here?" William proposes.

It's a couple of miles from her house, so Meredith bargains. "Do you want to go there on foot and take a short walk, or drive there and take a long one?" She boosts her case with her most winsome look.

He doesn't let her know whether it's common sense or her charm that wins. But he agrees, volunteering to drive. On the way they pass a farm shop. William asks what it's like.

"They do the best sausages in the world."

"In the *whole* world?"

"Yes. Even my mum agrees." And that appears to be the end of the matter as far as she's concerned.

They've gone for several walks and she's starting to enjoy them. He calls it exercising without exercising. Meredith isn't so sure about that, but she likes the time together and the feeling of intimacy without sex. She's never really felt this closeness with a previous boyfriend. Initially she found the walks hard going, partly due to her unfitness and partly due to her footwear. She's let William talk her into purchasing a pair of light, modern walking boots. With practice, and the benefit of her daily exercise routine, she's begun to get the hang of them.

The days lengthening and the ground getting firmer help too. They are into March now. The first wild flowers are blooming, and birds are starting their courtships. Meredith feels sense of a kinship towards them as she and William amble along. "It's nice coming for a walk. I sometimes think we just—"

"And going for a walk would preclude?" His grim features transform as she has seen them do so often: first the corner of his mouth, then his eyes. The humour is as infectious as always, and the lascivious nature of his expression becomes increasingly unmistakeable.

Meredith laughs. "No one else believes you're such an animal, do they?"

"Whereas you ..." He raises an eyebrow.

"You're the one hinting at alfresco sex."

"No, I'm just the one suggesting that I'm game if you are." There's a definite challenge in his eyes.

"I most certainly am not!"

But something in her eyes must suggest that she might be persuadable—he begins to unbuckle his belt.

"It's an even bigger no if you're proposing to spank me with that in public!" She backs away but can't help smiling. Why is he so naughty? And why does she love that so much?

"Whoever said anything about spanking?" He finishes pulling the belt from his jeans. "That would be too noisy and much too difficult to explain."

She sees that the belt has holes punched along the entirety of its length, and soon finds out why. He snares her wrists and tightens the loop. His face is all smiles. She still trusts him, though if anyone had tried this with her a few weeks ago, she would have screamed.

He tightens the loop still further and secures it with the buckle. It doesn't hurt, but there's no way she can break free."Hey!" Meredith is uncertain whether this is still a joke, though the restriction of her limbs is familiar and not at all unpleasant.

He holds her in a strong but gentle embrace. With one hand he uses the long, loose section of the belt like a lead to pull her hands first one way, then the other. He kisses her below her ear before whispering, "It's okay if *no* means *pineapple.*"

Meredith takes time to answer. It feels good being held like this. but it's broad daylight and it's outside, and there might be people coming past. A part of her wants to do this, but there's no way she'll be comfortable. She doesn't want to disappoint William, but ... "I think it does mean *pineapple.*" Even before the word is fully out of her mouth, he's unbinding her wrists. "Sorry," she says without looking into his face.

"Hey! There's nothing to be sorry for." William hugs her close and fiercely. "I'm pleased and proud of you." He kisses her forehead.

"But I thought ..."

"Listen, we can't do some things if you won't say 'enough' or 'not that'. I can't be certain to spot the difference between 'make me' and 'don't make me' every time, so you have to help."

"But I don't want to lose you."

"You won't lose me by telling me what you think and feel. And if you feel or think you're not comfortable with something, I value you telling me." He coils the belt around his hand and slips it into a pocket in his fleece then gently places his hands on her arms. "Promise me you'll say no when you need to."

Meredith mumbles a yes without looking up.

"Now say it looking at me."

She looks up and repeats, "Yes," a little louder. There are the beginnings of tears in her eyes. He dabs them with a cotton handkerchief that appears in his hand. He kisses her, then takes her hand and leads her further through the woods.

She feels foolish and more emotional than she understands why, but she promises again as they go. He slips his arm around her shoulders. However, tenderness doesn't stop him entirely. The next time they pass a quiet-looking glade, he nudges her shoulder, nods at it, and winks conspiratorially.

"You really would, wouldn't you?"

"I refuse to answer on the grounds that it would incriminate me." And he laughs once more, though he doesn't make any further move to persuade her.

On their way back, they drop into the farm shop to get some of the fabled sausages. He takes the opportunity to buy other things as well—onions and parsnips for a casserole. Meredith suggests a roast dinner. This results in more purchases and a rejig of the shopping. Meredith pays for the things for dinner and for her fridge and freezer. William pays for the things he wishes to take home. William suspects their antics are the cause of some amusement to the older woman at the till, and mentions it to Meredith on the way out.

"What makes you say that?"

"Her face went from a 'gooey over young love' look to 'what the fuck' when we split the shopping into two lots." He can't help laughing.

Meredith plays his words over. It's the first time she's heard him say *love* in that sense.

They cook a casserole of chicken thighs and farm shop sausages. They also roast a whole bird, combining preparation for the two. By the time they sit for dinner, Meredith feels exceedingly virtuous, despite the sweet roast parsnips and juicy chipolatas accompanying her virtuous chicken and steamed vegetables.

When they get upstairs, Meredith is initially disappointed to find that he doesn't demonstrate some new excitement. Still, she's fulfilled by the old-fashioned kind.

27

Meredith Goes Shopping

On Saturday, unusually, Meredith is awake before William. She lies in the toasty warmth of her bed, her mind getting itself together, her body reliving the day and the night before. The echoes of their passion are unbidden but most welcome. Nerve memories spark lazily through her. She thinks she ought to put coffee on, but it's so warm.

Instead she looks across at him. One arm and shoulder stolen from a Michelangelo outside the covers. The sparks grow in intensity, and the corners of her mouth turn up. Who would have thought? So handsome, so civilised, but such a bad man. She stifles a chuckle, not wanting to wake him, then reaches out, almost touching him, but refrains. Once again she doesn't break this silent moment.

Eventually, he stirs before she tires of watching him, and she slides towards him, kisses his shoulder, slips her arm around his hip. She clasps the stiffness she knows she will find there, strokes its silky outside gently as it has stroked her insides so often. She delights in the softness of the skin in contrast to the hardness of the shaft. "Shall I make coffee?" she asks, open to the idea, but warming to other thoughts.

"Mmm, if you want to" comes the sleepy reply. But a strong hand reaches behind him to caress her thigh. His muscular haunches press into her hips.

She kisses and then bites his shoulder. "Hey!" he exclaims. His stroking hand delivers a sharp slap and he turns, flipping her easily onto her back.

She relishes the sense of powerlessness."Is that a no thank you?" She giggles, playfully struggling, forcing him to press her down more firmly.

He easily manoeuvres both of her wrists into one hand, but doesn't speak. He has that boyish look though. She makes a pretence of resistance as he presses his legs between her own. She spreads further and presses her hips up in invitation. She wonders at the way such a stern man can turn that exuberance on, and at how both sides of him play chords inside her body.

He positions himself at her entrance. Despite finding her already receptive, he teases her with the shallowest penetration, sliding just the head of his cock in and out. She makes to bite him again, but he's too quick and she's held too firmly. The mischief in his eyes matches that she feels in her heart. His free hand teases her breasts as he continues his slow rocking. He takes gentle hold of a nipple and asks between smiling lips, "What do you want?"

Meredith struggles more forcefully but just as helplessly. "Fuck me, you arse!" she snaps. His fingers tighten in response, causing her a mixture of pleasure and pain. "Ow!"

"Pardon? I didn't quite hear that." His fingers pull and squeeze.

The pitch of her voice rises. "I said fuck me!"

"Um, fuck me who?" The tension and pressure edge higher. The pain radiating through her breast begins to overwhelm the pleasure.

"Ow! Fuck me, sir!" The pressure and tension ease, and he enters her fully. "Bastard!" she whispers, and he laughs.

He kisses her. "Only so long as you want me to be."

She's not sure she does want it, but her body does. His hips build a rhythm, and his skilled fingers work to ease the pain they have so recently caused.

She's surprised and delighted that he simply takes her for a change, no drawn-out teasing. He wants and needs, and she is more than happy to let his need fulfil her own.

As usual he is the first to rouse afterwards. Kissing her, he mutters, "I suppose I'll have to go and make that coffee you promised me."

Feigning being hard done by, he pinches a nipple lightly before leaping out of bed. She admires his retreating bum as he heads towards the kitchen.

She stretches languidly, using the extra warmth of the patch he has just vacated. She inhales his scent from the pillows and enjoys the touch of the sheets on her skin. She doesn't sleep naked except when she is with him, but his body heat and the additional closeness ... The downside is that getting out of bed seems less appealing.

After a few minutes, she makes the effort anyway. She grabs a robe and follows him—and the smell of fresh coffee—to the kitchen.

"We'll be able to get most of what we need at one of the warehouse sports shops in the retail park," he says over breakfast. This reminds her of their plan to get her fitness wear and exercise kit of her own. Today is another day of brave new Meredith. She isn't escaping the New Year's resolutions that in prior years have melted away in shameful embarrassment by now.

"Shall we eat lunch out?" he continues. "It's a beautiful day." She's only too happy to agree and get out of the washing up. She loves his cooking, but is not overly enamoured of his talent for using every utensil in the kitchen to produce his marvels.

Meredith takes the unseasonably good weather as a perfect excuse to wear one of her new dresses. She's certain he'll like the tailored shirt dress, *Size twelve*, she proudly thinks, with its button front and loose skirt. The navy is striking against the blonde of her hair.

She's duly pleased with his reaction when she finds him in her living room. She happily twirls for him while he admires her curves and kisses her appreciatively, as he releases her from his embrace he says, "Turn around and bend over the table for me, please."

Meredith laughs. "Is the dress that good?"

"Yes, but this is for something else." Devilment dances in his eyes. "You wanted to not miss out on excitement ..."

She tries a knowing look. It just makes him smoulder back in that way of his that sets her wanting to play and before long she feels heat rising inside her, so she steps to the table, turns to face it, and bends, conscious that they have played here before as she does.

He lifts her skirt high, fully exposing her underwear. Taking hold of the waistband, he lowers her panties and lets them fall around her ankles. "Step out of them and spread your legs, please."

"I thought we were going shopping?" She does as he asks, thinking *It's going to be one of those mornings* and *This is more fun than shopping for fitness stuff* and *Yes! The dress is definitely a hit!*

He laughs. "They don't open till ten, and you're not quite ready for the trip yet, young lady."

She isn't quite sure what he means, but she doesn't think to stop and question him. At that moment he enters her. She wonders that she is so easily ready for him.

Taking his time, William reaches around to use his fingers on her while kissing and nibbling the back of her neck. Meredith allows herself to drift with the building pleasure. He takes her close and then back again, increasing and then slowing the rhythm of his hands and his hips. She knows he knows—knows how to tease and how to please. She trusts in her own knowledge that he is not in the habit of leaving her disappointed.

But this morning, that is just what he does. He withdraws from her and removes his magical digits, causing her to protest and seek to rise.

"Not so fast, young lady," he says. The strength of his hand on her back holds her in place. She feels something smooth against her vulva, feels him press it into her, feels her body close around it. He gently tugs it.

"Hey, what's—"

It buzzes into life.

"Oh!" The vibration against her G-spot returns her to the edge.

"Now you may put your feet back together."

As she does, he slips her panties back over her feet and pulls them up her legs, taking the time to caress her thighs. He settles them over the device's protruding tail.

Finally he lowers and smoothes the dress's skirt, "Stand and turn to face me." He hasn't made a move to spank her offered bum through the entire process.

Meredith, to her embarrassment thinks this, and to her surprise finds herself wondering whether she is happy or sad that he hasn't.

"Now you're ready."

They take his car and he doesn't waste the opportunity to play with the remote control device whenever they stop at lights or a junction. He changes speed and pattern, keeping her heated but not allowing her to tip over, cheerily makes small talk all the way, as though nothing else is happening.

By the time they reach the retail park, she's almost at wit's end. He doesn't take pity on her. Silencing the tormenting device as the car comes to a halt, he leans across to kiss her briefly. She allows him to, even leans in towards him as he does so, but whispers, "I hate you." And it is only half in jest.

He ignores her words, cheerily hops out of the car, and bounces around to open the passenger's side door. He hurries her along while she, in contrast, is slowly seeking to gather herself.

"We really should pick up some things..." He emphasises *the word things* in a way that leaves no doubt as to what they will be for.

She agrees, though with some trepidation.

"I have to pick up some other bits. I've made a list of what you need to look for," he announces as they walk into a sports shop. He presents her with the folded list and a basket, then turns away. She feels the egg inside her come to life. If she weren't already off balance, she would have refused right there.

Instead, she unfolds the list. She can't believe her eyes. He's instructed her to shop for a table tennis bat, lead ropes, a pair of ankle straps, a riding crop, and a dressage whip. The thought of buying this last item fills her with dread; she has never been under one but has seen and heard those he owns. The whistling sound his make as their long thin shafts pass through the air is enough for her. And she has to arrange for an exercise bench to be delivered— all while a remote-controlled egg buzzes away inside her.

The place is huge, like a warehouse. Meredith can't believe he's sent her in alone without any idea what some of these things look like or where to find them. She has no idea even how to arrange home delivery. She looks around at his receding back, and freezes. She is sure that she can hear the egg buzzing away, and that everyone else must be able to hear it too.

The sound of her phone chiming — once, twice, three times — breaks the spell. Grateful for the distraction, she takes it out and inspects it. They are messages from him.

Trust yourself. I trust you and now you must. X.

Again he's inside her head, he seems to climb into her mind at will! Jesus, he could mess with her so badly if he wanted and she worries she would have no defence against it. She's certain he could reduce her to a wreck; at times she has been sure he was about to do so, but he always somehow left her feeling safe, with him beside her, atop whatever precipice she had feared and faced.

Ankle straps, cable attachments, back right. Lead ropes and whips, equestrian upstairs.

This message is accompanied by sample pictures of the items. The third message gives the part number for the bench, with instructions to order it last, and not to have the other items delivered.

As Meredith makes her way to the back of the cavernous store, she catches sight of her reflection and is reminded again of how she's changing. The woman in the mirror is slimmer and stands taller, even though a part of her wants the floor to swallow her up. The mirror also confirms her earlier opinion that the navy shirtdress suits her to a tee.

She finds a large display of metal bars, rope hoops, plastic and metal handles, and there; a selection of sturdy leather and nylon bands with D-ring attachments. She's struck by how many different ones there are. *Do so many people spend their time in the gym?* asks one voice inside her. Another counters with *Or tied up?*

For a moment she considers asking him which ones to buy, but dismisses the notion. She examines the options, rejecting one leather pair as too loose and another for their hard edges. She settles on the most attractive of the nylon variety. Despite liking the pink and purple, she settles on a black pair as somehow more fitting. She has to reach up to take them from their high peg. As she does, the still-buzzing egg moves inside her, causing an unwanted thrill.

There is no instruction concerning the table tennis bat, but there is a large table set out in plain view. Walking to it, she finds an even more bewildering choice. There are hard plastic outdoor bats, thin and flimsy ones, and thick, padded ones. She considers messaging him. The thought that his most likely reply is *It's your bottom* prevents her. Bad enough that she knows what these things are for, without further reminder. Instead, she touches each in turn.

She dismisses the outdoor bats with their hard textures, embossed makers' names, and plain plastic handles. She passes over the padded ones somewhat more ruefully. The pimpled variety feel flimsy to the touch, though she can imagine their impact. kneeling close to the floor and finding the device inside her shifting once more, and doing so in a way that its movement forces her to stop and gather herself, she finally selects one with a nicely shaped handle; a lightly padded, smooth side; and pimples on the other.

She realises as she puts it in her basket with the cuffs that the movement and tasks are combining with the egg to affect her. She walks up a flight of stairs, and this brings an entirely new set of sensations. Her body has no way to escape the internal stimulation at each step upwards and, halfway into the climb, the vibrations increase, forcing her to stop. Meredith clasps the handrail and almost drops her basket before their strength fades again. She looks around, cheeks suddenly flushed, expecting to see his knowing smile and fearing to see someone else looking at her with curious eyes.

She reaches the safety—*ha*—of the mezzanine. Following his directions, she quickly locates the equestrian section. Shy of the whips, she selects the lead ropes first, surprised by their softness and how thick they are. She's grateful that she has to neither bend nor stretch to take them from their peg. Next she puts her laden basket down while she looks at the whips. *These are meant to be used on horses, and here I am, fighting my own arousal and actually contemplating buying them to be used on myself.*

Contemplating the selection she's already Meredith feels certain it would be impossible for anyone to look at them and not know *exactly* what's up. Her face heats despite the coolness of the store.

As she stands before the display of horse whips, her basket and its guilty contents at her feet she has a sense that she's being led along a dark and dangerous downwards path, never able to see what is around the next corner, never able to quite refuse the tug of curiosity that draws her on despite her misgivings. Yet with each turn, her sureness in the rest of her life has grown. With each descent, her confidence in the face of the unknown has burgeoned. Her body has rewarded each submission. She stands mortified, listening to the barely audible buzzing inside her as though it were a fire alarm and her responses war within her.

She almost rebels. Almost. How many times has she *almost* said no, *almost* run, *almost* cried out *pineapple*? And how many times has she cried out in pleasure not long after?

Meredith jumps as a strong hand touches her arm. "You're doing well." His bass whisper brings her down from the ceiling, glad that she only *almost* screamed. She looks around for relief from her solo mission, but he's already moving away.

Returning her focus to the task at hand she decides the crops feel less intimidating than the long whips. She's familiar with his collection and doesn't wish to disappoint, but also does not wish to leap too far. She touches the handles, shafts, and slappers of several. The soft leather of one particular crop. She recalls his fondness for stroking her body and thrills internally. Taking it from its hook, she flexes it and finds it neither foolishly flexible nor too scarily stiff. Before she has time to second-guess herself, she resolves that this is the one for her and places it in the basket.

As she bends to do so, she gets two surprises: her arousal has risen further, and bending almost causes her to lose control.

Unlike the items already there, there is no way the crop will fit entirely inside the basket. Looking up, Meredith realises that the dressage whip will stick out still further. She reaches toward the shortest one that looks nicely made and is struck by her hand's reluctance to pick it up. Taking a calming breath she overrules it and takes up the whip with an effort of will, swiftly placing it beside the crop before heading back to the stairs. Again her thoughts intrude: *I'm choosing items to be spanked with. He's so devilish! I want to please him, but oh, how it feels!*

Going down the stairs is no easier than climbing them. She is now desperately aware both of her ongoing arousal and of the fact that she is walking around with two whips. She distracts herself by looking around for the customer service desk, seeing it she's pleased to see that the clerk on duty is a girl.

Once back on the ground floor and aiming to finish and escape as soon as possible, she takes a long stride, but the movement inside her quickly persuades her to revert to smaller steps. William is at play again, and the pattern of vibration changes. Trying to make her way nonchalantly and in a straight line, Meredith walks towards her destination.

The clerk is perhaps eighteen or nineteen, and looks the type to have a genuine interest in sports. She's sorting through a pile of small items as Meredith arrives and takes a moment to greet her new customer. Meredith doesn't mind and takes that time to gather herself.

Finally she looks up and smiles apologetically. "Hi, can I help you?"

"Er, yes. I'd like to order an exercise bench," Meredith replies. "I have the part number if that makes it easier?"

"Certainly. Would you like to pay for the rest of your shopping at the same time?"

Meredith who had put the basket on the floor, out of sight picks it up and places it on the counter while trying not to make eye contact. "Thanks," she says, trying to look anywhere but into the helpful girl's eyes. The motion inside her grows stronger again. she consciously controls her breathing and silently vows to kill William—but not until after she has cum.

"You have quite an assortment!" exclaims the clerk.

Meredith's eyes immediately flick to her in alarm and guilt, but there's no hint of knowingness in her youthful face."Yes, I've started getting in shape, and I'm trying a variety of things," she explains.

"I love horses. Have you been riding long?"

Meredith knows nothing about horses or riding, despite having several items from the equestrian section in her shopping. For an awful moment imagines herself trying to blag it and eventually humiliating herself by blurting out the true purpose of the items she is purchasing. Without quite thinking consciously she says, "No, I've just started, but you're right, they are wonderful creatures." She's grateful that her mouth has come to her rescue rather than digging a deeper hole for a change.

"I'm afraid I haven't any large bags here. I'll just go and fetch one," says the girl, and she moves to the other end of the counter.

Meredith focuses on breathing. She feels the patterns inside her change once more, building to a peak and then pausing. Images of herself dissolving in a blissful orgasm mix with thoughts of hitting William as hard as she can.

The clerk returns with a bag large enough that only the business ends of the two whips will protrude. Meredith thanks her and is relieved as the vibrations fade away to a more bearable level.

She sets off to find William. He's at the main tills, seemingly oblivious to all she's been through as he pays for the fruits of his own expedition. She joins him, interested to see what he's selected.

He turns as she approaches, always so aware, and kisses her. The boy scans William's items: sports bras, knickers, leggings, tops, and sets of dumbbells and exercise bands. In her heightened state, Meredith feels an urge to crush herself against William, but resists it. She sees the total of what he's spent and determines to insist on paying.

He offers his arm as they depart. "You were marvellous," he says. "We'll drive to the main shopping centre to get the rest and then eat, shall we?"

"I need to go somewhere to clean myself up before I sit anywhere," she protests in a whisper.

He feigns innocence. "Why, what's wrong?"

She glares at him. His games may be exciting, but she's not backing down on this. "You've been driving me crazy for an age, you bastard. I am not soaking this dress and then walking around!"

He laughs and gets another dagger stare in response, "Oh, okay. There's a coffee shop here. I'll get espressos while you freshen up."

As they approach the shop, he adds, "On the condition that you taste yourself while you do."

Her eyes tighten in annoyance as she looks at him. The vibrations becoming more intense again as he smiles his devil smile.

"Okay!" She surrenders, exasperated, and the vibrations recede. She leans towards him and whispers, "But when we get home, I'm going to ravish you and then I'm going to kill you."

There are plenty of tables free in the coffee shop. He selects one with comfortable chairs in the front corner and places his bags down. Without asking him, she put her own bag down and picks up the one of his with the sports underwear in it. William's face turns quizzical, but a defiant glint in her eyes cuts off any further response. He heads to the counter, and the vibrations cease.

Once inside the rest room, Meredith looks into the mirror. She tries to process the events of the day. While it's true that she is unbelievably turned on and felt a thrill of triumph as she escaped from the sports store, with her prizes she was and is far outside her comfort zone. The fact that he put this thing into her without even asking hits her. And she allowed him to do so! She resolves to set limits on his behaviour towards her, and decides quite firmly that she is angry with him.

That decided, she checks her reflection again, straightens her hair and admires the dress once more before going into the bag. She notices the quality of the leggings. The tops are not overly revealing. The knickers are soft and smooth. Takes off the pair she's wearing. As she suspected, they are soaking. She tucks them into the plastic the sports ones were packaged in, and start to put the new pair on.

She pauses, then rifles through her handbag. With some relief, she finds a sanitary pad and applies it to the new undies. As she pulls them up, her fingers brush the vibrator's tail protruding from her, and She realises that she hasn't even seen it.

Curiosity gets the better of her and she lifts her dress and pulls at it tentatively. The device inside her presses down inside her. She considers removing it. She's *already almost* decided not to obey his instruction to taste herself, though she enjoys both her own taste and the sense of decadence, though she knows he knew this perfectly well.

A previous boyfriend complained about her fondness for her own taste, and ever since she has refrained—until William came along and encouraged her to delight in it. He delighted in bringing her to orgasm with his fingers, then presenting those fingers to her lips before kissing her and telling her how sweet she tastes.

Deciding that disobedience would be both petulant and self-denying, she slides two fingers into herself. *Oh God, I don't think I've ever been so wet!* She resists the temptation to finish herself off, though it would only take a minute, and sucks her fingers. Then pulls the sports knickers and their protective lining up.

He's just setting their two cups down when she returns. He smiles one of those smiles, lit with boyish delight, and it is hard to stay angry. He kisses her and whispers, "Good girl, you taste divine." He sits while she blushes.

From her own seat opposite, Meredith can clearly see that she is not the only one who is aroused. There's swelling in his trousers. Speaking at a normal level, William asks, "Do you like the things I chose?"

In truth, she does. But, following through on her decision, she replies, "They're just fine, but I can't let you keep buying me things. How much do I owe you for them?"

"Nothing!" He seems genuinely surprised. "If you want, you can buy things for me. Besides, the things you bought were for me to use."

He seems serious and not at all contrite. *The things you bought were for me to use* flares in her mind. She had indeed bought items for him to bind her and—

And here he is, talking as if that were normal! She's not sure if he is entirely genuine or being a complete bastard.

She takes a sip of the surprisingly good coffee "Well, then, I'm going to start by paying for lunch," she insists in her best trying-to-be-firm voice.

He acquiesces without complaint. "Very well. That's kind of you, and I accept." His hand slides into a pocket. The vibration inside her restarts for a few moments. This sends a wave through her, pulling her mind back to how close she is. It gives her pleasure—and takes the edge off her little triumph.

"So, what's next?" she asks him warily after draining the last of her espresso.

"You said you wanted to look at a couple of bits of lingerie, so I thought we'd do that next. There are a couple of items we'll have to go to a specialist shop for. Then lunch and home. Seeing as how I've planned the morning, I thought you could choose what we get up to this afternoon." He smiles into her eyes and turns up the vibrator inside her as he does so.

He takes her hand as they walk back to the car. They deposit their purchases and drive the short distance to the main centre. Fortunately they only have to drive over two speed humps. He takes them slowly; she nevertheless feels both deep inside her.

"I'm not sure I should be buying more things till I've finished my diet," worries Meredith aloud.

"You need something pretty that fits perfectly," William says firmly. "You don't have to buy the store. Just get one set that you like." Ever practical, "I would offer to …" He winks and Meredith laughs. She's not used to pampering and is proud that she stands on her own two feet. She's glad he's not being too much of a dick about it.

The shop he chooses is more of a fashion boutique than anywhere Meredith would normally buy underwear. She recalls with chagrin that some of what she's purchased in supermarkets while picking up her groceries. Catches her reflection in one of the store's many mirrors as she enters and, seeing a her slimmer, smartly dressed self on the arm of a handsome man she straightens, and tells herself that she's the new Meredith she has wanted to be but never quite got around to becoming.

The more outlandishly cut and coloured displays are placed near the entrance to attract the eyes of men desperate for last-minute gifts. She steps past these and into the shop. It's been years since she's been somewhere like this to shop for herself rather than to search for a present. Therefore, despite constant low-level distraction inside her, she makes up her mind to enjoy this indulgence and makes multiple circuits of the wares.

After what she hopes William considers an excessive time, she selects a bra that each of them has admired. It's lacy and strappy but not excessively revealing and has a front clasp, which she knows he will like, discreetly hidden behind an embroidered flower. She selects knicker-style bottoms with a matching flower motif. She pretends to consider thongs that have the same decoration, and makes a show of rejecting them. She doesn't look, but hopes she senses a moment of disappointment from him.

Meredith is less keen on their next port of call—the mall's one intimate store. She hasn't set foot inside a shop like it other than to replace her simple vibrator. Oh, and one very giggly occasion with Jess, when her friend was due to be a maid of honour. Their only purpose then had been to get items to embarrass the bride. Knowing the items he's already had her buy in a regular store, the prospect of going in with her rather spanky boyfriend leaves her feeling far from giggly.

Sensing her nervousness, he pulls her to the side just before they reach the entrance, and kisses her deeply. The vibrations inside her tell her that he has played with the remote control yet again. Its vibrations combine with the kiss and the pressure of his body against hers and she rapidly approaches the point of no return. Barely holding on she begs,

"Oh God, please don't, William, not here! In urgent gasps, I'll scream the place down!"

He relents. The device slows and his embrace relaxes, then pulls back, smirks, and twinkles. "Are you feeling brave?" But doesn't wait for a reply before leading her in.

She follows in a daze. Once past the threshold, William hands her another folded list and whispers, "I'm proud of you. Just get the assistant to help you with the last few things. I'll be back in no time."

Moments later, Meredith, cheeks flushed and eyes dilated, is presenting the folded piece of paper to a stylishly dressed woman assistant and saying, "Please, can you help me find these things?"

Shopping List:

~~Riding crop~~
~~Dressage whip~~
~~Table tennis paddle~~
Soft flogger
Conventional paddle
~~Lead ropes (2)~~
~~Ankle cuffs~~
Wrist cuffs
Rechargeable vibrator

The woman's eyes widen, then fix on Meredith with an appraising look. Meredith looks down, unable to face her gaze. Seeing the contents of the list for the first time, her cheeks flame even brighter. She wishes the tiled floor would open up beneath her. Glancing back up at the woman's face, she expects to see a look of horror but is surprised to be confronted instead by what she can only describe as a conspiratorial smile. "Of course, my dear." The woman speaks in a clear alto, her accent hinting at continental origins. "Let's get you a basket, shall we?"

Meredith follows her, a sense of gratitude melting away the worst of her mortification. The woman seems to think the list is perfectly normal! Now that the peak of Meredith's arousal has passed she studies the woman, who is athletic and in her late thirties. She has dark hair and wears her staff black elegantly as she moves with quiet confidence around the store.

First, the woman takes her to a display at the rear, away from any browsing customers. Meredith looks at an array of floggers, recognising similarities between those on display and those in William's collection. She is somewhat surprised to find the store has fewer types than he does! As in the sports store, she is unsure which to choose and looks to the woman for guidance and sees her name tag this time: *Annette*.

Annette takes pity on her. "Are you familiar with these things at all?" she asks. "If not, then I suggest choosing the one that feels softest to you. Otherwise, choose the one most similar to the one you enjoy most."

"Yes, um …" Meredith thinks, *OMG, I just admitted that my boyfriend uses these things on me! Whatever must she think of me?*

The woman smiles warmly. "It's OK. You'd be amazed at the people who are a little adventurous. Provided you play safely, it's all quite normal."

Still blushing furiously, but warming to Annette's kind attitude, Meredith touches the samples. There's a faux leather one with long falls, and some shorter PVC ones. The leather one is heavy. Unable to quite believe she is hearing herself say it, she asks, "Do you have a lighter one like this, or one like this with shorter falls?" She uses the term for the whip's tails automatically, proud to display such casual familiarity.

"So you're not a complete novice then," Annette suggests, allowing one eyebrow to rise slightly, ""But this is your first relationship like this?" Her tone is light but questioning, and her guess accurate.

"No, my boyfriend has lots of things," Meredith admits, still blushing. She doesn't respond to the second observation—or was it a question?

"And you're using one of them now?" The older woman's lips purse in an almost successful attempt to stop herself smiling.

"Oh no! You can't hear it, can you?" Meredith's embarrassment returns. "It's remote-controlled, and he's left it running."

"Don't worry, I can't hear a thing." Annette smiles. "I'm just a bit more in tune than most people. Do you mind me asking if this is a game, a test, a punishment, or a reward?"

Annette's way of speaking makes Meredith feel as though she's almost a third participant in … well, what is it? Meredith herself is not sure. Again she doesn't answer the question, though this time it's because she doesn't know.

"We might have something more to your taste in the stockroom. The long-tailed one is in the sale. If you want, I can have a look when we've picked up the rest of your list, and you can have the other for the same price."

Meredith allows herself to be led along to the paddles. Here she finds her choice simpler. A plain black one with nicely rounded edges and differently textured sides reminds her of her first spanking orgasm, and that memory makes her mind up for her. There aren't any leather cuffs as nice as William's, so she chooses the pair that most closely resembles the ankle cuffs she purchased earlier. That leaves just the vibrator she realises with relief.

Annette continues, "You don't have anyone else you can talk to about these things, do you?"

"Not apart from my boyfriend," Meredith admits, finally drawn into this charming woman's efforts at conversation.

"Would you like my number? Just for if you want to chat?"

"Yes, thank-you. That would be nice." Meredith responds after a short pause as they arrive at the large section devoted to vibrators. The selection on offer is huge. The stipulation that the device must be rechargeable immediately allows Annette to rule out most. This leaves some attractively finished (and reasonably proportioned) vibrators. Meredith chuckles at the thought that she is buying a vibrator while using one. From the look in the assistant's eyes, she shares the joke.

"Do you—" Annette pauses "—normally—" another pause this time with a look and the barest hint of a smile that doesn't make it past the corners of her eyes, ""—like to use yours inside or out?"

Meredith realises she's blushing but replies, "Oh, definitely outside! I don't like to—" She stops short. Given her current situation, the caveat may seem ridiculous to Annette, but that can't be helped. That's how Meredith is.

"The best choices are a wand or a clit vibe." Annette directs her attention to several small pebble-shaped toys and others with bulbous heads.

Thanks to her experience with William's collection, Meredith is in familiar territory. "I like the wand with the curved handle," she says and puts her hand on the display model. It has a familiar silky texture that her fingers—and other parts of her—have grown familiar with over the last few weeks.

"Good choice, and that means you're nearly done with your *task*." Annette smiles conspiratorially. "I'll just pop into the stockroom to see if we have that other flogger." She lowers her voice and leans towards Meredith before continuing, "And if you need to, you can use the changing room while I'm gone to take the edge off."

Meredith is shocked at and almost tempted by the offer. If she found it possible to stay quiet while she came, and if she weren't desperately keen to share her orgasm with William, she would have leapt at the offer, well, also if she weren't too shy to …

Instead she chooses to wait by the till, trying not to think sexy thoughts or wonder at Annette's awareness of her condition. She also tries not to think too much about the toys she is buying.

Annette emerges from the stockroom, holding a handsome chocolate-brown flogger with short falls made of real suede. "You're in luck. This is the last of an old line. It was more expensive, but the packaging was damaged."

Meredith's fingers enjoy the softness of the suede. Her mind imagines it against her, and she likes the picture. "Thank-you. I'll take it, if I may."

William arrives just as she is paying, announcing his presence to Meredith's body by increasing the vibrator's pace and changing the pattern once more. Meredith leans heavily on the pay desk. Her face betraying what's happening inside her. He puts his arms around her and kisses her neck before reducing the toy's intensity.

Annette can't help but smile. The customer has completely accepted the fact that her excitement had a knowing audience. While Meredith recovers, Annette turns a pointed look towards the handsome newcomer and says, "She's been *very* good. I hope you're going to reward her."

His smile and the light in his eyes assure Annette, as his stiffness against Meredith assures her. "Yes, she's lovely, and I most certainly intend to."

Normally two people talking about her in such intimate terms would set Meredith raging or longing to hide. But they speak with such gentleness that she responds instead by kissing William and smiling shyly and saying a fond goodbye to Annette. She leaves the store on his arm in a far more comfortable frame of mind.

As they walk into the aisle she asks, "Is it okay if we just pick up some things to eat at home instead of going to lunch?" He briefly squeezes her hand and smiles his reply.

When they arrive at the grocery, she looks at him. "Basket each?" she asks. Her eyes now challenging, whether through recklessness brought on by continual stimulation, growing confidence, or knowledge that relief is soon at hand. His face turns devilish. And she rapidly adds, "But no cheating, please!"

The vibrations surge again, driving her body's excitement upwards but rapidly recede, and William winks as he sets off into the aisles.

When he reaches the tills minutes later, Meredith is already there. She's collected two sandwiches, cheesecake, and a bottle of Fleurie. For his part William has managed to fill his basket almost completely. He stands behind her. "Is that all you got?" he asks, unloading what has to be the makings of at least two full meals.

She leans into him and whispers, "You're lucky I didn't just get us a bag of crisps to share, you tormenting bastard."

His response is yet another surge and the murmured words, "You're going to pay for that when we get home." The combination nearly sends her over the edge.

She waits, watching as his purchases are scanned: cheeses, cured meats, smoked salmon, peppers, cherry toms, green leaf salad, bread, bacon, eggs, mushrooms, sausages, pineapple (that makes her smile), and a chilled bottle of rose champagne."How on earth did you manage to pick up that lot in the time it took me to get us a sandwich?" she asks incredulously once he's paid.

"I thought we might need a certain amount of sustenance." He grins, bumping her gently with his shoulder.

"For the whole week?"

They make their way to the car. The comment earns her backside a swat and a change in pattern. Every change seems to get around whatever ability she's developed to ignore the vibrator's effects on her.

He opens the trunk. She goes to put her bags in, but he stops her.

"Take the cuffs with you into the car." Which, in her fuddled state, she does without question. Once in the car, he leans over to kiss her properly, his hands making free with her body, at first through the crisp cotton of her shirt dress.

She revels in his touch on her excited body for a while, but as he gets more adventurous, she laughs. "Hey, wait till we get home!" He begins to work on the dress's buttons, and her hands fly up to stop him. "Don't!"

He traps first one arm and then the other, undoing the buttons at the wrists and then holding them while he finishes opening the front of the dress without pulling the sides apart. He kisses her once more, this time slipping a hand inside to cup a breast.

"Just get me home or I'm going to kill you!" she hisses when his lips break contact.

She fixes him with a stare. He returns it steadily. The fingers inside her dress slide under her bra and capture a nipple, clamping down. In Meredith's excited state, the jolt shoots in all directions. She holds her breath and her pupils dilate.

William realises that he too is trapped by his constant teasing. The car is not parked somewhere private enough for her scream of release to go unnoticed. As her mouth opens to release it, he releases his hold.

She sits with her eyes closed as he smoothes her dress closed, but without doing up any of the buttons. His lips graze her cheek. "If you put the cuffs on, you can hold the remote." With that he starts the engine.

She rouses herself as he drives out of the car park. Once on the straight, he holds up the remote control, his thumb poised above the + button. "Okay, okay!" she says, too weary of fighting back the inevitable, but determined that it not happen in a public place.

The drive is mercifully short. Also mercifully, William does not insist she join the wrist cuffs together. So Meredith sits, clutching the remote, as the effects of his latest touches fade. Then the closeness of her home and her release begin to affect her. She's been waiting forever and has come close many times.

When she gets out of the car, she discovers that her sleeves cover the black material circling her wrists, and that the dress's tailoring and belt prevent it from opening so widely as to expose her. William retrieves the bags from the boot while she retrieves her keys. She opens the door with a sense of relief that she has made it back without letting go completely.

As the door swings open, he is so close behind her that she can feel his warmth. She barely has time to step in and kick her shoes from her feet before he pushes the door shut and puts the bags down in one movement and then his hands are on her, one making swift work of her dress's belt while the other slides the it from her shoulders. His arms circle her, pulling her to him, and she feels that he is as ready as she is.

One hand's clever fingers find the cuff's clips and link them. The others pull her new panties down. His leg presses at the back of her knees, and if he were not supporting her, she would have fallen. Instead, he lowers her to her knees. He forces her body forward while keeping her hands low, pressing her face and breasts into the carpet. He must have unzipped along the way, because the head of his cock presses immediately against her needy entrance.

Fearful that the vibrator will be pushed entirely into her, she takes hold of its tail with one hand. The other is still clutching the remote control. As he thrusts into her, she tugs the tail and presses the power button. In moments she lets out a cry that shakes the entire house while he drives himself into her again and again.

28

Waking in a Predicament

Meredith surfaces on her sofa as William places a heavily laden tray on the coffee table. She's under one of her throws. Its wool is slightly itchy against her skin. She purrs and smiles up at him as she recalls their homecoming.

When she goes to move she finds that her hands are still bound. Waking more fully, she realises that other than the cuffs she's naked, and that the cuffs bind her wrists more tightly than before. He must have removed them and re-bound her. "You didn't have to tighten these or clip them back together you know.'," she says, reaching her bound wrists out toward him as he bends to kiss her.

After the admittedly enjoyable kiss, he replies, "It was too tempting not to ... and you didn't object."

"Was I fully awake at the time?"

"No, you weren't." He smiles and kisses her again, still not moving to free her.

"You took the time to get yourself dressed properly, I see."

"I did," he confesses, all innocence. "But then I was the one getting food ready while you slept."

She realises that the now fully discharged egg is still inside her. "You could have removed the vibrator at least!"

"I thought it would wake you if I did, and besides, I wasn't sure how you'd want to clean it. The red or the fizz with lunch?" he continues conversationally, "I got the champers from the refrigerated shelf but it could ideally use a bit more chilling."

Meredith is still holding her arms out to him, expecting to be released, but he makes no move to free her.

Reluctantly she rolls onto her back, uncovering herself to his gaze. She flushes, always so conscious of her nudity, though he seems oblivious to his own whenever he is unclothed. He doesn't look away—he never does—as she pulls at the vibrator's tail. It gives her a final wave of pleasurable sensations as it emerges.

"Where shall I put this?" she asks, holding the warm, wet toy in front of her. She appears to have no intention of cleaning it with her mouth, so he proffers a hand towel which she takes and with some difficulty dries the vibrator and her hands before wrapping the vibrator in the cloth. She then raises herself somewhat awkwardly to a sitting position and, leaning forward, put the bundle down beside the tray.

"Can you at least remove these and let me put something on before we eat?" she finally pleads.

He kneels by her. His hands take their time enjoying her body. "Why? Are you cold?" His touch leaves her breasts and, bypassing her cuffed hands, finds her mons. One palm presses there while his fingers hover millimetres above her labia.

Meredith feels a temptation to rotate her hips and bring them into contact. "No, but—"

"If you let me make you cum again, I will take them off," he offers playfully. His fingers are already toying with her folds, and her body is responding. The devilment in his eyes tells her she'll have no peace until she lets him do so.

He takes her silence for consent and lifts her unresisting, cuffed wrists above her head, enforcing her sense of vulnerability and powerlessness. William turns her and lays her full length along the sofa pinning her arms above her head while he kneels. He kisses her breasts and her lips as his fingers delight in her wetness. It's not just that he knows how to please her, inside and out. It's his confidence and her certainty of the eventual result. She feels at times as though the interaction is between him and her body, while she is just there for the ride.

Her nipples become engorged. It's like a switch he has found in her.

When he holds or binds her body taut, her inner feminist tries to rise but... His probing middle and index fingers inside her and thumb outside close around her pubic bone, pressing under her hood. It's a way nobody ever touched her until she met William. He applies tension slowly, creating a sensation akin to a luxuriant yawn throughout her body. Thought fades further with each ounce of force he uses. Meredith's internal political debate is short and one-sided as she feels something inside her open like a flower.

His right hand prescribes the minutest of circles, tantalising as it declares ownership of every nerve ending. He sucks her left nipple into his mouth; the tips of his teeth drag over its sensitive bud as he releases it. "How many times did you deliberately tease me today, my sweet?" he asks, taking her by surprise.

When she does not answer, his teeth nip her sharply, eliciting an exclamation. "I didn't hear your answer, my sweet."

"What do you mean?" she asks, knowing it's not a good strategy—in one way.

He quite deliberately bites her left nipple again, then leans forward and bites her right. "How many times in the lingerie shop?" he asks before tenderly kissing it.

Meredith smiles and blushes at the same time. "Did you notice?"

He holds her naked body stretched out. His clever fingers expertly working her to the edge again and again. She tries to remain silent, knowing how the sounds she makes delight him and encourage his teasing, but numerous squeaks and groans escape her lips nonetheless.

"Then there's the matter of an appropriate reward for completing each of the tasks I gave you." His lips return to her breasts. Senses her urgency as the movement of her hips grows more frantic, he eases the pressure he is exerting through his hands, drawing an exasperated moan from Meredith.

"Ah, ah." William's lips leave her. "We have also to discuss the threats to kill me— "his teeth rake across her nipple, though not hard enough to cause any pain, "—and how good you were not taking the opportunity to, er, relieve the pressure." He leans up to kiss her mouth this time, and she opens to him.

His hand becomes more insistent again. As he feels her muscles tense, he breaks their embrace. "So do you want to eat handcuffed or cum before?"

"Just let me *cum!*"

The response earns Meredith a light slap to her vulva, which almost sends her over the edge. "Ow! Bastard! Please!" The curse and the plea leave her mouth before she realises, earning her mons a second swat. Her "Ow!" this time is louder and more heartfelt.

Panting and frantic, she cries, "Please may I cum, sir?" The plea is far louder than she intends. His thumb on her clitoris and fingers inside her clamp down and circle as his gaze bores into her.

In moments she is writhing in his grasp. The way her arms are still trapped above her seems to draw the waves of pleasure through her body. They roll over her, crashing from her pelvis and stomach to her breasts and onward. Time stops as the hands controlling her body keep her convulsions going. She hears her own voice bouncing back at her from the walls.

After a timeless time, he senses her tiring and relents in his onslaught. He releases her wrists and wraps her in his arms.

As reality returns, his lips tenderly brush hers. He presents his fingers, still laden with her scent, to her mouth. Her lips part and she sucks them reflexively. He withdraws them and kisses her. His nimble fingers unlink her cuffs, though he doesn't remove them from her wrists. He traces around where they circle her slender limbs. "Now, food!"

Meredith is surprised at the sudden rush of hunger that hits her. She is now grateful for his extensive food shopping efforts; a sandwich would neither suit the scale of her hunger nor the intimacy of the moment. William has not only laid out the items he picked up, but has also raided her larder.

She fails to persuade him to allow her to dress or in any way cover her nakedness. The aromas of cheeses, cured meats, smoked salmon, and crusty bread overwhelm her shyness. The tastes of Somerset Brie with onion marmalade and an English green salad explode in her mouth. Hunger and a well-loved feeling heightening her sense of taste. The cool Fleurie's fruitiness feeds her hunger too, though it also awakens her thirst making her grateful for the chilled sparkling water.

While eating, she is almost completely distracted from her nakedness, but his touch reminds her again, keeping her aware of her situation and maintaining her arousal. A cycle develops: his touch excites her, and her embarrassment builds.

He goes to the kitchen and returns with slices of warm pork pie finds that she's wrapped the throw around herself. "Did I ask you to cover yourself?"

"No, but ..."

He patiently removes it despite her protest. His hands cup her breasts, working her soft flesh and hardening nipples with familiar skill.

As it does so often, her body pauses under his touch. She lowers and squares her shoulders, offering her breasts to him. As he teases her sensitive flesh, he fixes her with his sparkling gaze. His hands release her, but his eyes still hold her in place. The glint in his eye is joined by an upward quirk at the corner of his mouth.

He holds a small silver clip up in front of her. "To remind you," he says. His fingertips pinch her left nipple and pull gently. She feels something slide around her nipple, and looks down to see the clip around it. "I bought you these as a treat."

His hands release her breast, but the clip stays, and with it a pleasant pinching sensation. He moves his attention to her right breast and repeats the process. Finished, he kisses her mouth, leaning her back against the sofa. As he presses his weight onto her, the solidity of his chest against her clipped nipples sends jolts of pleasure through her and she feels a tightening inside. Her legs separate willingly and his hand moves between her thighs. He finds her ready and slips two fingers inside her eager body before breaking the kiss.

"And if you cover yourself again ..." His free hand pinches one clip, slowly increasing the force. The pressure rises, and at first so does her pleasure. Then, for a brief instant before he lets go, it crescendos to a distinct stab of pain. "I can tighten these." The unexpected after-effect of the pain is a warm wash of joyous heat spreading through her breast and beyond. She feels herself clutching the fingers inside her as the wave spreads.

He once more finds her mouth welcoming, her body giving out clear signals that she is not certain she wishes it to. But it feels so good.

She feels empty when he removes his hand and presents his wet fingers to her mouth. Her lips accept their intrusion and her tongue laps her taste from them. They pull from her mouth and again a flickering of loss passes through her before his lips brush her own.

"Now eat while it's still warm." The warmed pie is excellent and leaves Meredith's hunger, at least for food, sated. She watches William finish a last morsel. "Do you want a break before dessert?" he asks finally.

She most certainly does. They clear the remnants together, and she catches her reflection in the mirror. Her decorated breasts look exotic. normally she's shy of looking at herself, but the bright clips hanging from her nipples turn mere nakedness into an erotic display. Her nipples seem more delicate, and stand prouder atop her breasts.

Though nothing overlooks her kitchen, Meredith still feels intensely self-conscious. She never walks around the house naked, and the clips and William's presence greatly increase her awareness of her nudity.

They load the plates and cutlery into the dishwasher, and the copious leftovers into the fridge. He steps behind her. As his strong arms encircle her, she leans back and closes her eyes allowing him to move her legs apart as his hands claim her once again. He touches her however and wherever he pleases, playing with her body and the clips. The image from the mirror rises in her memory. An exotic creature in the possession of this strong man.

His fingers enter her, her body granting its own permission. She moves to greet the intrusion. Again he doesn't continue long enough to give her release. Meredith's mouth opens reflexively to accept his wet fingers, but this time he places them in his own mouth before turning her head and kissing her full on the lips.

"Now, if we aren't having dessert yet ..." He pulls on the nipple clips, eliciting a yelp from Meredith. It's a dare and a challenge. The feeling is on the edge between pleasure and pain, and growing in intensity as he pulls.

"Ow! No!"

"Is that a safe word?" he taunts without breaking eye contact.

Meredith's body is alight, *Why don't I say the word?* she asks herself. *Pride? Lust? Masochism?* The mysterious link between her breasts and sex is flashing brightly. She stands her ground but stays silent as her nipples are stretched slowly out in front of her.

"Follow—" he pinches more tightly "—or say it." As he continues to pull, her feet begin to move towards him, guided as much by her rising desire as by his tormenting.

The silent part of her mind wonders at the compact he seems to have with her body and its desires. Her arousal mounts and her voice does not protest. He leads her, and with ginger steps and sparks of pleasure and pains coursing through her, she follows him up the staircase. *I'm in control. I can stop this with a word. I'm being led like a slave around my own home. No, worse than that.* She can't imagine even a slave being led around by the nipples in so explicit a display of control and submission.

She yelps another "Ow!" as they pass the turn onto the landing. But her insides clench in ecstasy at every motion and every thought. her feet move on and her internal monologue continues, *I'm choosing my humiliation at his hands. When he is not here, I will lie awake and revel in the memory.*

A few 'ouches' and a few 'oos' later, they arrive in her bedroom. He must have laid out each of the new toys on her bed while she slept. She sees, with her eyes and feels with an internal clenching, that the charging cable is attached to her new vibrator. There is also a new set of make-up brushes *so that's what he was doing when it abandoned me.*

William stands her so she faces her bed, and finally releases his hold on the clips. The tension disappears, and she finds herself missing it— misses having her own breasts used as reins to guide her. He steps behind her and reaches around to caress her now tender orbs with both hands.

The two lead ropes are tied around the stout legs at the foot of her bed. She stands nude save for the cuffs on her wrists and the clips on her nipples. The crop, whip, flogger, and paddles lined up on her duvet seem far more threatening now that she is unclothed. Again her body's responses are an odd mixture of nerves, fear, and wanton expectation. All secondary to her desire to have him inside her.

She feels his hardness behind her and holds her breath as she dares to press herself into him. She is rewarded with a telltale pulsing as his cock nestles between her buttocks. The knowledge of his lust is strangely reassuring when she is in his power. Her lips open, and she edges her feet apart as her body anticipates that hardness sliding into her.

William is pleased with his efforts. The scene is as he wishes, and he's delighted by her obvious response. He feels her heart quicken at the sight of the restraints and instruments of discipline. Her body surrenders to him, wantonly aroused. There are perfect moments she gives to him: her cries of pleasure and of pain, her joy at his taking of her, and perhaps most of all these moments in which she silently offers herself up to his tenderness and cruelty.

His hands on her breasts relish the softness of her globes, the stiffness of her clipped nipples, and the pounding of her heart. Slowly, gently, he loosens the clips and removes them. His ears enjoy her groan of pain as the blood rushes back in and their sensitivity soars. She moans in pleasure as he lovingly caresses her tortured flesh.

His will enjoys the way he centres. His pleasure in its dominion overpowers his instinct to simply throw her on the bed and take her as he wishes. "Sit, please." His voice is steadier than he feels.

Meredith turns and sits on the bed, blushing as she becomes aware that he will see proof of her wetness on the covers. She looks down so as not to meet his eyes, but she needn't have concerned herself; his first action is to guide her unresisting mouth to his erection. Her cuffed wrists join it in benediction as he allows her a languorous minute of enjoyment.

She cannot fathom why the act of sucking him eases the aching lust his body awakens inside her, but it does. She takes him in, holds, sucks, then pulls back far enough to allow her tongue to circle the head. She playfully probes the opening of his foreskin. Her efforts are rewarded by the tiniest slick hint of his salty-sweet pre-cum. She releases his cock from the confines of her mouth and reverently draws his foreskin back, then kisses the taut skin of his glans as she might her lover's tongue.

William allows her to continue. She and he both need this. But he only allows her to do so for a time, he has other plans. Taking up the ankle cuffs, he kneels and secures each of her legs. He runs his hands up her calves and the insides of her thighs before laying her back. In his turn, he tastes her with his skilful mouth. She wonders that some previous partners have been unable to find her clitoris or urethra. She delights in his tongue's exploration of both, then curses that skill silently when he chooses not to grant her the release she desperately needs.

His lips move to her mons and then her breasts. He's patience itself. He enters her slowly, her body clenching around him as she writhes. His thrusts are measured, his rhythm intoxicating, but he does not drive into her with enough force or urgency to push either of them over the edge.

Meredith almost doesn't care though. Eagerly she drinks her own taste from his mouth. The fullness of him inside her does more to ease her urgency than sucking him did. When, eventually, he withdraws, her body yearns towards him. Her emptiness cries out like a lost child. She remains ready and open to him. Despite her emptiness, her excitement rises.

"Please lie face down with your hips on the pillows in the middle of your bed."

It occurs to Meredith how the excessive courtesy in William's deep voice when giving her orders affects her. In her mind, these are never requests. It is as though the words bypass her mind altogether. Her body responds outwardly by complying and inwardly by—Oh God! How it responds inwardly!

She turns and positions herself as instructed. Her sensitised nipples send excited messages as her breasts take the weight of her upper body. Her bum is elevated and tilted, offering herself lewdly. The sense of exposure rises sharply as he secures her ankles to the ropes at the corners of the bed, spreading her legs at a ninety degree angle and opening her vulva widely to his gaze. She recalls every time his hand has caressed, entered, or struck her exposed, vulnerable body. The memories wash through her.

He undoes the clip that links her handcuffs and uses it to secure them around one of the bars at the head of her bed. *I'm helpless now, at his,* her mind capitalises he word as her insides fill with its warmth, *mercy, cruel though it may be.* She tests the strength of her bonds, more to assure herself that she is indeed powerless than out of desire to escape them.

He caresses her derriere with each of her newly acquired instruments of torment in turn starting with the soft flogger. The sensuous suede strands delight her skin. She says a silent word of thanks to Annette, her "co-conspirator" for her kindness. She marvels at her eagerness to feel its kiss. She realises how her captive body is responding. She flushes and then glows at the realisation of his skill at reading her responses.

Next she feels a silky stroke, then a flat, straight edge. She decides it is the paddle. She remembers lying across William's knee, shivering in trepidation, just a few weeks ago. The way the pillows raise her hips prevents her from pressing herself into the bed, but her movement makes her response clear to him.

The table tennis bat in its turn offers two new sensations. The pimples are rough as he rubs them gently across her buttocks. The smooth side is cold against the skin of her thighs. *He's never used something quite like this on me.* Her mind reaches out to torments unknown, and her rebellious body warms to her imagining.

The soft suede falls of Annette's flogger return. Oh, my they are as soft as any in William's treasure trove of a playroom. Imagination, memory and sensation unite, *like being beaten with warm, liquid chocolate.* He caresses her with them long and slowly, delighting in the way she uses the little movement he has allowed her to retain to follow them and open herself to them. He trails the falls tenderly along her folds. They carry her wetness from vulva to bum. At this gentle touch, it is the cheeks of her face that burn. *This is so wrong but so wonderful,* her guilty mind tells her as it files away the sensations and the fantasy for moments when she is alone.

Her reverie is brought to a sudden end when the tip of the riding crop slaps her hood and mons lightly but loudly. She yelps in surprise. The rush of sensation has her panting. Despite her response, her expectation, and her fear, that blow is the only one that lands. He proceeds to caress her: calves, inner thighs, outsides of breasts, and, yes, mons. The soft leather of the slapper and the smooth springiness of the shaft explore her vulnerable body in leisurely fashion.

Finally she feels the long, thin, vicious-looking dressage whip. As with the crop, he does not merely caress her thighs and derriere. He draws the tip of the wicked thing along the length of her wide-open inner labia from hood to urethra to inner lips he runs it back and as it makes its way it draws her hood clear of the infinitely sensitive pearl it protects. A wild thought breaks loose in her mind: he'll bring this feared tool of pain down on her with all the force at his disposal. And she herself bought the torture instrument!

In her imagination she's writhing in agony and cumming with greater force than ever. Waves of pain and pleasure washing away the barriers between the fantasy of light that she has lived since becoming William's lover and the fantasies of darkness from her best and worst dreams.

Meredith hangs there even after she feels the whip's touch end. She senses his weight next to her. His hands trace her body with confident caresses. She's floating, adrift, helpless, but somehow completed. She has so far borne only a single blow from any of the five implements, but her nerves are popping and frizzing.

His final gentleness is one brief kiss to her shoulder. In the respite, her consciousness tries to swim to the surface.

Whack.

Her body leaps in shock more than pain. The table tennis paddle has crashed into her left buttock. She groans.

Whack. It strikes her on the right. The sounds reverberates in her bedroom as her helpless body bounces on her bed.

She's now expecting and prepares herself for further blows. She can't quite bring herself to think about wanting them. But he takes her by surprise, as he so often does, caressing her rosying skin, eliciting rivulets of pleasure.

He slides an arm around her hips, lifts her slightly, and lowers her again. She feels something pressed between her and the pillows hears and feels it buzz into life. Her new wand? Her body and bonds hold it in place. She wonders, not for the first time, how he became so practiced.

Pressing her hips downward brings the hood of her clitoris into contact with the vibe's head. He hasn't turned it up high, and he has set it to a frustrating, undulating pattern of vibration—enough, she fears from experience of past torments, to get her to the edge and keep her there without giving her the slightest hope of release. She presses her hips as low as she can, but no, she's certain. *He's such a bastard*, her silent voice taunts and she's once again powerless to do anything about it.

He caresses her thighs and buttocks. "Six to each cheek, my sweet." She braces herself.

Whack.

Whack.

This time there is a little more pain and a little less shock. "That's two now." Again the caressing touch, and again she floats in her world of sensations. She does not consider saying *pineapple*. Rather, she pushes her mons onto the wand and in so doing tilts her buttocks invitingly upwards.

William, not being a man to ignore such an invitation, does not do so.

Whack.

Whack.

She calls out. The blows have landed on the sensitive skin where her thighs and buttocks meet. This time his caresses last longer. He slides his thumb into her, and his fingers close around the head of the wand, pressing it more closely against her and her body at first shakes in response. Her hips begin to rock reflexively and he allows her to continue. Her breathing becomes more shallow, when he detects the tell tale sign of her holding her breath he stops and takes his hand away.

Whack.

Whack.

This time he returns to the rounds of her buttocks. Though there is more pain than when he last struck here, the sensation is still more one of shock and stimulation, when his touch returns she gets closer still.

"That's four apiece." This time he uses his hand in leisurely fashion, much to Meredith's frustration. Her rising excitement still means that he is only able to refrain from making her cum for so long, and so again he has to take his hand away.

A brief whimper escape her lips and when he caresses her fast-warming bum with the paddle, she makes to move away from it, though with the way she is bound there is nowhere for her rosy cheeks to hide.

Whack.

Whack.

Her gasps come swiftly and are almost as sharp as the sounds of the paddle striking her. Her bottom glows brightly. His soothing caresses are nearly uncomfortable. Her body longs for the expected return of his hand to her entrance. Once more he brings her to the edge, and once more she whimpers at the loss of his skilful touch a moment before her need is satisfied. This time her whimper is more fearful; she's certain the final blows will genuinely hurt.

He makes her wait for them. As she does, she reflects on the fact that she is being beaten with a piece of equipment from an innocent game. The thought distracts her and lessens her resistance.

Whack!

Whack!

Meredith really does cry out this time and hears him place the paddle down with some relief, and much expectation. She knows his habits and his skill, to both her pleasure and...

His hand returns to her sore buttocks but makes no move towards her pussy or the buzzing wand.

When he does not immediately move to satisfy her, she wiggles as enticingly as she is able. "Sir, please ..."

"I haven't heard you thank me for today yet, young lady."

He pauses. All patience, he caresses. In that pause and patience, she finds the simple words. "Thank-you, sir."

Her words complete the moment, complete her submission. She hears him undress, senses his weight on the bed and the reassuring solidity of him. Meredith feels the residual soreness of her skin as his smooth hips meet her upthrust buttocks and melts as he fills her emptiness, rises as his mass presses her down. He forces the head of the wand tight against her. She winces and then purrs as his hands find her breasts, still hypersensitive from the effect of the clamps.

Their earlier exertions have eased his own urgency and he takes long, slow delight in her first orgasm, moving inside her with his accustomed irresistible force yet with no hint of frenzy. After, his strength and endurance allow her to revel in their closeness until she feels her own need rise once more. Only then does he unleash his full power and take his own pleasure in full.

29

Laying as One

They lie intimately together for an age after the age they have spent on pleasure. He releases her wrists but makes no move to free her ankles. She is glad that he does not, as it would break their union. She cherishes this closeness even more than she does their intensity. Indeed, the heights of that intensity make her cherish this all the more.

Eventually his practiced fingers free her ankles and he leaves the bed, to her disappointment. He returns a moment later with towels and tenderly wipes the perspiration from her body. He covers her with the duvet before wiping himself down. Then he joins her and allows her to curl herself contentedly under his heavy arm. She feels the energy, excitement, and exertion drain away in his warmth. The last thing she registers is an amused musing on what tiring work this lying down can be.

As for him, he strokes her hair tenderly, enjoying her dozing and before long joins her.

Thus, when the uncomfortable angle of his head causes him to stir, rather more of the day has passed than he'd intended. He rouses her with gentle kisses. Her first response is to ease herself even more closely into his warmth. "Might one interest you in a spot of dessert, young lady?" he enquires in a voice that suggests a morsel would be nice, but lingering would be equally enjoyable.

"Mmm… What did you have in mind?"

He grins. "Definitely that, but I thought we might have some food first. There's the cheesecake you picked up, fruit, cheese, or whatever you have in the freezer."

"Wine?" she asks coyly, and gets a lightly pinched nipple for doing so.

"Yes, there's also wine!" he says in a theatrically exasperated tone. "That will go better with the cheeses." He rolls her off his arm and rises in a fluid motion. Meredith watches his peachy bum as he walks around the bed, but makes no move to get out of it herself.

William puts a robe on and ties the belt. Noting that she has not moved, he sweeps the duvet onto the floor. "Hey!" she exclaims, reaching too late to grab it. "No fair!"

"I know you and bed, young lady!" He reaches out to help her up, meeting her pout with a steady look. It's an unequal contest, and she relents, allowing him to help her up with the grace one might show a duchess rather than a recently spanked and thoroughly naked girlfriend.

She gropes for her robe, but he prevents her from getting to it. As her mouth opens to complain, he swats her backside. "Not till *after* lunch," he says sternly.

Her shyness at being naked is quelled by her body's responses to his spank, his tone of command, and the unspoken promise in his eyes. While she doesn't demur, she also doesn't follow. He threatens, "Would you rather I led you by the clips or by your hand?"

She responds with a lowering of her eyes and rising colour in her cheeks. Silently taking his proffered hand, she allows herself to be led downstairs.

While they the cheese and biscuits, Meredith works up her courage to break the spell of silence she feels she has fallen under. Oddly, rather than making her more self-conscious, his frequent caresses help. He pours her a glass of the Fleurie and kisses her lips before passing her the glass. It is as if he has returned the power of speech to her in the moments their contact lingers. "Can I ask you something?"

"Of course." He sets his attention on her.

She sips her wine to gather her confidence. "Why won't you let me get dressed?" She blushes again and holds her glass so that her arm covers her breasts.

He smiles at her discomfiture. "We had a deal. You get to do what you want *after* lunch." He grins mischievously as his hands find her body once more. "And I fully intend to enjoy myself until then."

It seems unfair to her, but it feels so nice to have him touch her. The aroused state in which he is keeping her softens the edge of her embarrassment. "But you're dressed!" she says sullenly.

"Yes, I am, aren't I?" He lifts the glass from her unresisting hand and embraces her, pressing his robe against her nakedness. He kisses her deeply.

A part of her wants to stamp her foot at the shameful aspect of her situation, but the textures of the material against her skin are delightful. Annoyance loses out to the part that melts into the sensations and his embrace. He turns her around and continues to kiss her over her shoulder while his hands make free. Meredith can feel his amorousness isn't only affecting her; she rocks against him and purrs as his body responds with a readiness of its own.

Her nipples stiffen again under his caresses, though he doesn't touch her breasts yet. In other relationships, she spent time wishing her partners wouldn't rush. With William, she holds herself in anticipation. He spends time stroking her sides. It's nice. She hadn't realised so many parts of her body were sensitive. Most men make the comforting leap for the obvious. She has missed out on so much.

He runs his fingers across her belly and teases her mons. She shifts her feet a fraction further apart as he traces her ribs, all the while kissing. Whenever she opens her eyes, she finds his blue-green gaze twinkling wickedly at her.

His fingers stroke her swollen outer labia and she leans back contentedly into his ongoing kiss. In this moment, she is, for the first time she can remember, comfortable with her own nudity. The languid caresses of his ring- and fore-fingers continue while his middle finger is tantalisingly cocked just shy of making the desired contact with her.

After almost too long, he draws this longest digit along the length of her opening, brushing over her hood. With each pass he spreads her wetness a little more and lingers a little longer. Eventually he presses under the hood to her pearl, then circles slowly and teasingly. Meredith, torn between her desire to press backwards against his hardness and forward against his touch, sways between both and braces herself for her coming orgasm.

He snakes his arm under her breasts and sets his strength to support her. He does this when he makes her cum standing. She remembers the first time he did so, when he made her watch herself in the mirror. The memory is more exciting and less humiliating than it felt at the time. Of course, she muses, she's grown to love the reassurance of his strength around her.

She abandons herself to sensation as his rhythm rises. He circles, teases, slides slick fingers between her folds, draws her hood up, and pulses her pearl against her pubis. He takes her close, keeps her close. Then he withdraws his touch.

She teeters. Her cry is one of loss instead of the expected rapture. While her mouth is still open, he slides two fingers between her lips. Instinctively she sucks them, which he allows her to do for several long moments before taking the other two into his own mouth. The hand below her breasts presses her mons, squeezing her into him and emphasising his own arousal. He holds her like this until the quaking in her insides fades.

He takes her chin gently between his fingers and turns her face towards him while he sets about caressing her body once more. This time he touches her breasts, and she is thankful. His firm touch meets their softness and makes its way to their wildly sensitive buds with aching slowness. As he toys with them, they send delicious sparks through her that reawaken her need.

Again he takes his time, taking pleasure in her responses. He releases her lips, and his own seek out her neck and shoulders, trailing delicate kisses from her ears to the nape of her neck. The mewling of her voice when he touches her is something he cannot hear enough.

She comes towards a peak far more swiftly this time. Frustratingly, his hands slow, and he holds her release tantalisingly out of reach. He takes her close, once, twice, and a third time. Her knees almost fold at this last, and his arm takes a share of her weight.

Slowly he turns her around. He kisses a tear of frustration from her eye and holds her close. "After dessert."

She wails.

"All good things ..." His lips purse in a teasing smile and he pats her naked bottom. When she remains sullen, he takes hold of her nipples, gently squeezing and tugging. "Come to those who *wait*, and if you remember, I said you could choose something *after* lunch." He emphasises each stressed word with a tightening of his fingers before giving her lips the most chaste of kisses.

His handling of her body—as well as his blend of command, humour, and tenderness—weakens her resolve and finally wins her over. In any case, she can always attempt the smallest and quickest cheese course of her life. So she gets biscuits and plates ready, making certain to wiggle her bum at him as she does so. There being no harm in trying to get him to hurry up too.

Still conscious of her nudity, she prefers not to sit at a table. She asks William if they can sit on the sofa. He cocks his head to one side and approaches her. Before she realises what he's doing, he runs a finger between her labia. Naturally, after his continual attentions, he finds her receptive. Smiling, he raises the glistening finger between them. "Of course, but you might want to sit on a towel!"

He tosses a hand towel to her and pointedly sucks his finger. Her cheeks flame in mortification.

Despite their frenzied activity, Meredith's excitement and need prevent her from taking too much time over eating. She contents herself with two small crackers with Brie and a sprig of ruby grapes, while she sips her wine and finishes before William. They're sitting close. He pauses frequently to run gentle hands across her skin and she floats warmly on the wine and touch until she has a mischievous thought.

Draining the last of her Fleurie, she stands and conspicuously places the empty glass down with soft clink. "I've finished my lunch now."

He looks up at her roguishly. "But I haven't finished mine yet."

This doesn't deter her. In a bold moment, she places a cushion on the floor by his feet and kneels in front of him. Looking him in the face as if daring him to stop her, she open s his robe. "Well, I'm not stopping you."

William is torn between making her wait and desiring to take his own pleasure. Her minxish action wins him over, and he shifts to allow her access. "We might have to discuss this later, young lady." The thought does not deter her nimble fingers in the least and she continues returning his smile.

She finds him hard. His taste is faintly edged with her own, a combination that she always finds evocative. She runs the tip of her tongue around his foreskin and then teases inside. Using her hands, she draws the foreskin back, exposing the tip of his glans. She runs her tongue along the tiny, sensitive lips of its opening. She is rewarded by a further stiffening and draws his foreskin further back. The glans now has the glossy smoothness of full erection. She fixes him with a coquettish look while she strokes slowly up and down, the pad of her thumb pressing on its underside.

He decides that he's not going to get any peace. He takes his last Stilton-laden biscuit into his mouth in two bites and strokes her hair. "Are you trying to get into trouble?"

Meredith chews her lip, pretending to consider this. "I might be." Taking his question as permission, she encourages his legs apart and she makes herself comfortable as she sets about the task of repaying him, if only a little, for all the teasing she has endured today.

William seldom cums through oral sex. But Meredith prides herself on her ability, and the position affords her comfort and easy access. She sets her full attention to the task, pleased that it is now her turn. Her hands concentrate on his shaft while her tongue circles the outer edge of the shining head.

Having promised to allow Meredith her choice of activities after lunch, William successfully resists the temptation to do as he'd planned— make love with her. He holds himself mostly still and quiet under her tender onslaught. She knows the usual sensitive places—the frenum, the dark ring around the head— even just over half way down the sides, and also those more specific to him.

Concentrating on his pleasure, she feels her own heat rising again. The character of this arousal is different, more a general warming. She's reminded that hers is usually the more passive role in their relationship. She may be nude and on her knees, but the sense that she has control is a pleasant change after the hours of surrendering herself, no matter how much she has enjoyed doing so.

She smiles to herself as the stifled sounds he makes and the touch of his hand on her hair convey his enjoyment, reminding her of the times she has sighed and squirmed in response to his attentions. Her hands, her mouth, and her eyes control his pleasure. Now that she knows so well he joy of abandoning herself she appreciates this on a different level and savours that appreciation...

★★★

William caresses the sleepy Meredith's derriere, and she wiggles an encouraging response. She normally wakes in a filthy mood—but then, until recently, she normally hasn't awakened from the kind of night that would put a girl in a good mood. He scooches up behind her, reaching his clever fingers around, and her legs move to accommodate them. There is none of his usual teasing; he methodically brings her to orgasm. It's something that confused and almost upset her when he first did it. She still finds it a little disquieting, a statement of ownership in its own way as profound as any spanking. When he chooses to build things up, it feels that she is more involved. She still isn't quite sure of her emotions about it that he can and does just bring her to orgasm on the spur of the moment even if her body is, obviously, fine with it.

After she crests, he gentles her, then playfully tickles her. When she struggles, he easily straddles her, his weight and strength making the task of holding her still simple. Meredith writhes and laughs under him, eventually squealing, "No fair!"

William rolls her onto her back and resume tickling. Her squeals become more desperate. Then he allows the character of his touch to change. He bends forward and kisses her shoulder. When she cranes her neck, he kisses her lips. She feels his hardness against her and without further warning, he slides into her.

Meredith gasps into his kiss, unused to her body being so ready and also unused to a man so able to read her. She kisses him with greater fervour.

Hi moves inside her with easy strokes of his hips before asking conversationally, "Is it your turn to make the coffee?"

Meredith sighs in exasperation. She *knows* she made coffee on Saturday. "I think it's your turn."

William accelerates his strokes and she happily rocks against each, moaning softly. He takes the weight of his body on one arm. Using the fingers of the other, he tweaks a nipple, making her yelp and whispers, "Are you sure?" In her ear.

She kisses him then bites her lip in response to his love-making, but manages to reply with a yes though she means it to be firmer than it sounds.

He thrusts again, and this time stays deep. His hand finds her other nipple and pinches, making her gasp. In spite of the stab of pain, she smiles when he says, "Are you fibbing, young lady?"

Meredith holds her tongue and composes her face until he resumes his rhythm then responds as coyly as she is able, "No." Looking as coy as she can, she adds, "It's definitely your turn, sir."

She makes no effort to defend her breasts. Instead her fingers trace down his back, delighting in the play of his heavy muscles as he moves inside her.

"Hmm," he growls, thrusting especially forcefully into her. Then he withdraws, rolls her over, and spanks each cheek before re-entering her from behind. "I thought pinkest bum made coffee?"

Meredith pushes back against his passion, panting out, "I think it's the peachiest."

He builds and maintains a vigorous rhythm. "First cum? That was you!"

"You can't," she gasps, "change the rules."

He takes her wrists, pins them easily, and reaches to the bedside to retrieve the cuffs. He puts a one on each wrist while still rocking inside her.

Meredith giggles, liking this turn of events very much. "You definitely have to make the coffee now, fuck face—I got no hands!"

William links the cuffs around attachment point at the head of the bed before withdrawing from her. He places his left hand gently but firmly on the small of her back and whacks her rosy bum four times, to a series of ouches and mmms from Meredith.

He grabs her ankles and slips a knicker vibe onto her, then turns it on low—too low to get her off. He gives her tempting rear one last swat before heading for the kitchen.

Meredith squeaks, "Don't leave now!" Only to hear him laugh and feel him use the remote control to change the vibration pattern. She thinks, *Oh fuck!* when she realises he's not coming back. Aloud, she calls, "You're an arse!"

William hears her as he's putting the kettle on. He takes his time before walking back upstairs. When he gets there sits beside her on the bed and caresses her bum gently then, without a word of warning, he lands a heavy swat on each cheek. Meredith shrieks in surprise. He stands, pausing only to change the pattern of the vibrations again before returning to the kitchen.

This time Meredith submits to her fate. She writhes alone on the bed, attempting to get enough stimulation to achieve her goal, but gives up her fruitless efforts after a few minutes. William returns with a tray bearing fruit juice, croissants, and a cafetière. She barely notices until the smell of the coffee reaches her.

He puts the tray down on the bedside and sits beside her again. He patiently tears off a small piece of hot croissant, adds butter and jam, and offers it to her. Meredith opens her mouth and allows him to feed her. He thinks about teasing but decides not to and gives her the morsel. She enjoys its buttery sweetness and says, "Thank you." Seeing his face darken, she adds, "Sir."

He prepares another bite for himself and eats it, absent-mindedly stroking her body as he chews.

"Are you going to uncuff me, sir?" Her question earns her another whack to her bottom, eliciting an "Ouch!" Then he offers her a sip of fruit juice as if nothing has happened. She accepts it but mutters "Arse!" earning her bottom another swat.

He takes a sip himself. "More croissant?"

Meredith tries sulking but, getting nowhere, finally gives in, "Yes, please." He raises his hand once more. "Sir." He feeds her. "Thank you— sir." William kisses her and takes another piece for himself.

He works through both croissants and glasses for fruit juice in the same fashion, while the vibrator works its way slowly through Meredith's grasp on normality.

William plunges the cafetière. That task completed, he turns his attention back to his captive and further teases her. She quickly begins to mewl, lifting her hips in the air in supplication.

William enjoys her pleas for a moment before moving the fabric of her knickers aside and entering her. He is rewarded by her vocal and physical response. He turns up the vibrator, and she murmurs, "Oh, sir!" He builds up a rhythm inside her and Meredith pushes back, breathing shallowly as his strokes become ever harder.

His vigour make her wonder whether this is a reward for her submission, a punishment for her cheekiness, or a need of his own. Soon it doesn't matter. "Close … sir," she pants. "Ahh, harder, sir!" His hips bounce her off the mattress with each thrust. then meeting her and driving her down once more.

She buries her face and holds her breath.

Pushes back against him…

Her body stiffens and convulses internally as he holds deep inside her. He feels her trembling and maxes out the vibrator's power, drawing a guttural cry from her as she climaxes. Her hips rock reflexively as her body seeks to draw out her ecstasy and milk his own.

He wraps his arms under her and holds her tightly as their breathing slows each listening to the beating of each other's heart.

Eventually Meredith speaks, "Told you it was your turn." She says with a giggle.

He undoes the Velcro of the cuffs and withdraws from her. Instead of pouring the coffee, he lies back.

She looks at him expectantly. He whacks her bum again. "Pour me some coffee, girl!"

She rubs her bum, kisses his shoulder, and smiles. "Yes, sir!" But once she has turned her back on him, she rolls her eyes. She pours two cups, smiling. Of such little victories …

"Good girl." He'd lay odds that she has rolled her eyes, but he's not certain.

Meredith decides to push her luck once more. Cocking her head to one side, she asks, "Milk?" She knows that he drinks it black. There isn't even any milk on the tray.

He considers sending her downstairs to get some, but instead simply raises an eyebrow, looking disappointed. "Never!" It broadens the smile on her face. Meredith hands him his coffee and he takes it, returning her smile at their private joke.

She gets back into bed and nestles against him. "I'll have to change the sheets."

"We may as well make that really necessary then," he responds, looking lewdly at her.

30

The Loneliness of Difference

Willliam left earlier, so Meredith has the bathroom to herself and completes her ablutions without being tickled, brought to orgasm, or otherwise made love to. It's much easier, but she misses the attention and its attendant benefits.

As she showers before work, Meredith reflects on how sensitised her skin is. And that despite their experimentation with her new toys, there isn't one mark anywhere on her. *I've been beaten to within an ace of screaming, but there's nothing to show. And even if there were, my credit card records clearly show bought each and every one of the instruments I was beaten with, except for my lover's palm.*

Her hands, as they scrub, evoke the memory of those instruments. She recalls his hands and lips caressing and kissing, taking her past the point of screaming as they move over her body under the streams of hot water. Sensations linger on her thighs, her buttocks, her breasts, and her mons, all alive with echoes.

Once dressed, she gathers her weekend purchases and hastily stashes them in the bottom of her wardrobe. *I'll have to find a proper place to keep all of these!* It's one thing to buy them and experience them while immersed in a sexual high. But in the light of a Monday morning, the thought of anyone else, even her window cleaner, seeing them strewn around her bedroom is quite another.

She gets into her car. As she sits, her body reminds her of his spankings, and she feels herself tighten deliciously inside. The sensation repeats as she draws the seatbelt across her body. *I'm so adventurous.*

As she is driving to work she can't stop thinking about her stock of guilty items. It's one thing to have William's house as a den of secret delights. But her own home has stayed primly outside such decadence—until now. Now, even when she's curled up contentedly with Netflix on the telly and a cat on her lap, she'll know a whip is there.

A flicker of doubt arises in a corner of her mind. *Have I gone too far?* Even the pleasure she usually takes in her car's handling isn't enough to recover the mood of the morning for her.

Work is almost a welcome distraction. Emily is in an unusually subdued mood. For once she isn't full of tales of her weekend adventures, having spent the last two days visiting relatives. Meredith has an unusually combative thought of telling her the lurid details of the days spent with William. The thought dies swiftly at the memory of Emily's recent kindnesses. Any brief triumph would be outweighed by the suspicion that the story would be around the company by close of business. Handing a colleague such power would certainly risk ruining the improved relationship among the team.

It is one thing, she is sure, to revel in her mind and her private life in her adventures, but it would be quite another to risk having them the talk of the office. "Mine was quiet too," she says instead. "My boyfriend stayed at my place for a change. We did a bit of shopping and went for a walk."

Emily seems to be a little cheered by this. "Didn't you get up to anything?" She smiles delightedly at Meredith's glow of embarrassment. Meredith's lips may be able to keep themselves sealed, but her face is not so skilled. "Good for you! At least yours wasn't quite totally wasted." She disappears before Meredith can process this unexpected response.

Then there's Sophie, the young PA they share. The girl is nursing a head, but Meredith doesn't pull her up on it. They all had at one time or another. And Sophie is far too young for Meredith to want to confide in her. There's the fear of shocking her—and the fear she might not be shocked at all. One never knew. William seems to regard her responses as perfectly normal. Given Emily's boasting and the way one or two friends talk, Meredith is beginning to feel that she might have been alone in missing out on life. so hard to know what is "normal" these days!

On reflection work colleagues, are too involved in her life outside of her relationship with William to talk about the more exotic side of their relationship.

The morning rolls on, as does the afternoon. William messages to say thank you for the weekend and to suggest she stay at his place on Wednesday. She agrees, the travel is a pain, but he's done several midweek runs to her place.

As the day nears its end, Meredith looks forward to dinner with her mother—though she certainly can't imagine taking her mother into her confidence about the heightening of her relationship, or at least its details.

Eating with her Mum saves the bother of cooking, and their long walk with Roley in the lengthening evening light is very pleasant. Even if she is distracted trying to think of a better place for her new toys, which she currently has hidden at the bottom of the bottom drawer in a chest, beneath her once-worn ski suit.

On Tuesday, Meredith makes a decision. If she can't talk to someone she knows, then she will talk to someone she doesn't. The woman from the sex-toy shop had said Meredith could phone, after all. She checks, and yes, the woman's card is still in her handbag. The logo on the card, a lacy mask, is definitely risqué, but not so much as to shock. The name is given as *Mistress Annette Rohde*.

Meredith looks at the card for another minute, wondering if she should wait until lunchtime. Then she thinks that it's likely the shop will be quieter early. She picks up her mobile to begin dialling the land line number listed and closes her office door before dialling.

The call is answered on the third ring. A young-sounding woman answers. "Good morning, Intimate and Confidential. How may I help you?"

"Um, good morning. May I speak with Annette Rohde?"

"Who may I say is calling?"

"Um, Meredith. I came into the shop on Saturday, and she gave me her card."

"One moment please."

The phone goes silent, and in that silence Meredith feels uncertain. She should have done as William suggests and made a list of points before the conversation. Her mouth feels dry.

The voice returns. "Can Mistress Annette call you back?"

A relieved Meredith answers, "Yes, of course." She gives her details when the girl asks and then hangs up, feeling a small sense of accomplishment. She makes a cup of coffee in the staff kitchen, and returns to her office to set about making that list.

About fifteen minutes later, her notes are made up and Meredith has just resumed working when her mobile rings with a number her phone doesn't attach a name to. Her nervousness rises. "Meredith Webb," she says calmly, but her heart is pounding.

She's somewhat disappointed when a male voice she doesn't recognise announces itself as calling from Decathlon Fitness to make an appointment to deliver the training bench on Wednesday afternoon. She asks if she can call back to confirm.

She's still arranging to work from home on Wednesday when the phone rings again. She answers on the first ring.

"Good morning, Meredith. This is Annette. I hope you are well."

Meredith has heard the voice only once before, but recognises it easily."Yes, I'm fine. It's just that, well, you were so kind and knowledgeable, I wondered if we could talk?"

"Are you sure everything is all right?" Annette presses lightly. Meredith detects a note of concern in her voice.

"No, no, everything really is fine. Better than fine. It's just that, like you guessed, I'm quite new to all this, and I don't really have anyone I can talk to, and, well, after what you said on Saturday, I wondered if it'd be okay if we met for a coffee sometime?" Meredith silently thanks her notes as she stumbles through her request.

Annette suggests meeting at the weekend, but Meredith has plans to go to William's house. Annette then says that she could see her briefly after work on Thursday. Meredith gladly agrees, and they settle on a coffee shop. She hangs up with a sense of satisfaction and relief.

She concludes her arrangements to work from home, offering to do so just for the afternoon. She shows Mr Rossi the client presentation she's preparing to give on Thursday. He's impressed, he also says it would be sensible to work at home the whole day.

Flush with success, Meredith rings William to let him know about the delivery. Slave driver that he is, he suggests changing their evening plan so he can stay at her house and put the bench together. He enthuses about the new exercises he can show her. Meredith is grateful/not grateful. She loves the changes in her body, but not exercising. Nevertheless, she feels a sense of achievement at having made and re-jigged so many plans before lunchtime.

She spends the afternoon proofreading and arranging with the print room to produce handouts and DVDs of the material. She finishes the day thoroughly pleased with herself, even remembering to stop at the supermarket. William's messianic approach to home cooking doesn't seem so bad now that she's seeing, feeling, and receiving compliments on the changes in her body. She's also too is getting more skilled at meal planning and cooking.

Her home seems large for one. It always does after William has been there with her. She wonders how he feels when he gets back to his big, empty house.

A few moments later, she feels the familiar rubbing of a feline head against her leg. Aggy meows for attention. Aggy always makes the idea of having the place to herself, with a big TV and purring companions, seems very homey indeed.

There's a half bottle of Rioja in the cupboard. William is there in her head: *"If you can't leave a bottle half finished, then only have half bottles to hand."* He's an arse, but a well-meaning one—and he's hers. He's right too—the half bottles from a specialist knock the tiny ones from the supermarket into a cocked hat!

She pours herself a glass and is struck by how hungry she is. She sets to work preparing her dinner. Practice, habit and knowing how good it will taste have made prepping chicken much easier. She cooks it and, pleased with the results, takes a picture of her plate. She sends the photo to William. As an afterthought, she sends a copy to Jess as well: *"Thank you for your support, hugs x."*

After she eats, she settles herself comfortably and calls William. He's home too, and switches to video call. He says nice things about her dinner but, seeing the elaborate preparations in his kitchen, where he's standing, makes her think she could do more. He explains that it's 'prep night' after spending the weekend at hers as a hissing erupts from one of the pans on his stove, and she half listens to him as she plays with Pog.

★★★

Working from home reminds Meredith why she doesn't like working from home. She thinks she's spending her time fruitfully, but she's deprived of her usual reset techniques between tasks—fetching a coffee or talking to colleagues face to face. Messaging services are good, and her own coffee is better, but the social interaction is what works for her.

The delivery man struggles into her hall with the package. As William is coming over later, she takes pity on him and doesn't ask him to carry it into the spare room.

The quiet and the absence of colleagues messes with her sense of time. She doesn't realise how late it is until she tries to contact Mr Rossi and finds he's left work for the evening. realising she packs up promptly and rises, finding that she has sat still so long that her legs are stiff.

On arriving, William kisses her and compliments the smells coming from the kitchen. But his eyes quickly move to the package occupying much of the hall. It reminds Meredith of her own reaction when he brings a toy bag over. She notes with regret that he doesn't have one with him. She has her own collection, of course, but misses the sense of anticipation. Instead, he's carrying a toolbox.

"You want to put it together now, don't you?" she asks, surrendering to the inevitable. *He's as much of a child as I am sometimes.*

His face lights up. "Well ..."

"You already know what it is; you gave me the part number! What's in it for me?" She's going to let him, but she's going to have fun first.

"If I put it together, you can use it!" he says, pretending he's being helpful. "There's a new exercise I was going to show you."

She doesn't particularly want to learn a new exercise, and he knows it. It isn't as if she hasn't already won her bet with Jess.

He smiles boyishly and gestures with the toolbox. "Where shall we put it?"

She gives in. "I thought the spare room. It's big enough so I can use the bench, but it won't be in the way." Before she finishes speaking, William has flipped the heavy box up with ease. She pities the delivery man who struggled into her hallway wonders how people get on delivering equipment for people like William.

Once the packaged bench is upstairs, William opens his toolbox and lifts out a Stanley knife, neatly slicing through packing straps and tape.

While he does Meredith examines the toolbox. His home, apart from the toy room, kitchen, wardrobes, and gym, shows signs of what Meredith regards as "male pattern untidiness". It's a matter of what is important to him. Tools are obviously another thing he values; the box is as pristine as his gym.

The bench comes with a Allen key and a pressed spanner, like flat-pack furniture, but William will have nothing to do with either. He works with his own tools with a happy fascination and easy confidence that remind her of the way he uses toys on her. He uses a powered tool to initially screw each bolt and then tightens manually with a ratchet. As he tightens bolts, she sees muscle flexing through his shirt as the checks each in turn. It's not enough to indicate he's forcing, but she's certain nothing on the bench is going to fall apart under her weight.

Watching him puts Meredith in the mood for something other than exercise—well, less formal exercise, anyway.

He tidies the tools away and asks, "Do you want to train before dinner or after?"

Meredith fixes him with a look. "After!" She says meaningfully, "And not just after dinner!" She hugs him. "Thank you for putting it together, but there are more urgent things ..." Her look is meaningful and earns her his rueful acquiescence.

31

Action Stations

When the alarm goes off, Meredith finds that she has moved to the side of the bed he must have abandoned in the small hours, on his way to Heathrow. The pillow still smells of his hair.

After showering, she has a choice to make between the new dresses. Though she prefers the new shirtdress, she selects the red A-line because Annette has already seen the other one. Their coffee date is tonight. She briefly wonders why that's important to her, but files that thought for later consideration and gets on with the business of the morning.

She's in work early, as is now usual for a day when she has a client meeting. There's time to clear her inbox and messages before she reviews her presentation, she is already word-perfect with it. She's equally adept with the answers to the battery of "what if" questions William has bombarded her with, as well as strategies for answering any question she does not know. She has time to send a mischievous message to William, asking in faux innocence when they will be going shopping again.

Emily is also in earlier than usual, and looking her best. Meredith is increasingly of the view that Emily is nicer than she has given her credit for. She compliments the way Emily looks in her figure hugging pencil skirt suit. It's something Meredith would love the confidence and figure to wear.

They travel by train to the meeting. To Meredith's relief, Emily doesn't make the same show of excitement she did for the in-house run-through. They test each other with hypothetical questions for the first few minutes before settling to talking. They unite over criticism of the way coffee tastes from paper cups, and then joke about stitching up Adrian for his antics.

Having prepared so thoroughly and (as they agree) both looking a million dollars, they arrive expecting things to go well. Still, they're surprised by how smoothly the presentation flows. Of the two questions they aren't able to field on the spot, one is something they need management agreement on, and the other Meredith handles with a William technique, assuring the questioner that they will check and get back. She's proud of how easily she does it, and delighted when, after the meeting, she realises that Emily has emailed both questions to all attendees and copied Mr Rossi.

Normally after these things, Meredith is relieved to get out. This time she's almost strutting. Emily definitely is! When they leave, there's genuine warmth from the clients.

Emily winks at her and mouths *We are so boss.* when they turn the corner, she says, "Oh my God, that was *amazing.* We have *got* to celebrate."

It's rare that Meredith wants to spend time with Emily, but she does. The timing is terrible though. She checks her phone. She can manage a quick drink before meeting Annette, she supposes. This is a new situation—two worldly women wanting to spend time with her, and neither of them is Jess! "I can't stay out for long; I'm meeting someone. But we can have a quick drink tonight and celebrate properly next week?"

Emily looks disappointed but agrees to defer. "With any luck we can get Marco to stick a card behind the bar," she jokes.

Emily sees a mini-supermarket just before the station and drags Meredith in. A brief disagreement about white or red ensues. Meredith assures Emily that she'll love Fleurie, referencing William's excellent taste. They buy the wine, nibbles, and some wine glasses.

Emily takes the mention of the new boyfriend as an invitation to be curious. When they're sat on the train and enjoying their first glass, she asks, "So Mr All Work isn't all work then?" And the two have their first chat about men in which Meredith feels like an equal, even without letting on the details.

Meredith is so engrossed that she doesn't notice a message from William until she checks her phone before getting off the train. She replies, *"Brilliant, so good, with colleague, talk later <3"*

The cafe's quiet when Meredith arrives. Checking the time, she realises she's early, so she sits nervously at a table, sipping espresso and feeling overdressed. She wonders if it's foolish that she's meeting a virtual stranger to talk about her strange, exciting relationship with her strange, exciting new man. She's wound up and a bit tipsy from her day, and bursting inside with experiences, fears, and a thousand questions she has no idea how to ask.

She's realises she has chosen the table that William would have: a corner table with a clear view of the room and comfortable seats.

Meredith feels relieved and excited when Annette arrives. She has begun to live this adventure, but she has not spoken a word about it. Somehow this will make it more real. Annette is more attractive and even more elegant than Meredith remembers.

Annette is precisely on time. Her eye quickly picks out Meredith. She pauses at the counter and takes a moment to observe. Registering Meredith's eager wave, she gives the barest nod, though she has to concentrate on not smiling in response to the eager grin that spreads across Meredith's face.

Sitting in her red dress against the monochrome decor Meredith could have been posed where she is by and artist. Annette definitely thinks she sees what the boyfriend sees in Meredith. There's an innocence, a nervousness—and something more. She sits straight, with an air about her, a little more so than at the weekend. Annette smiles as she orders. At the weekend, of course, Meredith had other things on her mind.

Annette pays without waiting for her order and walks over to the table, allowing her mouth to form a tiny smile at the blonde woman sitting there.

Meredith relaxes when Annette approaches. She notices that Annette doesn't bring a drink with her. She realises she's paying attention to details. William *is rubbing off on me.*

"I ordered another espresso for you. That's right, isn't it?" Annette says, lowering herself gracefully into a seat.

"Yes, thank you, and thanks for meeting me." Meredith is grateful when the barista arrives, carrying a tray with a tiny glass pot and two cups. He neatly lays out their drinks, then nods to Annette. "Ma'am."

Annette replies, "Thank you, Peter." She smiles briefly, though without releasing Meredith from her gaze.

Registering Meredith's nervousness, she injects more warmth into her smile and says, "It's a pleasure, my dear. I trust your, ah …" She pauses and looks even more intently at Meredith. "Your boyfriend rewarded you adequately for your performance on Saturday?"

Annette is herself rewarded by a rush of colour that causes Meredith's face to match the red of the dress she is wearing. Much to Meredith's surprise, Annette's laugh is light and musical. "Well, then, my dear, you must tell me all about it!" She leans forward a fraction her eyes shining with encouragement and curiosity.

Meredith slowly recounts the details of her car journey home and arrival. Annette makes a perfect audience for her tale, listening but also asking about her feelings and responses. She allows Meredith to enjoy her experience and celebrate her adventurousness through the telling. Each time embarrassment threatens to overwhelm her, Annette's sure eyes, gentle smile, and conspiratorial questions give her courage.

Annette's interest becomes particularly intense when Meredith relates her experiences with the flogger. She is delighted when Meredith refers it as "your flogger" and at her description of Williams use of it on her.

The barista approaches again, cleans a nearby table and departs. Meredith stops talking and Annette looks up. "It's okay. You can trust Peter's discretion completely." She smiles as she says this, and Meredith thinks she recognises that smile. Her curiosity is piqued.

"You don't mean he …" She can't find the words.

"Does things to me?" Annette finishes for her with a laugh. "Um, no. I'm a bit more like your boyfriend."

Meredith's confusion must show, because Annette adds, "You might say that Peter and his wife are mine, at least a little, in the same way that you are William's."

"But …"

"I did tell you in the shop that it's fine as long as nobody gets really hurt."

"But he's a man!"

"And you think some men don't find letting someone else be in control exciting?" Annette asks, warming to Meredith's discomfort. "Men and women can be much alike in that respect."

"And his wife?" Meredith is still trying to get her head around this revelation.

"She's not a man, she's a woman," Annette teases. "But yes, you aren't the only woman in the world who likes to let go either."

"Do you spank them?" Meredith whispers.

"Only if I want to and they want me to, or if they break an agreed rule." Annette smiles an odd little half smile; "But that means they either want me to punish them or want to be reminded to do something that is good for them."

"So if they don't do what you say, then ..." Meredith wonders at her own innocence. She's wanted to talk, yes, but had no idea that she'd have her eyes opened in this way.

"If you want to know more about Peter and his wife, then you'll have to ask them. You can tell them they have my permission to tell you anything they are happy to." Annette's tone is light, but her clipped Eastern European accent and firm set of her mouth let Meredith know that this part of the conversation is at an end.

They each sip their drinks. Questions and reticence bubble inside Meredith's mind. Responding to the pause, Annette asks, "How long have you been with your William?"

"Two months," Meredith answers, working it out. She wondered that it has been such a short time. "But it feels longer."

Unable to resist the tease, Annette asks, "In a good way?" She enjoys causing another pretty blush. "I think I can take that as a yes. Your cheeks are very expressive. A person can find that very charming, you know." She takes another sip of tea. "Would you like to tell me how William introduced you to the lifestyle?"

"He didn't. Well, I found his things and ..." The flush returns to Meredith's face.

"And?" Annette speaks softly but with a trace of command. She tilts her coiffured head a fraction and her brown eyes twinkle, making Meredith think of William.

"And, well, I asked about them, and he used some of them on me." She looks down. "He was so stern and so gentle. It was beautiful." Her voice trails away, as her body remembers. Another crack appears in Meredith's reticence. "And then I asked him about other things, and ..." She lowers her eyes and says no more.

Annette decides to help her out. "And on Saturday you walked into my little shop?"

Meredith thinks that she can understand how Peter and his wife would find happiness in pleasing the owner of that voice. She shyly meets those brown eyes. "Yes," she confirms simply.

"Do you mind if I ask whether you have a safeword?" Meredith looks blankly at her. "A word you say when you want to stop."

"Oh, yes! It's *pineapple*." It sounds sillier than ever when she says it out loud to someone else.

"And have you ever used it?"

"No. Well, yes. Um." Annette waits patiently. "Not exactly."

Annette changes her angle, smiling conspiratorially. "That sounds like the beginning of another good story."

Annette's words are like a key again unlocking her tongue. Meredith tells her about the walk, and William suggesting they get up to something in the woods. "Then he held me and whispered that it was okay." She reaches for his exact words. "He whispered, 'It's okay if *no* means *pineapple*'."

By the time she finishes, Meredith feels emotionally drained. She expects to see scorn on Annette's face, but instead she sees a caring smile. "I'm glad you have one, dear. That's a very important lesson he taught you about using it. You're lucky your first dom understands. It's a lovely story. Never forget it, or the lesson."

They sip in silence for a moment. The coffee is good, and Meredith feels glad to have got some things off her chest. She is as peaceful inside herself as she is after a session with William. She can certainly see why Peter and his wife might want to do as Annette asks.

"So *this* is all normal?" Meredith asks, her voice little over a whisper. "That's what wanted to talk to you about."

There's no teasing in Annette's smile as she replies, "Perhaps not everything is *normal*, but then normal is different for everyone. If he doesn't do anything you are not willing to do, then yes, your relationship is as normal as any in the community—and a lot more normal than many outside it."

They talk companionably for several more minutes. Annette's parting words are "I'll call you if you like, and we can have dinner next week?" Meredith happily agrees.

As Meredith drives home, she muses on their conversation, her feelings, and her relationship with William. Foremost in her mind are the thoughts *I'm not crazy* and *This is normal*. There's a strong undercurrent of delight. The sophisticated and elegant Annette appears to be a new friend, and one who is impressed by her adventures. The other woman's acceptance and appreciation not only validate Meredith's experiences, but make them just that little bit more exciting.

32

Little Black Dresses

hen she gets home, Meredith thinks about doing her exercises, but decides to eat first. The meal is simple enough to prepare a portion of a ragout she and William had cooked together. She proudly thinks of how organised she is becoming. Not long ago, tonight's meal would have been a takeaway, and Meredith would have eaten far more than she should then washed it down with a bottle of wine.

She heats the ragout and adds freshly grated parmesan, black pepper, and a few leaves from her new basil plant. Five minutes' work doesn't look at all bad, and it tastes divine.

As she eats, she thinks about not doing her exercises. Then she thinks about Peter from the coffee shop, and how Annette would respond if he were remiss. She considers Peter's wife and wonders what she's like. She fancifully imagines one or other of them having to bend over Annette's knee, just as Meredith has done in play over William's. Would the other watch and count out the punishment? Meredith wonders if William would punish her so. She knows that he dislikes it when her self-discipline slips for too long.

The thoughts, though not entirely appealing, are entirely erotic to her. She imagines having to explain her failure to bother with twenty minutes of simple exercises or go swimming. Such lapses after he has taken such trouble to plan the sessions and teach her!

In the end, despite her efforts at self-distraction, her sense of duty wins. She performs the scheduled routine and finds that she feels better for having done so. She even refrains from rewarding herself with a cigarette. Instead she phones William to report that she finally thinks she's improving then basks in the double glow she feels at her own satisfaction and at pleasing him.

When he asks about her day, Meredith realises that she hadn't remembered to call him earlier. It takes her a moment to rewind. As she doesn't speak as quickly as he expects, William changes topic, in case the day went badly. "Seeing as how we skipped lunch out last weekend, would you like to eat out somewhere formal on Saturday?"

Her first thought is of their private, intimate meals together, with languid interludes between courses. But it has been a while since she dressed up and ate anywhere fancy, and when he points out that they had never managed to make lunch out the previous weekend she relents, despite privately she holds him entirely responsible for that.

That settled, she brings the conversation back round to the tale of her afternoon and delights in his praise. He really is a very good listener—for a man.

Only when she has hung up does it strike her that she has now agreed to go out for two evening meals—one with Annette, one with William—but doesn't have anything appropriate to wear that fits. An hour later, her fears are confirmed. A tear brims in her eye as the last piece of evening wear hits the wall. She curses William for the short notice and her wardrobe for its inadequacy.

Meredith pauses, gets herself a cup of herbal tea, and reasons that her two new day dresses look good. She has a clear lack in her wardrobe, and she will need something in the way of evening wear that fits now.

She turns her PC on. A few minutes later, she is shopping online. With her nerves still frazzled, the task seems impossible. There are so many black dresses!

Grabbing her phone, she messages Jess: *"Help, I'm going out on Saturday night and I have nothing to wear!"* Usually Meredith's the calm one, but this is Jess's field of expertise.

Her friend helps her narrow the search down with some simple advice. She eliminates those that are too revealing, too old, or too young. There's no way she is going to wear something skimpier than her sexiest nightie outside. A long-standing fear of tripping over the hem of a full-length frock eliminates more choices.

Eventually, she settles on a pretty knee-length pencil dress with lace sleeves and enough décolletage to show off her ample bosom—but not so much as to make a spectacle of it. She selects it for her basket and continues idly browsing.

As she does one dress she'd previously discounted as being too revealing catches her eye again. It's a sleeveless wrap-around with a plunging V, and walking would reveal a good deal of the wearer's left thigh making just a bit too much of everything. A few weeks ago she wouldn't have dreamt of seeing herself in it but...

She ponders and pulls up the pictures of two dresses next to each other. The pencil dress is less eye-catching from behind, but the cleavage of the wrap-around is much more noticeable.

She loves the wrap-around but is still not certain that she dares to wear it. so, when she finds herself hesitating she adds it to the basket, and sends the links to Jess.

As she considers her decision the lacy sleeves on the other dress give her a thought, she has a black shawl she loves, which she could wear over the wrap-around. It would match the dress and preserve her modesty.

A few minutes later, her friend messages to buy both. She promises to tell Meredith what she honestly thinks if Meredith models them in selfies.

Meredith arranges next-day delivery to the office and trusts to her friend's advice. She can take both to William's, along with the next best thing from own cupboard, so that in any case, she'll have something.

It's late, and she has yet to pack for the weekend. She shuts down the computer before she spends all night worrying over the right outfit. Hurriedly she packs jeans, tops, underwear, and make-up, glad that she now keeps toiletries and a few things at his home. Things may not be *serious* yet, but he has set aside a drawer (other than the ones in his playroom) for her use.

★★★

When the package arrives, Meredith sneaks into the bathroom at work and tries both dresses on. She really isn't sure she dares wear the wrap-around, even though it suits her better. Jess, on receiving the pictures, is adamant on behalf of the wrap-around.

Still hesitating, Meredith goes into Emily's office and shows her. Emily says, "I think I prefer the— Wait, is it for a man or for work?"

Learning that it's for dinner with a man, she declares, "Wear the wrap-around if you want to get laid."

Meredith's face must betray her, because Emily bursts out laughing. "Oh, Meredith, we'll make a star of you yet. Is tonight or Saturday?"

"Saturday. He says we're going somewhere fancy for dinner."

"Lucky old you. Some guys' idea of 'nice' is metal cutlery. Is it the same man?"

"Yes," Meredith admits, hoping not to have to answer too many questions.

"Mr Ideas?"

Another treacherous blush confirms it.

"Well, I think he's very good for you. Definitely wear the wrap-around."

The important business of the day dealt with, they also pick out the CVs that interest them.

★★★

The excitement of her new dress does something to offset the misery of the drive. The saving grace, with the journey ending at William's house, is the certainty that she will be welcomed with enthusiasm and a fine meal she has no need to cook for herself.

William asks about the new dress when she carries the bag in, but she saves the great unveiling for the big night. There are some surprises for her at the house too. For starters, when she heads upstairs to freshen up, she notices there's a shiny new lock on the playroom door. She smiles, filing the information away to tease William about. His old television has also gone—or, rather, moved to a wall in the dining room. When she comments, he leads her into his media room, in its place a gleaming fifty-five-inch Sony. "After seeing yours, the old one seemed ..." He laughs.

Meredith is in a playful mood. She eats quickly, and when he asks how she wishes to spend the rest of her evening, she feints towards the new television, pauses, and then races up to his playroom, lock and all.

★★★

Another benefit to the drive the night before is the chance of a lazy Saturday together. The weather cramps their activities, though with the way rain affects her hair, she prefers it during the day than later. Anyway, spending the day indoors with William is, in Meredith's view not exactly a hardship.

Dressing that evening brings each of the lovers a welcome surprise. Meredith glows with pride at William's response to her evening dress, but she's sure his dinner suit eclipses her—he looks like a cross between Bond and a Bond villain.

William's "eat somewhere nice" turns out to be a performance of *The Magic Flute* at the Royal Opera House, followed by dinner at a Michelin-starred restaurant with an Anglo-French menu. Their seats, a gift from his grandfather, are in the dress circle, and the restaurant, set in an exclusive London hotel, is grandiose, making Meredith glad of her new finery.

Despite her best efforts, Meredith can't help laughing when William has a club sandwich with his interval drink. It's sweet when he admits that he doesn't want to embarrass her by ordering two mains in the restaurant later.

It's the first time she's seen an opera with surtitles. The story is familiar to them both, yet neither speaks German fluently, and there are parts Schikaneder's clever libretto neither knew. They agree that Sabine Devieilhe as the Queen of the Night is magnificent (that aria!). They reluctantly tear themselves away from a series of curtain calls and make their way to the restaurant.

Meredith initially thinks to have the lamb, but it's served with sweetbreads and she's not quite that brave. She opts for sea bass instead. William chooses turbot. He persuades her to try a white wine with their meal. Though it doesn't alter her preference for red, the Chablis's lemony and floral notes are a joy with the fish.

William makes her laugh by saying how glad he is that the opera was a traditional production, not a "camped up" one. He's such an odd mixture of adventurer and conservative. She agrees that the costumes and set added to the grandeur of Mozart's music.

Meredith is unable to resist asking William for further details about his new television. He take her comment in good part he tells her how impressed he is with her 4K screen and how surprised he was when he first saw its image quality. "It was a lot better. I'd have to be a fool not to admit that. So while you were away in Italy, I did something about it. I even got to get my tools out." He grins his best grin.

"And the lock?" she enquires innocently.

This time he actually laughs out loud. "I didn't want you to never be willing to allow your friends to visit my house."

On the drive home, Meredith looks across at him, so handsome and confident as he guides the heavy car along increasingly quiet roads. Closing her eyes happily, she recalls an earlier drive with him. Lulled by the smooth movement and passing lights, she dreams of that evening and …

She wakes as he stills the big engine on his drive. She feels guilty that she's slept, but the rest means that she has the energy to enjoy herself. They undress each other and finish their evening off in style before lapsing into a restful sleep together.

33

Teasing

When William stays at Meredith's house the following Wednesday, it's the first time he's come over when, instead of Meredith waiting to see what toys he's brought, she is able to lay out her own. Retrieving them from their hiding place, laying them out for him to use, and savouring thoughts of the evening ahead are an altogether different thrill for Meredith.

Meredith even feels a glow of pride in her own audacity. She is still barely able to believe that she had the nerve to buy all of these things. Of course, William persuaded her, and Annette, her new friend (is she a friend, she wonders) definitely helped. But she, shy Meredith Webb, did it!

They have developed a routine when he travels to her house for the evening: tea, exercise, taking turns in the shower and kitchen, and eating together. Inevitably, the cats show up while food is being prepared. It feels as if they've been doing it far longer than they have.

Dinner is either at the table or, more usually now, in front of Netflix. Though William isn't as fond of television as she is, he's happy to share some of her rituals when he's in her home. Tonight the informality of the sofa wins out.

"Would you like to try something new?" He asks his eternal question as clearing up turns into flirting. Wondering what he has in mind, Meredith gives her usual answer.

He takes his time with the restraints she bought. She always feels a wave of warmth flowing through her as she offers her wrists to be bound.

The same is true when she feels the stroking of the flogger's soft suede falls. She thinks how deliciously naughty she is and they are, and how their bond has grown intimate and strong.

He teases her mercilessly but refuses to grant her release. At one point, she cries out, "Just *let* me!" But it is not until afterwards that she recognises the exasperated voice as her own. And he doesn't let her.

Before, no matter how many times he's teased her to the brink, it has been a prelude to pushing her over it. This is different. She finds it hard to get to sleep. Every time she shifts, she feels unfamiliar and uncomfortable with her lack of release. When she moves, he simply edges her again, leaving her yet more frustrated.

He allows her to pleasure him. She takes her time, despite her own frustration, and uses all of her skill. Pulling his skin back, she swirls her tongue around his glans, pulses it against his frenum, and attends to his every response. In their few short weeks together, she has come to know his body far better than she knew her own before they met. She takes pleasure and pride in using that knowledge for his benefit, and in the sense that she is reciprocating the pleasure he gives her.

She wonders, as he tantalises her again, if her feelings towards William's way with her body are similar to those of her previous boyfriends with regard to her skills.

In the end, exhaustion gets the better of her and she sleeps. She wakes only as he kisses her, apparently before he departs for work.

He doesn't always leave straight away, however. She has never imagined having morning sex on a work day. He introduces her to the notion—a decadent one, to be sure, but then, he's a decadent man. Although he has to leave early, he makes quite sure that she is awake, rousing her with kisses and using his confident, clever fingers to edge her again. His devilish eyes glint into her sleepy ones. She murmurs a complaint, but he hushes her and strokes her hair.

He gets ready to go while she naps, and returns to the bedroom with coffee to edge her once more. This time she really does complain. He spanks her and says, "Wait for the weekend." She is due to go to his house.

"I make no promises!" she calls out defiantly as he closes the bedroom door.

A moment later, it re-opens and his head comes around it. "That's as maybe, young lady, but I most certainly do," he says darkly. The meaningful look in his eyes does things to her insides.

She lies there for a while, contemplating finishing what he's started. She wonders what those "promises" would involve were she to do so. She's sure he would discover her transgression of his order, but thinks she might enjoy the promises anyway. Her hands brush her breasts. One hovers over her mons. The thoughts are almost tempting enough.

Instead she gets up, and even behaves in the shower, although her body is alive under the hot water and soft suds.

Downstairs she finds that William was in a generous mood in some ways at least—there's a prettily laid out plate of melon and wafer-thin ham under a meat-safe, as well as a flask of coffee and a round of sandwiches for her to take to work.

Work goes well despite her lack of sleep. She's feeling supported, and she also has the sense that she's organised again. Mr Rossi calls her into his office and cheerily commends her work and initiative. He confirms that the new client is happy with their efforts and wishes to go ahead with their proposed pilot scheme. He also asks her about her plans for the future, which is odd, because her annual review isn't for ages.

She sees Emily head in to his office shortly after she leaves it. After Emily emerges, John goes in. Meredith is still wondering if there's something going on when Emily stops by her office. "I've never seen the old boy so happy," Emily marvels. "Did he tell you anything?"

"Just that he's happy with us, and we have even more work."

"Well, if it's any help, I've been doing some checking online, and I think they've advertised for a junior and an IT trainee."

Working together as a group makes the afternoon fly, past, and provides a useful distraction from Meredith's anticipation of her next dinner appointment.

At home after work, she bathes, does her hair and make-up, and puts on the same dress that she wore for the weekend with William. She summons an Uber and waits. After a few minutes, her phone announces the car's imminent arrival, so she wraps her shawl around her shoulders and makes her way out.

She arrives early at the restaurant and goes to the bar to order a calming cocktail. Once again, Annette arrives precisely on time. She smiles as Meredith rises and kisses her cheek. Her gaze travels over the new dress. "Very nice. Give me a twirl."

Meredith is taken aback. Surely Annette can't mean to have her do that in the bar? She doesn't move.

Annette waits for a moment, then raises a single finger and makes a spinning around gesture, looking at Meredith pointedly as if rebuking a recalcitrant child. Mortified, but unable to think what else to do, Meredith slowly and awkwardly rotates. Completing the turn, she is rewarded by a radiant smile. "You are a gem," Annette declares. "Your William is lucky."

Unused to such praise, especially from someone so elegant, Meredith's glow of embarrassment turns into one of pride. "Thank you. It's new."

They take their table and order, talking of ordinary things while waiting for their starters. Then the conversation turns to the matters uppermost in Meredith's mind.

"What did you mean when you said Peter and his wife belong to you in the same way I belong to William?" The wine, dim lighting, and bonhomie in the quiet restaurant make it easier for Meredith to form the question than she expected.

"My poor choice of words." Annette's phrase seems mocking, but her tone is far from it. "You let William do whatever *you want* to you, and you enjoy that. That's how Peter and his wife are with me. Does your William take things very slowly, and keep checking to see if you want to carry on when he does something new?"

"How did you know that?" Meredith feels herself colour and in grateful for the dim lighting. It's as if this woman has spied on her.

"I didn't know, but I hoped. You seem happy together, and he handled the situation in my little shop sensitively. Some people use this sort of relationship to bully, and a person new to it is very vulnerable if they're not careful or cared for."

"Sometimes I can feel myself waiting for the next thing," Meredith offers, wondering how to explain that William is gentle and patient. "What exactly did you mean by rules? What you said about that struck a chord with me."

"Let me give you an example. If someone has trouble controlling their alcohol use, then they might give up control of how much they drink to a partner or friend who will make better decisions for them. It can also be something silly and fun."

Meredith looks at her empty glass guiltily. "I'm afraid I need that sometimes."

"Sometimes or often?"

"I drink more than I should; I know that. And then there's the smoking. I know it's bad for me and William hates it." She goes on to tell Annette about the deal he made with her about smoking when they went out for dinner.

"Why don't we play a game to see if you like rules?" Annette suggests. It seems innocent enough, so Meredith nods. "As you've already played one with William about your smoking, how about drinking?"

Warily, Meredith says, "Okay" Butterflies start in her stomach. They fly loop the loops when Annette smiles her response.

The elegantly dressed brunette summons a waiter with the merest tilt of an eyebrow. Meredith wishes she could do that. "My friend has had enough wine. Could you bring a bottle of water?"

"Sparkling or still, madam?"

Annette looks to Meredith, who says, "Sparkling, please."

The waiter tops up Annette's wine glass before he departs.

"Can I ask you something?" It's harder for Meredith to work up courage without a glass or two more, but then, she's learning techniques—work and life meet again.

"Of course, though I may choose not to answer." Again the older woman talks with her eyes as well as her words.

"This is going to sound stupid." Meredith pauses. "Why does this feel like a date, but not like a date?"

The corners of Annette's mouth turn upwards. "Can I be frank?"

"Yes. I asked, so…" She doesn't add *So it's my fault if I hear anything I don't want to*, but the words are there.

"If you're attracted to me, or want me to be attracted to you, it will feel like a date." Annette sees the shock in Meredith's eyes, and also feels her fascination. "However, it's not a date, so it doesn't." Seeing that Meredith is still uncomfortable, she adds, "It might feel that way if you want me to like or approve of you too. And then there's our little game …" She gives a gentle smile.

This makes sense to Meredith, who, though she's uncertain why, very much wants this woman's approval. "But you've brought me to dinner and we hardly know each other."

"Oh, my dear, you and I know each other better already than you know some colleagues or friends who have been in your life for years." It's Annette's turn to stop and think. "Let's get some things clear. We share a particular interest, if from different sides. I invited you to dinner, and I offered to pay because I like you and find you interesting. You have come to dinner, I presume, because you like me and find me interesting."

As Meredith still seems to be in listening mode she continues, "By buying you dinner, I may claim your charming company for the time it takes us to eat, so long as I treat you respectfully. I may claim nothing more. By accepting, you are offering me nothing more. I hope we can continue to be friends. If not, I recommend that you find at least one other friend whom you can confide in. As for dinner? If we had decided on the spur of the moment to come and you hadn't offered to pay your share I would consider you a leach, and I would have nothing more to do with you. If you wish to return the favour by buying me dinner or a drink sometime, then I will be only too pleased to accept."

Meredith smiles. "That reminds me of something William said."

"Then he must be a special man. Someday I should like to meet him properly."

Her smile sets Meredith thinking that this woman, like William, must be quite confident of how clever she is. *How did they get that way?* An image of a separate room in school for darkly mysterious boys and girls who will grow up to make peoples insides melt forms.

She decides that Annette is right; the two of them should be friends. "Yes, I'd very much like to return the treat and buy you dinner." She's less sure how she feels about Annette and William meeting though.

After their mains, Annette again summons the waiter. Anticipating their needs, he brings the dessert menus. Meredith looks longingly at the variety of decadent offerings before selecting a lemon sorbet.

Annette nods her approval. "Is our game fun so far?" When Meredith goes to answer straight away, she raises a hand. "No, think about your answer and then tell me."

Meredith closes her eyes to help her concentrate. it had been liberating to hand over the decision, and she's only had two small glasses, so if she'd driven she could have saved herself the cost of taxis.

Meredith ponders on, and thinks about how she feels when she lets William take control, and how she sometimes teases him to make things more intense. Then frames her thoughts into words. "Umm, it's sort of liberating." She lets out a shy half laugh. "I know we aren't playing a game with food, but if we hadn't been playing, I think I'd have given in and ordered the chocolate torte with salted caramel— rather than thinking of what I should have— though I must confess, there's a temptation to push things by ordering a sauterne and see what happens."

There's something faintly predatory in the way Annette's face responds to Meredith's confession. "That's called bratting, and if you were mine, there would be consequences." There's a faint—and faintly delicious—edge to Annette's voice. For a moment, Meredith's insides thrill to the notion of being this woman's prey.

They finish their meal. Annette insists on taking the bill and ordering coffees. "Remember, you can choose the restaurant and pay next time," she says when Meredith protests.

Meredith flushes slightly at forgetting, and thanks her.

"And how do you feel about letting go now?" Annette uses her encouraging voice, and Meredith finds it irresistible.

"Before, I didn't even know I could let go that way. When I first let William use those toys on me, my heart was pounding. But I trusted him, and he was so gentle." Meredith pauses, thinking how she's changed, how much more confident she is now, in herself, in William and in her body. "I don't know about in general, but with William it's like being at the start of a rollercoaster that ends in a cuddle." She looks down and chuckles. "Squealing and all."

"See, you had had enough to drink." The sophisticated woman takes a sip of wine and smiles. "And letting go now?"

Annette's comment is like a caress. Meredith realises this is a similar feeling to what she sometimes experiences with William. But with William, she only lets go sexually. "It's different, but similar. With William its..." She stops but can see Annette's mind fill in the rest, "It all works on trust, doesn't it?"

"Yes, it does." The coffees arrive before Annette has time to finish her answer. She uses the interruption to frame her thoughts in relation to what she knows of Meredith's experience. "It's like a parachute jump. You've been fortunate, I think. A lot of people don't deserve or know how to handle and reward your kind of trust." Meredith thinks she sees genuine concern in the woman's eyes. "It can be intoxicating to give it, but it's very easy to get into trouble or hurt."

Annette tests the temperature of the coffee, then drinks. "It's easy to fall in love with the thrill of falling, but the most important thing is to know that the parachute works. In this case the parachute is the person you hand over control to." She looks seriously into Meredith's eyes. "You have to learn to know you're safe and free before you let yourself enjoy the sensation of not being." She takes another sip, "One reason I've asked so many questions is to make sure you're being careful. You weren't. Luckily, your boyfriend was."

"You're very kind. I'm still learning. This is all new and very different," Meredith admits. "I didn't realise how complicated it all is — I still don't. I didn't even realise it existed until I met William."

As she finishes her espresso, she looks back. She's never imagined William doing anything wrong while they've been together. She's never imagined letting anyone else do anything kinky to her. But how easily he could have!

It's late and there's a chill in the air when they leave the restaurant. To Meredith's embarrassment, Annette insists on seeing her into a taxi, then kisses her cheek as they part. As she rides home, she contemplates the ease with which the other woman waved down a cab.

The cold has convinced both of her cats to settle in. By the time she gets home, Pog is fast asleep in his favourite spot by the radiator in her living room. Aggy stirs and mewls as Meredith gets into bed. Whether it's the late-night coffee, the frustration William has left her with, Annette's questions, or some combination of the three, Meredith finds it hard to get to sleep. She lies awake into the small hours while her mind takes flights of fancy in which she or others surrender themselves.

Annette's reassurances that other people do it and that she considers it normal is comforting. It builds Meredith's willingness to let the fancies flow. Her imagination is captured by the woman's hints at a wider world of submissives and dominants, though she's certain she'll never step into it. Only the recollection of William's admonishment stops her from touching herself.

Instead, she messages him, even though she isn't certain he'll still be up.

I wish you were here.

Is everything OK?

Yes, I had a lovely evening, but I wish we could …

Meredith leaves space for his mind to complete her sentence, just as he so often does, knowing how erotic she finds it.

Feeling amorous?

More than.

Well, you're coming down tomorrow, aren't you?

Meredith hasn't confirmed whether she is going down on Friday or Saturday yet, but she's sorely tempted to brave the traffic. While she's considering it, he messages again.

Unless you want to wait till Saturday?

He's just so cheeky, she thinks.

★★★

Rising bleary-eyed to the insistent noise of her alarm, Meredith checks reality in her head and is pleased that it is Friday. Once sleep came, her dreams had been vivid and varied.

Shortly after her alarm goes off her phone pings with a text message.

You good for the weekend?

Her thumbs, faster and more awake than the rest of her reply,

"I had a lovely time, but yes, we have unfinished business.

If you're that keen...

you still have the knickers I bought you.

What do you mean?

William messages her a picture of the remote control device and a smug emoji.

You're so bad! I can't wear them at work!

[Shrug]

Change into them at the end of the day [angel, devil]

Meredith looks for a "hands on hips" emoji unsuccessfully and settles for sending him a GIF.

Got to get ready, I'll talk to you later!*"*

He's so brazen! But she toys with the idea of taking the knickers with her. Whether it's the tiredness, the unfinished business or the conversation, she isn't sure.

As usual, she takes her coffee upstairs to finish while she gets ready. She has a bag to pack for the weekend, so she spends longer at her drawers than usual. Her eyes fall on the neat travel case *those panties* and the toy fits them came with, and, she slips it into the bag—after all, doing that only gives her the choice.

Because she's tired and because it's Friday Meredith picks up coffees and croissants for herself, Emily, and Sophie. As she eats, Meredith realises how long it is since the three of them did this. She likes the slim new her, but this is a nice change. The sweet buttery treat gives her an energy boost after her poor night's sleep.

Their continuing busyness helps her through the morning, as does the arrival of the first batch of CVs for the new junior position. She and Emily agree on two that interest them and let Mr Rossi know. He asks if they are okay with working through lunch. They've both done it regularly for the last few weeks, and they reason that, on a Friday especially, working lunchtime is better than leaving late. So they agree.

It comes as a pleasant relief when lunch turns out to be a new process group, catered with a nice selection of sandwich trays. They're joined by John and Anders, the technical manager, though not by Mr Rossi, who has a directors' meeting. The two guys are good company and seem enthused. Meredith apologises for stealing their thunder—she says she feels she's getting more credit than she deserves. She finds out that she isn't the only one to whom Mr Rossi has been talking positively. And she isn't the only one who has raised similar ideas. "We're all getting something we want out of this," John assures her.

All four are enthused and motivated, which makes for a productive session. They feel justified in agreeing to John's suggestion of a short stroll to their usual watering hole before starting their afternoon's tasks.

Getting back to work, Meredith's thoughts return to William, aided by some suggestive messages asking if she's been a good girl and promising to reward her. They make her cheeks flame even when alone, but it's really bad when one makes her blush while she's with Emily. Her colleague's laughter persuades Meredith to ask him to stop.

Even without the continuing messages, she thinks about their words the night before. Deciding it would be nice to initiate things herself for a change, she sneaks out to her car and fetches the discreet box from her weekend bag.

At the end of the working day, Meredith says good-bye to Emily and Emily smiles and tells her to have fun with her saucy smartarse before departing.

Such a moment! Meredith slips the box from her desk and looks at it. She wonders if she's brave enough. Thinking of William's delight, she asks herself if Jess has ever dared to do something like this. Finally, she imagines telling Annette about it.

She heads to the rest room.

It's one thing to put vibrator panties on in the privacy of her home. Sneaking into the rest room at work to do it is quite another. The cubicle door that she's relied on without thinking for the last three years suddenly seems flimsy. Her normally deft fingers are clumsy. Oh God, what if she drops the toy while putting it in, and it bounces under the door?

Meredith manages to change into the panties and slip the toy inside without incident. She goes back to her office to get her things. There she has an idea. She unzips the empty box and sends William a picture of it.

Driving with the vibrator in place, even without it being turned on, is an effort. It was one thing being in the passenger's seat with the hardness pressed against her, but driving! At least William and the remote control are miles away—not that she can imagine him endangering her by... She holds her breath at the thought. And the memories. Then she sets the satnav's destination and messages him with its estimation of her arrival time.

Working the accelerator, clutch, and brakes presses the smooth surface of the toy against her, and the stop-start rush hour traffic forces her to keep changing gear. She realises within minutes that there's no way she can safely make the whole journey. She reluctantly turns into a side road and finds a quiet place to slip the little treasure from its pouch.

When Meredith arrives at William's house, she is already in a state of high excitement, fuelled by days of denial and the dreams that followed her conversation with Annette. The dreadful Friday rush hour fails to dampen her mood or her ardour. She draws up on his drive and checks that nothing overlooks the place where she's parked. Then slips the toy back into place.

Meredith arriving with the vibrator already in place is a pleasant—, a more than pleasant surprise for William. He imagines her putting it in and thinking about him. He smiles all the way down to the core.

Even before her hand reaches the bell, his door swings open and his grinning face greets her. The hidden toy bursts into life while he lifts her easily in his arms. The effect on her is electric.

The look in his eyes when he sees her body responding is worth the nervousness and embarrassment she's been through. It's even better than the vibrator's effect on her body after the day of denial and fantasising. The combination is another thing that goes further than she's travelled before into her sense of self. *Trust*, her mind replays to her, and she does. She's been ready for him and for this since the moment she made the decision to change into the lace panties and slip the little purple toy into their hidden pouch ...

She wants him to take her there and then. She can see in his face and feel through his trousers that the feeling is mutual. But he doesn't let either of them take things so swiftly. He insists on coffee and dinner. He caresses her hand or thigh at every opportunity, brushing against her, flirting, and giving her brief bursts of vibration and making eye contact that lingers achingly.

Even William's patience and love of the build-up has its limits, however. Their conversation fades. Their exchanged glances lengthen. Their touches linger. Finally, in silence, he reaches out to take her hand and lead her upstairs.

Meredith holds back a fraction as they pass the playroom door. He looks at her enquiringly. "Would you—"

"No, but ..."

"Would you like me to tie you?" His voice is so gentle.

And she nods. So he leads her in to select her bonds.

Standing before the displays and drawers is always an exciting experience for Meredith. It's like visiting a chocolatier, only more intimate. Her whole body responds. With thoughts of the last few days bubbling inside her, the feeling is stronger still. The urgency of her need wars with the fascination. She considers ropes, but the comfort, ease, and familiarity of cuffs — the gleam of steel and the scent of leather — call to her.

Her decision made, she reaches out to touch, smiling, caught in fantasy. *Harder or softer?* she wonders. She selects heavy, softly padded cuffs with bright steel fittings for her wrists and ankles. She offers them, and by implication herself, to him, and she feels herself glow. He takes them with gentle hands. He takes her with firm kisses. She melts, anticipation flooding her senses. When the kiss ends, she follows him into his bedroom.

William lays the restraints on the bedside cabinet and turns to face her— tall, strong, assured, and with tenderness in his eyes. They stand in stillness by his big, comfortable bed. Its crisp white sheets and duvet contrast sharply with the black of the cuffs. A voice in Meredith's head asks whether he knows how he creates the many different intimacies he does.

She faces him shyly, despite knowing him well now, and smiles her anticipation as he bends to kiss her. The little toy, so close against her, hums into life as their lips meet, and she gasps. His wicked eyes twinkle at her.

"Not yet," he admonishes in a deep murmur. His teeth nip the inside of her lip lightly. She's ready for him to use the remote control to drive her over the edge. Or perhaps he'll throw her on the bed. She's more than ready—but clearly he intends to tease her further.

His fingers deftly undo the buttons of her blouse and slide it from her. She feels less self-conscious about him seeing her now. Her hands twitch with her desire to undress him too, and to hasten the rewards she's certain are coming but his stern look makes it clear that she is to wait. When her face betrays her frustration, he grins. However he doesn't relent until she is standing in just her panties and stockings.

Only then does he allow her to take his shirt off. His skin is always so warm. No matter how many times she touches his shoulders, she still feels that she is touching a sculpture as much as a man, just as she did that first night.

Having spent so much time thinking and talking about the emotions attached to the act, Meredith finds herself intensely conscious of the implications and of her body's responses. Offering each wrist to be bound is now a profound step in a courtship dance. The polished leather and gleaming steel of the cuffs make them look like jewellery and his gentle, focused attention while binding her is as intimate as any embrace.

She watches his strong hands work and feels his assured gentleness and imagines that she has broken some rule, that she is offering herself up for punishment, and a surge runs through her. He looks up, the blue in his irises bright, and she fancies he senses her thoughts.

★★★

"So, did you like it?" His voice is soft.

"Mmm, like what?" Meredith asks through her pleasant haze.

"The waiting."

She cuddles into him. "I don't think I'd want to do it often, but it was very intense." She kisses him. "It made me feel very aware."

He grins. "Well, we won't be doing it all that often. Making you cum is too much fun." Those wolfish eyes burn into her, and she's ready again.

Until she met William, Meredith had gone her entire life without sharing that with anyone. If anyone had suggested that just a few short days of celibacy was a task, she laughed. She supposes she didn't miss driving until she got a car, or drinking until she discovered red wine. The denial is not something she enjoyed for itself, but, oh, wow, the reward. She hugs him and relishes the bear-like strength and warmth of him. It's made her even keener to …

She's reluctant to broach the subject and break their blissful silence. But she also senses that this is the time. "How do you feel when I don't follow my diet or skip my exercises?"

"What do you mean?"

Meredith halts to gather the thoughts that have been bubbling in her head since she started talking to Annette. Her heart is pounding so hard that it almost stops the words from coming out of her mouth. "Does it make you want spank me?"

"Well, um …" William doesn't know quite how to respond. Yes, it drives him up the wall. Yes, he would sometimes be all too happy to tip her over his knee and spank her for her self-destructive behaviour. But for all his experience, he'd never actually spanked her except as an elaborate form of foreplay. "Yes, I suppose it does. I'd not really thought of it like that before." He halts again, examining Meredith's face and finding it earnest. "Why do you ask?"

Here ends Book One